Pavel Kornev

THE HEARTLESS

*thank you for being
my reader!
Without you books
are nothing!
PAVEL KORNEV*

SUBLIME ELECTRICITY
Book Two

Magic Dome Books

The Heartless
(The Sublime Electricity Book #2)
Copyright © Pavel Kornev 2016
Cover Art © Vladimir Manyukhin 2016
Translator © Andrew Schmitt 2016
Editor: Barbara D. Jenkins
Published by Magic Dome Books, 2017
All Rights Reserved
ISBN: 978-80-88231-34-9

TABLE OF CONTENTS:

ONCE, THIS WORLD was dominated by *the fallen*. But humanity cast off their tyrannical rule and created a mighty Empire with colonies spread out across the globe. The power of the metropolis is stronger than ever before, but its past is dark and its future cloudy. Old secrets are capable of destroying in one moment that which took years to create. After all, nothing can save humanity from treason, not armadas of battleships nor bomb-laden dirigibles.

The key to one such secret, by happenstance and inheritance, has fallen into the hands of Leopold Orso, a former police investigator who now works as a private detective. His *illustrious* talent allows him to bring other people's fears to life. Unfortunately, though, it cannot help him extricate himself from the web of another's scheming. Defeat threatens to result in imminent death. Victory beckons with the ghost of a chance to escape with his life. His soul is plagued by painstakingly forgotten memories. And to think all Leopold ever wanted was to come into an inheritance that was his by birthright.

"Nerves, nerves, my heart is stitched of thee!"

From the song "Heart" by Steamphonia
(Russian Steampunk Band)

PART ONE
MOOR

Tempered Steel and Gelled Kerosene

1

N IGHT. DARKNESS. Speed.
Peril.
The engine blared out a heartrending bellow. The armored car was racing down a rain-slicked country road, every minute and even second threatening to fly off the shoulder and get stuck in the mud or, even worse, slam into a tree or flip over. Time and again, the tires bounced up on a bump, then plunked down into a pothole. The steering wheel was banging up and down, trying to break free of my hands. I had to grasp it with all my might or I risked losing control.

My first misstep would almost certainly be my last.

Speed. Peril.

My legs had long gone numb. My back was shooting with unbearable pain, and my eyes were constantly tearing up. But I was glad to be rushing off to my uncle's estate in the middle of the night, relieved to be done with the formalities in the Chinese Quarter so quickly. Ramon Miro, on the other hand, had been complaining about our trip from the very beginning.

His normally red-tinged face was now nearer the color of cream. The former constable was splayed out like a starfish, afraid to fly out of his big seat on our next little jump, and clearly struggling against a bodily urge to vomit. He strongly doubted the possibility that the unknown strangler would be in front of us, and told me as much without end until he was finally overcome by nausea.

"Stop and clean the headlights!" He demanded.

"I can see the road just fine!" I retorted, not wanting to lose time.

"It's make or break time!" I repeated to myself mentally. Another of my grandfather's sayings. "It's make or break time, no looking back now!"

We had to make it. Make it or die trying!

Fortunately, now that we were outside city limits, the rain had become less intense. The country road mostly ran through fields, making detours around the little forest glades. All that was left for me was to look out for potholes and keep the pedal pressed to the floor, pushing the engine for all its horsepower.

It was crackling madly, just gulping down the trotyl granules. The unsecured cargo in the back was rattling loudly, as well. I couldn't even hear my own thoughts, but I did make out a question from Ramon.

"No!" I screamed back, not looking away from the road for even one moment. "I have no idea who strangled the Judean!"

But it definitely was no human. The hands of mere mortals could not cause frostbite, nor leave ice burn on the skin. Aaron Malk had been killed either by infernal beasts or an *illustrious* gentleman. It was probably one of the bank robbers who tried to work me over.

Who precisely was not important. What was important was beating him to my uncle's estate.

The killer now knew for certain where to find

the lightning-rune aluminum box and, if we didn't get there first, Count Kósice would be parting not only with it, but with his very life. The last part, to be perfectly honest, wouldn't have especially bothered me. The problem was that, if it came to that, the chance of us meeting the same fate surpassed all rational bounds.

If the *illustrious* gentlemen got their hands on the aluminum box, the malefics would come after me. Failing that, I'd have to keep running from the mysterious bank robbers. But if I had the box, I could take control of the game; my only real chance of overcoming my opponents was to make some more progress in the investigation.

Just then, a front wheel plunked down into a pothole. The self-propelled carriage lifted off the ground, then slid into the mud; at the very last moment, I regained control and straightened out the armored vehicle just before it drove off the shoulder. We came very close to turning over in a ditch.

Ramon made a convulsive gulp and moaned out:

"I hate you, Leo!"

I just snorted:

"Think about the three thousand..."

"I've earned it already!" My hulking partner cried out immediately in reply. "My job is done! But now, you've dragged me along on this long-shot adventure!"

"The hunt for the werewolf you also thought a long-shot adventure, right?" I replied, easily finding an answer.

But Ramon Miro wasn't quite as verbally adept. He stuck his finger into the loose seam of his blood-soaked cloak and asked in an accusatory tone:

"Do you think this is normal?"

I had nothing to parry his indisputable conclusion with, so I didn't even try.

"We need to figure out why all this started! If we find out what's riding on this horse, we'll be showered in gold!"

And again, Ramon was ruthlessly precise in his wording.

"That's you!" he declared. "Not me! You'll be showered in gold, not me."

"Don't worry. I won't leave you out in the cold," I promised him, noting a few flames flickering to my right and warning him: "We're past the station. We'll be there soon."

Ramon went silent.

Having thrown all the dogs and people nearby into a panic with its loud chattering, the armored car dashed between tenant's farms, drove around an oak glade and finally rolled right up to the manor.

"We're almost there," I warned my friend. "Get ready."

"Turn off the headlights," Ramon advised.

"There's no use," I refused, not even so much because I was worried I would fly off the road, as much as because of the engine's clapping. Only a deaf person wouldn't have heard that.

Or a dead one.

That was the very thought flickering through

my head as the armored car came to a stop before the closed gates of my uncle's manor. In the guard-post window, there was a dim light flickering, but the late old man didn't think to glance outside and ask why the police were visiting at such an unearthly hour.

Something wasn't right.

"Something isn't right," I said to Ramon.

But before my warning, he was already hidden behind the smoke-shrouded hood of the armored car, pressing the stock of his Winchester to his shoulder.

"What am I even doing here?" he moaned.

"You're covering me!" I reminded him, and got out of the vehicle. "Don't yawn!" I warned my friend, running around the self-propelled carriage, throwing open the back door, and tossing my cane in. In its place, I pulled out a semi-automatic carbine and a few cartridge pouches full of loaded clips.

"The glasses won't affect your vision?" Ramon then asked.

I lifted the smoky eyepieces and snorted:

"What do you think is better?"

My partner's reddish face lit up in the darkness with the luster of my shining eyes. He admitted:

"On. Put them back on."

I lowered my glasses back onto my nose and carefully walked up to the gate. Then, my rifle propped on a crossbeam, I commanded Ramon:

"Come on!"

My hulking partner jumped over the fence in

a flash, undid the latch and opened the path onto my uncle's property.

"The guard-box!" he whispered, warning me.

"You first!" I sighed out just as quietly in response.

I didn't want to loudly announce my presence, regardless of the warning shot I risked from a manor guard.

Covering one another, we walked up to the cracked-open door. There, Ramon peeked inside and immediately recoiled.

"Dead," he said, adding: "Broken neck."

"Curses!" I swore, hesitating for a moment, then ordering: "Wait!" and hurried to the armored car.

I removed the steering wheel and threw it in the rear, then climbed in after it. I felt around for the box of grenades I had strapped down under the seat, took out two and twisted in the fuses. Then, I hung a massive padlock on the tailboard and returned to my partner, now much calmer and more put together, my knees not shaking in the slightest.

"We should call for backup!" whispered Ramon, greeting me angrily, having completely forgotten his recent dismissal.

I didn't stick my finger in the wound, though, just shook my head:

"I think we're too late."

"Where did you get that idea?" asked my hulking partner, growing surprised.

"The dirigible is gone," I told him, pointing to a lonely signal light on the docking tower.

The airship's signal lights were nowhere to be seen, along with the white oval of its balloon.

"The murderer might have flown away on the dirigible," Ramon posited.

"All the more reason not to worry," I snorted and started off to my family mansion.

My hulking partner came behind me, but quickly stopped and declared:

"Either the Count or the killer flew away. There's no reason for us to go in!"

"Come off it!" I exclaimed, trying to bring my partner to reason. "We have to figure out what exactly happened here!"

"Why the devil do we have to do that?"

"In order to have an elementary understanding of who we're searching for! And also, if the Count flew away on the dirigible, the strangler must be somewhere nearby. What if we can get him talking?"

"No," Ramon cut me off. "That's a bad idea."

I looked at the silhouette of the mansion. There wasn't a single light on. Next to it, there was a stable and an overgrown garden that could have hidden a whole company of soldiers. I mentally agreed with my friend.

It really was a bad idea. Bad and very dangerous.

But I said otherwise out loud.

"Either we go together," I shrugged my shoulders hopelessly, "or you wait for me in the car. But know that, if I don't come back, the Judeans won't pay you a centime for the werebeast. Think about that!"

"Curses!" Ramon swore, wiping his sweaty face and nervously glancing at the darkened mansion. "Aw hell!" he relented. "Let's go!"

With a quiet chuckle, I went first down the path, stopping when I reached the fork toward the stable, but didn't turn down it, not wanting to waste time. The mansion was luring me in.

Luring? I caught myself on that thought and even slowed my pace.

My excitement faded as if I had crossed over some invisible boundary. The world once again acquired dimension. The silhouettes of the buildings and the trees of the garden no longer seemed like carved plywood theater props strewn carelessly about the lawn. The understanding rolled over me that this was all happening in the here and now.

My fear returned.

I froze in place, listening to the silence of the night. Without the sound of our boots splashing in the puddles, the silence would have been grave-like. The only other noise was the horn of a steam train somewhere very far in the distance. But it felt like it was coming from another world; all the armored trains of the Empire taken together wouldn't have been able to help us now.

"Leo!" Ramon whispered quietly. "What's going on?"

I shrugged my shoulders to settle my imagination's unwelcome playfulness, and walked on. My family manor grew up out of the darkness like a black titan. Soon we were able to see the door. It was thrown wide open.

"I'll be damned if that isn't an invitation!" Ramon sighed. "'Will you walk into my parlor?' said the spider to the fly!"

My laconic, hulking partner's strained nerves had loosened his tongue, and I found it necessary to reassure him, so I handed him one of my grenades.

"Take this."

"You just can't wait to blow this whole place up, can you?" Ramon joked, looking around apprehensively. "Maybe we should just burn the house down now and not waste time."

"Excellent idea!" I grumbled, slowly and carefully stepping up onto the veranda. "Cover me!" my friend called out, first to cross the threshold.

We stood in the entryway, looking around in the darkness, then I flipped the light switch on the wall, but the electric bulb on the ceiling didn't turn on.

I hung my carbine on my shoulder, took my Roth-Steyr from its holster and requested:

"Torch!"

Ramon handed me his pocket torch; its bright beam swept through the entryway and immediately picked out the body of my uncle's butler from the darkness. Also, someone's legs were sticking out into the hallway in a pair of badly abused ankle-boots.

After stepping over the night guard's body, we walked into the guest room. There on the sofa was lying the parlor maid with her head thrown back. The color of her bloodless face was now no different from that of her white apron.

"Damn it!" Ramon Miro sighed.

"Quiet!" I hissed at him, listening to the silence.

On the other side of the wall, there was a cricket chirping quietly, but that was all. I couldn't hear anything else.

"Follow me!" I commanded and started walking up to the second floor.

The bright beam of the torch danced and jumped from side to side, easily illuminating the dark corners. At the same time, I couldn't leave the thought that someone's cold eyes were watching us from the darkness.

Wishful thinking? Who the devil could say...?

We walked right past the second floor.

"First, let's check the Count's office," I decided, walking further up the stairs.

To my great surprise, I lost all desire to continue pursuing the unknown strangler; I was filled with the urge to turn around and run away without a second thought. And I don't even know what exactly stopped me from taking that shameful step, the left-over passion still raging in my blood or the fear of looking foolish.

I suspect it was more the second.

We walked up to the third floor. I walked into the hall and froze like a dead person when the I saw the flickering of a kerosene lamp in the flung-wide doors.

And a shadow! The shadow on the floor in front of the door was throbbing slightly, either crawling away in one direction or slinking away in the other. There was someone in the office.

The torch now off, I stuck it in my pocket and pressed my pointer finger to my lips. Ramon nodded, letting me know he'd seen the shadow, and was gathering strength for the fight.

I held onto my Roth-Steyr with both hands and walked forward. Walking soundlessly on the carpets leading down the hall, I stole up to the door and took a bounding leap into the office. Once there, I immediately stepped aside, making way for my partner.

I didn't shoot; I didn't see any person. There was just paper strewn about, and filing-cabinet drawers snarling up at me from the floor.

But I made a mistake! Initially, my gaze just slid right over a figure sitting at the desk, as if it was just another shadow. The flame of the kerosene lamp was quivering behind the immobile man, turning him into a black silhouette like one of the slippery fish swimming thoughtlessly in the aquarium at the far wall.

I could only make out a cloak and a hat with a wide flat brim; nothing else.

Shadows, what a damned nuisance!

I drew my pistol, putting the stranger in the crosshairs, but before I managed – or got up the resolve – to pull down on the trigger, there came an unpleasant whistling half-whisper, just as ghostly as the shadows:

"It's no use!" The sentence echoed in my temples with a vile sting. I froze indecisively with my pistol raised. Ramon, though, didn't hesitate.

His Winchester burst forth with a deafening thunder. Its dual spark tore the shadows filling the office to shreds, but the malefic wasn't moved in the slightest.

He made a theatrical pause, then looked at the bullet in his hand and said carelessly:

"You're just wasting perfectly good cartridges."

Angry at the setback, Ramon clanked down the lever of his Winchester, throwing the spent casing onto the floor. But I stopped him, repeating the strangler's words:

"It's no use!"

The mysterious figure set the bullet down on the edge of the writing desk. Not only was it covered in frost, it was also deformed; the stranger's bony fingers had crumpled the aluminum jacket.

"Good decision," the malefic laughed. Then, with a magician's gesture, he pulled a box made of light-gray metal from thin air. I saw the lid. It was engraved with a jagged lightning rune. "I suppose this will be of interest to you, *illustrious* Mr. Orso?"

"Perhaps," I answered cautiously, guessing how to act.

Move from a position of power or show him how reasonable I could be? Attack first, or try to come to an agreement?

The bullet he crushed in his fingers made the first option seem futile; the ruthlessness displayed by the strangler had taken away all hope for the second.

So, what to do?

Ramon started walking in one direction away from the door. I went the other. The kerosene lamp was now not at the strangler's back but, even so, the dense shadows under his hat formed an impenetrable veil, hiding his face better than any mask.

"Guess where the Count is," the malefic commanded me calmly; he was stubbornly ignoring Ramon, instead turning to face me.

I made sure the desk was between us, and demonstratively holstered my gun.

"Even if the Count is in hell, I won't be too broken up," I answered, not especially bending the truth.

"Perhaps he is in hell," the strangler chuckled. "Would you like to take a look?" he asked, extending the box. He immediately pulled his hand back, though, as if teasing.

"Take a look?" I asked in incomprehension. Licking my lips, I asked: "Under what conditions?" I asked and immediately realized I'd just made an unforgivable mistake. Perhaps even a fatal one.

The strangler's relaxed demeanor was immediately replaced with predatory interest.

"You don't know what's inside, do you?" he asked, even taking a step forward. The flame of the kerosene lamp before his face forced him to stand up straight and move back, though.

For the first time, his whistling half-whisper did not cause a biting echo in my head, so I was able to formulate my answer more carefully in opposition to my previous, rushed bluntness.

"Do you?" I asked, watching a fiery moth wriggling on the window. "Do you know?"

"That doesn't matter," the malefic answered, and the shadows around him started moving like a constrictor wrapped around a circus performer.

One of the ghostly tethers slid up to Ramon and twisted around his ankles; my hulking partner froze half-step, and the barrel of his Winchester, originally pointed at the strangler, suddenly shook and began to turn in my direction.

With a fated sigh, I removed my dark glasses, but the glow of my eyes didn't throw the malefic off in the slightest. He just laughed:

"And just what do you think you're going to do, *illustrious* one? Scare me to death?"

"Take you with me to hell," I answered, and threw the lamp on the floor in a careless motion.

The glass immediately shattered. Kerosene poured out all over the office and caught fire. The flames reached the curtains almost instantly, flying up to the ceiling. The haphazardly strewn papers, turned over drawers and furniture then also caught in their turn.

Ramon threw his Winchester away and tore off his flame-ensconced cloak. He ran into a chair and started rolling on the floor looking like a human torch. The fire cut *me* off from the entrance door and chased *me* into the corner. But the strangler didn't lose his presence of mind. Or was it that he lost his mind in fear? In any case, he dashed toward the exit right through the fiery room.

I glanced at my timepiece, waiting for the right moment, but Ramon extended his hand to me and, begging, rasped out:

"Come on, Leo!"

Having decided not to test my partner's patience, I took the carbine off my shoulder and struck the aquarium wall with its buttstock. The water that poured out onto the floor instantly put out the puddle of burning kerosene and an impenetrable blackness took over the office again.

"Fires of hell!" Ramon whispered through his parched lips, peeling himself from the wall. "That hurt like hell!"

"Silence!" I hissed at him, walking over to the door and looking into the hallway, but the strangler's trail had already gone cold. I tried to listen for him, but the dense silence just rang in my ears.

Ramon stood next to me and whispered out barely audibly:

"Did he get away?"

"He got away," I confirmed just as quietly.

My hulking partner wiped off his perspiring brow and fell back into the armchair, sapped. He'd been struck by just a little echo of another's horror, but even still looked like one of the fish from the now empty aquarium.

"Will he be back?" Ramon asked when I turned on my electric torch and started studying the chaos I'd caused in the office.

"No," I stated confidently in reply. "But if he does come back, he'll see a burning house."

"How'd you do that?"

I just laughed:

"It's all my *talent*, old buddy. Or have you forgotten?"

The strangler was afraid of fire; I noticed him jump back from that kerosene lamp. He was obviously scared. All I had to do was pull on that thread at the right time to turn the puddle of burning kerosene into a raging fire.

Can terror magnify a threat? Indeed!

The aluminum box glinted up from the floor in the light of the electric torch; I pulled on my gloves and picked it up, but the lock was broken and the box was empty.

"Curses!" I swore, not hiding my disappointment.

"What are you on about now?" Ramon shuddered.

"Nothing."

"Nothing at all?"

"That's right!" I snarled. In a fit of anger, I threw the box into the corner and walked around the office, but I still hadn't come to any definite conclusion on who was responsible for all this mess: was it the Count, and he'd fled, or the malefic who'd come after his soul?

"Leo, we need to get out of here!" shouted my hulking partner, trying to hurry me along as I shuffled through the burned papers strewn about the floor, now wet from the spilled water.

"We do," I agreed with him and stuck the bullet the strangler had crushed into my pocket. "But first, let's check the house."

We went through the whole mansion, but there was no one on the third or second floors, and all the servants down below were dead. The strangler was enviably methodical. He hadn't left anything behind.

"Where is the Count's family?" Ramon asked as we walked into the guest room.

"His daughter's at a boarding school, and his wife's at the spa." I answered. "Continental Europe. Neither we nor the malefic will reach them now. Well, at least we won't. That much is for certain."

"Will you search for the Count?"

"What do you think?"

"It's your business," Ramon replied, not trying to convince me one way or the other. He then suddenly pointed to the body of the servant girl spread-eagled on the sofa. "Hold up!"

"What is it?"

"Point the torch at her neck!"

I did what he said, and immediately noticed two dark blue spots on the dead pale skin.

"Well, tear me to pieces!" Ramon gasped. "There was a vampire here!"

An unpleasant chill ran down my spine; I forced myself to touch the dead girl. The body had already gone cold, but unlike the other victims, this one had just started to get rigor mortis.

"What have you dragged me into, Leo?!" Ramon whispered in fear and anger. "Malefics and vampires, just think! Even in Europe, there are practically no vampires left.

All the more so here!"

"Well, the werewolf flew in from the New World, so why couldn't this vampire have done something similar?" I muttered.

"What for? Why the devil would he do that? What's happening, Leo?"

I dismissed my partner's concern and hurried to the exit.

"Let's get out of here! It's getting light out already!"

"No, just a moment!"

"You just can't wait to get behind bars, can you?" I asked with a frown, looking my friend from top to bottom.

"Alright, we can talk later!" he decided. I just had to head for the exit, but he grabbed my hand and stopped me: "Are you sure the malefic was alone?" he asked and first looked outside, his Winchester at the ready.

"Why wouldn't he be?" I asked, surprised.

"How could he get through so many people all alone?"

"The shadows," I reminded him. "He had the shadows helping him. You almost shot me because of one of them, remember?"

Ramon was clearly shaken by the unpleasant memory. He loaded another cartridge into the tubular magazine of his Winchester and muttered:

"In any case, don't yawn!"

I nodded and took the semi-automatic carbine from my shoulder. The strangler definitely wouldn't be hurt by a rifle, but vampires tended to surround themselves with mortal helpers. So, I had to be careful with the weapon in my hands...

The high veranda of the mansion faced east. At the very horizon, the clouds were already turning a shade of faint pink, and I said quietly:

"It's getting light out!"

My hulking partner nodded, letting me know that he had heard my words, but not lost vigilance; he didn't believe the legend that vampires could be hurt by sunlight. To be perfectly honest, neither did I. So, in no particular hurry, we walked back to the armored car, not taking our eyes off the trees and bushes near the path.

The birds had already begun their normal morning bickering. From the tenant farms, I heard a rooster crow. The risk of meeting a random passerby was growing with every minute. Approaching the gates, we threw back the latch and ran headlong for the car.

Ramon took a prudent look under the self-propelled carriage and gave a nod:

"All clear!"

Then, I opened the tailboard and threw my rifle in it and taking out the steering wheel in its place. My partner ran up and extended his Winchester.

"Take it," he said.

I accepted the gun and groaned out:

"Dolt!"

"What are you on about?" Ramon shuddered.

"The casing!" I screamed. "You left a casing in my uncle's office! Fingerprints!"

"Curse me!" Ramon exclaimed, going bed-sheet pale. But he immediately overcame his moment of hesitation, grabbed the wheel from me and got into the car.

"Let's go back! Now!" he shouted, affixing the steering wheel to the column.

"Start it up!" I called out, and jumped onto the passenger-side running board.

The engine chattered to life; to the jingle of its very frequent popping, the armored car drove up to the gates, easily tossed them aside and drove onto the grounds of the mansion. When it hit, we shook hard, and the self-propelled carriage even went off-road onto the grass. But Ramon managed to turn the wheel in time and get back on track.

A moment later, we had arrived at the mansion. There, Ramon sharply braked, jumped out of the cabin and ran at breakneck speed into the building. I ran around and sat in the driver's seat, turned the car around to prepare to leave and raised the front armor sheet, which had been down on the hood until that point. Driving at night with an obscured windshield wasn't possible, but now, it was getting light out. The villagers were all waking up, and the last thing I wanted was for some eagle-eyed tenant to describe us to a policeman

The front door slammed again, and Ramon ran fervently down from the veranda into the car.

"Drive!" he shouted.

"Did you find it?"

"Yes!" he replied, catching his breath. "Drive, I said!"

And so, we drove. We didn't stop until we reached the city, not even to pour water into the radiator. Eventually, though, we found a dark passageway in the back yard of a factory to park the vehicle in.

Ramon ran to a station on the neighboring intersection with a bucket, and I started pacing around the self-propelled carriage, massaging my cramped legs and looking all around. My back was in unbearable pain, my head felt full of molten lead, and my arms were shaking in exhaustion. I felt out of sorts, but not at all because of my personal wellbeing.

There was something else bothering me.

"What should we do with the self-propelled carriage?" I asked my partner after he'd come back with water. "Everyone knew the Count and I were at loggerheads; I wouldn't be surprised if they came to search my place today or tomorrow."

"Is that even possible?" my hulking partner asked in surprise.

"What do you think?" I furrowed my brow.

"No!" he waved his hand in annoyance. "What about the quarantine? How will they get inside?"

"Sooner or later, they'll find an *illustrious* person with immunity to the Diabolic Plague. The armored car is direct evidence. We left too many tracks at the estate."

"Get rid of it," Ramon suggested.

"Not an option," I refused. "We might need it again."

"Leo! This tin can could land us behind bars."

I didn't even listen.

"Your cousin from Foundry Town..." I snapped my fingers. "What if we brought the armored car to him?"

"Are you crazy?" Ramon's eyes grew round. "I'm not bringing family into this!"

"What about the coalhouse?"

The man began thinking, then nodded.

"You know, there are a couple other abandoned packhouses there," he muttered. "There's no way anyone will go into them before fall."

"Do they have separate vehicle entrances?" I clarified.

"Some do, yes," my friend confirmed. "Let's go!"

By that time, it had long been light outside and the recently-awoken people on the street were looking curiously at our police armored car, caked in mud from wheels to roof. Fortunately, there weren't many people in the outskirts near the coalhouse where Ramon now worked as a guard. Our only company was a pair of chatty mutts.

Ramon pointed at the set of gates, told me to wait and ran out. When he came back, he was holding a heavy keyring.

"Don't worry," he reassured me, undoing the

rusty warehouse lock. That old drunk wouldn't wake up even if a ship's cannon went off next to his ear.

"Make copies during your shift."

"Of course."

The gates gave way with a ghastly screech. We had to put all our weight into throwing them open. I then drove the armored vehicle into the interior of the sooty packhouse. I turned off the engine and extended my partner a hand, all my energy sapped:

"Thank you! You really helped me out."

Ramon clenched my hand in his massive paw and asked:

"When will you be retrieving the reward for the banker's killer?"

"I'll deal with it this morning," I decided, looking at my timepiece and correcting myself: "Actually, it might be closer to lunch time."

"Don't draw it out," he demanded. "Alright?"

"Don't you doubt it," I promised, taking my cane and getting out of the cabin.

With our combined strength, we managed to close the warehouse doors, but only barely. Ramon put the lock back on, rubbed some coal dust on it and took a look at our handiwork.

"This will be fine," he decided.

It would have been good to take the right key off the ring now, but my weary thoughts got all mixed-up. My eyes were starting to close all on their own. The sleepless night and jitters had squeezed all the juice out of me. The only thing I really wanted now was to lie in bed and close my eyes.

So, I just waved my hand and headed home. Sleep.

BUT IT WASN'T so easy to get to bed.

Elizabeth-Maria knocked me off course. She examined me closely then declared in a tone that wouldn't bear objection:

"A glass of tea would do you good."

I looked at the reflection of my pale and peaked countenance, turned away from the mirror and nodded:

"Alright, make up a pot."

"You'll drink it in the kitchen. I hope that at least can teach you to come home on time!"

I didn't start a fight over it; I just wasn't in the mood. I silently hung my dusty jacket on a hanger, placed my cane in the umbrella stand, then got out of my mud-caked boots and walked into the kitchen.

I took a seat at the window, finished the hot sweet tea and stared thoughtlessly at the wet, black trees of my garden.

"I'm starting to see that coming back in the morning is a habit of yours!" the succubus noted pointedly as she lit the stove.

I stayed silent. I didn't want to talk, or move. Even the bed no longer called to me with the promise of slumber. It now seemed impossibly far away.

I sat at the window and drank tea.

Elizabeth Maria stopped trying to make me

talk and set a thick cast-iron pan on the fire. She poured oil in, added spices, and the kitchen immediately filled with the smell of exotic goodness. A few minutes later, a glob of meat was slapped down on the red-hot metal, but I didn't pay the hissing and sizzling sounds the slightest bit of mind. Only when the girl set a plate of barely cooked steak before me did I express my incomprehension:

"Don't you think this is a bit rich for breakfast?"

"Look at yourself, you're all skin and bones!" the girl objected. "Also, I suspect this is not breakfast for you, but a late dinner."

"Where'd you get the idea I wanted to eat?"

"You smell of death," Elizabeth-Maria answered calmly, "and for a man, killing is but the prelude to a substantial repast. Even if you're killing something like yourself. It's an ancient custom."

"Like myself?" I asked, making a face. "Today, we killed a werewolf. A ghastly monster."

"Do you suppose you're so very different from him?" the girl couldn't resist joking back.

I squirmed.

"Yes, I do!" I threw out sharply. "I am very different. Is that clear?"

"As you say, dear," Elizabeth-Maria shrugged her shoulders and took a bottle of sherry from the drawer. "Yes, that reminds me! The red wine is still disappearing. You better bring your light-haired monkey to reason before I cut his hands off."

"The leprechaun and I haven't been able to find a common tongue recently," I shook my head.

To be honest, my childhood imaginary friend's trickery was now driving me totally crazy. I hadn't thought about the rude pipsqueak for many long years, and now couldn't get my head around why on earth he'd suddenly popped out of my subconscious. It scared me, because it meant I might lose control over my own gift. No nightmare I'd ever created before had stayed in the world for so long. No fantasy had seemed so real.

Elizabeth-Maria was just a clever succubus, but what was powering the leprechaun?

I had no answer to the question.

"That pipsqueak drinks like a horse," the girl complained, taking a seat opposite me with a glass of fortified wine and setting a dish of sauce before me. "Eat!"

I was about to refuse, but my stomach suddenly moaned out in hunger. And though I had never especially cared for undercooked meat – and when I cut into the steak, blood came out – I had to admit that it wasn't at all bad. The spicy sauce had a flavor I couldn't place, but it was surprisingly subtle, and went with the steak perfectly.

"Have you ever heard of the Convent?" I asked the girl, cutting another bite of meat.

"The Convent?" Elizabeth Maria asked in confusion and sipped the wine, trying to hide her puzzlement. "Ideologues," she said after a pause so long I wasn't even really expecting her to answer.

"Ideologues?" I didn't understand.

"Typical malefics are simply happy to sell their pitiful little souls in exchange for a little bit of power and mortal prosperity. These are not like that. They tell tales of old. They want to bring those times back."

"Is that so?"

"That is precisely so," she attested. "And why do you ask?"

I just shrugged my shoulders, not telling her the dying werebeast's final words.

"Don't get involved with the Convent," Elizabeth-Maria warned me. "They're dangerous. Extremely dangerous. If you cross their path, they'll kill you and eat your soul."

"Where's all this sudden concern for my soul coming from?"

For a moment, from behind the imaginary exterior of a sweet-looking girl, her true appearance stepped out, revealing an infernal creature with the fiery red eyes of a hellbeast. They burned into me with unconcealed hatred.

"If they eat it, there'd be nothing left for me!" the succubus announced.

But it was very easy for me not to play along. I had a good understanding of fears and could say for certain that the succubus was afraid. And that she was afraid on her own account, not mine.

"Weren't you summoned from hell by a

malefic?" I squinted. "Was he from the Convent?"

"I don't want to talk about it."

"You ran from him and he's searching for you. Is that right? What would happen if he finds you?"

"You won't manage to get into my head, Leo," Elizabeth-Maria said with a sweet smile. But I wasn't ready to change the topic.

"Perhaps he even put a bounty out on you." I posited, looking the succubus right in the eyes.

"You don't understand the first thing," the girl sighed. "Leo, you and I have an agreement. And that could only mean one thing..."

"And just what is that?"

"He is long dead," Elizabeth-Maria stated. "He pulled off his own head. You can't even imagine how great it was!"

"Please, spare me the details! We're at the table!"

"It wasn't I who started this conversation," the succubus reminded me dryly. "And no, he wasn't from the Convent. The arrogant twerp! Smart people choose devils and minor evil spirits as *familiars*. With them, you can do whatever you want! But he chose a succubus! The arrogant upstart!"

"But minor evil spirits don't give as much power, isn't that right?" I asked, surprised. "What's the good of that?"

"Power?" the girl laughed uncontrollably. "The source of power is the divine fire of the human soul. *Familiars* serve a different purpose."

"Please enlighten me, then."

But the girl had already finished her wine and gotten up from the table.

"Finish eating and go off to bed," she demanded. After that, she went over to the neighboring window, looked at the dead garden and suddenly stated: "Pain."

"What? Excuse me?" I asked, pretending not to have heard her.

"Pain," Elizabeth-Maria repeated. "This world is a constant source of pain, but when one's master casts a spell, that pain is multiplied tenfold. Familiars absorb that pain. That's all. And not all the pain can be absorbed, just some. But even that causes unbearable suffering."

"Is that so?"

"Oh, yes! The burning tears your head to bits and pierces you through with hundreds of icy needles. Have you ever heard of Chinese water torture? The monotonous pain bears down on you and brings you to the level of an animal. When someone speaks to you, you can hear the words, but they mean nothing. In fact, you cannot even perceive that you really are hearing them."

"And are you suffering this pain now?"

"No, sweet Leo. Not at all. Thanks to this body," the girl said, turning away from the window and leading her hand from her chest to her thigh, "the pain left me. But it's around here somewhere. Look for yourself."

I nodded and got up from the table.

"Leo! Stay away from the Convent!" the

succubus repeated. "Don't make them angry. Don't talk to them. Don't look at them, and don't even tread in their shadows. Just forget they exist. That's my advice to you."

"Shadows?" I perked up my ears. "Shadows with their own life force?"

Elizabeth-Maria didn't answer at all, turning away toward the window again.

I hesitated, but in the end, I didn't pester her with an interrogation. I just waved my hand and headed into the bedroom.

Malefics, their familiars and a strange burning. The dead Kira and her companion. The strangler's shadows. All these things could have been part of something bigger, but my weariness was stopping me from sorting it all out. The only thing I had the energy for was crawling up to bed, climbing into it and putting a pillow under my head.

Sleep!

2

I WOKE UP in a flash. I just opened my eyes and felt a clear presentiment of misfortune. I grabbed my Roth-Steyr from the bedside table and hopped out of bed.

I looked into the kitchen and caught my breath with relief. There was no one there.

A bad dream?

But then, I saw that my window had been

left open. On the windowsill, there appeared the gaunt figure of a werefox; a bounding leap and she was already in the middle of the room.

"Long time no see," said the miniature-framed girl with a clear Chinese accent. Then, her smooth face stretched out into a ghastly snout. Her bared teeth shimmered back at me with a yellow glint. They were small, but extremely sharp.

That they were sharp I could be certain. And so, without any hesitation, I unloaded my pistol at the beast as she prepared for a jump. The bullets slammed full force into a wooden panel behind the fox's back. She herself leaped toward me, but even faster, I threw a hand forward and snapped:

"Enough!"

The beast evaporated. Just a stiff wisp of air remained, hitting me in the face, finally chasing off what was left of my dream. It was a nightmare, just a nightmare...

I subconsciously worried that the fox would try to get even with me, and my *talent* didn't delay in bringing that fear to life. Recently, my *talent* had gone totally out of control, no matter how unfortunate that was.

A knock came at the door; I unlocked it and let Elizabeth-Maria into the room.

"Another nightmare?" she asked calmly, having noticed the many bullet holes in the ceiling.

"Not at all," I objected, looking at the smoking pistol in my hand and shrugging my shoulders. "I was trying to draw her Imperial Majesty's monogram. That's all."

"At least you've got a hobby," the girl snorted and hid in the hallway. "Go to the range! You're a horrible shot!" she shouted, already down the hall.

Theodor came in to replace the acid-tongued redhead.

"Would you like me to fix it, Viscount?" he asked me, studying the mess I'd made.

"I suppose we could just hang a rug over it," I decided, taking out my extra clip. I then noticed that my Butler's skin was looking abnormally pale and asked: "Is everything alright, Theodor?"

"Naturally, Viscount," my servant assured me expectedly. His face was noticeably upset, though. It was as if some power accessible only to twins had made him sense the death of his brother.

It would have been nice to tell him about his brother's untimely end, but I hesitated, not sure how my servant would react to the news. Did he really need all these tribulations now? I wasn't convinced.

"You may go," I said, dismissing my butler without having come to any definite decision.

At one point, I'd be sure to tell him everything, but not now. Some other time.

Cowardice, you say? Nothing of the sort. Simple tact, and nothing more. One mustn't simply up and dump that kind of news on one's butler! He must be prepared for it first. I'd have to think something up...

Alright, so it was cowardice. What of it?

Who among us is without flaws?

I reloaded my Roth-Steyr, got dressed and left the bedroom. I went down to the first floor and looked cantankerously at my reflection in the mirror. But my suit was fitting perfectly as if it had been sewn to my exact order. Surprising even, considering my tall and lank dimensions. Trying to buy a suit when you looked like I did was pure torture.

"Leo!" Elizabeth-Maria called out to me from the kitchen. "Let's go drink tea!"

"Not now!" I refused, looking at the clock on the wall. It was already two in the afternoon.

"Leo!" The girl raised her voice.

I gave a heavy sigh and relented.

"Let's try to pretend we're a normal family," Elizabeth-Maria suggested when I had taken my seat at the table and was staring out the window.

I still had the urge to answer rudely but, by force of will, I held back the inappropriate outburst and just noted:

"That would mean we should act like master and servant, then. That seems most appropriate to our situation."

Elizabeth-Maria put two spoons of sugar in her cup and parried calmly:

"Many families have just that sort of interaction, dear. The husband – sovereign and the wife – his rightless slave."

I grabbed a piece of toast from the basket and took off the top from a jar of raspberry jam. I scooped it onto a knife and shook my head with a bitter sigh:

"A succubus suffragette. Where is this world headed?"

"I cannot claim that we have equal rights in hell, but we are certainly more tolerant of others' faults, dear. You mortals could learn a thing or two from us."

"Ugh, no thank you!" I snorted, finishing my tea and asking: "What do you know about vampires?"

The girl tilted her head to the side and stared at me, suggesting I go on.

"It's not such a hard question," I muttered, slathering my second piece of toast with jam. "You know, vampires! Fangs, pale skin, allergy to sunlight, an unhealthy obsession with others' blood. What do you know about them?"

"Are you planning a trip to Transylvania?" Elizabeth-Maria joked.

Or maybe she wasn't joking, and was totally serious.

"Why Transylvania?"

"Remember our conversation yesterday about the burning?" The girl stared thoughtfully at a glass of tea, then pushed it away from herself and went to get some wine; she had stashed a bottle of fortified red in the grain drawer.

"The burning?" I asked in surprise. "What of it?"

"Malefics experience the pain only when they are casting a spell. And that doesn't happen so terribly often. They can either bear it or force a familiar to suffer along with them. Werebeasts experience torturous pain immediately after they turn back into humans but, even still, they are infrequent visitors to New Babylon."

I nodded, agreeing with her assessment. Elizabeth-Maria continued:

"Underworld natives arrive to this world in their natural state. They rid themselves of the pain by clothing themselves in the flesh of others, taking human souls and bodies. Other creatures, the offspring of times gone by, either run from civilization, or become degraded, losing the last remnants of their mind. Only ghosts and magical conjurations do not feel the pain. In fact, they do not feel anything at all."

"Where are you going with this?"

"No one can bear such pain for long," Elizabeth-Maria declared. "Vampires cannot deny their essence and go back to being normal people, even for a minute. Vampires are not like the zombies raised by Haitian masters. They can feel pain. But their bodies are dead, and dead flesh has no defense against the pain."

"How long ago were you called to this world?" I asked, having caught a sense of sorrow flickering in the succubus's voice.

"It doesn't matter!" she snapped back in annoyance, waving it off. I put my eyelids together, shutting in the fell light glowing up out of my eyes. "It doesn't matter, Leo. The most important thing is that not a single vampire would come to New Babylon out of good will. It's akin to the most intricate torture. Only threat of death could make them suffer it."

"But still, where might I find them?"

"In Transylvania, Romania, or Zuid-India. Among the Egyptians or the Aztecs. In Cuba or the African Colonies. In the Siberian taiga, the mountains of Afghanistan or the endless Asian steppe. Anywhere but here. Not in big cities. Even in the provinces, the burning is too strong..."

But I was still being haunted by the bloodless body of my uncle's servant girl with two precise wounds on her neck, so I kept insisting:

"Where do you think I could find a vampire in New Babylon?"

Elizabeth-Maria looked in reply with unhidden doubt, then with a careless look shrugged her shoulders, clearly having lost all interest in the conversation:

"The bottom of a hole. The deeper the better. If one really did come to New Babylon, it would be in a leaden sarcophagus somewhere in the catacombs beyond the city."

"A sarcophagus?" I asked in surprise. "And why lead exactly?"

"If you come across a vampire, ask. Perhaps you'll even get an answer," the girl said with a detached smirk, now thinking about something else entirely. "What are your plans for tonight?" she suddenly inquired, twirling a lock of her red hair around her finger.

"I'm going to the circus," I said, standing from the table and removing the kerchief I'd stuffed into my shirt neck to catch dripping jam. "What of it?"

"I never took you for a circus aficionado."

And that was an accurate assessment; I didn't like the circus. Neither the circus, nor circus people.

Devil! If I really thought about it, there weren't many people on the planet, toward whom I didn't experience a certain antipathy.

Was I a misanthrope? No, more like a clinical introvert.

"A friend asked me to go with him," I explained. And when she came out after me into the entryway, in my turn, I inquired: "And the burning, what causes it?"

"The million-franc question!" the girl laughed, taking a little brush and starting to dust the shelves. "No one is sure, but in the time of *the fallen*, it wasn't around. Back then, the whole world belonged to us, and us alone."

"Yeah, yeah," I chuckled, going outside without a cloak or even a jacket.

The weather put a smile on my face. There wasn't even a trace of yesterday's tempest remaining. The sky was clear, though far off on the horizon there were clumpy, foreboding cumulus clouds gathering.

I started down from the porch and immediately was reminded by the discomfort in my leg that it was sprained. And even though it wasn't bothering me so bad today, it still seemed reasonable to go back home for Alexander Dyak's cane.

"You're fast!" Elizabeth-Maria snickered acridly on my return, not stopping her dusting.

"And you, I see, have really taken to

housework," I replied, going tit for tat and looking with surprise under my feet, only now noting the bare floor. "What happened to the rug?"

"The rug?" the girl asked in surprise.

"Yes, the rug!"

"Leo, do you take me for a housekeeper? How should I know about your rugs?"

I frowned and raised my voice:

"Theodor!"

"Yes, Viscount?" my butler asked, having come to my call.

"Theodor, did you take the rug from the entryway?"

"No, Viscount," my servant answered dispassionately and said nothing further.

Elizabeth-Maria stared at me with lively curiosity. With a no-less-interested tone, I answered her:

"And you say you had nothing to do with this either?"

"That's right," the girl confirmed.

I'm not sure why, but I believed her. And that put me all the more on alert.

I walked through the guest room, looking carefully underfoot and soon noticed a long reddish-brown splotch on one of the skirting boards, as if someone had tried hastily to wipe off some spilled red ink. Or blood?

"Look," I said to Elizabeth-Maria.

The girl gave a graceful curtsy, scratched it with her long nail, licked her finger and, perplexed, drew out her words:

"How interesting!"

"What is it?"

"Blood," the girl stated her verdict and added: "It's fresh."

Theodor's distant tranquility disappeared in a flash.

"Please!" he flared up. "Only the three of us have been in the manor. Others have no way of even entering! That must have occurred to you, Viscount!"

"And yet, the rug disappeared, and the floor is dirty with blood," I muttered, continuing to look around the room. At first glance, everything was in place. I didn't manage to detect any other traces of another's presence.

"Another one of your nightmares, perhaps?" Elizabeth-Maria purred.

"I do not know," I replied, shrugging my shoulders and looking into the hallway. "Theodor, bring me a lamp!"

The butler carried out my order and, soon, the uneven light of the bat-like bulb hanging down from my ceiling allowed us to discover another few drops of blood, smeared and partially dry.

I pulled my Roth-Steyr from its holster and chambered a round. Someone had been in the house uninvited, and I didn't even want to think why they had rolled out the rug. However, the blood on the floor didn't leave me much room for imagination.

Someone had killed someone else and then covered their tracks.

But who? And most importantly, who did

they kill?

Theodor armed himself with a poker from the fireplace. Elizabeth-Maria ran for the saber and we followed the bloody spots as if it were a trail of breadcrumbs. This person wasn't particularly precise, so it wasn't a difficult task to discover the reddish-brown spots.

We breezed through the pantry and closet, turned down the side corridor and Theodor hazarded a guess:

"The carriage-house!"

And he was dead on. The drops of blood extended right up to the door from the annex into the carriage-house; unlike many modern homes, my manor had a door directly from the living quarters into the vehicle storage area.

"Quiet!" I whispered, flinging the door open and stepping in with my pistol at the ready. Theodor quickly came after me and raised the lamp over my head, illuminating the dark garage.

The leprechaun, caught unawares, peevishly moved his accordioned top hat onto the back of his head, spit his rolled cigarette onto the floor and cursed:

"Bugger, what bad timing!"

And it was hard to disagree with him. We'd caught him with a fresh corpse laid out on a workbench, hacksaw in hand. It was, in fact, very bad timing...

"What the devil?!" I snarled and, ducking my head as not to hit it on the low door jamb, went down the stairs. "What the devil are you doing?"

The leprechaun didn't answer, though. He

tore off his kitchen apron and skillfully leaped out an open window.

I stuck my pistol in the holster and walked up to the body. Its throat was ripped open from ear to ear. The cadaver was unfamiliar to me, but I could say for sure that it was not an *illustrious* gentleman. In his dead eyes, the bloody murk of the curse that enveloped my house had already taken hold. The body of an *illustrious* person wouldn't have capitulated to the Diabolic Plague so quickly.

"Do you know, Leo...?" Elizabeth-Maria said, drawing out her words with an incomprehensible look on her face, slowly going through the tools the leprechaun had laid out: a hacksaw, a hatchet, a set of utility knives, a small hammer and a chisel, "your fantasies are quite a bit darker than I supposed..."

I cursed.

"This isn't my fantasy!"

"Your nightmare, then?"

"Come off it!" I retorted with a wave. I then went through the cadaver's belongings on the floor.

He had a wallet with a few hundred francs, a pair of gloves, and a pen-knife, which didn't arouse any suspicion. But the mask with eye slits, set of lock picks, small crowbar and glass cutter spoke for themselves.

Someone had tried to break in. What could I say? He picked the wrong house.

"It occurs to me that the situation is not unambiguous," I muttered, sticking the money in my own wallet.

"Alright. If you want to think so..." Elizabeth-Maria grinned, amused at everything.

Theodor remained imperturbable.

"What shall we do, Viscount?" He asked. "Get rid of the body, or inform the police?"

I paced through the garage, nervously tapping my fingers on the boxes and trophy weapons, then decided:

"Bring him to the icehouse."

"Fresh meat?" the girl cracked up laughing and threw up her hands. "Leo! Don't be so serious, I was only joking!"

"Alright, I guess," I muttered, spreading out the blood-soaked rug. "Theodor, help!"

Together, my butler and I lowered the corpse to the floor, wrapped it up and dragged it into the house. Elizabeth-Maria lifted the hatch, so all we had to do was lower the body down and lay it on the ice.

"This isn't right," my butler said, pursing his lips. "He cannot stay here!"

"You're right," I agreed, hurriedly leaving the basement; I didn't want to stay down there any longer than necessary.

"And what will we do with him?" Theodor asked, coming up after me.

"We'll think something up," I replied, shrugging my shoulders. My plan now was to bring the armored car back here later and take the body out of town.

Elizabeth-Maria lowered the hatch and inquired acridly:

"You don't want to ask your imaginary friend what he was planning to do?"

"I can get by without his advice, thank you very much."

"Viscount," the butler started. But I cut him off:

"Later, Theodor! I have business to attend to first."

Elizabeth-Maria adjusted my neckerchief and smiled:

"Dear, are you really saying there are more pressing matters than a fresh corpse in the icehouse?"

"Much more pressing," I confirmed, donning my derby-cap before the mirror and leaving the house.

3

MY ATTORNEY'S office was located in one of the faceless towers of glass and concrete that grew up from a new neighborhood in the northern part of the city, which was quickly becoming the center of the Imperial business world. Huge corporations bought whole floors of office buildings there according to their needs. Less well-off companies made do with just individual offices. The successful industrialists considered offices with a view of the historical part of New Babylon especially prestigious; my lawyer's place, though, might as well have been a windowless jail cell.

A recent graduate from law school, the red-headed and sickly pale young man tore himself from his papers and stretched out his lips into something resembling a warm smile. The greenhorn lawyer wasn't getting a single centime from me, either. He was satisfied just to have the status of Viscount Cruce's attorney, though he did think that gave him the right to do half-assed work. Normally, that didn't bother me. Normally, but not today.

When the young man began standing up, I pushed him back into his chair, myself taking a seat on the edge of the table.

"I've got an urgent job. It must be done without delay!" I ordered in a tone that wouldn't bear objection.

"But, Viscount, I cannot abandon my other clients!" the lawyer protested. He really did seem to have been working on some other papers before my arrival, too.

I set a check for ten thousand francs in front of him and smiled:

"Your commission would be ten percent."

My attorney studied the check and shot me a gaze of amazement.

"Ten percent?" he asked with badly hidden trepidation.

"Yes," I confirmed. "Ten percent of ten thousand. But you'll have to work for it."

The lawyer opened his notepad and inquired:

"Under what circumstances did you come by

the check and on what grounds was it protested?"

"Unimportant," I said with a wave and jumped back from the table. I then instructed:

"File a suit to recover the whole value of the check. And just in case, ask for an injunction against the Count's bank accounts, his suburban estate and his dirigible, *Syracuse*. Also, you must put out a search notice for the dirigible immediately."

"But, Viscount!" my attorney protested. "For a sum such as that, these are rather extreme measures..."

"If the suit can't make the Count pay in cash, we'll have no choice but to follow the accepted procedure and wait out the funds from the sale of his property. I wouldn't like that. Would you?"

The lawyer shook his head and bleated out indecisively:

"But the dirigible?"

"My uncle may attempt to flee to the continent by air. If we can deprive him of his means of transportation, he'll be a lot more ready to negotiate."

"And if he voluntarily pays the check..." my attorney started, nervously cracking his fingers, "will my commission remain in force?"

"Yes, the ten percent is yours no matter how this shakes out. But if you don't get to this right now, I'll have to hire someone else."

The lawyer jumped up from the table, adjusted his vest, grabbed his well-worn jacket from the hanger and reported back:

"I'm headed to court immediately!"

"Stop!" I yelled out, barely getting his attention in time. "First, draw up an official complaint. I'll take it to my uncle's attorney first so we can't be later accused of bad faith."

That was how anyone would have acted if they didn't know for sure that the Count had fled, and I was not preparing to give a reason to suspect me of knowing too much.

The lawyer went back to his table, loaded a sheet of paper into a time-worn typing machine and started clacking away on the keyboard with a mad speed, glancing from time to time at the check in front of him.

I didn't sit down in the wobbly visitor's chair, instead pacing from wall to wall. The uneven flickering of the electric lamp under the ceiling was having a bad effect on my nerves.

"There. It's done! Sign!" the lawyer said a quarter hour later, handing me the sheet.

I didn't sign anything, first studying the complaint in excruciating detail, telling him to correct a few typos and only after that placing my signature.

"If you lose that check, I'll tear your head off," I warned my attorney, placing the complaint in my inside pocket.

"I don't doubt it for a second!" he said insightfully. "I'll send it to my notary's office for safe keeping."

"Please do," I nodded. "And don't dally."

"I'm already on my way!"

Not waiting for my lawyer, I went outside alone, stopped the first cabby I met eyes with and told him to bring me to Via Benardos, which is where my dear uncle's lawyer worked.

Maître LaSalle rented an office on the upper floor of a building that looked a lot like a piece of pie from the outside: its facade was of a normal width, but the side walls met in a sharp corner, allowing the architectural abomination to fit between the two neighboring buildings. If desired, I wouldn't even have to jump from rooftop to rooftop. I could just walk.

A finicky watchman at the entrance wanted to know the purpose of my visit, then relayed it up the listening tube to the lawyer's assistant. Only after getting the go-head from him was I allowed inside. There were no elevators in the building. I had to take the stairs, which snaked around an internal courtyard all the way up to the fifth floor. The view out the windows revealed a tiny, dark space reminiscent of the inside of a well.

The lawyer's assistant met me in the entryway and tried to impede me with questions. But, feeling annoyed, I waved him aside and barged straight into the lawyer's office.

"Viscount Cruce!" said the lanky, if not to say frail gentleman of fifty years with surprise, looking up from his papers. He handled the affairs of several members of the old aristocracy. They were all still well off, but had long ago burned through their former influence. "To what do I owe your visit?"

I turned to the pushy assistant standing in the doorway and barked out:

"Make yourself scarce!"

"Leave us," Maître LaSalle ordered. Then, he reproached me: "Have a bit of courtesy, Viscount! Nothing costs so little and is valued so highly as common courtesy."

"You may find that to be so, maître, but I prefer cash," I parried, tossing the complaint on the table. "Ten thousand francs, for example."

The lawyer clipped his reading glasses on his nose and started studying the document; I didn't want to loom over him, so I went over to the window, which looked out onto the neighboring building with a rusty rail of a fire escape. It revealed a view of one of the side streets, narrow and curving.

"This must be some kind of mistake!" my uncle's attorney then exclaimed. "A mere misunderstanding!"

"I do not agree with that assessment, maître," I shook my head, continuing to stand at the window, "but in any case, there's nothing stopping you from getting in touch with the Count and speaking directly."

"Have you brought the check with you?"

"What do you think?"

"What claptrap," the lawyer muttered, picking up the phone and asking to be put through to Count Kósice's manor. Soon, he threw down his phone and told me: "The line's malfunctioning."

"What a shame."

"Where did you get the check, Viscount?"

"That's not important. It's got his name on it."

"Then I place your right to it in doubt. I also have doubts on its authenticity and the very fact that it was refused in the first place!" the lawyer said, putting forth three mutually exclusive arguments with glee. But I couldn't be deterred so easily.

"I guess you'll have to convince a court of that, then," I smiled.

"This is plain abuse of the legal system!" the lawyer objected. "The demand for an injunction on his property, bank accounts and means of transportation over such a trivial matter is simply laughable!"

"Get in touch with the Count, maître," I recommended. "Get in touch with him and insist that he meet with me as soon as possible. The longer this goes on, the worse it'll get."

The lawyer got up from the table and said very quietly and distinctly:

"You'll come to regret this, Viscount. You will regret your negligence very much."

"Whatever happened to courtesy!?" I exclaimed, leaving the office. "Maître, remember your courtesy!"

I didn't try to catch a cab on Via Benardos. I immediately turned down one of the side alleys and walked through the arch onto a quiet boulevard to the Emperor's Academy. Thankfully, the broken feeling in my leg wasn't bothering me quite as much today. And also, I was in no rush.

In the end, it took me ten minutes to reach Leonardo-da-Vinci-Platz. When I entered *Mechanisms and Rarities*, Alexander Dyak was reading a paper.

"Leopold Borisovich!" the inventor cried out, glad at my arrival. He walked around the display case and extended a hand. "Allow me to congratulate you"

"On what?" I perked up my ears.

"On a successful end to the experiment, naturally!" Alexander Dyak burst out laughing, then faltered. "Or was it not you that brought Procrustes to his doom?"

I took a fateful sigh and corrected the inventor:

"It wasn't Procrustes."

"If you say so, Leopold Borisovich, if you say so!" said the shop owner, nodding his head several times. "I trust you haven't forgotten my request? The timeframe is very important for science..."

As surprising as it was, I hadn't forgotten the inventor's request and, while still in the opium den awaiting the police, I had written down a full chronology in my notepad from the first shot to the werewolf's last breath.

"Here you go," I said, handing him a piece of paper taken from my notepad. I then grabbed a newspaper from the display case and immersed myself in reading but, beyond the flashy headline "Procrustes Dead!" there was nothing concrete in the article. The inspector general's prohibition against talking to the press was being rigorously observed. Only one of the coroner's assistants hadn't managed to hold his tongue about the fact that the bite marks on Isaac Levinson's servant matched the jaw size of the werebeast shot down in the Chinese Quarter.

My name was not mentioned.

"Staggering, just staggering!" Alexander Dyak muttered to himself, studying my notes. "There's quite a lot to think about here."

"I'm afraid werebeasts are rather infrequent visitors to New Babylon," I smiled.

"The world isn't confined to just New Babylon," the inventor shrugged his shoulders, turning the sheet and hiding it in the pocket of his frock. "How's the cane?"

"Above all praise," I answered, not exaggerating one bit. "But today, I've come to you with a new request of an applied-science nature."

"Very interesting," Alexander Dyak replied, curious. "What is it this time?"

"Fire," I told him. "I need a compact device capable of creating a powerful flame."

"A flamethrower?" The inventor asked in surprise. "Leopold Borisovich, do you need a flamethrower?"

"I have a flamethrower," I admitted with a smirk, "but it's too bulky and uncomfortable to carry..."

"Tell me what you need it for," said the inventor, waving his hand. "I'll help you if I can."

So, I told him about the ghastly strangler, his shadows and fear of fire. I didn't mention exactly where our tussle had taken place, and why I was worried I'd meet him again, though.

And worried I was. Fear is a weapon. Fear can kill, but some things are much more deadly than fear. For example, black magic. One time, the malefic had run from the fire. But that trick wouldn't work again. As soon as I tried, he'd tear my head off. A being capable of snatching a ten-caliber bullet out of thin air was nothing to trifle with.

"Quite a serious task!" Alexander Dyak gasped, shaking his head. "I am familiar with the construction of a flamethrower. There's nothing complicated there. But a compact portable flamethrower..."

"I know," I nodded, "it's not easy..."

"There's the combustibles tank, the compressed-nitrogen tank, the jet pipe," said the inventor, enumerating the necessary components.

"I don't need a full flamethrower," I reminded him again. "It only needs to work one time, like in an emergency situation!"

"A single-use flamethrower?" Alexander Dyak started thinking. "What can I say Leopold Borisovich? It's never a bore with you!"

Just then, a couple of students came into the shop and I hurried to bow out.

"Come by tomorrow at the same time," asked the inventor, walking over to the customers: "What can I help you with, young ones?"

I went outside and bought a fresh edition of the *Atlantic Telegraph* as I walked toward

Emperor Clement Square, feeling too stingy to spring for a cab.

THE RECENT SPOT of bad weather had been to the city's distinct advantage. It had washed the dust and ash off everything. The fresh wind blew away the smog and smoke of the chimneys, and the puddles and many streams were drying out before my eyes. It was very sultry out. On the horizon, there were new black clouds starting to form in wisps. They looked dark and evil.

The bad weather was threatening to return, but for now, the sun was still shining in the sky. The city-dwellers were walking down the boulevards and across the squares, sitting on cafe verandas and admiring the sheen of the freshly washed glass in front of the expensive stores.

On Emperor Clement Square, there was even a suffragette demonstration. Fifteen ladies were rhythmically shaking signs with calls for equality; the curious onlookers, newspapermen and police gathered around them were much higher in number. I walked calmly around the crowd.

Much more calmly than before. The usual public that gathered on this street was well-to-do and stylish but, in my new getup, I no longer felt like somebody's poor relative. The shoes I was wearing were so shiny with fresh polish that it seemed I had gotten them done at one of the nearby stalls not five minutes earlier.

I walked into the hotel *Benjamin Franklin*

with a confident victorious air, carelessly nodding at the porter as I announced myself:

"Viscount Cruce for Mr. Witstein."

"One minute." The receptionist went through the list, made a call and pointed me to the elevator. "He's been expecting you, Viscount."

Abraham Witstein came out into the main room of the Emperor's Suite with his face red from a recent shave. On the coffee table, there was a pile of fresh press. On top of that, I saw today's edition of the *Atlantic Telegraph.*

Apparently, I needn't have bought one...

"Viscount!" the Judean exclaimed with a smile. "Am I to understand that you come today bearing good news?"

I placed a deformed ten-caliber bullet on the table, the same one I'd dug out of the wall of the opium den, and confirmed his supposition:

"The news is even better than you suppose."

"What is that?" the banker asked, getting on edge as he stared at the rumpled lead ball and torn aluminum jacket.

"This is the bullet that struck Procrustes," I told him. "This ruthless monster was long considered uncatchable but, when he came after Isaac Levinson and his family, a certain private detective followed the beast on orders from the Witstein Banking House and gave him a one-way ticket to the underworld. Mr. Witstein, I trust you have nothing against this version of events. It is the one I told the police."

The Judean took the bullet, turned it in his fingers and placed it back on the table, pursing his lips.

"We were quite emphatic that you should not allude to our enterprise..."

"Do you prefer the story that a private detective killed an out-of-town werewolf who had it out for your company for no reason?"

The banker thought over my words and waved his hand:

"Viscount, pay no mind to my grumbling. You did everything as you should have. I've already received a call from the police saying the bites match up, so I'll give the order to pay out the three thousand francs..."

"Five."

Abraham Witstein smiled:

"My dear Leopold, if my memory doesn't deceive me, you were promised three thousand francs for the killer dead."

"Mr. Witstein!" I exclaimed, melting into a no less false smile in my turn. "Do you really think you can compare some run of the mill werebeast with Procrustes himself? The whole city is humming, abuzz with the name of your banking house..."

"We weren't chasing fame!"

"That's good, but judge for yourself: who in their right mind would try and rob the very bank responsible for bringing the most terrifying legend in town to justice?"

"Not the most terrifying," the banker corrected me. "Not even close."

"Alright then, the most terrifying legend of recent years," I agreed. "Is that of no interest to you?"

"Five thousand?"

"Five thousand!"

"And that's all? No monthly payments?"

"Blackmail runs deeply counter to my nature," I assured the Judean. "If you do not value my efforts at five thousand, what can I do? Pay three. I'll just compensate the remaining two with the kind of cheap fame you have no desire for. Declaring that the dead werebeast was not Procrustes, but just some nameless New-World emigrant would stir up quite the sensation, I assure you! I don't exactly have clients lining up, so I'm telling you the pure truth and nothing but."

"But your ego would far prefer going down in history as the killer of Procrustes, isn't that right?" Abraham Witstein chuckled.

"So, you see why this could never be blackmail, then. I stand to lose incomparably more than you, if the real story were to come out."

"Do you really need money this badly?"

"That's all a question of how my labors are valued," I replied, leaning back in my chair and admitting: "I mean, another two thousand couldn't hurt."

The banker called his bodyguard. The balding big-nosed Judean halved a packet of hundred-franc bank notes, counted them out and handed me the agreed-upon sum. I watched him in a most careful manner, so I didn't have to check the accuracy of the count. I just stuck the pile of bills into my wallet and stood to my feet.

"It was nice working with you, Mr. Witstein."

He looked sourly in reply and clarified:

"Our work together will continue, though, right?"

"Unofficially," I reminded him.

"Unofficially," the Judean confirmed.

Then, I bowed over him and said quietly:

"If this information gets out in any way, I'll deny it, but unofficially, one of the robbers is already dead. In total that's two of the four."

Abraham Witstein sized me up with his piercing gaze and asked:

"What happened to him?"

"He was careless with explosives."

"Is that all?"

"For the moment," I answered. "And now, allow me to take my leave. I have a great many pressing activities planned for today."

"Keep me informed," the banker said after me, getting up from his chair. "Alright?"

"Without fail," I promised, squeezing his outstretched hand and walking down to the first floor. There, I looked thoughtfully toward the bar but, although my wallet was now swollen with hundred-franc bills, I chose not to squander my money and just left the building.

The sun was peeking out from between shaggy black clouds, just as before. Steam was rising from the wet causeway. I didn't leave the square. I took a seat on one of the benches not far from an equestrian statue of the founder of the Second Empire, got out my half-empty tin of sugar drops and tossed one into my mouth.

So, the Emperor's brother had done something and now, sixteen years after his death, it was coming to fruition. But what?

A box, a thunder rune, many *illustrious* gentlemen. Was it a conspiracy? Perhaps.

There was one thing I could be absolutely certain of: I knew nothing. And the faster I figured this all out, the higher my chances of remaining alive.

The main question now was which of the threads to pull first in order to unravel this ball of twine with the least amount of effort. My attorney was already bending over backwards to find Count Kósice and, if my uncle hadn't yet managed to make it to the continent, sooner or later, he would find him. I had two directions I could put my efforts into now: trying to search for the strangler or trying to track down the gang of *illustrious* gentlemen.

Though they no longer possessed the mysterious contents of the box, they definitely did know what exactly was supposed to be inside. And in matters such as this, information is worth its weight in gold. Other than that, both the strangler and bank robbers had it in for me and, to my eye, the best defense would be a pre-emptive attack. The potential threat had to be eliminated.

Now the question was whether the bigger threat was the malefic or the *illustrious* gentlemen.

I even decided to toss a coin, but had a

change of heart and headed for the magistrate. It would be incomparably easier to find the *illustrious* gentlemen; I decided to start there.

Incomparably easier seeming, at least. I had the perfect plan: determine who owned the warehouse I'd blown up, find that person and use them to track down the robbers. I knew the approximate location of the plot of land. There was little else to do. I had to spend a few days in the archive, go through a few half-tons of ancient documents and, after working up an allergy to paper dust, find the information I needed in the very last box I thought to open.

Not such a charming perspective.

But money is often capable of performing real miracles, right? One hundred francs was enough to get one of the quick-thinking clerks interested in finding me the right documents by this evening. After negotiating for another fifty if he actually found the documents, the young man got lost in the archive. I went back outside and started thinking about what to do with myself before the day came to an end.

I could consider my work as a private detective finished, so now, I could either head for lunch with a clean conscious, or go on a walk around the city and enjoy the day off. I certainly didn't want to go back to my mansion with a corpse in the icehouse. And I had to refuse taking a bit of exercise down the Yarden Embankment because of the pain in my leg. The cane saved me from being totally lame, but getting around was still a chore.

Albert Brandt was expecting me at six. Ramon Miro was probably still sleeping before his shift. To my great surprise, I realized I had basically nothing to do.

A strange sensation. I wasn't used to it.

I stood for a bit on the steps of the magistrate, went down to the sidewalk and hopped into a steam tram headed for Newtonstraat.

I had one more thing remaining. It was unpleasant and even somewhat dangerous, but it wouldn't have been good to let it go. Quite the opposite, in fact. The earlier I stuck a feeler in this direction, the higher my chances of success would be.

I didn't go into the Newton-Markt. I headed from Ohm Square directly into *The Blue Ostrich*.

Every department of the metropolitan police had their own preferred meeting places. Low-level constables disappeared after their shifts in one of the nameless liquor bars nearby, CID constables preferred drinking in *Archimedes' Screw*, office clerks had *The Green Fairy* coffee shop, and the detectives of Department Three met up in *The Blue Ostrich*.

It was considered one of the most tranquil establishments in all New Babylon, and I sincerely hoped that the serene atmosphere would keep the person I was going to see from physically assaulting me. It would be devilishly unpleasant to end up behind bars because of a fight with a police detective.

The Blue Ostrich restaurant took up the first

two floors of the building on the corner of Newtonstraat and Ampère Boulevard. From the outside, it had no noteworthy features except the ostrich on the sign, which was a noble shade of royal blue, the same as a police uniform. There was music playing inside. The interior was adorned with potted palm trees growing up to the ceiling, and it smelled of expensive tobacco. Department Three really knew how to relax in style.

The maître d' gave me a courteous smile and inquired:

"Have you reserved a table?"

"I'm expected by senior inspector Moran," I said, fudging the truth. "Is he already here?"

"Yes, he is," the maître d' confirmed. "Would you like me to take you to his table?"

"If you'd be so kind."

My arrival was not to Bastian Moran's liking. Not in the slightest.

Before him, there was an untouched stuffed grouse in pineapple gravy; the senior inspector looked first at the appetizing dish, then shifted his gaze to me and, without a doubt, came to the conclusion that the grouse and I absolutely did not pair well.

"Don't worry, Bastian. I won't keep you from your meal long," I smiled, taking a seat at his table.

"Will you be ordering anything?" the maître d' clarified.

"No, he will not," the senior inspector answered for me. And when we were left alone, he pursed his lips. "You know, Viscount, you're the last person I was expecting to see here today."

"Life is full of surprises," I said back with a shrug of my shoulders.

"Have you come to spoil my appetite?"

"Nothing of the sort. I thought I could be of service."

Bastian Moran set aside his knife and fork, wiped his lips with his napkin and nodded:

"I'm listening." He was clearly hoping to get rid of me before the grouse went cold.

I took a police report from my inner pocket and handed it to him.

"Where'd you get this?" Bastian Moran asked in confusion, quickly looking over the papers.

"Wrong question," I shook my head. "You should be asking how the bank robbers got a copy of a police report."

"I suppose the newly minted private detective before me doesn't have an answer to that question," the senior inspector noted reasonably, slapping his hand on the table. "I'll ask you again: where did you get this?"

"I was attacked," I answered, not especially bending the truth. "In the course of the fight, these papers were dropped by one of the criminals."

"And what became of the attackers?" asked the senior inspector, staring at me with the unblinking gaze of a boa constrictor.

"They got away. Otherwise, why would I come to you?"

"And why did you come to me, Viscount?"

I threw my gaze over the bright room with huge floor-length windows, a dance floor and an orchestra stage, then put one leg over the other and said calmly:

"There's a rat in the Newton-Markt, senior inspector. And I think it's in your best interest to find him."

Bastian Moran rolled the report into a tube and banged it on the edge of the table.

"And what do you care, Viscount?" He smiled poisonously, adding, "beyond the desire to aid in the pursuit of justice, naturally?"

"Expecting to be stabbed in the back is not conducive to mental balance."

"So, you wanted someone else to solve your problems for you, eh? Or are you implying I was involved in this regrettable incident?"

"The thought has crossed my mind," I nodded, changing he topic: "I suppose you are aware of yesterday's events in the Chinese Quarter?"

"Did you come here to brag?" he asked.

I then set a round ten-caliber bullet on the table. Its aluminum jacket bore clear fingerprints from the strangler.

"The fingerprints of the man who killed Aaron Malk are on this metal."

The senior inspector's eyes grew dark.

"Where did you get that bullet, Viscount?" he demanded.

"It's called work. You might consider acquainting yourself with it one day, instead of just wearing out your pants in an office," I smiled, getting to my feet. In parting, I wished him a "bon appétit" and headed off for the exit.

Bastian Moran stayed at the table, but was now looking at the stuffed grouse without the slightest interest. It positively warmed my soul.

As I stepped out onto the veranda, I measured up the distant titan of the Newton-Markt with my gaze, took out my tin of sugar drops and threw an orange-flavored one into my mouth. The clouds carried through the sky like whitish shaggy cotton. The fresh wind chased the smog and furnace-smoke from the city. It was surprisingly easy to breathe today, even despite the vapor rising from the earth.

I stood for a bit, enjoying the pleasant sour taste, then waved a hand at a cabby rolling through the intersection and told him to drive to the municipal library.

Once there, I slipped the badly sun-burned man a few coins, but didn't enter the temple of knowledge. Instead, I walked up onto the terrace of the neighboring cafe. There was a vision of grouse with pineapple gravy dancing before my eyes, and I could no longer sate my hunger with sugar drops alone. I needed something more substantial.

Also, the very thought of just sitting for a bit in a wicker chair and doing absolutely nothing was quite attractive. I could forget about all my cares and just drink a cup of coffee in the very middle of the work day.

Wasn't that a dream?

I ordered Viennese coffee, a few Belgian

waffles and an ice cream with maple syrup. I leaned back in the chair and realized that I was suffering from a critical lack of fresh press. Without a paper, the appearance of a world-weary lounger just wasn't complete, and I'd somehow managed to lose the issue of the *Atlantic Telegraph* I bought earlier.

I looked out onto the street, snapped my fingers and found a boy nearby with a stack of papers under his arm and satirical magazines sticking out of the side of his bag.

"*Atlantic Telegraph*," I asked him.

The kid handed me the paper I requested, getting ten centimes in return, then walked down the street, loudly informing passers-by:

"Storm warning! Hurricane coming! Dirigible flights to the continent canceled! Anarchists blow up police armored car! Read all about it! Blood-soaked horror and imminent storm!"

I went back to the table and began leafing through the news as I waited for my order. But there was nothing new about Procrustes in the paper. Just rumors, as before. The Newton-Markt was keeping stubbornly silent.

They brought my coffee, crispy waffles and two scoops of ice-cream with maple syrup on top. In no particular hurry, I ate my food and leafed through the paper. The hurricane was expected any day now. After I finished my meal, I just sat and drank my coffee.

But I was no longer unoccupied, not at all. I was thinking over my next steps and considering my opponents' possible moves. I wasn't expecting the malefic strangler to attack any time soon. What did he need me for? But then the gang of *illustrious* gentlemen had serious intentions. And it wasn't at all certain that Bastian Moran's forthcoming activity would get them to lay low. He might have been working for them, after all.

Paranoia? Nothing of the sort. The bruise on the back of my head and electrical burns on my arms and legs were clear evidence of the fact that I was currently quite far from mere paranoia. But sure, I did have a slight, if natural, mistrust of those around me.

I paid up and headed into the library. Once there, I spent some time filling out a library card and set about shuffling through old newspaper files. I was looking for any mention of people who died with the characteristic bite marks on their neck. But there was no mention of such happenings in the crime blotter from any paper in the last five years. Elizabeth-Maria was right. Vampires must have tried to avoid New Babylon. And if not, they were devilishly good at covering up their foul misdeeds.

After killing a few hours, I tossed my gaze at the clock face and ordered a few books on the founding of the Second Empire. But I was disappointed: though there were dozens of thick tomes written on the great Rie brothers, Emperor Clement and Emile his constant chancellor, I wasn't able to glean anything useful from them.

They all just told slight variations on the same official story I'd heard my whole life: a group of people fighting for freedom and justice rose up in rebellion against the tyranny of *the fallen.* And though the Emperor himself had been given every imaginable biographical treatment, his younger brother had always occupied his shadow. Even as chancellor, he wasn't such a public person and, after his sudden end, everyone simply forgot about the great Duke of Arabia. I supposed the fact that he was disliked by the widowed Empress had at least some part to play in that.

One thing could be said absolutely for sure: of those who took part in the rebellion alongside the Rie brothers, the survivors now numbered in the single digits. Their generation was gone now. Those who had known Emile Rie as chancellor numbered incomparably higher, but I was hardly likely to track down anyone involved in his secret by going down that route.

And there was definitely some kind of terrifying secret tied up with the lightning-rune aluminum box.

"In respect to the memory of Emile Rie..."

What the devil did that *illustrious* gentleman have in mind?

What kind of respect? What did that have to do with anything?

I headed to the magistrate, still not having found an answer to the questions hounding me.

I ARRIVED to the magistrate just as it was closing. I walked into the vestibule, looked for the clerk whose palm I'd greased and was unpleasantly surprised to find a sour expression on his handsome mug.

"Alas, Mr. Orso," the young man sighed, "I'm afraid I cannot help you..."

"Listen here, my good sir!" I grabbed him by the arm and pulled him toward me. "Our agreement was mutually beneficial. Don't complicate things!"

"I checked the archive," the frightened clerk whispered back fitfully. "The land you asked about is currently in abeyance. You can check yourself, if you like!"

"Where are the documents?"

The young man adjusted his frock and pointed at one of the doors.

"After me, please," he said in an official tone.

We walked into the office. The clerk there rifled through a desk, opened a dusty folder and handed it to me.

I quickly made sure that the documents were about the right property. Its last owner really had died half a century ago. With unhidden disbelief, I looked at the civil servant:

"How is this possible?"

"I do not know," he replied, shrugging his shoulders. "The plot of land has simply been forgotten!"

"Do such things even happen?"

"Back then, stranger things were known to happen."

"Perhaps." I wrote the address of my attorney on a sheet in my notepad, tore it out and handed it to the man. "If you do manage to find something out, I'd be much obliged."

"By all means," the clerk nodded, sticking the paper in his pocket.

And I went outside empty-handed.

Twilight had already crept up on the city. The street lamps on the alleys leading to the magistrate were starting to turn on. The black clouds on the backdrop of the darkening sky seemed to be made of cut black paper. A steam tram grumbled loudly across the square. A few carriages and a police armored car rolled past.

I followed it with my watchful eye and headed into the *Charming Bacchante*.

My mood wasn't suited for an outing to the circus, but Albert Brandt would never forgive me if the valuable ticket went to waste on my account.

4

WHEN I GOT UP to the poet's apartment, he was standing in his underwear before a mirror shaving, dipping a straight razor from time to time into a basin of soapy water on a stool. His evening attire was on the couch. In a glass on the table, there sat a beautiful carnation for his lapel. And do I even have to say that his lacquered ankle-boots at the door had been so thoroughly polished that it hurt the eyes?

"Leo!" Albert grew happy at my appearance. "You're always so punctual, it's impossible! The cabby will be here in five minutes."

"Did you order a carriage?"

"This is a society event!" the poet snorted. "Being late, or arriving on foot is bad form."

"As you say," I chuckled, taking a seat on his ottoman.

"That's why I shaved all on my own!" the poet bragged, wiping his cheeks with a towel.

"Your arms don't ever just twitch?"

"You're mean. Who raised you?" Albert reproached me, taking his suit and going behind the screen to get changed. "What's the news?" he shouted, already out of view.

"A storm warning's been announced. They expect torrential rain and lightning."

"Is that even news?" the poet snorted. "What about Procrustes? Who has he killed now? I was working all day today. I didn't even go outside."

"Procrustes is dead," I informed my friend.

"Come off it, Leo!" he replied, not having caught my meaning. "If only you knew what a royalty I've been promised for this poem about him, you'd be dripping with envy."

I felt my bill-swollen wallet and had a fit of laughter.

"That's not very likely."

"Oh, come off it!" Albert said with a wave, coming out from behind the screen dressed to the nines. "And take your billiard ball already. Why the devil'd you even drag it down here?"

"Are you saying I should bring it to the circus?"

"Throw it away if you must. I have no need for it whatever."

"You're grumbling like an old man," I said, refusing. Then I asked: "Are you not going to wear a cloak?"

Albert looked out the window, looked up at the sky and agreed:

"Sure, a cloak couldn't hurt."

"Remember the storm warning!"

We left his apartments and went down to the first floor. Very soon after that, the carriage the poet ordered drove up to the cabaret.

"To the old circus!" Albert declared, and he took us off down the narrow streets of the Greek Quarter, which were dark and still quite deserted.

The twilight had grown denser. The sky was finally stretched over with clouds, and the wind had grown stronger and brisker. The temperature had also dropped noticeably.

The movement on the street wasn't very intense yet, so getting to the square near the Yarden Embankment with the old circus at its center took us just ten minutes. The old circus building was circular and had a stone dome lined with archway entrances.

There were so many people gathered outside of it that we couldn't get through.

In the light of the street lamps, the honorable public was sauntering down the alleys of the square and embankment. Some were asking for an extra ticket, some were selling tickets that had never been "extra" in any sense at three times their listed value. There were several divisions of equestrian police maintaining order. Near the fence, in front of the entrance to the circus building, constables' uniforms shone out like beacons.

"Full house tonight," I noted, getting out of the carriage.

"These scalpers are gonna get rich," Albert agreed.

We went onto the square and stepped past the many carts and stalls of the street sellers providing something to tide the viewers over for the show.

"We'll eat inside," the poet decided.

I didn't argue. Enjoying concessions at the circus was a tradition. Going to the circus or theater and not stopping by the refreshments area was bad form.

Curses! What an obtrusive concept!

Standing at the edge of the square, I cast my gaze over the stone titan of the circus and gave a shiver.

"Yeah, this place is also giving me chills," Albert nodded. "Ghastly things have been done here. Ghastly."

There were rumors that, when *the fallen* ruled, a certain portion of the audience would not return home after a show. And though no documented confirmations of such occurrences existed, the stories had tickled the nerves of several generations of New Babylonians. Thirty years ago, the authorities even built a new circus building. This one was bright, airy and spacious. Nowadays, the only groups that performed at the old one were traveling collectives and independent troupes.

I didn't pay particular attention to these rumors, I just felt something strange in the air, that was all. The ripples of long-gone fears? Perhaps that was it.

"Extra! Extra! Procrustes kicks the bucket!" came the sudden call of a boy darting between the people in the crowd with a stack of papers. "Extra! Extra! Read all about it! Procrustes shot down in the Chinese Quarter!"

Albert Brandt immediately acquired the fresh edition of the *Capital Times*; it consisted of just a few pages and was entirely devoted to the legendary murderer. The poet read the headline in the light of the gas lamp and exclaimed:

"Curse me, Leo! He's dead!"

"I tried to tell you," I chuckled back significantly.

The poet considered my affirmation and stared at me with clear disapproval.

"I thought you were talking about..." out of delicacy, he didn't remind me of my father, which meant he couldn't be that angry, "bygone times! Not about the present-day murderer!"

"I said what I said."

"Here, it's written that Procrustes was shot by on-duty police."

"In the inspector general's place, it would be at the very least stupid to say otherwise."

"Am I to understand that this wouldn't have transpired without your involvement?"

I nodded.

"Tell me!" demanded the poet, looking around and immediately correcting himself: "No, wait! Let's go get some food!"

"They won't let us in yet," I told him, but the spectators crowding in front of the circus didn't slow Albert down one bit.

He moved decisively forward, getting through to the wide stone steps without particular effort. And once there he coughed, clearing his throat, and in a low and cracking voice demanded:

"Let me through!"

And the people, not really aware of their actions, started making way. We didn't have to curse or fight our way to the front. My companion's *talent* worked easily on the circus patrons and made us a path through the crowd.

With the guards, that wasn't going to work, though. And Albert didn't even try. Such tricks could easily lead to him sitting out the show in the neighboring police station.

"I'd like to speak with the manager, if you'd be so kind!" the poet asked. If a note of bossiness slipped through in his booming voice, the constables didn't pay it any mind. Then, one of the doormen suddenly left his position and ran to fulfill the *illustrious* gentleman's request.

The crowd around started grumbling and shooting us unkind looks. Then, Albert waved his tickets in the air, letting them know that we weren't just taking advantage of our connections and walking in without paying.

"Calm down, ladies and gentlemen. Please, be calm!" he said in an easy and good-natured tone. "I'll be performing comical couplets today, and my friend is trying out for the role of tap dancer!"

Everyone around burst out laughing and, when the manager told them to let us in, no one said a word.

"Mr. Brandt!" said the circus employee, embracing the poet as he clapped him on the back like an old friend. "I'm devilishly glad to see you but, to my extreme shame, I must be going. So much to do! So much to do!"

"We'll talk later," Albert nodded carelessly.

I waited for us to be left alone, and elbowed my friend in the side.

"So, that means I'm to be a tap dancer?"

"Well, you have got a cane," he said with a thoughtless hand wave and walked through the old-ad caked vestibule. "We have to hurry, my young friend. We must be inside before the ravenous crowd gushes in!"

I walked after him and unwillingly shivered when Albert turned sharply and asked:

"Do you smell that? It smells like the circus! The circus is a special world, Leo! Circus people are not the same as you or me. They're a particular folk. A surprising lot!"

I didn't share my friend's inspiration one bit. In his time, my father had done business with some middle-man circus impresario, and I had spent just about as much time around "circus people" as I could stomach for one lifetime. There were good ones among them, but also some that were plainly wicked. All in all, I wasn't left with particularly pleasant memories.

"Have you ever been backstage?" the poet asked, stepping through the vestibule.

"I have," I confirmed, not saying that I had lived a few months in this very building and even taken part in setting up shows.

"A surprising world!" Albert said as he walked up to the concessions stand. He ordered a cup of coffee, a glass of cognac and a sugared lemon, then hurried me along: "Pick something, Leo. Pick something."

I asked for a mineral water with pear syrup and a bit of ice cream with nuts and told my friend about yesterday's skirmish with the werebeast in the Chinese Quarter.

"Alexander Dyak is simply a gem," I announced near the end. "I don't even know what I'd have done without his help!"

"Alexander has a good mind," Brandt agreed with me, then asked in reproach: "But, Leo, why didn't you tell me all this earlier?"

"I was afraid."

"Afraid?"

"Well, sure," I confirmed, pushing away an empty plate. "I was afraid of spoiling your inspiration. After all, you did recently tell me how delicate it is..."

"Leo, you're not a good person," Albert Brandt sighed, having picked up on the mockery in my voice.

At that moment, I heard the buzz of the crowd. The spectators managed to quickly fill up the circus.

I finished my mineral water and chuckled:

"So, am I to understand that the lady of your heart is busy this evening?"

"That's right, she couldn't make it," the poet confirmed with a dreamy smile. "But her and I already saw each other today. I gave her a huge bouquet of tulips. She's crazy for flowers."

"How original!"

"Leo, sarcasm doesn't suit you," the poet frowned, gulping down the last of his cognac and suggesting: "Shall we go?"

"Let's go," I nodded, as the second bell had already rung.

And, after grabbing a program and a pair of theater binoculars, we headed off to find our places.

As it turned out, the poet's unknown benefactor had given him a whole box, so we were to enjoy the spectacle in enviable comfort, causing the other spectators to look on us with unhidden covetousness.

"*Moon Circus* is five centuries old, can you imagine?" said Albert, his program open. "For a long time, they performed only in New Babylon, but for the last three hundred years, they've been traveling Europe. Some of their acts haven't changed since the day they were founded!"

"How educational," I snorted, looking at the stage and rows of seats, the majority of which were occupied.

The sawdust-covered ring was placed, as tradition dictated, in the very center of the spacious building. The dome looked very high from inside. There were no windows or lights on it, and the cables running down got lost in the murky shadows nearer the top.

"I've always liked learning new things," the poet shrugged.

"I've always liked learning useful things," I parried.

"You're a bore, Leo!"

"And you're a nuisance."

"I should have gotten a cognac," the poet sighed, just as the third bell rang.

Soon after that, the master of ceremonies walked into the ring. Then, the session orchestra started playing, as two grimacing clowns walked out on stage, one red and one white. A magician followed them, taking rabbits and pigeons from a top-hat, clearly not large enough to store such a great number of beasts. Next was a sweet looking girl, who climbed into a box, was closed up, then vanished. The following act was a pair of jugglers, throwing their flaming clubs back and forth. Nothing strange, everything like usual.

For me, it was all pure boredom. But then, the acrobats started. They performed without safety wires or a net spread out under them but, despite that, they pulled off such stunts under the domed ceiling that I was left frozen with my mouth agape.

The acrobats seemed to be flying. Really flying, with every second breaking the law of gravity. In times gone by, they would surely have been accused of witchcraft. Now, though, people were just staring in horror; the crowd would burst into applause, then wash over with waves of elated terror. Sometimes, I felt that one of the artists was out of step and would fall like a stone to the ground but, every time, there appeared a trapeze underhand at the very last moment, or they were caught by a partner with perfectly calculated timing.

That performance alone was worth visiting the circus.

"Breathtaking!" sighed Albert Brandt after the acrobats had finished bowing and were now off scene.

I was forced to agree with him. I had never seen anything like it.

The master of ceremonies came back out and announced:

"And now, ladies and gentlemen, we will have a performance from a virtuoso of scientific hypnosis, Maestro Marlini!"

The music went silent, and an imposing looking gentleman swaggered out into the arena. He must have been forty or forty-five years old to look at him. His hair was gray, and his face was swarthy. Unlike most magicians, the maestro didn't wear a tailcoat, but a simple business suit. He did not break any of the other rules of the trade, though. He started with simple tricks, guessing people's thoughts and forcing them to remember things long forgotten. Only after that did his assistants start to bring out props.

"I need a volunteer from the audience!" the maestro announced after his assistants had finished affixing a tightrope to two pillars some distance apart.

There was no lack of willing participants. They even had to draw straws.

"Now good sir, if you'd kindly attempt to walk the tightrope," the hypnotist said to an ungainly gentleman with a considerably sized beer belly. "You needn't fear, it's quite simple."

The volunteer lurched up onto the rope and, as could have been expected, jumped off after just two steps. The tightrope had already started swaying forcefully. Thankfully, it was less than a meter high.

"It really is quite simple!" Maestro Marlini declared. And, in confirmation of these words, one of the acrobats returned to the arena; with mocking ease, he walked the tightrope, bowed to the audience and ran backstage once again.

"Man is capable of more than he knows. All one must do is liberate his hidden reserves!" the hypnotist cried out when the screams and laughter had died down. "The brain is a unique tool. Very few are able to access even a quarter of its abilities!"

The audience started laughing again, and the hypnotist got a pocket watch from his vest and started swinging it on its chain before the reddened face of the embarrassed volunteer.

"Three! Two! One!" the maestro counted off loudly and demanded: "To the rope!"

The unwieldy gentleman calmly stepped onto the hanging tightrope, walked confidently across it to the opposite pillar, then walked back. Just before he'd reached the end, the hypnotist abruptly snapped his fingers, taking him out of the trance. The man instantly lost all confidence and nearly fell over as he jumped down.

"Voila!" declared Maestro Marlini, releasing the volunteer who was no less mesmerized than the crowd. He then called for another: "Well, does anyone remain, who dares doubt the power of the human mind?"

This time, the assistants brought out two stands. On one, there were three huge oranges. On the other, there were three felt balls of similar dimension.

"First, let me ask: do you know how to juggle?" the hypnotist asked a skeptically inclined old man. Based on his dashing appearance, he was retired military.

"No, sir," he chuckled back.

"We'll see about that." The magician took out the oranges and began throwing them into the air one after the other, tossing them from one hand to the next. "Watch and learn!"

"You can't teach an old dog new tricks," the volunteer said, shaking his head. But the maestro continued juggling the oranges. At some point, the old man became so far removed from reality that, as soon as the hypnotist asked, he closed his eyes and made a fairly skillful repetition of the hypnotist's primitive trick.

"Did you think we were done?" asked Maestro Marlini, leading his gaze over the silent audience. "Well, think again!"

He poured fire-starter fluid over the felt balls and struck a match on the side of the box; a colorless flame instantly rose up.

The old man threw, then caught the oranges over and over like a wind-up doll. And even when one of the hypnotist's assistants grabbed the fruits and placed them on the pillar, his hands stayed in motion as if nothing had happened.

Someone started laughing, and Maestro Marlini put a finger to his lips. Meanwhile, an assistant extended a gloved hand and grabbed one of the burning balls, throwing it to the volunteer still immersed in a trance. He didn't notice the change and started juggling them as he had earlier juggled the oranges. The audience gasped.

"Pain is all in our heads," the hypnotist declared at the same time. "But the abilities of the mind and body are limitless! Nothing mystical, nothing magical! Nothing but scientific knowledge!" He looked at the juggler and continued with a smile: "So then, we've been paying too little attention tonight to our charming ladies. Are there any valiant women out there in tonight's audience...?"

Before he managed to continue, a girl with an alluring figure came out into the arena, and my heart gave a moan. I recognized her. It was none other than Elizabeth-Maria von Nalz, daughter of the inspector general and the love of my whole life.

"Oh! I admire decisiveness in people, my lovely mademoiselle!" laughed Maestro Marlini, kissing her hand and gracefully removing the glove from her thin feminine hand. "No tricks!" he announced as he led his hand before the face of Elizabeth-Maria. Then, suddenly, he stabbed a long knitting needle right through her hand.

Everyone just gasped, and I jumped out of place.

"Sit down," Albert pushed me back. "Calm yourself, I've seen this number before."

This number? He put a knitting needle straight through her palm!

Seeing it had a sinister effect on me.

"Pain is in our heads!" the hypnotist repeated insistently, carefully pulling the needle out and, with an automatized snap of his fingers, broke the trance.

Elizabeth-Maria looked in astonishment at her hand, kissed the magician on the cheek and hurried back to her seat.

"So, you see," Albert Brandt noted phlegmatically. "Just a trick!"

At that moment, six assistants brought out several long troughs filled with red-hot coals. The light from above was turned off. An eerie crimson glow poured out of the improvised path into the semi-darkness of the ring. A piece of paper thrown onto the coals quickly went black and caught fire.

"Now, ladies and gentlemen, it is technically possible that there are undercover acrobats and jugglers in the audience. And it's also possible that our mademoiselle here could be one of the unique individuals that do not experience any pain whatsoever. But red-hot coals are another matter. I hope none of you suspect that I've planted a covert Indian yogi."

The audience replied with laughter, but not totally confident. Everyone was waiting for the culmination.

"Any volunteers? I need two people!" Maestro Marlini raised his voice. "No worries, we'll pay if this lands you in the hospital!"

This time, the audience's laughter was utterly nervous.

In the end, two people came up: a grown young man in a shabby suit from the back rows and a well-mannered pipsqueak with pomaded hair from the middle of the stands. Even if one were so inclined, imagining this duo as undercover yogis was quite beyond the pale.

"One thousand francs!" Maestro Marlini said to the younger of them. "One thousand francs if you make it to the end! And a hundred just for trying!"

Without hesitation, the young man took off his well-worn boots and socks, rolled up his pants and walked up to the glowing path.

"You may begin!" The hypnotist gave his permission. "Pray, begin!"

The young man bristled up nervously but, all the same, walked onto the coals. To my surprise, he made it a few steps, going faster and faster before he had to jump off onto the sawdust with his feet scorched black. The hypnotist's assistants immediately jumped over to him, put him on a stretcher and brought him backstage.

A grave-like silence came over the hall.

"Well?" Maestro Marlini turned to the second

volunteer. "Are you still prepared to risk it? Do you believe in the power of the mind as fervently as I?"

The short man swallowed spasmodically and started taking off his shoes. The audience started buzzing.

And again, the hypnotist took out his pocket watch. This time, it took him a minute or two to get ready. Then, the dandy walked calmly over to the red-hot coal path and walked across it from beginning to end.

The audience erupted into applause, and the master of ceremonies came quickly out into the arena.

"Inter-r-r-mission!" he   announced. "Ladies and gentlemen, after the break you can expect trained carnivores, miraculous tricks and the crowning number: splitting a lady in two! Hurry back for the second act!"

But everyone hurried off to the concession area.

I threw myself back into my chair and patted down my perspired forehead with a handkerchief.

"It's   all   just   tricks,"   Albert   reminded me. "Want   some   cognac?" he   offered   and immediately waved his hand. "Ah, that's right! You don't drink!" he said as he left the box, whistling quietly to himself.

I sat there for a bit then got up and walked the passage between sections to the exit. On my way, I suddenly bumped into Elizabeth-Maria as she hurried the other way. Her hat was adorned with a fresh rose. Her narrow waist was pulled in with a belt, and she looked unbelievably attractive in her fashionably-cut dress, white blouse and jacket.

"Good evening," I greeted her, not at all hoping she'd recognize me, but the girl unexpectedly slowed her gait.

"Viscount Cruce!" she exclaimed. "What a meeting! Daddy's devilishly ornery with you!"

"Is that so?" I babbled back. "Again?"

"Oh, yes!" Elizabeth-Maria came closer and whispered: "He'll never forgive the fact that you beat them to Procrustes."

"He told you that?"

"That it was you that shot the monster?" the girl smiled, orange sparks flying in her colorless white eyes. "Yes, he did! He couldn't keep from strutting in vexation!"

The inspector general's daughter started walking away and then I, in a fitful attempt to continue the conversation, blurted out:

"How's your hand?"

"Hand?" Elizabeth-Maria asked in surprise. She laughed back: "Oh, Viscount! Maestro Marlini is simply a genius! Just look for yourself!" she said, extending her thin palm. I touched it carefully and, barely holding back my shaking, said:

"Simply unbelievable!"

"I've been at all the maestro's performances. He really is unbelievable!" the girl said in admiration. "He's performing tomorrow at a reception at Baron Dürer's place. I'll be there, too. What about you?"

No one had invited me to a dinner party at the house of the aluminum king, but I just said mysteriously:

"I don't even know. I'm working on two investigations right now..."

"Oh, you must be there, Viscount. It will be such fun," the girl assured me and hurried down the corridor.

I took off my glasses and followed her with a persistent gaze. Then, I waited in line to buy a mineral water with syrup and took a seat on a free bench. The bell rang. Intermission was over, but I couldn't get up. I was too thrown off by the unexpected meeting.

My heart was beating unevenly with nervous breaks and bursts, at times causing my breathing to seize up. A cup of water helped to calm my nerves, but I didn't want to go back into the performance hall, so I stayed on the bench.

I just sat out the whole second act like that. When the audience finally thronged out to the exit, without even wanting to, I got up and grabbed Albert Brandt, surrounded by elated admirers.

"Leo!" he said in surprise. "Where'd you disappear off to? I completely lost you!"

"Nowhere."

"It can't be that Maestro Marlini made such a strong impression on you, can it?" the poet laughed. "Tomorrow, he and I will be entertaining guests at Baron Dürer's reception!" he said. He leaned in to me and whispered: "Unfortunately, I cannot bring you with me. I myself was invited by the aluminum king's personal secretary..."

I shrugged my shoulders, not at all upset by the fact.

And though I had slightly bent the truth in talking about investigating two crimes at once, Elizabeth-Maria would surely be accompanied to the reception by her fiancé. What need did I have to watch them and kick myself in vexation? None at all.

"Are you going to go home now?" I asked the poet.

Albert Brandt turned to his awaiting admirers and shook his head:

"No, I do not believe I am."

"See you tomorrow, then."

"The reception is at four," the poet warned me. "I won't be home the second half of the day."

"So, I guess I'll see you the day after tomorrow," I smiled. "I won't be available for the first half of the day."

We said our farewells; Albert led the admirers of his work into the nearest drinking establishment, and I went outside, stood on the top step of the circus entrance and leaned heavily on my cane. I just stood and admired the smooth black surface of the Yarden, reflecting back all the riverbank street lights.

"I'm surprised to see you here!" came a voice from behind my back.

I turned and found myself face to face with a slender gentleman in a floor-length cloak with a white scarf thrown carelessly around his neck.

Bastian Moran, may he die in an explosion!

But I didn't ask what the devil Department Three wanted from me. Instead, I smiled and quipped:

"Indeed! What a small world this is, senior inspector!"

Bastian Moran raised a steep eyebrow in feigned surprise.

"I wouldn't be hearing a note of sarcasm in your voice, would I, Viscount?" he inquired. "You cannot seriously suppose that you're being followed?"

"You don't look like much of a circus aficionado."

"True, but I am also not the type to thoughtlessly waste human resources on following such a predictable gentleman as yourself," the senior inspector noted. "Bearing in mind your friendship with a certain poet, I knew where to look. How your talented friend spends his time is a secret to no one."

"Is there a particular reason you were looking for me?" I asked, digging out the very essence of his reply. "Have you finally arrested the bank robbers' accomplice?"

"We have not," Bastian Moran answered calmly. "Yet," he added, looking around and suggesting: "Would you like to take a walk down the embankment?"

I didn't refuse. We left the crowd of viewers heading home after the show, and walked down the riverbank in the light of the gas lamps.

"When was the last time you saw your uncle, Viscount?" the senior inspector asked suddenly.

"Has something happened?" I stopped, leaning on my cane.

"Answer the question!" Bastian Moran demanded, all his courtesy instantly sapped.

I winced and stated unconfidently:

"The Count and I last spoke on the day of the bank robbery, senior inspector."

"And you haven't spoken since?"

"No," I shook my head. "I tried calling this morning, but the line was malfunctioning. I had to speak with his attorney. But, what happened?"

Bastian Moran took out a pack of Chesterfields, lit one up and looked at the river.

"An attack was made last night on your uncle's estate."

"Is the Count alright?" I immediately asked.

"Nowhere to be found," the senior inspector answered curtly. "Our current thinking is that he was not home for the attack."

"What rotten luck," I joked back unkindly and waved my hand. "Pay it no mind. I'm just angry."

"Considering the imbroglio between the two of you, Viscount, I'm afraid I have to ask what you were doing last night."

For a moment, I lost my place.

"You suspect me? Really?"

"We're following up on all leads."

I chuckled:

"This time, I'm lucky enough to have an alibi. At midnight, I was handing over the remains of Procrustes to detectives in the Chinese Quarter."

Bastian Moran nodded and made a fully expected clarification:

"And the second half of the night?"

"Ramon and I went back to my place. We went up to the top of Calvary and looked at the city, coming back to our senses. It's not every day that you kill a legend, you know," I said, smiling as I told the pre-agreed lie. "And though you might suspect Ramon of wanting to help me with a false alibi, it would have been impossible for me to even get out there."

"I suppose then that you were not a passenger on the night train headed in that direction, then?"

"No, senior inspector, I was not."

Bastian Moran took a last puff of his cigarette and threw the butt into a cast-iron ashcan.

"Alright," he nodded, not clear at what, and went silent.

"Allow me to ask," I then said. "What happened? It cannot be the same uncatchable gang that robbed that bank, can it?"

"What makes you say that, Viscount?"

"I don't believe in coincidences."

"The robbers were there, that much is certain," Bastian Moran confirmed. "The tire marks in the mud by the gates are identical to the ones we found at the scene of the robbery."

I nodded and returned to the river. I could see the little yellow lights of the carriages crossing a bridge over the Yarden. They were taking home audience members after the show. I suddenly wanted to be in one of them, not playing cat and mouse with an agent of the all-powerful Department Three, but just going home to my family or friends.

But the passing weakness left on its own. I sighed and asked:

"And now, you suppose my uncle was somehow connected with the bank robbery?"

"I don't suppose anything," Bastian Moran said with a dismissive wave, pulling on his kid-leather gloves. "I'm more interested in the check for ten thousand francs signed by your uncle. Where did you get it, Viscount?"

"Did the maître file a complaint?" I chuckled, not at all surprised by this turn of events, and certainly not afraid or thrown off balance. I didn't care at all.

"No," the senior inspector shook his head, "I just happened to find out about the suit you filed. And you know, Viscount? I do not believe in coincidences either. One day, your uncle's estate gets burgled, and the next there appears a check for a very large sum."

"The check was presented for payment long before this regrettable incident."

"And yet, Viscount, where did you get it?"

I took a deep breath and thought about whether or not to just tell the bothersome policeman to get lost. I decided it wasn't time yet, and shrugged my shoulders:

"The Count wrote me that check at our last meeting."

Bastian Moran gave a pointed chuckle and

encouraged me:

"Continue."

"We made a deal: my uncle writes the check, and I don't bother him with lawsuits on my inheritance for the rest of this year and all of next year."

"The Count got thirty thousand francs out of that," replied the senior inspector, demonstrating a deep knowledge of my financial affairs, "what did you get?"

"Fast money."

"And that was all? You got just a fourth of the eventual total. That doesn't look very smart to my mind. Was there something else?"

I replied:

"There was. I was planning to use this money to buy out my debts. My uncle was going to declare me an impostor, then Isaac Levinson would offer the creditors ten cents to the franc for them..."

"And the money would stay in the family?" Bastian Moran smiled. "Everyone walks away happy?"

"Not very ethical, but not strictly illegal, either."

"What went wrong, then?"

"Aaron Malk was supposed to cash the check. He was Levinson's assistant. But first, the bank was robbed, then Procrustes killed Levinson, and Malk disappeared with my money!"

"So, that's why you were looking for him!" the senior inspector figured, now fully convinced that my story added up.

"And you already know the rest," I said, turning away to conceal an inappropriate smile. "We found Malk dead. Before arriving at the police, I searched his body and discovered the check with a 'rejected' stamp on it."

"And so, you went to hash it out with your uncle?" Bastian Moran suddenly shuddered.

"Balderdash!" I laughed carelessly. "I decided to take the legal route and now, I've got my uncle right where I want him! The law is on my side!"

"And that is surprising," he said, thinking it over. "Why did your uncle do something so poorly thought out?"

"If you find him, ask," I shrugged my shoulders. "I'm intent on getting what I'm legally entitled to. That will be enough for me."

Bastian Moran nodded and clarified:

"Viscount, I suppose that Ramon Miro will corroborate your story, then?"

And I carelessly shrugged my shoulders again:

"Ask him."

"Without fail," the senior inspector promised, giving me a salute goodbye before he walked down the embankment. Soon, a closed carriage came out of the square with no distinguishing features. Bastian Moran flung open the door, climbed swiftly inside and rolled off into the night.

I'm sure that, if my answers hadn't been to his liking, I'd be rolling off in that carriage with him. But this time I wriggled out of it, tricking fate yet again.

I took a few deep breaths, calming my frenzied breathing. I took a drink from a water fountain and leaned my elbows on the embankment wall.

As surprising as it seemed, I wasn't at all worried when talking with the senior inspector. Not one bit. The whole time, I had the image of Elizabeth-Maria von Nalz before my eyes. I heard her voice, and smelled the subtle aroma of her perfume. It hadn't gone anywhere and now, in the most natural way, it was driving me insane. I wanted to howl at the moon and tear out my own heart in anguish.

Naturally, I didn't do anything of the sort. Instead, I stood and looked at the river.

Just stood and looked.

The clouds stretched out over the sky, obscuring the scattered stars and rising moon; the dark now enshrouding the city was broken up only by street lights and the gleam coming from shop windows on the opposite bank of the river. In the distance, I saw signal-tower lights way up high.

At night, you cannot see the grime. At night, you cannot see the gilding. Night makes equals of us all.

It looks down from on high, not distinguishing rich from poor. Love is not so forgiving of human flaws.

As before, the lights of the carriages were crawling over the bridge. Like the other circus patrons, I didn't want to walk around the city at night, either. I was also very afraid of ending up in an electric chair again, so I was careful in my selection of a cab, hiring only the third or fourth one that met my eye. And then, I only got inside after I had taken the safety guard off my Cerberus and stashed it in my pocket.

"Balsamo Square," I commanded.

We negotiated for a short while, then the driver gave the reins a flick and the horses brought the carriage down the night-time streets of New Babylon. I closed my eyes and remembered Elizabeth-Maria. The scent of her perfume, the softness of her hands, her voice and surprising, delightful eyes.

And she remembered the gangly Viscount. She remembered me!

She even realized that I had been the one to stop the legendary Procrustes. The thought even made me feel guilty for a moment. Only for a moment, though. Because no matter what, I didn't have a single chance. I was not a good match for her.

Not a good match, that was it.

5

BALSAMO SQUARE was surfaced with ideally even black stone, baked into place. At one point, a prison had towered here with powerful bulwarks and damp dungeons that plunged into the earth for many dozens of meters; and so it was until the mystic and adventurer Giuseppe Balsamo was transferred here from the Lion's Castle. He called himself the Count Cagliostro.

It is still truly unknown, whether Balsamo had magical abilities from the beginning or if he turned in despair to the rulers of the underworld once out of confinement, but the fact remains that the Count was the first to challenge *the fallen* and bear the force of their rage. He didn't last long, but bear it he did.

The rebellion lasted for two days. In the end, the authorities of New Babylon destroyed the prison down to its foundation and filled the basements with molten stone. Along the way, a few neighboring blocks went below the earth, but the main consequence of that incident was not at all the destruction; many historians are proponents of the theory that Cagliostro's example was the inspiration for the Rie brothers' rebellion a half century later.

There was anecdotal confirmation of that fact as well: Emperor Clement had personally attached the name Balsamo to the barren patch where the prison had once stood, even though the Count was not a scientists or philosopher, the professions typically honored in the Empire as the main engines of progress.

I didn't particularly like this area. It was too unquiet and eclectic, even for New Babylon. The ancient buildings leaned up against one another. The new constructions rose up intently with uneven gaps separating them. Everywhere around, there were iron grates underfoot, but they were not storm drains. There was another street below. Down there, you could see the windows of the floors left below ground. Through the grate, you could see people walking between bright streetlights and hear music playing.

The nearest way down was a little stairwell with collapsed stone steps. I went down it, my hand in my pocket squeezing my wallet. Once below, I walked down the underground street confidently and with determination.

During the day, light reached this level through the grates. Now, I could see shop windows and occasional gas lamps. There were plenty of people down here; the majority of them were unprincipled thieves and naive dreamers. Miracle elixirs from unknown masters and outright rapscallions could not be distinguished by taste or color; palm readers easily found scientific bases for their work in the writings of ancient scholars and the geniuses of the Renaissance era, while horoscopes were composed in accordance with the most recent astronomical discoveries. It wasn't a good idea to yawn here. Otherwise, you could be drawn into some unpleasant business before you even blinked. You'd find yourself buying a blood-purifying magnetic bracelet or an amulet to protect you from the evil eye made of meteoric iron.

"Sublime Electricity!" whooped out a plump character in a white robe not far away. His sleeves were rolled up to his elbows. "A scientific method of exorcising demons and removing curses with electric current! Just five francs!

Don't pass this by! Unique technology!"

His lathered assistant was zealously pedaling a generator, and the wires of the ominous looking armchair sparked with electric discharge from time to time.

I quickened my pace. I hadn't the slightest desire to sit in an electric chair by choice. It would have been doubly strange to pay for it.

A bit later, the din of the crowd was left behind. I turned down an imperceptible passage and descended a narrow stairway to the level below. Light didn't reach here at all. And even my good *illustrious* vision wasn't enough to be able to see sufficiently; in fact, the glow of my eyes now only inhibited me.

I flicked the wheel of my lighter, but the uneven flame immediately went out, and the sparks dissipated into nothingness; I was out of kerosene. I cursed and walked on, looking for the door I wanted almost totally blind.

I found it, knocked and, not long after, the door flew open hospitably.

"Leo, what a surprise," Charles Malacarre said with a shake of his head, letting me inside. "I didn't hear a thing from you for five years, and now you're a frequent visitor all of a sudden!"

It was pitch dark in the blind illustrator's residence and, after stepping over the threshold, I asked immediately:

"Do you have lighter kerosene?"

"Is that the only reason you've come?"

"What do you think, Charles?"

The artist laughed hoarsely:

"You need someone's portrait so urgently that it couldn't wait for tomorrow?"

The sound of a match being struck rang out, then the little fire was lit and a candle gave off its warm glow.

"You don't have t..." I tried stopping the blind illustrator, but he wouldn't listen, and took a seat at the table, sharpening pencils.

"Is it such an urgent matter?" he repeated his indirect question.

"I simply didn't want to sit where anyone could see," I answered, looking around the artist's shoe-box of a room.

A fireplace, canvases, cups containing countless pencils on the shelves, an easel, a few chests, a table, a bed. Nothing else. Just a pitcher of water next to the bed and a few chipped glass mugs.

"So, it's personal?" Charles snorted, and said: "The kerosene is on the shelf by the fireplace."

I started filling the lighter, and he thoughtfully muttered:

"I don't know if I'll manage..."

"Why not?"

"Your *talent* is shining so bright that it hurts my eyes," the illustrator answered, and I took his words at face value.

"What if I try to calm down?"

"I don't think that'll be of much use, Leo. It's about a girl, isn't it? You're young, your blood is hot."

"Come off it, Charles!" I laughed

uncontrollably. "I'm cold blooded as an adder!"

The artist sighed loudly, then asked:

"Think of something distant. I'll take what I need."

So, I laid down on the bed and stared at the ceiling. There were uneven patches of light flickering on it from the candle. It turned out to be quite the task to not think about Elizabeth-Maria.

The girl occupied all my thoughts. All of me.

The slate of his pencil scraped against the paper and, without waiting for Charles' bark, I started guessing where my uncle might be hiding, and whether the strangler would find him. My thoughts gradually started revolving around the lightning-rune box, then I remembered the undying werewolf. But in the end, no matter how I tried, I just couldn't shake the image of Elizabeth-Maria.

"Leo!" Charles Malacarre moaned out, setting his pencil aside. "It's simply impossible to work with you! You might as well be pouring molten gold into my head!" he shouted, standing from the easel and grabbing for the pitcher as he said: "Alright, take a look..."

I grabbed the candle, walked up to the portrait and froze, stunned in place.

Elizabeth-Maria von Nalz looked alive. Although the drawing was fully black and white, the orange specks in her *illustrious* eyes were shimmering, and it seemed that she was now smiling and would soon begin talking to me. The sensation was so real I got spooked...

"Leo!" Charles shouted, giving me a jerk. "Control your *talent*. Get it together!"

"I'm ok," I whispered, wiping my sweaty face with a kerchief. "Charles, this is simply amazing!"

"Love, love," he said, just shaking his head.

I took the sheet from the easel and rolled it into a tube. I felt more at ease on a deep level. I don't know if it was a peculiarity of Charles' *talent*, or a quirk of the human psyche, but every time the illustrator put my fantasies to paper, they dimmed in my mind, no longer able to tear my psyche to shreds.

The thoughts of Elizabeth-Maria stopped tormenting me. My mental clarity returned, and left me with the obsessive desire to see her again no matter the cost. Only then did I understand how close I was to trying to lie my way into the reception at Baron Dürer's tomorrow. It was putting me positively beside myself...

"Leo!" the artist called out to me, sharpening the day's dulled pencils. "There's something else..."

"Oh yeah?"

"Something else in your head..."

"What's in my head?" I frowned, because no one likes when other people dig around in your memories. And although Charles perceived only the brightest images, it made me feel beside myself for a moment.

The artist had a perfect understanding that the whole delicacy of the situation and continued without his previous certainty.

"I saw something," he sighed. "Something

I've seen before. With my own eyes. I haven't always been a blind mole, you know. One upon a time, I was young and sighted. Back then, the dames even called me handsome!"

"Alright then, what did you see?"

"A shade," the illustrator answered simply. "A person whose face I couldn't make out, neither then, nor now. His image only flickered in your mind, but it sticks in the memory..."

I involuntarily nodded. The strangler's image had also been cut deep into my memory.

"Charles, who is it?"

"I do not know," the blind artist answered simply. "In the time of *the fallen*, they were thought to have been servants of someone from the inner circle of the brilliant Rafael."

"They?" I asked in confusion.

"They," Charles confirmed. "Leo! The faceless shades served one of the most powerful *fallen*. The return of these abominations cannot be leading to anything good."

"I've only seen one."

"Where there's one, there are others!" the old man cut me off, his face gaunt and pale. "No one has seen them since the insurrection. No one, ever. There must be something serious afoot, if they've slunk out of hiding."

I tried to hide the nervousness that was now captivating me and reassured the illustrator:

"I hope that no one sees them again, then."

"Keep your distance from these creatures," Charles advised me. "Better to tell the authorities. This is no mere trifle."

"Alright," I said, not wanting to argue. "I'll think it over."

"Be careful," the old man begged me, shivering as he wrapped himself in a plaid. This greeting from his past had clearly knocked him off track.

"Without fail," I promised as I took out my wallet.

"I have no need for money!" the artist declared when he heard the bank notes rustling.

"Everyone needs money," I objected, setting fifty francs on the table and walking back to the door. "Take care of yourself, Charles."

"Leo!" the illustrator laughed. "You stole my phrase!"

"I know," I chuckled and walked out the door.

To the uneven flame of my lighter, I went up to the underground street one level above. There, I hurried to the nearest stairway. I did not want to stay underground any longer than I had to, and it had nothing to do with my difficult relationship with basements. I simply had to catch my breath and think over what I'd heard.

And though I tried not to show it, Charles's words had seriously upset me. If you believed the history textbooks, the brilliant Rafael was a towering figure even by the standards of *the fallen*. The assault of his suburban manor took several days, later becoming one of the most popular themes for battle paintings of the era.

It wasn't possible that one of that *fallen one*'s posse had escaped that and was now coming back more than fifty years later, right? Then again, why not? And how was Emilee Rie's aluminum box connected with that?

The unanswerable questions made my head hurt. Sharp bursts of wind were throwing a light drizzle into my face; I wanted to get home as fast as possible, lock the gates and lie in bed. Just forget all my troubles and problems, at least for one night. Sleep it off, and think over the situation with a clear head. Every day, it was feeling more and more unpleasant.

Servants of a *fallen one*! Just think!

But right after I got home, I wasn't able to go straight to bed; as had become tradition, I had to accompany Elizabeth-Maria for dinner. Thankfully, she was unusually taciturn and Theodor also brought the dishes from the kitchen like a quiet, speechless shadow.

Over the last few days, the butler had grown seriously depressed.

After finishing my dinner in grave-like silence, I got up from the table and only then did Elizabeth-Maria inquire:

"What are your plans for tomorrow, dear?"

"What's that?" I perked up my ears.

"I'm bored!" said the girl, stretching out her words. "Bored, Leo! Do you understand? I am not accustomed to being cooped up inside all the time!"

"There's nothing I can do."

"Perhaps we can go somewhere?" Elizabeth-Maria suggested. "You need to unwind!"

"Not an option," I shook my

head. "Tomorrow, I'll be spending all day out of town."

"All day?"

"That's right."

"And what am I supposed to do with myself?"

"Have you considered the library? Ask Theodor, he'll show you where it is."

"I know where your home library is!" the girl snapped, offended. "Leo, you're unbearable! Just think: how could one just sit and read for whole days on end? That would drive any person crazy!"

"Well, I do not know about that. Try catching the leprechaun, then. That might perk you up."

Elizabeth-Maria just furrowed her brow, but my butler supported me.

"Madame, I think you ought to try and find his treasure," he advised.

"More silver?" I sighed fatefully.

"Now the knives have gone missing," Theodor confirmed.

"That little imaginary bastard has earned a good spanking," the girl smiled dreamily. "It'll be nice to give him a crack him on the nose."

"He probably doesn't have a treasure," I reminded them. "He's a figment of my imagination."

"All leprechauns have treasure," my butler said, still stubborn. The disappearance of our silver had affected him to the depths of his soul. "Whether he's imaginary or not, it's in his nature."

"Perhaps I really will do that," Elizabeth-

Maria decided.

I just shook my head and went outside.

I went up into the kitchen, practically falling over in exhaustion, but I didn't forget to close the blinds. After that, I took off my clothes and flopped back onto my bed, instantly becoming immersed in a deep, anxious dream.

In my dream, I was back at the circus but this time, the whole building was devoid of even a single living soul; my only company was the leprechaun. I understood perfectly that it was all just a dream, so I left the box, went into the vestibule and again ran into Elizabeth-Maria von Nalz. I tried to grab her outstretched hand, but the girl laughed and easily slipped away. I followed her down the empty corridors, went behind the stage and, somehow, we ended up in the basement of my own house.

It got dark, quiet and cold.

Suddenly, an ice chunk caved in, crackled and, like the quicksand of legend, pulled me down into an icy hell, into the underworld itself...

I dashed, grabbed the lowest stair and tried to get out, but I found no measure of success. The icy whirlpool was pulling me down with an ever-growing force. My fingers were getting numb in the cold and slipping, breaking my finger nails. The pain was twisting and breaking my joints, and I certainly would have fallen into the black icy abyss, but then something lashed across my face.

Instantly, I woke up, flung the towel that had just been thrown on my face off, and sat up in bed.

"Bugger!" the leprechaun grumbled, sitting in an armchair with a book in his hands. On one armrest, there was a glass containing a burning candle. On the other, there was a half-empty bottle of wine. "You're distracting me!"

I took a few deep sighs and fell back on my pillow.

"Aren't you a bit too old for *Alice's Adventures in Wonderland*?" I asked the pipsqueak.

"Stop it!" the albino demanded, licking his finger and turning the page. "Sleep! You caught me!"

But sleep had already left me. I got up on an elbow and asked my fantasy:

"Who was that man you were cutting up this morning?"

The leprechaun stared at me dismally and grudgingly answered:

"Doesn't matter. He was creeping around. Being cheeky. Asking for trouble!"

I didn't reproach the albino for killing the burglar, but I also wasn't going to let the topic die.

"What did you mean to do with the body?" I asked the pipsqueak.

He cursed under his breath and kept staring at the book.

"What did you mean to do?" I repeated my question.

"See, Leo, this is the very kind of heartlessness that leads to stray animals starving on the street," the leprechaun answered without looking away from the book. He then demanded: "Bugger! Don't bother me when I'm reading!"

Stray animals? Had he been planning to feed the body to street dogs?

The last thing this neighborhood needed was somebody training the strays to be man-eaters!

I turned onto my other side, pulling my comforter tighter and said:

"Don't do that anymore!"

The leprechaun didn't answer, though. He just didn't have time: down below, something fell with a deafening clang. So much that it shook the floor.

"Bugger!" the pipsqueak exclaimed, even spilling some wine in surprise. "The cupboard?"

Sounded like it. In a flash, I jumped out of bed, grabbed my Cerberus from the bedside table, yanked my Roth-Steyr from the holster and ran for the door. I dashed into the corridor and nearly slammed into Elizabeth-Maria as she peeked out of her room.

"Out of the way!" I shouted at her as I dashed by, and the girl, in her nightgown, ran after me.

Headlong, I ran down to the first story, jumped across the kitchen into the entryway with the door flung wide and went back into the guest room. I stepped over the overturned cupboard and immediately caught a dark figure in my sights that was pressing my half-strangled butler against the wall. Under his hat with a wide flat brim, there were swarming shadows; the hands grabbing Theodor's neck looked a bit darker in tone than the average New-Babylonian's.

A Moor?!

"Let him go!" I demanded, not having made up my mind to shoot.

The strangler slowly turned toward Elizabeth-Maria as she came through another door into the guest room.

In the blink of an eye, the girl was at the fireplace, grabbing the saber down from the wall and throwing herself at the malefic. He jumped away from my butler at full speed and stepped out to meet the succubus, opening his hand in a protective gesture. The sharpened steel made contact with the flesh with a mournful wail and was flung back, having left just a little bleeding scratch.

I shot, aiming at the head; the Moor caught the bullet from thin air, threw a chair at the girl with another hand and flew at me! But, he tripped over the leprechaun, who had just appeared from out of nowhere. The strangler quickly jumped to his feet, but fell back down when the albino slit his tendons with a rusty kitchen knife. His flesh, which didn't give to normal steel, yielded with surprising ease. The blade rasped against his bones, but the strangler didn't even scream.

In a flash, the malefic was ensconced in shadows. They became an extension of his arms and flew out in all directions, threatening to reach me and enslave my conscience. Stumbling away from them, I took aim again, but then Elizabeth-Maria stepped forward. With the saber, she struck the Moor's neck with all her might. His head, cut clean off, flew from his shoulders and rolled across the floor.

"Simple as that!" the succubus snarled, with very little human in her voice.

After that, the girl's eyes, glowing crimson, stopped on the leprechaun. And he immediately held the kitchen knife out in front of him, and put his left hand behind his back like a born swordsman.

"You wanna dance, kiddo?" he asked, jumping toward her, then jerking back. "One-two!" With that simple maneuver, he came noticeably closer to the door.

"That's enough!" I croaked out. Then I added, now less loud, but somewhat more substantially: "He might not have been alone."

It worked. Elizabeth-Maria, the bloodied saber in her hand, pressed herself against the window. Theodor ran over to lock the front door. The leprechaun was still acting like nothing had happened. He picked up his accordioned top hat, shook it straight over his knee and spit on the floor.

"Bugger! There goes the rug!"

And in fact, the strangler's black blood had poured out over practically half the guest room.

"It's quite a bad time to be a rug in this house," the succubus joked and told us: "I couldn't see anyone in the yard, but there might be someone hiding in the garden."

"Why wait for them?" I snorted and turned to my butler who was dragging out a double-barreled hunting shotgun and a box of rounds. "Theodor, is everything alright with you?"

"My condition does have certain advantages," he replied, turning his head from side to side. "I don't need to breathe anymore, for one."

"And why is no one asking if I'm alright?" the leprechaun asked capriciously, but everyone had forgotten about him.

"You'd be better off shutting up!" Elizabeth-Maria advised him, wiping the saber blade on the hem of her already blood-soaked nightgown.

"Bugger!" the pipsqueak cursed and, filled with a sense of his own merit, went out the door.

And just in the nick of time, too. The succubus was already barely holding on as it was.

"You should have asked where he hid his treasure," Theodor suggested belatedly, lighting a gas lamp. But I just waved a hand:

"We've got enough problems."

After setting my pistols on the coffee table, I touched the sabre-severed head and looked at the cut with a measure of disgust. It was smooth and even, as if made by a guillotine. Elizabeth-Maria could clearly slash with unbelievable force.

"Anything out of the ordinary?" the girl inquired with a chuckle.

"It's cold," I answered, wiping my fingers on the rug.

The dead-man's skin was frigid and slimy,

like that of a reptile. And yes, the malefic was noticeably colder than a fresh corpse should have been.

Elizabeth-Maria went away from the window and kicked the decapitated head away.

"A Moor," she winced fastidiously, looking at the black face with a wide nose and meaty set of lips. "Leo, you've got a real talent for making friends!"

"What can you tell me about him?" I asked calmly.

The girl put the saber back over the fireplace and shook her head:

"Well, dear, now I see why you were asking about vampires."

"Just don't tell me that was a vampire. I can tell the difference between malefics and vampires."

"That's no malefic," the girl objected. "It's a malefic's servant. Leo, your grandfather's saber came in very handy."

"The leprechaun made the first strike."

"And that really is surprising," Elizabeth-Maria snorted, going down on her knees. She took the corpse's hand with a wide slice across the whole palm and called me over: "Leo, look!"

I squatted next to her and asked:

"At what exactly?"

"At his palm."

I asked the chalk-pale Theodor to bring a kerosene lamp and only then saw what exactly put the girl on edge. The Moor's palm was covered with the gray lines of old tattoos. The fanciful symbols were dotted the back side of his hand as well; they began at the fingers and went into the cuff of his spacious sleeve.

"An Egyptian message," I determined. "It looks to be an older form of writing."

"He isn't quite that old," Elizabeth-Maria retorted and asked: "Theodor, knife."

When my butler brought the sharp kitchen knife back from the kitchen, the girl split the sleeve all the way to the shoulder in a confident motion and smiled in self-satisfaction:

"Like I said!"

There were strange tattoos adorning his arm, and even crawling up his collarbone, but there they were fresh and clearly marked by swollen and inflamed skin.

"Curious," I muttered in perplexity.

"Leo, dear! You can't seriously have thought you were unique, right?" the girl laughed, looking expressively at my own tattoos. In just a few motions, she cut all the clothes off the headless Moor.

Beyond both arms, there were markings covering the heart region; then, Elizabeth-Maria went all out and turned the dead body onto its stomach. His spine was also marked with tattoos. They ended at chest height. The ones on his upper spinal bones seemed to have been made not so long ago.

"We're lucky the protection didn't go up to the neck," I said with a shiver.

"There are many ways of killing that which considers itself invincible," said Elizabeth-Maria, shrugging her shoulders. She then stood up straight and suggested: "Leo, go to sleep. We'll clean it all up."

"The last tattoos," I said, not moving. "How long ago do you think they were made?"

"Yesterday or the day before," the girl announced without the slightest hesitation. "In such creatures, everything heals in a matter of days."

I didn't argue with her opinion, just nodded.

"I need you to cut out some of the new tattoos for me," I warned her. "A few of the old ones wouldn't hurt, either."

Elizabeth-Maria looked back at me expressively, but didn't inquire about my strange interest in the dead man's tattoos.

"Sure thing," she promised, covering her mouth with her hand as she yawned. "And, if you'd be so kind, please imagine I've got insomnia. Mortals waste a surprising amount of time on sleep. It's... irrational."

"But nice," I snorted, taking my pistols from the coffee table and heading into the carriage-house.

There were itchy ants crawling up my back, but not because of the cold, even though I was walking through the hallway in nothing but my long johns. It was just that I had always considered my house an impregnable fortress. But now, for the second night in a row, there were unwelcome strangers just strolling about.

That scared me. Scared me and made me angry.

I considered such intrusions a personal insult, a shot to the heart, a deed somewhat more humiliating than even kidnapping me and torturing me with electricity.

I wanted to get revenge and wasn't preparing to wait for the dish to get cold. The Moor's last tattoos had been done in New Babylon, which is why I was planning on going straight off to find the artist who did them.

But first, I decided to prepare for new surprises. No, I didn't screw the wicks into the hand grenades. Instead, I cleaned the Madsen machine gun of grease and set about loading up ten clips of thirty bullets each. After that, I loaded another few magazines for the semi-automatic rifles and loaded a few Mausers. But I didn't bring them with me, and left them in a box on top of the other pistols.

Guns are no panacea, but they do tend to come in handy when you're out of other arguments. In the end, there was nothing to stop a vampire from sending normal cutthroats after my soul. In addition, someone from the *illustrious* gang could show up. I really needed to stay on guard.

But thoughts of guns and plans for revenge instantly flew out of my head. I just had to get up into the bedroom. The leprechaun was standing opposite my pencil portrait of Elizabeth-Maria von Nalz with a rolled cigarette smoking in one hand and an open bottle of wine in the other, clicking his tongue in perplexity.

I froze at the threshold, then shook off my

consternation and, setting my pistols on the bedside table, said pointedly:

"I wonder if you can be hurt by a silver bullet?"

The pipsqueak looked angrily back at me, but didn't walk away from the drawing. He then ran full speed to the chair and blocked me off with a book. He was not planning on leaving the bedroom.

I cursed out soundlessly, put out the gas lamps the leprechaun had lit and laid down in bed.

Should I kick my own fantasy out the door? Nonsense...

6

I WOKE UP to the sunrise. It smelled unbearably of tobacco and booze in the room. There was an empty bottle lying on the floor. The arm of the chair had spots of wax on it, but the leprechaun had disappeared: based on the flung-wide door, he had gone off to play on Elizabeth-Maria's nerves.

Last night's events still seemed like a bad dream. But no, they were no dream; when I got down onto the first floor, I saw Theodor, his sleeves rolled up, still washing the black blood off the parquet floor of the guest room. There was no longer a rug in the room.

"Is the body in the icehouse?" I asked.

"Yes sir, Viscount," confirmed my butler, the color not yet returned to his face. From under the high raised collar of his shirt, I could make out the lilac-black marks of the strangler's hand.

"Curses!" I exclaimed. "We'll soon have a proper mass grave in our basement!"

"Two bodies isn't so many," Elizabeth-Maria said, responding to the noise.

The leprechaun slipped past after her into the room, not able to hold back laughter and even wiping his dirty kerchief to dry his newly formed tears.

"I see the two of you have found a common tongue?" I snorted.

The pipsqueak carefully touched his swollen nose and grumbled:

"Bugger..."

"He grabbed my feet from under the bed," the girl answered my unasked question.

"Well, you're a hussy!" the leprechaun snorted, deftly hopping up onto the windowsill and staring out the window. Based on that, my imaginary childhood friend was no longer intending to hide.

Curses, look at the company I'm starting to keep!

Elizabeth-Maria sized up the pipsqueak with a hateful gaze, but didn't get caught on his words and asked:

"Would you like breakfast, Leo?"

"I'd have some tea," I decided and reminded her: "What about the skin?"

"Do you doubt my ability to remove human

skin?" The girl melted into a sweet smile, under which there was hidden something rarely unpleasant. "Well don't, Leo. I am quite skilled at it."

I walked into the kitchen. There on the table were many long strips of black human skin drying out; the succubus had clearly taken to the flaying with aplomb. My appetite disappeared in a flash.

"Your choice, dear," Elizabeth-Maria allowed. "Whichever piece you like best."

"Very funny," I frowned, nervously finishing my tea and asking her to wrap the first strip of skin in a rag.

The girl did what I asked, then took the two longest of the remaining strips and started weaving them together with such a mundane look you'd think she was doing macramé.

"What are you doing?" I asked, startled.

"Your grandfather's saber is nice," the girl smiled in an untoward manner, "but I wouldn't say no to a more reliable weapon. Some enemies are easier to strangle than cut to pieces."

"Does that skin have any special properties?"

"Oh, yes! My advice to you is that, when your piece of the Moor is no longer needed, burn it at once."

I nodded, took a couple honey cakes from the bowl and hurried out the door.

The image of a sweet girl created in my head was so convincing that watching her flawless little hands weave strips of human skin into a garrote was just beyond my abilities.

With a shake of my head, I went up to the bedroom, but I couldn't just drink tea in peace. Elizabeth-Maria followed after me with a rag in one hand and a half-made rope in the other.

"Drinking by one's lonesome is bad form," she noted, looking around the mess the leprechaun had made. "You could have called me."

"I don't think that's a good idea," I answered, tying my neckerchief.

"Will you drink with me?"

"I'd drink you both under the table."

The girl smiled and asked:

"You can't control him at all?"

I didn't answer, though, just stored my Roth-Steyr in my belt holster, stuck my Cerberus in my pocket and headed for the exit.

Elizabeth-Maria handed me the rag bundle and advised:

"You could stand to shave."

"Certainly," I called back, rubbing my scruffy chin with my fingers, but I still didn't waste the time getting myself in order.

I went down to the first floor, walked out onto the porch and looked at the sky. Up above, there were wisps of cloud darting about. They threatened to completely cover the sky in very short order, but there was no rain yet, just the shaking tops of trees and sharp gusts of piercing wind.

It was brisk; too brisk for this time of year. I could now feel the incoming bad weather without any storm warnings whatsoever. But whether the storm would break out this evening, or tomorrow or at the end of the week, was still a complete mystery. And so, I had a nearly impossible time figuring out what clothes I should wear into town.

I decided to save myself the new expenses and returned home to change into my old suit. I pulled boots on my feet, and threw my canvas jacket on over top. Only in the realm of headwear did I remain true to form, taking my derby hat down off the shelf.

Elizabeth-Maria was looking at me contentiously, but didn't make any commentary on my appearance, just asking:

"Should I expect you for lunch, dear?"

"No, I'll be back by dinner time," I answered and went out the door, exerting a certain amount of effort to hold back a "I hope."

The last thing I wanted was to burden myself with the excessive attention of the succubus. In recent days, the infernal creature had been behaving herself entirely incorrectly, and I was even starting to get the creeping suspicion that the image of a sappy beautiful red-head I created had started to make an impact on the underworld native. But I shouldn't delude myself. The only thing stopping the beast dwelling inside Elizabeth-Maria from tearing me to pieces was our agreement.

FIRST, I WENT to visit Ramon Miro.

Glancing warily from side to side, I went down Calvary to Dürer-Platz, caught a cab there and ordered him to drive to the coalhouses.

Ramon's shift hadn't yet managed to finish, and I found him at his guard post. My hulking partner threw himself back into his chair and was holding an icepack on his face. But when I appeared, he threw it on the table and winced in shame. Or was he wincing in pain?

I first noticed that my friend had a decently-sized bruise around one eye, and his nose was swollen. I leaned up to the doorframe and shook my head:

"Rough night, eh?"

My hulking partner stayed silent.

"Who did that to you?" I asked, reformulating my question.

"Doesn't matter."

"This isn't connected with our dealings, I hope? It wasn't our former colleagues working you over, was it?"

"Not them," Ramon declared and, his right hand raised, showed me his scraped knuckles.

It was a convincing enough argument, and I only clarified:

"Were you asked where we went after the Chinese Quarter?"

"Yeah, some red-headed goon came by. A detective sergeant, I think."

"He came here?"

"No, to my house. As I'm sure you understand, I didn't tell many people about my new place of employment."

"And what did you tell him?"

"Everything as we agreed."

"So, you fought with someone else?"

"That's enough, Leo!" Ramon flared up. "Stop!" He picked up his damp ice bag again, placed it against his cheek and asked: "How's the reward coming?"

I just chuckled back:

"The reward will come through soon enough. I'd rather you tell me what happened to your face."

Ramon sighed fatefully and confessed:

"It's from an underground fistfight. They paid me two hundred francs. Now can we drop it?"

"You need money that badly?" I grew surprised.

My hulking partner got up from the table and started pacing from corner to corner as he finished his water glass.

"My cousin, who has a workshop in Foundry Town," he sighed, "is planning to buy the building next to his. If I can find six thousand by the end of the month, he'll cut me in on the profits."

"Six thousand?" I snorted. "Well, well."

"One thousand I've already got saved up," Ramon said. "I'll scrape together another five hundred somehow. Three thousand from you, right? Nothing changed?"

I opened my wallet and pulled out my partner's share. Demonstratively counting the bills, I handed them to Ramon.

"Take this."

"Great!" Ramon's face instantly lit up as he raked in the money. "The Judeans didn't try to cheat you?"

"They're a business-like folk," I shrugged my shoulders and noted significantly: "So, that means you have to hunt down another fifteen hundred?"

"I can handle it," the hulk barked.

"Before the end of the month?" I questioned.

Ramon cursed out in anger and asked:

"Leo, what do you want from me?"

"I've got a job. Won't take more than a day or two. I'll pay five hundred."

My friend clearly didn't want to get caught up in another adventure, and he inquired without any interest:

"What kind of work?"

"As usual, I need cover."

"Have you tracked down the Count?"

"No, I am preparing to track down the strangler."

"Forget it!" Ramon exploded. "That degenerate would eat us bones and all without so much as choking!"

I peeled back from the doorframe, dusted off a dry old stool, sat on it and said just one word:

"Flamethrower."

"What?" the hulk was taken aback.

"Flamethrower," I repeated. "I have a flamethrower."

"And you're planning to use it in the city?" Ramon asked, making a "screw loose" gesture. "Have you gone totally mad?"

"I hope it won't reach that point. I took one such monster down last night at home without any flamethrower."

"At your house?" Ramon was taken aback.

"At my house," I confirmed calmly. "And I don't think he was the last. So, it's in your interest to help me burn out their nest. Just imagine the kind of nastiness they could dream up."

"Devilry!" my hulking partner exclaimed, then stayed silent for a long time. Afterward, he clarified: "You'll pay five hundred and you've got a flamethrower?"

"If we actually have to use it, I'll toss you another couple hundred. Even the inspector general doesn't make seven hundred a day!"

"He doesn't have to take these kinds of risks!" Ramon got down off his chair and walked around his post. "Alright, what about your uncle?"

"He's hiding, but sooner or later he'll have to reach out. I've got him right here!" I said, showing my friend a tightly clenched fist.

Ramon nodded and voiced his counter-offer: "One thousand per day."

"Five hundred."

"Leo, thanks to you, I almost kicked the bucket yesterday!"

"And who saved you?"

"And who lured me into that mess, more like?"

There was a certain rationality in my friend's words, but I wasn't going to pay such an insane sum.

"Five hundred, Ramon. Five hundred and not a centime more. I'm not financially solvent enough to offer better."

"Five hundred is too little," said my partner, not wanting to meet me half-way. "Why take such risks? Five hundred is two fights in the ring!"

"Sure, but think about what will become of your countenance after those two fights!" I reminded him, twisting my fingers before my face.

"At least I won't be strangled by a malefic!"

"Alright!" I relented. "You can have a thousand! But only if you have to shoot. Five hundred and five hundred. Agreed?"

"Hands in."

I got up from the stool and leaned on my cane.

"Get the armored vehicle in order and come after me to the *Charming Bacchante*."

"And the flamethrower?"

"It'll all be there."

I said. After giving Ramon a salute, I went outside.

IT WAS TOO EARLY to rustle up the right people, so after the coalhouses, I headed to Albert Brandt's.

But I didn't go up to see the poet. I first stopped into a barber shop not far away, then took a seat on the street table under the cabaret's awning and asked the owner's sleepy nephew to bring me coffee, sugar and a saucer of cream. I decided I'd put that with the croissants I bought on the way and have breakfast.

The weather went bad right before my eyes.

There were little ripples of molten lead scurrying about the canal. The wind blew down the chimneys, and the cloth awning buffeted. The sky finally was stretched over with dark clouds. I found it surprisingly pleasant to drink the sweet hot coffee with milk and feel like a normal person.

Albert Brandt appeared when there were just crumbs remaining of the croissants.

"You could have come up," he grumbled out, wrapped up tight with a blanket around his shoulders.

"You're already up?" I asked in surprise, looking at the time. "This is early for you."

"This is my kind of weather," Albert explained, going into the cabaret's bar for some mulled wine and returning to the table. "You look like you didn't sleep well, Leo," he noted.

"I didn't sleep well," I laughed back with a nervous smirk.

"Problems?"

I just held my finger above my head.

"Can I help in any way?" my friend asked.

"I'll manage on my own."

"Are you sure?"

"You understand, Albert," I sighed after finishing my coffee, "I feel like I'm running on a rail. And now, I can't get off. Either I run to the finish line, or I die. There isn't a third option."

"Is it all that serious?"

"I don't know," I laughed. "I just don't know. I'm just not sure of anything anymore. My *talent* has gone rogue, and it seems that everything around me is a figment of my imagination, and as soon as I turn around, reality dissolves into a gray slum."

The poet took a long sip of his glass of hot wine, then said as he looked out at the canal:

"Everyone is visited by such thoughts from time to time, Leo."

"But, unlike them, I could actually pull that off."

"I don't think you have such a twisted imagination," said Albert Brandt, shaking his head. "Leo, curses! Read the papers! Could you seriously have imagined all that? Explosions, strikes, wars! The world is falling apart. The world order is crumbling. The Empire is splitting at the seams! And the miracles of science? Every day something new happens, every day!"

"I do not claim the role of creator," I replied with a shrug of my shoulders. "I'm just moping."

Albert stared at me in determination, then finished his mulled wine in one long gulp and suggested:

"If you want, I could take you to Baron Dürer's reception."

"I want to, but I shouldn't," I refused.

"Why not, if I may ask?" Albert squinted, rubbing his sand-colored beard. In the end, his blue eyes lit up, as if my *illustrious* friend was intending to use his gift of persuasion.

I shook my head.

"First off, it wouldn't be very polite of me to impose on you," I announced to the poet. "You were, after all, planning to take the lady of your heart, right?"

"Incognito," Albert confirmed. "But that doesn't matter. True friendship, Leopold..."

"Second, I don't want to. I don't want to see Elizabeth-Maria with her fiancé."

"You could at least try..."

"No!" I cut him off. "I cannot. And third, you're forgetting about the rail. I'm not exaggerating when I say I'm not feeling right. These affairs cannot bear delay. I'll be busy today."

"You won't be free by four?"

"No."

"Alas. Dürer's receptions are simply unforgettable."

"The aluminum king can allow himself many extravagances," I shrugged my shoulders. "Do you know if he's related to *the* Dürer?"

"I have no idea," Albert replied, waving it off frivolously.

"Are you going to read the poem about Procrustes?" I then asked.

Albert started thinking.

"No," he decided. "First, I've got to whip it into shape."

I nodded, looking all around in contemplation, then glanced at the clock.

Ramon was late, and I didn't like that one bit.

But just as soon as I started worrying, around the corner came the armored vehicle to the crackling of its powder engine. The unwieldy self-propelled carriage crawled unhurriedly along the embankment and turned down the neighboring street; I then gathered my things.

"See you tomorrow!" said Albert, extending his hand to say farewell.

The poet held me back and warned:

"If you need help..."

"I know who to turn to," I laughed and walked off after the armored vehicle, leaning on my cane now not so much because my leg hurt as because I'd grown accustomed. My leg had almost totally stopped bothering me today.

When I'd climbed into the passenger seat, Ramon, sitting behind the wheel, noted with reproach:

"You were in no hurry!"

"You either," I said, tapping my finger on the clock face.

"I had time to wash the mud off the carriage while I waited for you," Ramon shrugged. "I filled the trotyl and poured water into the radiator, too. And plus, I had to go home to change clothes."

The former constable had chosen his clothing, a cloak with police patches removed and a peaked cap with no insignia, by design: many locals would not realize this was only a former police officer if we had to stop on a lively street or leave the car somewhere.

"I hope you didn't park the armored car in your own yard?"

"Who do you take me for?" the hulk objected, turning off the narrow street onto a boulevard. "I parked it two blocks away."

"We'll have to get rid of it," I

decided. "Otherwise, they might connect us with the robbery of my uncle's estate. We left tire racks."

Ramon gave a nervous shiver and suggested: "Well, maybe we should put it in the river?"

"Maybe, but it'll have to be at night," I sighed. After that, I told him: "Turn your head."

Ramon got surprised, but did it.

"You've got quite the bruise," I chuckled.

"It'll be gone soon," he frowned and barked: "Tell me where to go."

I told him the address, and my partner laughed:

"Well then, I'm glad we'll be in an armored vehicle!"

"I don't think there'll be problems."

"Leo!" Ramon gasped. "You're a quarter Russian, and already quite the handful. There are a countless number of such people there!"

"Let's go, already."

I'd decided that first, we would pay a visit to Sergei Kravets, the tattoo artist from the neighborhood settled primarily by Russians and Poles. The old man knew tattoos like no one else. It was another question as to whether he would be frank with us, though. I had big doubts on that account. But it was worth a try.

AFTER ARRIVING, Ramon acted like police normally act on raids. He blocked off the intersection with the armored vehicle, dragged out the semi-automatic rifle from the back seat and stood up near the car holding it ready. A light drizzle was now coming down, and that played into our hands. Patrolmen didn't like such weather, and even the most cautious among them preferred to wait out their shift in warm and dry liquor-houses. The risk of finding former colleagues today was minimal.

"Just don't take long," Ramon warned me, looking nervously around.

"If something happens, shoot into the air," I warned him and walked into the boot-maker's shop.

"It's been a long time, Leo," the old craftsman sighed bitterly. "I can't tell. Are you still a cop or not?"

"That's a complicated question," I answered, pulling out the wrapped piece of Moor's skin from my pocket. "I need your help."

"I see that's one of your habits," Sergei Kravets pursed his lips.

"I'll try not to bother you in the future," I promised and unfolded the fabric. "But now, I'm interested in finding out who might have done these fresh tattoos."

In shock, the old man stared at the piece of black skin and even backed up against the wall.

"Get out of here, Leo!" He demanded. "Just get out of here on good terms!"

"Please don't tell me this was your work."

Kravets caught his breath, dripping some kind of aromatic infusion into a cup with his shaking hand, and draining a few gulps.

"I didn't do this," he then sighed.

"But you know the man who did?"

"This is beyond the pale!" the old man flew into a rage. "You could get life in a work-camp for that, Leo! I'll tell you what that is! Egyptian magic! And also, you cut off a person's skin! Antiscientific activity, spying and murder! And you came with that to me? This is high treason!"

I looked expressively at the old boot-maker and gave a compassionate nod.

"All the more reason to be surprised, Sergei, that you keep such things in your workshop."

"Me?" Kravets was taken aback. "You brought it here!"

"Not at all," I shook my head.

"You can't do this to me! You aren't even a cop anymore!"

"Look outside..."

The old man just shrugged. There was no way he could've missed the crackling of the powder engine.

"Either answer my questions here, or in the Newton-Markt," I then told him. "I, for one, prefer to save us all time."

The bluff worked. Sergei Kravets frowned and grumbled:

"This is the last time I help you, Leo. The last time! Don't you ever come around again!"

"I don't remember this happening before..."

"This is the first and last time!" the old boot-maker cut me off. He took an electric torch from one of the shelves, turned it on and, in the electric light, the faded gray tattoos lit up silver.

"Witchcraft," Sergei grumbled. "I don't associate with such people."

"The tattoo was done by a malefic?" I inquired.

"Just the initial symbol," the old man answered. "That's how it is normally done. A malefic makes the anchor, and the other drawings just have to be attached to it."

"Do you know what's written here?"

"Some Egyptian filth," Kravets grumbled, pushing the package away from himself and starting to wipe his hands on a towel. "If you want to know more, find an Egyptologist."

"I want to know which of your colleagues made the last symbols."

"Do you think we all work together in a shop or something?" snorted the boot-maker.

"No, but the young learn from the old, and cannot hold their tongues. Also, these tattoo artists are true craftsmen. The previous style was maintained ideally. It's almost totally perfect."

"One might start thinking you know your way around this stuff."

"I do," I told him.

"What will happen to him? What will happen to the artist?"

"You're asking me? Maybe he'll live to a ripe old age and die surrounded by relatives and good friends, and maybe he'll drink himself to death or break his neck when he's up trying to clean the chimney. How should I know?"

"You mean to say you won't arrest him?"

"Not if he answers my questions."

I don't know if the old boot-maker believed me or not, but he didn't get stubborn, just told

me:
    "Tomasz Górski, goes by the nickname Razor. He's got a private practice on Nobel Road."
    "Doctor?"
    "Veterinarian."
    I figured out how to find the man, took the rag bundle and waved my hand to Ramon as I walked outside:
    "Let's go!"

7

NOBEL ROAD was five minutes away by car, but it took us at least that long afterward weaving about looking among the private homes of the area for a secluded spot to park. In the end, we drove the self-propelled carriage down a narrow alleyway and left it there, completely blocking off passage, then walked to the veterinarian's on foot.
    Ramon was armed this time with his Winchester. I grabbed the semi-automatic carbine and a couple hand grenades. It was clearly not unnecessary precaution, if you consider the fact that we might meet one of the stranglers here, or even their master.
    We walked in from the back yard, simply jumping over the fence, as the guard dog was thankfully held back by a strong chain. We barely managed to tie our neckerchiefs on our faces before some boy came out to see what the

commotion was; Ramon simply poked his butt-stock into the boy's stomach, pushing him back inside. I ran off after him, and we dashed through the rooms, rounding up the veterinarian's whole household. The vigilant boy, a plump girl, a fat aunt and a stammering helper were all driven into a closet with no windows or doors. Paying no mind to the crying and lamenting of the ladies, we locked them in and took Tomasz Górski to task. He was a tough old man, wrinkled and totally bald.

"Take the money and leave," he suggested, having taken us for robbers.

"My dear old man," I smiled, adjusting my dark glasses, "you won't be rid of us that easily."

The veterinarian grew pale, but was undaunted, making another suggestion:

"If you let the boy go, he can go withdraw more money from the bank. You don't want this on your conscious. Money isn't worth all this."

"Mr. Górski," Ramon then frowned, standing at the window and watching the gates, "your words could be taken as an attempt to bribe government officials in pursuit of their duty."

The dry official language of the affirmation made a mixed impression on the man: having stopped worrying about his property, he started turning his head in confusion, looking from me to Ramon and back again.

"But you're not in uniform, sirs," Tomasz babbled.

"This work cannot bear publicity," my hulking partner chuckled significantly.

And I smiled:

"Are you so burning with desire to visit the Newton-Markt, Mr. Górski?"

"No!" the veterinarian shuddered, then grew a bit calmer and declared: "Why are you here? I didn't do anything reprehensible!"

I simply unfolded my rag bundle and threw it on his knees. The old man started seizing up like an epileptic when he saw the black skin. He opened his mouth, but couldn't produce a single sound. He tried to stand, but reeled and we had to set him back in his chair.

"Do you understand what this could mean for you?" I asked compassionately after a truly theatrical pause.

"I don't know what this is!" the veterinarian yelped out. His voice was trembling so severely that any common jury would declare him guilty without even five minutes' discussion. "Take this filthy thing away!" he shouted, trying to throw the package on the floor. "I do not know, I do not know anything!"

I took a chair, sat opposite him and asked:

"Mr. Górski, just tell us everything."

"But I don't know anything!" the old man exclaimed, throwing the wrapped piece of Moor's skin from his knees, this time successfully.

I sighed and warned him:

"Do you really want to end up behind bars, Mr. Górski? Do you know what kind of sentence they normally give people involved in anti-scientific activity? You'll die in prison and never see your family again."

The veterinarian clasped his hands and cut me off:

"I don't know anything!"

"Who are you protecting, your family?" I clarified. "Do you think they'll be safe if you go to prison? Well think again, my kind sir! Anti-scientific activity! Espionage! Treason! Do you think this will not touch them? You are mistaken!"

"E-e-e-espionage?" bleated out the hiccupping veterinarian, seemingly about to go into a fit. "Treason? I know nothing about this! I never committed any treason!"

"That's not what we've been hearing," I assured him, standing to my feet and looming over the old man. I stared at him gloomily from my high height. "Having dealings with Egyptian spies, in current times, threatens the noose, nothing less. If you're lucky, your family will be sent off to a work colony, but whether you're lucky or not depends on you alone."

"I don't know anything!" the old man repeated his routine once again.

I felt his pockets, pulled out a keyring and walked over to the iron cash register.

"What are you doing?" the veterinarian gasped. "You have no right!"

Paying his pitiful babble no mind, I opened the lock, rifled through the cash and, to very little surprise, I pulled out from under the ledger a stack of Egyptian guineas. I counted the brand-new bank notes and declared:

"A hundred guineas. One hundred!" Then I

gave a weary wince and shook my head. "The fact that you are working with foreign spies has been established. Now, the only thing that could make this easier on you is coming clean."

"Either you work with us," Ramon said from the window, "or you'll disappear in the work camps. It's up to you."

The veterinarian drooped down and said indistinctly:

"I'd hardly be of any use to you. I was only paid to keep quiet."

"Tell us!"

"At night, it was the night before last, I heard my horses get spooked. I came out to check them and lost consciousness," Tomasz Górski told us. "I woke up in some kind of basement, or cellar. I was given the choice of working with them or death."

"Who?"

"Moors. I didn't see their faces."

"How many were there?"

"Four. I saw four."

"Did you give them tattoos?"

"Yes."

"All of them?"

"Yes."

"With what?"

"They had their own needles and ink."

After that, I asked him to describe the room he had to work in, but the veterinarian just kept saying that it was in some kind of basement, dusty and dirty with a sagging ceiling, stone columns and bare walls. There were no electrical wires there, just candles for light.

"On the way back, they blindfolded me. It seems it was some kind of catacombs. Three stairwells I remember for sure."

"Great!" I bolstered the veterinarian. "How long did it take you to get back to town?"

"An hour or two," Tomasz hazarded. "At first, it was a very bumpy ride, but then the road got better. They might have driven in a circle for a while, but I have no doubts that they brought me out of town."

"What happened next?"

"They let me out near home. When I took the blindfold off, there was no one around."

"Alas."

I walked up to the veterinarian and tore off a smart kerchief that just could never have gone with the rest of his severely-shaded outfit. On his slack skin, I could clearly make out a set of pale hand marks.

"Go about your life as usual," I then warned the tattoo artist. "Tell your family that we were robbers and got scared off by a random passerby. If you're asked to do more tattoos for these gentlemen, try to remember every word and every sound. You must figure out where you're being taken. Is that clear?"

"Yes."

"We'll get in touch with you," said Ramon, joining the conversation. "But if you go flapping your lips, you can be gotten rid of."

The veterinarian looked at us from under his eyebrows and said nothing.

— The Heartless —

I took yesterday's edition of the *Capital Times* from the table, knocking a pack of papirosa cigarettes and a box of matches on the floor. I walked over to the fireplace and threw the paper on the coals. When the paper started smoking and caught fire, I ordered the house owner:

"The skin!"

Tomasz Górski did as I commanded and even poked it into the fire with the poker, pushing the rag bundle further into the coals. The flame quickly grew a dirty reddish color. The unpleasant scent of scorching flesh dispersed throughout the room.

"Let your family out in five minutes. For now, just sit calmly," I warned him, sticking a stack of guineas in the breast pocket of the veterinarian's jacket. "Consider this your payment for good sense."

Then, I pointed Ramon to the back door. He jumped out after me and dashed through the back yard. This time, we didn't climb over the fence. Instead we undid the latch, calmly went out and hurried to the armored car.

The barking of the chained dog followed after us for quite some time.

"So, you said you filled the trotyl?" I asked my partner, getting behind the wheel of the self-propelled carriage.

"I did," he confirmed and, in his turn, wondered: "Do you trust him?"

"Tomasz? Yeah, I do. I don't think he works for the Egyptians. It just happened to come together like that."

"And you think he was totally open?"

"More or less."

I personally was convinced less by the veterinarian's words than by the marks left by the Moor's hands on his neck. No one would give a co-conspirator such an obvious brand. But as a reminder to a random person that they need to hold their tongue, such a mark seemed quite reasonable. Money and threats, the carrot and the stick. Nothing new.

"A hundred guineas is how much?" Ramon suddenly asked. "One thousand francs? More?"

"One thousand two hundred," I calculated mentally, steering the car to the exit from the alley as I joked: "It's actually a shame we're not robbers."

Ramon gave a nervous laugh; I think that thought managed to visit him as well.

"If they didn't do away with the tattoo artist," he said thoughtfully, "that must mean they plan on using his services again in the future."

"I think you're right," I nodded and revved the engine around a slowly moving cart.

"Shall we set up an ambush?" Ramon suggested.

I looked sidelong at my friend and snorted:

"Are you really prepared to watch for them at night?"

My hulking partner gave a shiver.

"What other option do we have?"

"Ramon," I sighed, "our only chance is burning out the vampire nest during the day when he and his servants cannot offer serious resistance. Otherwise, even the flamethrower wouldn't be of any use, and don't you doubt it."

Hearing me mention the vampire, my partner finally tired of the topic and turned away to the side window.

"We don't know where the lair is," he said some time later.

"I have some guesses," I assured my friend, parking the armored car in a hidden yard not far from the *Golden Bullet* weapon store. "Wait here," I told him, getting out from behind the wheel. "I'll be back in twenty minutes. If I take longer, don't worry."

"It's your money," Ramon called back blithely, prepared to sit in the cabin all day if it meant five hundred francs.

THE POMPOUSLY NAMED *Golden Bullet* opened early in the morning; there, I obtained ten ten-caliber bullets and just as many buckshot shells, then headed for the shop *Mechanisms and Rarities*. And though there wasn't a particular need for an improvised flamethrower for this little trip out of town, I didn't want to put all my eggs in one basket, relying exclusively on a salvaged piece of equipment that I hadn't even yet managed to test out.

Alexander Dyak had already opened his business by that time. What was more, early-bird shoppers had already showed up: a trio of students and a gray-bearded teacher, practically ripped from a caricature of an absent-minded professor. I didn't even go inside. I just looked through the glass and immediately continued to the neighboring coffee shop. There was an intoxicating aroma of fresh baked goods and ground coffee wafting out.

I drank a coffee at the bar. When I was finished, I asked them to pack me up some crumpets and poppy rolls in a paper sack and went back to *Mechanisms and Rarities* as the owner was already serving his last customer, the "professor" I'd seen earlier.

"Good morning, Alexander!" I greeted him as I walked in.

"Good morning, Leopold Borisovich!" the inventor called back, counting out change. He bid farewell to the silver-bearded old man, then set a sheet of paper torn from his notebook on the counter and slid it to me. "Your bill!"

"Help yourself!" I offered, pushing over the bag of pastries with its stupefying aroma.

"White flour is bad for me at this age," the man refused.

I set the sack on the counter and took the sheet covered in indecipherable handwriting.

"I had to buy some of the components in," Alexander Dyak explained.

I studied the list and rubbed the back of my head in perplexity. The list included a rubber disk, a galvanized tube, sockets, a five-liter canister of kerosene, a flare, a garden-hose nozzle, back straps and a compressed air tank.

In total, it was thirty francs and forty-five centimes.

"I don't see a 'work' entry," I smiled, getting out my wallet.

"Come now, Leopold Borisovich," the inventor said with a wave. "For me this was, if you please, a little puzzle. A way to keep the boredom at bay."

"And did you find any success?"

Alexander Dyak sighed bitterly:

"To be honest, I was hoping for a difficult task, but this was all quite elementary."

"The simpler, the safer, right?" I joked, setting three tenners on the counter and holding them down with a one-franc coin.

"Not exactly," the store owner corrected me. "By the way, while I was preparing your device, I got another idea. And it could be much more interesting to create."

I asked him to bring me up to speed, but the inventor just waved it off.

"No need for that now. Let's go take a look at your miracle weapon," he suggested.

We locked the front door and went into the back room.

The inventor walked up to the workbench and shook open a rag bundle containing a compressed air tank, gas burner and shooting tip all connected together. The top of the tank was ringed with an uneven weld seam as if it had been opened. In place of the stop valve, a nozzle was sticking out. A bit lower, under the corner on the bolted down socket, there was a pipe attached with an incendiary charge. Also attached was a handle with a trigger.

"It's all elementary!" Alexander Dyak declared and, the tank under his armpit, pulled the handle with his right hand. "Point it at your target, pull down on the trigger. The estimated range is up to fifteen meters. There should be enough to last around twenty seconds."

"Estimated?" I clarified.

"Well, Leopold Borisovich, testing the object under field conditions was unfortunately not possible."

"But it does work?"

"I guarantee it! The construction is elementary! When the incendiary charge is lit, the gases in the internal tube enter the tank and push out a rubber disk, which creates the excess pressure needed to release the gelled kerosene."

The unfamiliar word cut into my hearing and I asked:

"Gelled?"

"Let's skip the technical details," said the inventor, refusing to share this information. "Then, the flame of the incendiary projectile ignites the stream of kerosene and, though it happens at about forty centimeters from the nozzle, I recommend you hold the device with your arms extended."

The shop owner handed me the single-use flamethrower. I weighed it in my hand, evaluated its dimensions and decided a backpack would make a great addition to the kit. Otherwise, transporting it was sure to be a headache.

Alexander Dyak got out a backpack from under the worktable, and without particular problems, put the flamethrower inside.

"Thank you!" I said, squeezing the inventor's hand. "I'll be sure to give you a report on how it works!"

"That's up to you, Leopold Borisovich!" the shop owner said with a skeptical frown. "This is a pretty outmoded design. To be honest, I feel bad offering you such an imperfect solution. Coming clean, there simply wasn't time to work out a better idea I had."

"What was that?" I wondered.

"Compact incendiary charges with a very interesting formulation."

"Interesting, you say? And how much would it run me?"

"A hundred francs' advance. The rest will depend on the final size of the order," answered Alexander Dyak, not wanting to bore me with the details.

I handed him two bank notes of fifty francs each and asked:

"When can I expect the finished product?"

"Come by tomorrow," the inventor suggested, stroking his gray beard. "I'll think it over this evening, and tomorrow, I'll try to make a prototype. But it will depend on your requirements. Perhaps it is of no interest to you at all."

"Not at all," I assured the man. "I'm intrigued beyond all measure!"

"Oh, youth, youth," Dyak shook his head, letting me out into the sales room. "I expect you tomorrow, Leopold Borisovich."

"Alexander, you wouldn't happen to know anyone from the history department, would you?" I asked after that.

"The second half of my shop name can give you an unambiguous answer to that question," the inventor smiled. "And why do you ask?"

"I've got a question on the history of New Babylon, and I have discovered some regrettable gaps in my education."

"Are you looking for anything in particular?"

"Yes, information on a *fallen one* known as Rafael."

Alexander Dyak gave it some brief thought, then looked at the clock and ripped a fragment of paper from a newspaper.

"Go out onto the square, turn left and you'll see the coffee shop *Helen of Troy*," he said, writing something on the paper. "If you hurry, you'll be able to catch Juan Dominico Ramillo, the assistant head of the archeology department." The inventor folded his paper in half and handed it to me. "I don't think he'll refuse to illuminate you on this issue, Leopold Borisovich."

"Thank you," I nodded and headed for *Helen of Troy*.

On the coffee shop's veranda, to my unstated disappointment, I saw only ruffling notes and yellowed pages of library tomes. Nothing but students. Then, I went inside and immediately noticed a black-haired gentleman not much older than me, who was writing distractedly in a thick workbook.

"Señor Ramillo?" I asked him.

The assistant head of the archeology department looked at my none-too-presentable outfit with unhidden doubt and inquired coldly:

"With whom do I have the honor of speaking?"

I simply extended the paper I got from Dyak.

The historian familiarized himself with the missive and immediately dissolved into a smile:

"Take a seat, I beg you! A friend of Alexander's is a friend of mine."

I carefully set the backpack on the floor, lowered into the chair and immediately warned him:

"I don't think my question will take too much of your time..."

"Ask away!" Señor Ramillo allowed.

"I'm wondering about a *fallen one* known as Rafael. What can you tell me about his suburban manor?"

"I've visited it before," the historian said. "From an academic perspective, it's of little interest."

"Who owns it now?"

"I suppose it's public property. No one of sound mind would take such a burden on themselves."

"Is that right?"

"I can tell you one thing," the archaeologist smiled, "the grass doesn't even grow there." And he added weightily: "To this day."

I nodded, taking it into account.

"One last thing, Señor Ramillo. How do you

get there?"

The assistant head of the archeology department was amiable enough to draw us a map.

After giving him my heartfelt thanks, I turned toward the armored vehicle and motioned for Ramon, who was standing on the back street, carbine at the ready:

"Let's go!"

"Where to now?" he asked, getting into the passenger seat.

"To get the flamethrower."

"Did you find any clues?"

"I've got a hunch we should check out," I confirmed, starting the engine.

Much to my surprise, driving the armored car suited me. I liked the speed, I liked the power hidden in the engine. Even the particular clumsiness of the armored vehicle didn't spoil my impression. In fact, because of that, the construction seemed all the sturdier, and thoughts about accidental trotyl detonation had long since stopped making me wince at every loud engine clap.

But it's poor maneuverability on a flat road turned into pure torture on the way up Calvary. The engine gave forth a heart-rending roar. The wheels skidded in the mud. The car jerked forward unevenly, then skidded down a bit; our ascent went at a truly turtle-like tempo.

"This would have been faster on foot!" Ramon said, finally losing his cool.

"Do you want to haul the flamethrower on

your own hump?" I snarled, driving the self-propelled carriage across the bridge over the stream. "That's all, we've arrived."

Right after the turn, I stopped the car, got out and unlatched the gate. I then hurried through the black garden, dead and wet, directly to the carriage-house. First of all, I dragged the flamethrower out, then went back for hand-held mortar rounds. Finally, I dragged out the mortar itself.

"What's that all for, then?" Ramon asked, taken aback. "Are we going to make war, Leo?"

"I want to test all this in action," I explained, lifting the tailboard. "It'll come in handy."

"Well then, hopefully that kind of fortune doesn't find us," the hulk chuckled, throwing open the passenger side door and shuddering in surprise when he saw a blinding flash of lightning on the top of the hill. "What the devil?" he grew surprised.

"Business as usual," I said with a hand wave.

The tower on the summit of Calvary served as a giant lightning rod, and it was struck even in clear skies with envious regularity. And now, there was a storm at our doorstep, so the lightning up there was nearly constant.

"Alright, let's go," Ramon hurried me along.

I took a seat at the wheel, turned the self-propelled carriage to the platform before the gates and rolled down the hill. Every time I drove the unwieldy carriage, I got better and more confident, so now I drove down the lively street without particularly worrying that I might hit someone.

"Leo," Ramon sighed after we turned around on Dürer-Platz and got on the nearest route out of town, "I respect you immeasurably, and also you're paying me, but if you would be so kind, please tell me what you've got planned! Or just stop, and I'll get out!"

"Calm your nerves," I said to my friend. "A friend of mine reminded me that monsters like that strangler were once known to run in the retinue of Rafael the *fallen one*. We're going to check his manor. It's not far from town. We'll be back before sundown."

"Do you think that's their nest?"

"I think it's worth taking a look."

The street to the bridge was fully clotted with carts and carriages. A no less dense stream was coming the other way. Also, a steam tram was leaning on its horn, demanding they all make way. Not wanting to waste time, I turned down the neighboring street. I drove around the deadlock on small alleys, going by one crawling cart after the next.

"Why there exactly?" Ramon asked after thinking over my idea.

"Such creatures don't particularly like New Babylon these days. Haven't for a while," I explained. "If they've returned to the city, something extraordinary be happening. They didn't even have time to prepare. It's logical to suppose that they might try to hole up somewhere familiar."

"Where did you get that idea?"

"The unfinished tattoos," I reminded him. "The tattoos were so important for them that they even had to find a local artist. But note that they did bring the implements and ink with them. This was no planned return. It must have been impromptu."

"But why out of town exactly?" my stubborn companion continued. "Why in the manor of the *fallen one*?"

"I asked someone who knows vampires, and they told me vampires prefer to stay underground, the deeper the better. And sure, there are catacombs in the city, but they're so packed with homeless and thieves down there you can't even walk."

"What's stopping them from renting a place?"

"A master who doesn't come out during the day and his Moorish servants? Do you think Department Three would overlook something like that? Their investigators practically till up the soil with their noses trying to root out Egyptian agents. And also, they brought the veterinarian out of town."

"Or so he said."

"That's why we're checking."

"What are we checking? The *fallen one*'s manor? The new owner won't even let us get near!"

"There isn't any new owner. They say the grass still doesn't even grow there."

My hulking partner nodded and turned to

the window.

Sometime later, the thick development of the city was left behind and the armored car rolled down a wide road. Alongside of it, there were high fences for warehouses and small factories. We gradually started encountering less and less loaded-down carts, and began seeing gardens and private houses instead.

Ten minutes and we were out in the expanses of the suburbs. Then, they were also left behind. All around, there stretched out fields and groves of fruit trees, oranges, lemons, and olives.

When I saw a pond flash behind a tall wall of poplars, I drove off the road right through the meadow to its bank, all overgrown with reeds. A band of trees was blocking us off from the street, and from the other side, as far as I could see, there stretched out an endless field, so I could stop worrying about prying eyes.

"What are you doing?" Ramon, surprised, got out of the car after me.

"Testing the weapons," I answered, throwing open the back door of the armored vehicle. "Have you ever used a flamethrower before?"

"There can't exactly be an art to it," my hulking partner muttered as he started sifting through ammunition.

I helped him attach the tanks of my trophy flamethrower to his back, fastened the belt, screwed out the valves and pointed at the pond:

"Try it out."

Ramon lit the burner, then pulled the mask

onto his face with its round glass eyepieces and walked down the shore in search of a gentle slope to the water. He stood at the very edge of the pond and a stripe of smoking flame shot out toward the reeds. In surprise, the squat man panicked and released the trigger too quickly, so the fire went out without doing any harm to the plants.

"Scatterbrain!" I laughed amiably.

Ramon swore to himself and, taking his past experience into account, let forth a long stream of burning kerosene on the reeds. He then led the nozzle from side to side, increasing the zone of effect. The high stalks caught on fire and instantly burned to ash. A pillar of thick smoke stretched upward and the water in the pond grew cloudy.

The hulk put out the burner, pulled off the mask and headed back for the armored vehicle.

"Let's go! We need to get out of here!" he hurried me along.

"Just a second," I called back and pulled the hand-held mortar out of its wooden box. I didn't fully charge the drum, just placed elongated rounds in three of the tubes. "Move back!" I said to my partner and aimed at a small oak growing on the other side of the pond about fifty meters away.

Ramon cursed out and started taking off the tanks; I plunked down on the trigger, it gave a quiet thud and a band of smoke extended over the pond. A moment later, water mixed with mud and seaweed was flying up into the air. I undershot.

I pulled the handle, turning the drum, and made a correction in distance before I repeated my attempt. This time, the explosion took out grass much farther away and significantly to the left of the tree.

"Leo, let's go!" Ramon shouted.

"I'm coming!" I called back, the wooden stock a bit better braced against my shoulder this time. I pulled down the trigger again. The smoke trail went a bit higher. The round landed in the thick canopy of the tree and immediately blew up; the foliage was sliced through by shrapnel flying in all directions.

I put the mortar back in the car and closed the trunk.

"I think I more or less got the idea," I said to my partner, getting into the car after him.

"Let's go!" Ramon demanded. "We aren't far from town! We might get caught!"

It wasn't like I was planning on going slow, though. The path ahead wasn't short, and there wasn't much time left before sundown.

The car, its powerful engine growling from time to time, got up on the road and rolled forward, gradually picking up speed. There were occasional potholes and they shook us hard, but that didn't stop Ramon from dozing off. No bump could keep him awake. Simply evidence of a sleepless night. And to be honest, my eyelids were sagging as well.

Ramon woke up forty minutes later after I had passed a few villages and turned onto a rural road. I had just found a convenient way to drive onto the field. One of the orientation markers made by the archaeologist on the map was a memorial stele on the side of the road. It was behind us. In front of us, there was a tall hill that grew up gradually out of the gray mist and drizzle. We had to go around it on the right.

"Is there much longer to go?" asked my hulking partner, yawning so wide it was a miracle he didn't dislocate his jaw.

I immediately wanted to yawn as well.

With some effort, I overcame that urge and steered the car onto the roadside as I told him:

"We're close."

"Are you sure?"

"Yes."

The car rumbled as it rolled down the steep slope and jumped up onto the overgrown soil. In places, there were stone blocks peeking up from the earth. Half a century ago, this path had been paved. In some places, huge trees had managed to grow right through the stones, forcing me to drive through the field or steer the car straight through a bush.

Ramon was clutching a handhold above his head, with every bump cursing like a drunken dock-worker. But I couldn't care less about his groaning: all my attention was going to steering the armored car.

Where before, there had only been trees growing on the sides of hills, now they started coming down into the flat areas as well. We drove over the edge of a young grove, maneuvering amongst the underbrush. It would have been impossible to take a shortcut through the washed-out field after the rain, because the heavy armored car would have surely gotten stuck and sunk in.

An eerie sense that I recognized this place started crawling over me. No, I had never been here before, but some kind of tension in the air was bringing up associations with the atmosphere of my own home.

The same curse? No, this place had no curse. Just a weak echo of former times.

The self-propelled carriage finally made it around the grove and Ramon couldn't resist a surprised whistle. And it really was impressive. Before us, a hundred meters away began a black patch of dead earth as if some kind of evil magic had burned all life there.

Just black dirt, mixed with very old ash.

After stopping the armored car on the very edge of the former property of the brilliant Rafael, I got out of the car and, without particular surprise discovered empty bottles in the grass, soaked packs of cigarettes, old bonfire pits and other traces of a great many picnics. But, based on the lack of tracks in the mud, none of the fanciers had the nerve to walk any closer to the building.

I shared this finding with Ramon, who just shrugged his shoulders and walked calmly onto the burnt-out earth. In no hurry, I went back and pointed to the lack of tracks.

"It's not all so easy," he snorted, "right?"

I didn't answer, carefully looking around. Behind us, there loomed a steep hill. In front, there was a stretch of burnt land and the towering ruins of a former residence. From behind them, there peeked out the silhouette of a half-destroyed castle.

"Well?" I turned toward the car. "Ramon, are you ready?"

He got into the car, and I pointed it at the manor's dilapidated fence. There had once been a paved road here, and the armored car rolled over the surface surprisingly smoothly, not at all bouncing on the uneven potholes.

The echoes of old magic didn't get stronger as we got deeper into the property. As before, they were barely noticeable and obviously could not harm anyone. The curse on my mansion burned incomparably stronger.

When the armored vehicle passed the gates, Ramon got out his Winchester from behind the seat, checked it and set it between his knees, its stock on the floor.

"What are we searching for?" he asked, looking out the side window.

"Any clues," I answered, turning to the ruins, meeting me with a heap of crumbling and burned brick. "First of all, we'll check the basements."

"We'll have to find them first," moaned Ramon. He warned me: "Don't drive up close. Let's get out the flamethrower first."

Considering my friend's apprehension well grounded, I stopped the vehicle and got my

Winchester.

"You go, I'll keep watch."

While Ramon was dealing with the tanks and belts, I was strolling not far away, carefully looking from side to side. Then I called him to the nearest ruins:

"Cover me!"

Ramon rushed after, but I had already gone through the empty door frame, stood back up straight and waved my hand:

"All clear!"

The collapsed ceiling had filled the room to the top with crumbling rubble; only incorporeal spirits could possibly have had a lair there.

We returned to the armored vehicle; Ramon stood on the running board and held onto the open door as I steered the self-propelled carriage toward the neighboring building, which had suffered even more than the first in the assault.

This one was shot through everywhere from what must have been quite close range. The reinforced stone walls had borne it, but there were quite a lot of divots in them. Everywhere around, there were bits of sandstone and tile fragments. We didn't find anything interesting inside.

"Leave the castle for last?" Ramon asked when I steered the carriage around the fully destroyed administrative buildings to a semi-circular marble amphitheater.

"Yes," I confirmed. "For last."

The sun, which now was shining through the layer of clouds as a pale spot had already begun to slightly dip toward the horizon but, considering the destruction all around, checking the whole estate couldn't take that much time.

Unlike the other buildings, the amphitheater had practically not suffered in the assault, and we even managed to walk around the internal rooms. Inside, we discovered just trash-strewn cages and went further.

In the end, making a full rounds of the property took a little over an hour, but the only cellar we found was underwater, and the entrance to the underground floor of another building was blocked off by collapsed ceiling. No matter how much we circled around, we didn't manage to find any other ways down.

So then, we drove up to the central building. The palace met us with the basin of a huge pool containing empty pedestals that had once been topped by statues. The walls had burn marks, the roof was collapsed and the windows of the upper floor were broken unevenly. The central stairwell's marble steps had all been displaced by the explosion and were jutting out unevenly and menacingly; we walked up it and froze at the entrance to the spacious hall.

"Are you ready?" I asked Ramon.

In reply, he swung the spigot of his flamethrower.

"I am."

Inside, it was empty. Just bare rock walls and that was it; not even the stucco under the ceiling remained. And also, the ceilings themselves gaped in places with dark gaps. The palace had taken a lot of damage in the assault.

We went carefully from room to room in search of a way down into the basement. When I looked back, I discovered without particular surprise that we were leaving tracks; the floor was covered with fine gray-ash dust.

The first hatch in the floor was found, as expected, in the kitchen. I turned on the electric torch I'd brought with from the armored vehicle and pointed it at the stairs.

"I'll go first," Ramon decided.

I hesitated briefly, then wrestled back an uncomfortable shiver. How I hate basements! And I went in after my partner, intently holding my torch to the side.

The basement was spacious and absolutely empty. The only things there were iron hooks sticking out of the walls and ceiling. Some of them were sagging, and absolutely all were rusted completely through.

Ramon and I quickly exchanged glances and went hurriedly back up. Perhaps, somewhere, there really were secret passages here, but finding them now would involve knocking on walls. A fool's errand.

"The basement is too small," Ramon decided. "There has to be more to it!"

"You're right," I agreed with my friend.

So, we kept going and immediately ran into a pile of collapsed flooring from overhead. We had to crawl out the window to get into the next room, which had caught our interest from outside.

Our efforts were rewarded with a huge hole

in the floor. Ramon stayed standing at the wall. I carefully walked over to the hole, looked down and said:

"It seems this was the arsenal."

"And?"

"It was totally filled in."

We went past a few rooms with floors sagging down into the basement, checked the left wing of the palace and stared skeptically through a window at the utterly demolished right wing.

"Climb in there at your own peril," Ramon decided.

I nodded and called him after me:

"Let's go! We haven't checked everything here yet."

The last way down into the basement we found was blocked off by a collapsed beam, but we still managed to squeeze through the narrow opening. From there, the passage was open, but Ramon had to take the tanks from his back to crawl behind me.

When he had dragged the flamethrower in after himself and put it back on, I went first down the stairs, squatting, and pointed the flashlight down a darkened subterranean corridor.

"Looks like we found it!"

"I do not understand why you're so glad," grumbled my hulking partner.

I ignored my friend's griping. Letting him through first, I took up the rear, my Winchester propped on my shoulder. It was extremely inconvenient to use both the rifle and the torch at the same time.

Soon, we found a side branch and turned down it, looking over the room and its fallen ceiling. From there, we went into the next small room and found a way down to an even lower floor.

"That way?" Ramon sighed.

"Yes!"

He went first down the choppy stairs and soon stopped to wait for me. I joined him and shined my torch over an even surface of black water that came almost all the way up to the ceiling.

"Perhaps they have a boat," Ramon suggested.

"I don't think so," I decided and took a step back.

My partner's theory really did have something to it, but I was already shaking all over with the desire to get out under the open sky.

"We'll leave this for last," I announced. By this point, I was decently worked up, in that it was now near five in the evening. In some places, we'd had to walk over rubble, and in others, we'd had to find a detour, then go down one level. The worst places even had knee-deep water.

But in the end, we found nothing and no one.

The only thing I did find was the pressure of an increasing sense of danger, the whispers of half-forgotten fears, and the shivering of my veins at every unexpected rustling. And not only I was nervous. Ramon was also on edge. He was looking around constantly with an irritable expression and pointing his flamethrower in all directions.

So, when he heard my suggestion that we set the search of the lower level aside for tomorrow morning, he latched onto that idea with unhidden joy.

"It will start getting dark soon," he shivered.

I nodded. It would be totally ghastly here at night.

So, we rushed to the exit. We came up from the basement and, not getting lost in the palace, went outside under the measured drizzle sprinkling down from above through the first window we saw.

Ramon put out his flamethrower and caught his breath with relief.

"Maybe there's no one here," he declared, letting the rain fall on his flushed face.

"Maybe you're right," I sighed, hiding my electric torch under my jacket.

We exchanged glances and walked to the armored car we'd left by the central entrance. The blackness of burned-out earth spread out from all sides and the complete silence affected the nerves in a surprising way, encouraging us to get out of there quickly and never return. It was scary to even think what had happened here on the day of the assault.

We found the self-propelled carriage just where we'd left it. Ramon threw the flamethrower into the back quickly, closed the tailboard and jumped into his seat. I pressed down on the pedal right after that, and the armored car rolled back to the road.

The farther we got from the ruins, the calmer I felt inside. So, when the earth burnt by the rage of *the fallen* was left behind and the wheels started squelching in the rain-soaked field, I stopped the armored car and got out.

"Leo, what happened?" Ramon asked in surprise, himself still shivering slightly.

"Nothing," I called back and threw a sugar-drop into my mouth. I spun the half empty tin in my hand and asked: "Are you alright?"

"I am," my partner confirmed, shrugging his shoulders. "But I'd still like to get out of here!" and reminded me: "By the way, what about my money?"

I counted out five hundred and looked around. The hill with its overgrown shrubbery was an eyesore, but I wasn't able to figure out exactly what about it bothered me so much.

"What do you think, scatterbrain?" I asked him as he stashed the money in his wallet.

He looked at the ruins and shrugged his shoulders indefinitely. His fear to return to the cursed property and his desire to get another five hundred francs were clearly being weighed against one another. But in the end, he gave a fateful sigh:

"I don't know, Leo. I just don't know. We didn't check the basement all the way, but it was full of water..."

"That's all true," I called back, pointing to the hill. "Ramon, look up there. Does something seem amiss?"

The hulking man removed his cap, stroked the back of his head thoughtfully and shook his head:

"No."

"The bushes!" I suddenly realized. "There's a gap! Look there, the bushes have been cut down!"

"Not a bad vantage point," Ramon decided after taking a look. "Shall we check it?"

"Of course. But we don't need to bring everything this time. Let's stay light-weight. No flamethrower."

"Are you sure?"

"Yes," I confirmed as I threw on the backpack containing Dyak's single-use flamethrower.

We drove the armored car into a glade, put a lock on the door and started walking up the steep slope. Getting through the bushes was quite the strenuous activity due to the thickly overgrown briar, and only thanks to a washed-out ravine were we able to get nearer the top without wasting the rest of the day.

The top of the hill was capped with tall Lebanese cedars. Under the canopy of their shady crowns, neither bushes nor grass could grow. There was just dried out brush everywhere, and a layer of rotting needles giving a spring to my step. It was dark, damp and spacious, so the rest of the way took no more than five minutes.

"I hope you inherited the gift of tracking from your New-World forbearers." I joked, leaning against a shaggy cedar trunk in order to catch my breath and give my sprained leg a rest.

Ramon grabbed his Winchester and called me after him.

"Let's go!" he grumbled. "It'll be dark soon."

Ten minutes later, we found the cleared-out area and evaluated the view that revealed itself from there.

"It's an excellent firing position, I'll tell you that," said the hulk, impressed.

We walked a circle around the top and soon discovered another clearing. This one looked out on the country road that led us here.

"That doesn't mean anything yet," Ramon decided. "Anyone could have done that."

"It's all very suspicious," I said, not agreeing. "You'd never find a better vantage point of the area."

"Your point being?"

"You and I are missing something."

I stood up on the edge of the clearing, looked down below and noticed a few cigarette-butts a bit down the hill.

"Where are you going?" Ramon shuddered when I, grabbing the roots sticking out of the ground, started climbing down to the clue I'd discovered.

"Just a second!" I called back, picking the butts out of the grass.

They were fresh. I gathered five, made sure they were all the same, with a characteristic flavoring in the middle of the filter, and kept one for myself as I extended a hand to my partner. Ramon pulled me back, saw what I found and shook his head:

"Anyone could have been smoking here. Anyone."

"You think so?" I snorted, demonstrating the name on the filter.

"Ethereal," Ramon read, looking closely at the small script. He gasped: "You can't mean, they're Egyptian?!"

"They are," I confirmed. "Judge for yourself. What is the chance someone just happened to be smoking these contraband cigarettes in the same place we're now looking for the den of the Moors?"

"We're missing something," my hulking partner reminded me, then shuddered and looked around nervously. "They could have seen how we got here!"

"During the day?" I doubted.

"We have to get out of here!" Ramon continued to insist.

I thought about it, but didn't get stubborn. We followed the familiar path quickly to the bottom of the hill, loaded up the armored car and flew away.

Inside, I felt a mess. The den of the Moors was somewhere nearby, but, if their leader really had belonged to the retinue of the brilliant Rafael at one point, finding his lair would be very difficult. I'd be out of money in a few days, and what then? Acting alone in such matters was pure suicide. Doing nothing, though, was the same.

"Devilry!" Ramon cursed as the armored car

gave another jump on the rural road, all beaten up by cart wheels. "My back!"

"Did you get hit in the kidneys yesterday?" I couldn't resist mocking him.

"No," the hulk winced. "That flamethrower has ghastly heavy tanks. It strained my lower back."

"Five hundred francs," I reminded him. "You know how many wagons of coal a worker has to unload to earn five hundred francs?"

Ramon got offended and turned away. He stayed silent like that the whole rest of the way to town.

And it should be said that I wasn't feeling like talking either: evening fell quickly, a fine mist was coming down, the wheels were slipping and the armored car was going out of its way to fly into the ditch. Driving the self-propelled carriage no longer seemed like fun to me due to the uncomfortable sitting position and the strain causing constant pain in my neck and shoulders.

That was precisely why, when the suburban lights started beckoning in the distance, I stopped the armored car on the margin and asked my partner to take the wheel.

"Where should I go?" he asked, getting moving.

"Take the armored car back to the warehouse," I ordered him, " come pick me up tomorrow morning. The earlier we get started the better."

"Back here?"

"Yes."

Ramon nodded with a sour look and asked: "Shall I drop you off at home?"

"No, just let me out on the way," I answered, sitting back deep in the uncomfortable seat and closing my eyes.

My head was just splitting.

8

WHEN I GOT back home, it was already nine o'clock. I could have ended my business early but, despite my migraine, I decided not to give myself the indulgence and spent a few hours in the public library groping for information on the estate of the brilliant Rafael and its surroundings.

In the end, before poking around in the submerged palace basement, I got the idea to check the ruins of the cemetery chapel and catacombs. The little church was of such ancient construction that no historian had any idea when exactly it had been erected in the center of a field open to the four winds near the residence of a *fallen one*. But even more than the chapel, my interest was caught by the nearby underground. It seemed there should have been an entrance to the catacombs on the eastern slope of the hill whose top Ramon and I had visited today. And despite all the caution I could muster, I just couldn't call that a mere coincidence.

For that very reason, I decided to start with

the catacombs. But tomorrow was another day.

AS I WALKED up onto the veranda of my manor, I was nearly falling down in exhaustion. And as soon as I had my jacket, damp derby hat and dirty boots off, I heard a thud and a shrill cry coming from the dining hall.

"Grub!" shouted the leprechaun. "Grub, now, bugger!"

Marveling at the depraved audacity of my imaginary friend, I walked into the room and grew even more surprised when I discovered Elizabeth-Maria setting the table while the pipsqueak banged a spoon, repeating his chant:

"Grub! Bugger! Grub! Bugger!"

"Chill out!" I demanded.

"The vanquisher of Moors needs grub!" the leprechaun immediately shot back, but stopped slapping his spoon on the table.

Elizabeth Maria looked at me gratefully and went into the kitchen.

"How is Theodor?" I asked when she had returned and placed a huge dish on the table.

"Your butler cannot bear seeing him," the girl said with a nod at the leprechaun. "As soon as he does, he starts to shake."

To my view, Theodor had taken the disappearance of the silver too close to heart. In life, my servant had been distinguished by pedantry and an unhealthy commitment to principle, but after his death, convincing him to compromise had become an utterly impossible affair.

So I just shrugged my shoulders and headed off to wash my hands.

When I was back, the leprechaun had a napkin tied around his neck and was licking his lips in anticipation of a big meal. Elizabeth-Maria, meanwhile, set down a dish of stewed meat.

"Faster! Move your ass, bugger!" the pipsqueak hurried her along, fidgeting on the chair in impatience. After receiving a plate, he sniffed at it, poked the meat with a table knife and cringed: "Rat poison!"

"Come off it!" I demanded, but he had no intention of calming down.

"Bugger! Leo, this is rat poison!" the leprechaun repeated, tearing the napkin from his neck before he scurried away, grabbing a wine bottle off the table in passing.

Elizabeth-Maria looked angrily after him, then said in a sweet little voice:

"Rat poison in the meat? Not at all! There is rat poison in one of the wine bottles, though. And which one that is, only I know!"

The leprechaun turned in the door frame, puffed out his cheeks indignantly and cursed out:

"Shrew!"

"Bon appétit," the girl smiled, no less sweetly than before.

She was in rare form today.

I, on the other hand, was feeling somewhat low, so I slogged through dinner in silence and asked my butler to bring tea to my quarters.

"As you say, Viscount," Theodor nodded as

he cleared the table.

"Leo!" Elizabeth-Maria called out to me before I managed to leave the room. "How is this possible?"

I turned around in incomprehension.

"What exactly are you surprised at?"

"The leprechaun. He's too real to be from your imagination. What is giving him his power?"

"Treasure!" Theodor immediately called back. "Where there's a leprechaun, there must be treasure. It's all in the treasure!"

The girl nodded in contemplation:

"Maybe it is a treasure. What then? It will be a glorious hunt."

"Just don't tear the whole house down," I demanded, having no doubt that I would soon discover the surreptitious allies rapping away at the walls, or perhaps digging up the garden.

And why not? I then, with a calm heart, headed into the bedroom.

To my extremely great relief, there was no leprechaun in the room. The only trace of his recent presence had been an empty bottle, cigarette butts and wax on the arm of the chair and those had already been cleaned up by my butler, who couldn't bear the mess.

The portrait of Elizabeth-Maria von Nalz was lying on the desk; I looked at it until the aching pain in my chest became unbearable, then laid down in bed. I didn't even put out the light, just closed my eyes for a second in anticipation of my evening tea. Next thing I knew, Elizabeth-Maria was nudging me awake in the morning.

"Leo, the police have come for you!" she said, relaying some extremely unpleasant news.

I shot up like I'd been stung, but immediately remembered Ramon and the car and laid back down.

"I'll be right down," I promised the girl, and she left the room, wrapped up tight in a long, warm robe.

My sleepiness cast off, I took my jacket, threw it on as I walked and trudged down to the first floor, fostering the hope that my derby hat and boots had managed to at least slightly dry out overnight.

Theodor really had thought to dry them out, but there was a gusty wind blowing outside sprinkling down a fine, miserable rain. Putting up my jacket collar did little to help, if not to say it did nothing to help at all. The rain just flowed right down past the collar. I hurried through the dead garden, still more homely and frightening than before, jumped past the gates and vanished into the armored vehicle, taking shelter from the bad weather.

"Dog's weather," Ramon grumbled.

"They came around to my house last night," my hulking partner mumbled out and started getting out from behind the wheel, but I stopped him:

"You drive."

The gloomy rainy weather was having a bad effect on me. I felt as if my head was filled with cotton, my eyes were stuck together, and even the cold rain wasn't able to chase off the remnants of my dream. I wanted devilishly to sleep.

Ramon didn't argue – it was five hundred francs per day! – just wound the engine. Meanwhile, I found a more comfortable position in the seat. My eyelids were already closed, and I fell asleep before we were all the way down Calvary.

I woke up from a jolt as we went past the pond from yesterday. With a bark of the engine, Ramon steered the armored vehicle around a cart and asked:

"Where do we go from here?"

I just nodded.

"Leo!" My hulking partner objected.

"Straight!" I waved a hand and tried to stretch out my numb legs, but the front seat was not made with my dimensions in mind. "Did you read the papers this morning?"

"No," he shook his head. "I wasn't feeling up to it."

"Alas."

Forty minutes later, I noticed a familiar monument sign and asked him to turn down a country road. Then, Ramon himself saw yesterday's hill and turned his head, looking for the grass we'd crushed down with our tires. The massive armored car clunked heavily through a shallow ditch and rolled directly over the uneven field with its whole frame shaking.

"Straight into the basement, then?" Ramon asked.

"No," I shook my head, "first, let's check the

catacombs. You can get into them from the other side of the hill. What do you think?"

"Doesn't seem like a coincidence," my friend shared my doubt, steering the armored vehicle up to the very edge of the cursed estate. He confidently drove around the hill and choked the engine, not wanting to try driving up the gentle, but severely overgrown slope.

The door thrown open, I slipped out and looked thoughtfully at the bushes. In their green cover, I couldn't make out a single gap.

"There!" Ramon suddenly shuddered. "The ravine!"

"Let's check it," I decided and pulled out the single-use flamethrower backpack from under the seat, followed by the semi-automatic carbine.

My hulking partner grabbed his Winchester and got out after me. After locking the armored vehicle, we headed into the ravine Ramon had noticed and soon discovered it was no ravine at all, but a rain-washed road. The tall bushes growing up along the edges had intermittently interlocking tops, forming real arches, but between the massive stone slabs there grew only sickly grass.

"We could park the armored car here if you want," said Ramon with a heavy pant in the middle of the slope.

"We could," I agreed, in that the slope was in fact quite gentle. "But what's the point?"

"I mean, I just," my hulking partner shrugged his shoulders. "Technically..."

A few minutes later, we were out on a little

square set with stone blocks. On its far side, there was a black cave entrance looming.

"Wanna go back for the flamethrower?" Ramon asked, looking around cautiously.

"Wait," I asked him, taking a hand grenade from my pocket. "Cover me!"

The hulking man got his Winchester at the ready, then I walked up first to the cave in the hillside, slunk in and immediately took a step back, having discovered a practically sheer drop underfoot. The grenade back in my pocket, I worked the torch hanging off my belt free and pointed it down. The bright beam showed just uneven walls made of unhewn stones. The light didn't reach the bottom, though, leaving me to wonder just how deep the pit went.

Ramon threw a small stone down, listened and hazarded:

"Fifteen meters, no less."

"And how should we get down there?" I asked, perplexed.

Though the hole went down at a shallow angle, the uneven stones could serve as decent hand- and foot-holds. But with the gigantic tanks on my back, the risk of falling off surpassed all reasonable bounds. Climbing down with just a single-use flamethrower, though, seemed a most dubious undertaking.

"Do you really think we should be poking around down there?" Ramon snorted. "We've got a box of grenades in the trunk. Let's blow it up and just end this!"

"There are other entrances."

"Let's find them, then."

"Ramon," I sighed, "your optimism brings me unspeakable joy, but the catacombs might be dozens of kilometers long for all we know."

My hulking partner spat in disappointment and asked:

"How did they even get here?"

"Christians used to bury their dead in them."

"Right under a *fallen one*'s nose?"

I shrugged my shoulders, turned off the torch and walked down the hill.

"What now?" Ramon asked, approaching me.

"There should be a rope in the trunk. Let's try going down."

"What are we gonna tie it onto?"

The bushes growing on the hillsides didn't inspire confidence, so I decided to bring the armored car up closer.

"There's a hook on the back. We can tie it to that."

So we did. We did not have the wherewithal to back the vehicle up the hill, though. First, we drove onto the stone square before the cave and there turned the self-propelled carriage to face away. Thankfully, there was plenty of room to execute such a maneuver without a hitch.

After that, I helped Ramon strap into the flamethrower as he doubled over in pain and pulled out a bundle of strong rope from the vehicle.

"Do you think it's long enough?" I asked my

partner, lifting the carriage back shut.

"We're about to find out," replied my hulking partner, tying a heavy spanner to the end and chucking it down the hole.

Before the metal clanged out on the stones below, just a third of the bundle managed to unravel, so I calmly stretched out the other end of the rope to the armored vehicle and tied a knot around the low iron hook.

"It's ten meters," Ramon said, refining his initial conclusion. "Listen, Leo, what if we lowered down the flamethrower separately?"

I thought over the suggestion and nodded:

"Let's!"

We pulled out the rope, freed Ramon of the tanks and slowly lowered the huge device into the catacombs.

"Go!" I hurried my partner, handing him the torch.

The hulk hung it on his neck and confidently slid down after the flamethrower. I waited for the rope to go slack and came down after him.

"Everything alright?" I called down to my partner.

"Yes, come down!" Ramon called back in a rolling echo.

Then, I grabbed the rope and leaned over the hole. The tips of my boots slipped over the damp stones, but I soon found a place to rest my feet and slightly support myself. It got easier from there. I latched onto the rope and pushed off the uneven wall as I slipped down.

"It'll be easier on the way up!" I declared, jumping onto the stone floor as the hole above suddenly lit up with the crimson spot of a burning cigarette. It smoldered in the darkness for a moment, then flew downward, past me, erupting into sparks on the stone floor.

I lifted the hand-rolled cigarette butt, caught the aroma of the leprechaun's preferred tobacco and caught my breath with relief. I looked over at Ramon, pressed into the wall in terror, and said with a wave:

"Pay it no mind."

"Who was that?"

"Do you remember the midget from the opium den? The one you chased down the hall?"

"Why the devil has he followed us?!" gasped my stocky partner.

"He works for me," I said, slightly overstating our relationship.

"You must be joking!"

"Forget it!" I demanded and started saddling up the flamethrower tanks on Ramon's back.

"Devilry!" my partner sighed. "This is gonna tear my back off soon!"

"Need I remind you of your wages?"

"Are you going to hold that over my head for the rest of my life?!" Ramon flared up. "Come on! Find someone else to help you!"

"Don't shout," I replied, and shined the torch at the passageway under the hill.

The stone walls here were cut smooth. The ceilings were three meters high, and the walls contained no empty niches or doors. If dead had once been buried in these catacombs, it had been somewhat farther from the entrance.

"Go!" I ordered Ramon.

He got the flamethrower ready for combat, and went first down the passageway. I stepped off after him. I supported the grip of my Winchester in my left elbow, and held the torch in my left hand. The pointer finger of my right hand was at the trigger. I was ready to open fire with no delay whatever. I even removed my dark glasses in order not to miss a thing, no matter how minor; in any case, the beam of the electric torch gave away our approach much earlier than the glowing of my eyes.

"It's empty here," Ramon whispered.

I went silent.

The underground labyrinth had already begun to affect my nerves. The paths stretched out farther and farther under the hill; from time to time, we found ourselves at an intersection and turned left every time. Ramon, meanwhile, was also making marks on the walls with a piece of limestone he'd thought to bring. However, the upper level of the catacombs wasn't all that bewildering. I remembered the path perfectly without any markings needed.

We hit upon a stairwell going down ten minutes later; Ramon sighed noisily and went first down the stone steps. I lit his path from behind.

The second level down was palpably different from the one above it. The wide passages were replaced with tall narrow slits. The ceiling got lost in the darkness. The light of my torch didn't even always reach it. There were grave niches in the walls everywhere; the broken stone tablets that once covered them were lying around underfoot.

The ancient burials had been looted with a particular carelessness.

Often, we came across incomprehensible messages on the stones. From time to time, Christian symbolism met the eye; most often, it was carved fish in the walls and conjoined chi rhos. Often, they were deformed by relatively fresh cuts.

"Nothing was left untouched here, huh?" Ramon asked, his voice muted to a barely audible whisper.

"I guess not."

"Well, where are the bones, then?"

"I have no idea," I answered, not having any clue. "The catacombs could have been demolished centuries ago."

"And yet, something isn't right here," my partner muttered out, glancing at a small space to the side with niches one over the other. The highest of them was in the form of an arch. "Family tombs?"

"Yes."

We went further, and started encountering such rooms more and more often. Then, the hallway led to another stairwell.

"Should we go down, or finish checking this floor first?" Ramon asked.

"Down, down, down," I answered decisively.

Under my boots, the wet stone steps started

to get slippery. The air seemed incomparably mustier, with some kind of very unpleasant smell.

"Do you think this is some underground gas?" Ramon said in alarm. "If this is methane, we'll blow up!"

"And if it isn't, we'll suffocate," I snorted. "Drop the panic! Follow me!"

And again, we found ourselves going down narrow passages with countless rows of empty niches. It was cold and melancholy here. The hair on the back of my head moved not even from fear, but from the expectation of an inevitable death. I wanted to drop everything and run back up and out. Though it was drizzling up above, and you couldn't see the sun from behind the clouds, it was better to have bad weather and a cold wind in your face than the terrifying must of the subterranean.

We soon started to see bones. Their white surfaces shone up at us here and there, until we discovered a whole pile of remains in a spacious underground room. And it would have been nothing, but the floor there was covered in a bone dust as if someone had been breaking open joints in an attempt to get to the marrow.

"Quite a lot of bones," Ramon whistled when the light of the torch hit on a gnawed shin.

"These must be from long ago," I decided and walked further.

After that, there were bones lying around everywhere, and it became clear that the upper floors had been cleaned out not at all by raiding marauders, but some creature that resided in this very structure.

Bhuts!

"Devil take those grave robbers!" I muttered to myself, but Ramon didn't hear me.

"I hope these burials were dug up long, long ago," he whispered out. "And they all died peacefully, from hunger."

"Better to hope for the flamethrower," I suggested.

"Have you noticed that there aren't any skulls?"

"Yes."

And in fact, the light of my torch had hit upon fallow ribs, spines, radiuses, tibias, and other bones, but from the skull, only lower jaws. We hadn't seen a single cranium.

"I don't like all this," Ramon sighed.

The terrifying atmosphere of the catacombs was making an impression on him as well. But to be honest, all these narrow little passages, countless niches and ceilings getting lost in the darkness, the confusing labyrinth of pleated passages and bone-filled rooms could have brought anyone to a panic.

Then we found the skulls. There was a huge, lovingly constructed pyramid of them towering in a spacious room.

I was blatantly thrown off. What was this for?

Was it a reminder of the inevitability of death, or clear confirmation of the madness of the creatures that dwelt here?

"Let's get out of here!" Ramon rasped out. "Fast!"

I walked around the edge of the room and turned down the next narrow passage. And just then, a raw-boned creature ran down from the ceiling, its appendages splayed out. The bhut was unnaturally thin and had smooth skin stretched out tight over its joints and ribs. Its dry lips didn't come all the way down over the scavenger's powerful teeth. Its eyes shimmered with a sullen flame.

I made this all out in one moment, and then my left arm jerked the barrel of the Winchester up all on its own and a heavy leaden bullet slammed right into the charging beast.

The bhut flew off to the side. It latched its sharp claws into a niche, somersaulted and gracefully landed on its feet. It crouched down in preparation for another jump, and I hurriedly plunked another bullet into him. The scavenger flew back.

A moment later, it threw me back. Ramon grabbed me by the collar and pushed me behind him, then blasted the bhut with a stream of burning kerosene. It hadn't the slightest chance to dodge in the narrow passage. The flame reached it instantly and lit it on fire like a bundle of dried twigs. A piercing howl rolled through the basement then died down. The scavenger was filled with agony, almost immediately deprived of strength, and went silent. It burned away completely. Not even bones remained.

While it burned away, Ramon and I stood

back to back, getting prepared to deflect another attack, but none followed. It seemed, if anything was still living in these catacombs, it wasn't tempted by the opportunity to sample fresh human meat.

Strange.

"Was it alone here, or something?" Ramon asked in surprise when he'd calmed down and was able to judge the situation more or less clearly.

"They say, if you put rats in a barrel and don't feed them, only one will remain alive," I answered with a nervous chuckle. "It must have run out of dead bodies long ago. Who else was it supposed to eat, if not its own?"

"I sure hope you're right," my partner said with a shiver. "By the way, you owe me a thousand, now!"

I shot him an expressive look, but didn't say anything and kept walking. But the passage came to a dead end. I had to go back. We looped around the human-bone-filled hallways for ten minutes, then came out into another room, just slightly smaller than the first; in the middle of it, we found a stairway down.

"This just never ends!" Ramon moaned out in sorrow.

I pointed my torch at my timepiece. We had spent just over two hours down here, but it felt like the beginning of our third day in a row. My nerves were on the very edge.

So, I didn't get into it with my partner, just commanded him curtly:

"Follow me!" I said, and started down to the next level of the catacombs.

Down there, to my surprise, instead of another narrow little corridor, we were met with a wide passage lined with columns. And, on the walls, there were no longer burial niches, just complex geometrical patterns carved into stone. The air grew drier and the stench grew stronger.

"Do you think this is it?" Ramon whispered with an incomprehensible expression, looking reckless and at the same time confident.

"Let's see," I said, not wanting to guess prematurely. Just then, the torch beam passed over a cave-in.

Then again, it wasn't so scary here. A few of the stone columns were leaning, and a few were fallen, but they didn't collapse to the ground, just stayed propped against the wall, leaving just a small slot below.

"Don't start me on fire," I warned my partner, ducking and walking to the other side of the cave-in. Ramon crawled through after me with untold effort. But he made it.

Right after the cave-in, we stopped to catch our breath, and I checked the grenades I had in my pockets, loaded up my Winchester and changed out my torch's electric jar.

"Are you ready?" I asked my partner after he was done fiddling with the flamethrower.

"Yes!" he called back, and we walked on.

Ramon was aiming the tip of his flamethrower from side to side in agitation. I was carefully checking every little shadow behind the columns that stretched down along both walls of the underground corridor. Then we came out into a small room, and I had to strain to hold back from delighted cursing: in the middle of the room, on a small platform, there was a stone sarcophagus. A stone sarcophagus lined with time-darkened lead leaf!

We found it! Had we seriously found it?!

I stuck a finger to my lips, giving Ramon the command to keep quiet. Then, I walked up first to the sarcophagus and got out a grenade.

"Get ready!" I exhaled nearly silently to Ramon, who was standing next to me. I dug my hands into the unyielding stone lid, applied some effort and, in one sharp burst, moved it half way off and jumped aside.

I immediately cursed out loud, but now without any elation. Insofar as I could tell, the sarcophagus was empty.

Ramon confirmed:

"There's no one there."

I returned to the shrine, and tore off the metallic mesh covering it from inside in annoyance.

"Devil! He got away!"

My hulking partner noted reasonably:

"At least we found the right place."

"One of his spots, nothing more, nothing less," I said bitterly.

"I don't know, though. The room totally fits the veterinarian's description," my partner reassured me. He then moaned out: "Devilry! My back hurts so bad!"

"Let's take a breather," I suggested. Then, feeling downhearted, I leaned my Winchester against the sarcophagus and sat on the lowest step.

Ramon took off the tanks, laid them carefully on the floor and stretched his back out with delight. Then he gave a slap to the massive sarcophagus top and asked:

"What's the lead for? There's some kind of mesh, too..."

"Who knows?" I grumbled back.

Then my inquisitive partner took the torch, pointed it inside and exclaimed:

"There's a whole storage area in here! Candles, barrels, some kind of little case!" After some brief thought, he went inside and broke the briefcase lock with his knife. "Woah!"

"What's that?" I asked as I got to my feet.

Ramon shook a thick pack of Egyptian guineas and handed them to me.

"A bunch of money, Leo. There's a whole bunch of money here!"

"And it doesn't belong to you..." came a lifeless, rustling voice from the doorway.

Almost dropping the torch in fear, my hulking partner turned and pointed it: the malefic had caught us off guard. The shadows hiding under his wide-brimmed hat dispersed, not having the strength to stand up against the electric light.

The Moor covered his face with a black hand and took a step to the side. Just then, two more stepped out of the darkness to his aid. They started going in different directions, coming around the sarcophagus in a semicircle. And I just froze in place, not knowing what to do.

The flamethrower was lying on the floor.

On the floor. The flamethrower.

The other flamethrower was in a backpack on my back, so I'd never reach it in time, either. And the big one was on the floor. On the floor...

So then, I tossed a grenade underfoot.

I just pulled out the stubborn pin and hurled it. I jumped into the sarcophagus, braying out to Ramon:

"Get down!"

My hulking partner dove into the sarcophagus after me, lifted the stone lid and had just barely put it in place when the explosion thundered out! It felt like we were inside a bell at the top of a tower just as the clock struck noon, now competing with all the neighboring towers for dominance. I lost consciousness for a moment; then I came to my senses and immediately coughed out the acrid char seeping in through the narrow crack.

Ramon started writhing; he sat up on his bottom and wiped the blood from his nose. It looked purple-black in the light of the torch.

"Well?" he asked.

As soon as I saw the words on his lips, I noticed; there was a ringing in my ears. I didn't answer at all, just directed my pointer finger up.

With our joint efforts, we moved the unwieldy stone top aside and stuck our heads into the black smoke filling the room. On the floor, there were a few puddles of kerosene still burning, as well as three charred figures.

I coughed my lungs out, then got out first and helped Ramon after me. Even all concussed, he didn't forget to take the money-filled suitcase with him.

"The flamethrower is all fucked up," he rasped out in a coughing fit.

"And we will be too, if we don't get out of here," I rasped back as I started hobbling to the exit. "We'll suffocate!"

"I don't believe you'll have time to suffocate!" said a stylish-looking man in an expensive suit as he fitfully smoothed out his sooty mustache. He took a step out of the darkness and bent down over one of the Moors as he calmly lit a cigarette on the malefic's still smoldering outfit. "You won't have time, Viscount. That much I assure you!"

I agreed with him immediately, and without a word.

We wouldn't have time.

PART TWO

LAZARUS

Hand Grenades and the Fifteenth Element

1

T HE HUMAN MIND is an abyss full of riddles, but the body is frequently a bigger mystery. Time and time again, we find our thoughts racing, yet the spinal column has already started giving commands. We are all slaves to reflex. And there's nothing bad in that; quite often, it saves our lives.

But, when I saw the bony body of a gentleman with a soot-covered face step out from the darkness, just barely brighter than pitch with the small puddles of kerosene still burning down, I didn't listen to what he had to say. My body reacted all on its own.

In the space of an instant, the massive sarcophagus was between us.

If the vampire – and yes, it was clearly a vampire! – was in fact amazed at my agility, he didn't express it in any way. He just gave a contemptuous snort, pressed his cigarette in the corner of his mouth and started wiping the flakes of ash off his jacket lapels with a kerchief. Unfortunately for him, though, he was just rubbing it deeper into the expensive fabric. He was in no hurry, and it was no wonder: the only way out of the subterranean hall was behind him.

I cursed, pulled the backpack out from behind me and, under the cover of the shrine, started undoing its stiff clasps. Thankfully, I was able to free the single-use flamethrower before the vampire threw himself on the attack. Ramon stood up nearby, and grasped his Webley-Fosbery with both hands.

The vampire was in no rush. With a fastidious grimace, he threw his soiled kerchief underfoot and smiled:

"Allow me to introduce myself: the name's Lazarus."

Then he frowned, and hid the sharp needle fangs under his upper lip. Now, only the dead black eyes remained to remind me that the creature before us was no human, but a supernatural being.

I had a perfect understanding of how infinitesimally small our chances were of escaping this alive, but all the same, I found the strength in myself to joke:

"Not *the* Lazarus, I hope?"

The vampire shook his head:

"My boy, I'm not so stupidly gauche as to go around claiming such things but the name is, in fact, no coincidence. Just as the Savior returned the biblical Lazarus from the dead, so too was I returned to life in a similar fashion. But I came back on my own, with no help. Now do you understand why the name seemed appropriate?"

"Moniker, surely. That's no name, it's a moniker," I objected, squeezing the flamethrower tank under my elbow all the harder.

The face of my opponent remained utterly fearless in response to my claim. I couldn't sense any aristocratic delicacy in him. He more closely resembled a very successful businessman or theater impresario. His thin mustache was fashionably curled. His brows were plucked. His expensive suit was a shade of crimson with a fresh carnation in the buttonhole.

He was a well-groomed man of average height and solid build.

A normal person.

But that impression was all spoiled by his eyes. The black dead eyes dashed the image of an honest citizen to pieces; they were an unambiguous sign that it was all just a mask that hid your worst nightmare behind it.

Not death, no. Helplessness.

A normal person had no way to withstand a creature that called itself Lazarus. *Illustrious* gentlemen, it should be said, did not either.

"A moniker?" asked the vampire, tilting his head as he thought over my words. He then shook his head. "No, it's no mere moniker," he stated. "As the popes of old would take a new name on their enthronement, I also chose a new name as I stepped into my new life. My name truly is Lazarus now. I have no other. Over the long centuries, this name has become a part of me. It means incomparably more than the one I was given by my parents."

The vampire waved his hand carelessly and started walking around the sarcophagus; we took a step back, not allowing him to get closer. The path out of the room was now clear, but a rash attempt at fleeing could end in nothing but a torturous death. Man could never compare in speed with an otherworldly beast.

"Maybe it's time for a grenade?" Ramon whispered to me.

But Lazarus overheard.

"Are you trying to ruin my suit once and for all?" he snorted as he stepped over the Moor's smoking body. "Go on! Throw your grenade! Viscount, I already have a long list of grievances against you. That won't make it any worse."

"A long list? Would you allow me to inquire as to its contents?" I asked, not having made up my mind to start up the flamethrower.

The vampire was acting strange. He wasn't afraid of fire. Or, to be more accurate, I didn't sense such a fear in him. He walked around the puddle of burning kerosene in utter calm. He didn't even lean away. And he was smoking! He was smoking a cigarette!

"Oh! Most of the list you know perfectly well!" Lazarus declared. "But in essence, Viscount, you shouldn't have meddled in our game. Such things are not forgiven."

"What kind of game precisely, if you could illuminate me?" I asked.

But the vampire just shook his head.

"This is no time for conversations," he declared.

Then I pulled down on the lever, igniting the starter. And a moment later, Lazarus was on the attack! In one blistering burst, he jumped over to the sarcophagus, but a stream of gelled kerosene had already struck him in the face. The igniter hit the flammable liquid, and it caught; the vampire was splashed with flame, and he spun in place, embraced head to toe in lapping fire.

"Run!" I roared to Ramon, myself stepping

back, continuing to shoot the flaming mixture at the disoriented bloodsucker.

The flame roared. An unbearable fire flew into his face, but Lazarus still wasn't about to fall over. His clothes were almost totally burnt up. Not a trace remained of his hair. But, at that, the vampire was still standing, and even found the strength to move against the stream of flame.

Twenty seconds of hellfire did no damage to him at all, but in that time, Ramon and I managed to get to the room's exit. And there, the flamethrower gave its last portion of kerosene and went out. It did, however, keep sprinkling flaming sparks from the igniter into the darkness.

Lazarus spit fire and gave a hoarse, fitful laugh:

"You'll need a bit more to stop me than plain old Greek fire!"

I didn't listen to him, just turned and ran as fast as I could.

From behind, I heard the rapid clatter of his footsteps, but I didn't look, just grabbed a hand grenade from my pocket and ducked into a narrow opening under a column. And when I jumped out the other side, I only had the pin in my fingers.

"Run!" I shouted to Ramon as a muted explosion blasted out behind us. The columns couldn't bear it, and sagged down, interring the vampire in their wreckage, but I had no certainty they would hold him for long.

"Run!" I shouted out again and ran for the exit.

Ramon darted behind me without delay.

We flew up the stairs; the acrid char was replaced by a musty basement smell, and I finally managed to take a little breather. Coughing and hacking, I cleared my lungs and throat, let Ramon out in front and, with renewed force, ran after my partner. Skipping the beam of my electric torch over the walls, I saw here and there the white marks Ramon had left. And that guiding thread helped us not get lost in the underground labyrinth, and carry ourselves to the exit.

It was just a little foresight, but it had just saved our lives.

And we really did get out just in the nick of time. When we had run up to the charred remains of the bhut, from somewhere in the distance, there came the echo of a new landslide, followed by an utterly inhuman wail full of hateful rage.

The cry, echoing at a rapid frequency, stuck into our backs like dozens of ghostly knives, spurring us on like a pair of horses. I was catastrophically low on breath. My legs felt like they were filling with lead. My sprained foot was exploding with pain at every step, but I ran, ran, and ran, trying not to lose sight of the bright torch spot jumping around in front of Ramon.

I simply cannot imagine by what miracle I had the strength to run the rest of the way to the catacomb exit. Obviously, fear helped; there was more than enough of that.

At the sheer drop, Ramon waited for me and

gave me a boost. I grabbed the rope and climbed up. My low weight and long hands and legs gave me a decent advantage, and I got out of the cave far in advance of my partner. But, despite how much I wanted to fall to the ground in exhaustion, I didn't just lie there once up. Instead, I grabbed onto the rope and started pulling Ramon after me.

Another echoing ghastly wail flew up. I got startled and nearly fell back down. The vampire was closing in on us. Closing in!

I grabbed my partner by the hand, pulled him up and ran to the exit. I jumped out headlong from the cave and dashed to the self-propelled carriage, but then Ramon caught up to me, knocked me off my feet and pressed me to the ground.

I gasped in fear and pain and, just then, the machine gun in the rear of the armored car started thundering. The burst of fire passed right over my head and exploded into a cloud of stone shards in the depths of the cavern. The high-caliber bullets whipped against the vampire like a deadly lash as he climbed out of the catacombs. And though they didn't knock him off his feet, they did throw him back, slowing his pace.

Lazarus jumped aside, but the cave didn't really offer anywhere to hide. The machine-gun burst eventually reached him there, too. I shoved Ramon off me as he pressed his head in his hands and shouted into his ear in a vain attempt to overcome the deafening thunder of the shots:

"Get in the car!"

Ramon started to get out of the zone of fire, climbing into the vehicle; I crawled directly toward the armored carriage and, when I was already almost up to it, the Gatling gun went silent. The electric wire, with a measured buzzing, continued spinning the barrel block, but there were no more bullets.

In one moment, I jumped into the back of the carriage. The leprechaun's elated cry piped up from behind the machine gun: "Bugger! Bugger! Bugger!" With the last of my strength, I barked out:

"Ramon, drive!"

I heard the clap of the doors and, just then, Lazarus came out of the cave, broken down but alive, insofar as such a term could ever apply to vampires. The charred remains of his once-expensive suit were hanging off him like pitiful rags, but neither fire nor high-caliber bullets could do any real damage to the inhuman beast.

Lazarus made an unintelligible, rage-filled scream and started running again.

I, calmly, as if this were a training exercise, loaded another belt of bullets into the machine gun and, after clapping the top shut, grabbed the smoking handle of the Gatling gun when the vampire had already overcome half the distance between us. I pushed down the knob with my thumb and round casings flew in all directions, bouncing off the car walls. The leaden lash whipped Lazarus across the chest, making him fall the earth and roll.

The car's engine gave a jump and a number

of very frequent rattles. The heavy self-propelled carriage, picking up speed at a mad pace, raced down the hill. A sharp jolt moved the sights of my gun, allowing the vampire to get to his feet again and throw himself on pursuit, but I instantly readjusted my aim and thrashed him with another short, calculated burst. And I did so again and again until we finally made it away and the bloodsucker was lost from view behind the trees.

All that time, the leprechaun was standing on the opened tailboard of the car and waving his hand with a mocking middle finger.

The situation was obviously funny to the pipsqueak; I though, wanted to kick him in the ass so he'd fall out.

And I would have done so, but I had no strength remaining.

None at all.

RAMON DROVE up to the suburbs without stopping. And he would have driven further, if the water in the radiator hadn't nearly boiled off. So, he just drove down an unpopulated little village street that crossed the road, stopped and threw back the hood. He leaned up against the armored car and let the rain come down on his uncovered head, having lost his peaked cap at some point.

With round casings ringing out on the floor, I jumped out of the rear I'd spent the whole ride in and raised the tailboard, hiding our machine-gun installation from curious onlookers. Then I threw my face to the sky, took a heavy sigh and walked up to my partner. The leprechaun joined us as if nothing was going on, took a seat on the running board and set about rolling a cigarette.

"What is that?" Ramon asked, pointing at him.

"A friend," I answered curtly and threw a sugar-drop into my mouth. After what just happened, I was still shivering.

"A friend?" my hulking partner clarified.

I nodded. Then Ramon shook his head and extended his hand:

"My money?" And when I'd counted out his thousand francs, and he'd hidden them in his pocket, he suddenly declared: "This is it for me."

"What do you mean?" I replied, not understanding.

"Forget my name," Ramon demanded. "I never intend to do business with you again, are we clear?"

"Ramon, what's gotten into you?"

"What's gotten into me?" the squat man grew red in anger. "First, I was nearly done in by the werewolf, and now this abomination! It was a miracle we escaped, Leo! A miracle! What will happen tomorrow? You wanna go hunting for demons? It'll have to be without me!"

"Wait..."

"No!" Ramon shouted back abruptly. "I'm not gonna be waiting this time. And I'm not gonna be risking my head anymore, either! I've had enough!"

"Come off it!"

"Leo! Are you even listening to me?" Ramon asked, exasperated and holding his hand out before him. "You're not the same person I used to know, Leo. You used to be cautious, with plenty of foresight. You didn't used to rush headlong into any old adventure!"

"I just want to figure this all out!"

"Then go figure it out! Figure it out on your own, and leave me out of it!" Ramon demanded and added for some strange reason: "Devilry, your eyes have even changed! They aren't just glowing, they're burning! Leo, something's wrong with you!"

I got my glasses with round darkened lenses out of my pocket in silence and clipped them on my nose. Ramon snorted, turned around and walked out. He didn't even look back one time.

"Bugger, what a scene!" the leprechaun rasped back, forgotten by all and smoking a hand-rolled cigarette. "A right tragedy!"

"You shut up," I grunted, chasing him off the running boards.

The pipsqueak ran over to the hood and shouted after Ramon:

"Jackass!" then turned to me stuck a thumb up.

I just frowned, threw open the armored car door and a heavy pack of Egyptian guineas fell out under my feet with an untouched bank package.

I was immediately reminded how glaringly Ramon's cloak pockets had been bulging, and it became clear that he and his cousin would no longer be having a problem buying the neighboring manufactory. They just didn't want to get caught up in currency speculation: an attempt to sell Egyptian guineas could even land one in jail. What was more, every second black market speculator worked as a police informant.

With a hopeless sigh, I threw the money on the passenger seat, then put down the hood and got behind the wheel.

"Are you gonna be driving?" the leprechaun asked, himself concentrated on pissing in a drainage ditch.

"Bugger! I'm car-sick!" he called out without turning around.

I just snickered, slammed the door shut and started up the motor.

I was getting pretty sick of that Lazarus...

2

IT TOOK ME twenty minutes to get to the city and, all that time, I was thinking over what to do next. But the thoughts crawling into my head were one more joyless than the next. Beyond the thoughts about rope nooses, strychnine and the metallic flavor of a barrel stuck in my mouth.

No, I didn't at all consider suicide a decent way out of all this, just the most painless. And though the vampire had long parted with emotions and the word "revenge" was now for him just an empty sound, my position was only made worse by that. A pragmatic person wouldn't tear off some unfortunate *illustrious* gentleman's head in a fit of rage; a pragmatic person would first tear out the arms and legs so that others wouldn't want to.

And what to do? Drive home?

Curses!

That was the first place the vampire would look for me when he got to town, and I was not at all sure that Elizabeth-Maria would manage to stop him. Though the succubus in human form had enviable strength and lightning-fast reflexes, she still wouldn't be able to tangle with Lazarus.

I couldn't go home, at the very least, until I found a proper weapon. Sure, perhaps I'd never find one that could kill him for certain, but I at least wanted one that could do irreparable damage.

Garlic didn't even cross my mind. Perhaps, a newly-turned bloodsucker would squirm a bit if he met an enemy with that strong, characteristic aroma, but Lazarus didn't scare so easy. A wooden stake might have done the trick, but I was hardly likely to catch the vampire asleep now. Lure him out under open sky? Devil, he ran out of the catacombs and didn't even wince!

Maybe, direct sunlight could hurt him, but the sky was full of thick dark clouds at present. Somewhere, an uproarious blast of thunder rang out. On the horizon, from time to time, I saw white, branching flourishes of lightning.

Bad weather had come to New Babylon, and it was making me feel just as gloomy inside as the sky looked up above.

Antiquated methods couldn't help. The most recent scientific discoveries for fighting vampires were of little use. Copper, silver and lead couldn't harm the living dead. With a titanium knife, I could theoretically cut off Lazarus's head no problem but, in practice, it would have been simpler to just slice my own veins, not torture myself and burden others with picking up my remains after they're strewn about the street.

Electricity? Yes! Electricity was destructive to all infernal creatures, but how long would Lazarus remain paralyzed after a shock from the battery hidden in my cane? And most important: I simply had no idea what I could do while he was stunned. Even armed with a wooden stake or titanium blade, I had no desire to get up that close to him, immobilized or not. I was under the firm impression that such a short-sighted act would be akin to a very roundabout suicide attempt. Alexander Dyak's miracle bullets couldn't harm this undead monster in any way. Kerosene was also powerless, so what could I do?

All in all, I'd reached a dead end.

But I didn't tear out my hair too quick. I parked the armored vehicle in a now-familiar yard not far from the weapon store *Golden Bullet* and headed to visit Alexander Dyak.

I locked the self-propelled carriage and started walking to *Mechanisms and Rarities* in nothing but my jacket, not having brought my charred coat. Midway there, the rain grew noticeably stronger. I had to hide under the overhang of a street cafe, and ask them to bring me a large pot of Indian black tea and an order of cinnamon buns. Thankfully, there weren't any other visitors, and the stench of the smoke, still clearly on me, wouldn't be bothering anyone.

I began eating breakfast, and immediately a chill came over me.

I got scared. It just then hit me that, only because of happy coincidence and my imaginary friend had Lazarus not caught and disemboweled us just now. It was just that it had hit Ramon a bit earlier.

The buns were nearly gone, but the rain simply wouldn't stop, so I ordered another tea and continued sitting and watching the gurgling puddles. I didn't want to go anywhere, or do anything.

Apathy was weighing heavily on me.

I should have been fleeing the city, but I was just too deeply mired. I'd managed to annoy too many people. Lazarus would be searching for revenge, the gang of *illustrious* gentlemen – the contents of the aluminum box...

The box! It dawned on me that I'd left it at my uncle's estate!

Cretin! The investigators had probably already connected the Count with the bank robbery and now half the metropolitan police was searching for him! Devil!

I cursed out to myself, throwing a rumpled fiver on the table and hopping out of the cafe. The rain was starting to slightly calm down, and it seemed reasonable to take advantage of the lull and return to the armored car.

Plans had changed. If I had to stay ahead of my former colleagues, it followed that I should drop everything and concentrate on finding the Count. If only my attorney had found a clue, if only he had found any trace at all...

I drove up much too quickly and even almost put a hole in a fence with my bumper. I immediately forced myself to calm down and not step on the gas, no matter how much I wanted to make up for lost time. And that was exacerbated by the fact that the main apologists for the Sublime Electricity, Tesla and Edison, would be coming to town tomorrow, so the streets were just teeming with cops. There were constables standing like beacons at every intersection and driving all around in their self-propelled carriages; some were calling for people not to make crowds on the streets, others, on the other hand, were rounding people up to check their identity.

I hadn't had the pleasure of seeing the metropolitan police this active in all my years of service, but now, my armored car didn't attract any attention from either the locals, or my former colleagues. There were plenty of armored vehicles on the streets of New Babylon as it was.

I just had to not get in an accident. That would be a right laugh...

With that thought in mind, I nervously shivered and even started coming up with explanations in my head in advance for where exactly I found the self-propelled carriage that once belonged to the bank robbers and for what great reason I hadn't brought it straight to the Newton-Markt, but they turned out not to be needed. I drove through the historic center with no issues. Thankfully, amongst the high buildings of the business district all rushing up into the heavens, the activity grew noticeably sparser. The few cabs on the road made way in good time, and police officers started meeting the eye with reduced frequency.

After driving around the tall building that housed my attorney's office, I left the armored car behind some dumpsters and tied on a neckerchief in an attempt to give my appearance at least a shade of respectability. My efforts were in vain though. The guard at the door had his nose buried in a newspaper and didn't even look at me. I walked calmly past his post to the third floor. While I walked up the steps, I mechanically checked my Roth-Steyr and Cerberus and even grew surprised at how deeply that habit had ingrained itself in me in recent days.

With a bullet chambered and the safety off, I felt much calmer. Paranoia? No, it was just that I'd made too many enemies...

Opening the door without knocking, I walked into my attorney's hovel, stood in the middle of the room and leaned on my cane.

The young man gave a shudder, glanced at me over the newspaper and immediately started squirming about as if his tender bits had been smeared in turpentine.

"Viscount!" he said after throwing away the

morning edition of the *Atlantic Telegraph*. Then, he shot up from the table, saying: "I did everything just as we agreed yesterday and yet, this morning, I got a message from your uncle's lawyer!"

"And what did it say?"

"It's addressed to you. I'd already called the courier, but fortunately, hadn't yet managed to send anything..."

I accepted the thick paper envelope. The address was written in an unfamiliar, sweeping handwriting: "To Leopold O., deliver to named recipient only;" for added security, it was sealed with an unused postage stamp, which looked untouched.

I inspected the envelope carefully, shook out the titanium blade of my folding knife and lifted the flap. I got out the letter, and with a certain measure of surprise, read the laconic missive:

"Four o'clock PM at the maître's. Come alone."

There was no signature, but there was no need for one: I recognized my uncle's handwriting easily.

"Is something the matter?" my attorney asked in surprise.

I shook my head.

"Everything is fine," I reassured him, hiding the letter in my pocket. All necessary documents on the inheritance should be prepared today by four o'clock in the afternoon.

"They've all been ready for some time!" the young man replied. He then fussily pulled out a thick stack of papers from the top desk drawer. "It's all here!"

I looked through the documents and, turning through them, asked:

"If you would be so kind, stay in the office today until at least seven. If need be, I'll send a courier for the papers."

"Viscount!" my attorney called out for me indecisively. "As for the commission..."

"Everything remains in force. Ten percent of the sum is yours," I assured the jurist, not at all doubting that my uncle wouldn't pay a single centime of the contested check.

To be perfectly honest, I simply didn't understand what the hell now made him want to meet with me, so the honesty of his intentions raised a mass of questions.

Why? What did he need this for?

In my place, an overly self-confident person might think he had his opponent cornered, but I personally considered such a supposition far-fetched. After searching the Count's damaged manor and finding the aluminum box with the black runic lightning on top, the investigators would have no choice but to declare a search for the Count, so any legal actions on my part wouldn't mean a thing now. And what was more, my uncompromising relative had set the meeting himself.

If I were a paranoiac, I would suspect malicious intent and even the desire to lure me into an ambush, but I knew the Count wouldn't be able to extract any profit from my death. And that meant he needed something from me.

But what?

With that very thought in mind, I climbed into the armored car and thoughtlessly stared at the rain-covered windshield.

Nothing. I had nothing that could interest my uncle, and recognizing that simple fact made me nervous and threw me off balance.

I looked at my timepiece. It was showing a quarter to one. There was more than enough time before the meeting, so I decided to drop by Alexander Dyak's. Not for a shoulder to cry on, nothing of the sort. But it couldn't hurt to find out what the inventor had spent his one-hundred-franc advance on. I still needed weapons to use against the vampire.

I started up the motor and got on my way.

WHEN I DROPPED into *Mechanisms and Rarities* a quarter hour later, Alexander Dyak was discussing a gold coin on the counter with the same assistant head of the archeology department from yesterday, and I didn't bother them. I just greeted the man and shook the tiny droplets of rain from my derby hat.

"Leopold Borisovich, one minute. We're almost finished," the shop owner warned me.

He talked a bit longer with the archaeologist, then the pair struck hands and Señor Ramillo, smiling radiantly, walked over to the exit. The inventor looked just as satisfied as his customer.

"A successful deal?" I asked, leaning on the cane.

"Mere trifles," the inventor shrugged his shoulders and asked: "I'd much rather hear, Leopold Borisovich, how things are going with you."

"Questionably," I snorted back.

"Problems with the flamethrower?"

"No, no!" I assured Alexander Dyak. "The flamethrower did its job, but the kerosene wasn't as effective as I would have liked."

"Is that so?" the shop owner asked in confusion. "Did it not light?"

"It lit, but it couldn't burn a vampire."

"Well, well, well!" the inventor replied, tapping on the counter with a pencil. He then rubbed his gray beard and demanded: "Tell me everything in order. Each detail is important."

"For science?" I joked.

"Leopold Borisovich!" the inventor drew out his words in reproach. "You and I are working on a strictly utilitarian problem: how best to eliminate the living dead. Believe me, it isn't nearly as much fun as studying the effects of radiation on a body with heightened regenerative properties. You cannot write respectable scientific works on this material."

"I beg your forgiveness."

"Think nothing of it!" Alexander Dyak extended me a little sign and asked: "Hang this on the door, would you. And try to remember. I implore you, try to conjure up every detail."

The stenciled words on the little sign read: "Experiment in progress. Call in case of emergency."

When I hung it outside and locked the door, the inventor and I immediately went back into the work room. There, I lowered down into a chair with relief and leaned my cane against the wall. Alexander Dyak, meanwhile, started writing down my tale of the fight with the vampire in his notebook.

"What can you tell me about him?" he asked me near the end.

"Other than the fact that he introduced himself as Lazarus and gets his clothing from a very respectable tailor?" I chuckled.

"Any detail could be the key to the riddle!"

"He wasn't afraid of going outside under clear sky and mentioned that he was a few centuries old. Perhaps, he was somehow connected with the brilliant Rafael, and had spent the last few years living in Egypt."

Alexander Dyak looked at me somehow strangely, but I didn't pay it any mind, and snapped my fingers.

"And also, he called kerosene 'Greek fire!'"

"Greek fire?" the inventor shuddered. "Are you certain?"

"Absolutely."

"I may have spoken too soon then, when I called this assignment not quite as entertaining as the one with the werebeast," the shop owner muttered out thoughtfully. "An ancient being that has become impervious to the open flame of burning kerosene. I'm sure this was not a natural trait, but an acquired one."

"And what does that give us?"

"It's generally accepted that burning is the simplest method of destroying any unclean spirit, including vampires. Wooden stakes aren't merely last century, they're a holdover from deep antiquity. Nothing but stories."

"But that bastard won't burn!" I exploded.

Alexander Dyak just laughed.

"Everything burns, Leopold Borisovich. What's important is choosing the right catalyst."

"What, excuse me?"

"I suppose you've heard of phosphorus?" the inventor asked out of turn.

I nodded:

"Matches."

"That's right," the store owner confirmed. "But when producing matches, red phosphorus is used, and it isn't as dangerous as white."

"I didn't know there was more than one kind."

"White phosphorus," Alexander Dyak continued, "is extremely flammable. It auto-ignites when heated to any temperature over thirty-five degrees Celsius, can you imagine? For that reason, it is generally stored in airtight jars, underwater, and not exposed to light."

"What would light do to it?"

"Prolonged exposure to light turns white phosphorus into red," the inventor explained. "And you know, Leopold Borisovich, I am more than sure that your Lazarus will not have taken the care to make a protection against phosphorus."

I considered it and clarified:

"How hot does it burn?"

"Extremely. And also, the products of its combustion are toxic."

"That's not actually a good thing."

"What can you do?" Alexander Dyak shrugged his shoulders. "With the money you gave me, I bought a certain quantity of white phosphorus and with it, I could load up to two dozen hand grenades."

"And have you tested this?"

"I left that for you. Remember, I said its combustion products are toxic." The inventor rifled through a box and pulled out a cylinder that appeared to be made of aluminum. "Take this!" he said and suddenly threw me an incendiary grenade.

I barely caught it; even so, I was soaked with sweat.

"Don't you think we should be worried about accidental detonation?" I reproached the shop owner.

"We should," he confirmed. "But first, we need to fill it with the incendiary material and install a detonator. I suggest we make it an electric."

"Ah!" I caught my breath with relief and spun the nearly five-centimeter-diameter and fifteen-centimeter-long cylinder in my hands. On the lower end, there was an iron ring mounted on a spring.

"It doesn't have a safety clip," Dyak warned me, "so I implore you: be as careful as possible. It takes quite significant effort to remove the pin, though, so you can carry it in your pocket at ease."

I returned the aluminum cylinder to the inventor and reminded him:

"First of all, you have to fill it."

"Why not?" the inventor shrugged his shoulders and took the top off a tank in the corner. After scooping some water out with a little shovel, he filled a cavernous porcelain mortar, poured a bit of boiling water in and started setting out his tools: pincers, a scalpel, and some kind of strange clips.

It put me beside myself.

"This all seems very dangerous."

"Not at all," Alexander Dyak reassured me. "You just need to observe certain safety procedures. For example, cutting white phosphorus must only be done underwater. And in no case should it be touched with the bare skin. It can burn."

The store owner pulled on a rubberized glove and deftly pinched up a bar from the water tank with his pincers. It was yellowish white and strongly reminiscent of everyday wax. The phosphorus was dropped into the porcelain mortar. The inventor measured out the necessary amount with an iron measuring stick and cut away the extra with his scalpel.

"Unscrew the body," he commanded after laying the shortened bar on a piece of soft scruffy fabric.

I hurried to carry out his order and

unscrewed the cover. Inside the case, I discovered a rubber puck with an ignition aperture.

"The hermetic seal is very important," the store owner told me, wiping little droplets off the bar. "And it's also very important not to allow the white phosphorus to crumble. Even the tiniest piece could start a fire."

With the same scalpel, he placed the white phosphorus into the thick-walled body and set the dense rubber puck on top. He then stuck the elongated detonator into the top and screwed it in tight. After a slight shake, he was left satisfied with his work.

"Take a look, Leopold Borisovich," he said as he extended me the incendiary grenade.

I gave it a shake with a certain apprehension, but the rubber disk was holding everything firm.

"Try it out!" allowed the inventor.

"Thank you," I smiled, stashing the grenade in my jacket pocket. But I immediately got it out and placed it in my coat. Then, I asked: "When will the others be ready?"

"I can make up another five right now," the store owner told me. "The rest depends on your ability to pay."

"Wait up, Alexander," I said, not understanding. "You mentioned the number two dozen!"

"Sure, I've got the white phosphorus for two dozen, but the bodies and detonators cost a pretty kopeck. Uhh... I meant to say they are quite expensive. I can make more if you're prepared to pay."

I winced. After the ruinous settling of accounts I'd just had with Ramon, I didn't want any new expenses now. On the other hand – I'd already paid for the white phosphorus, and it would be at the very least wasteful to throw the investment to the wind. At my next meeting with Lazarus, a lack of ammunition could be a truly fatal mistake.

But that reminded me! My ammunition!

"Alexander, could you fill any round with white phosphorus?" I asked the inventor.

He shrugged his shoulders.

"Within the bounds of reason," he said, drawing out his words tentatively. The light bulbs on the ceiling suddenly started flickering. The shop owner shuddered and gave a sniff. "It can't be another short, right?"

I also tried to smell, but didn't detect any notes of burnt rubber.

"A power fluctuation," I supposed, donning my derby cap. "I'll leave you for five minutes. I'll be right back."

"Alright, alright," the inventor nodded. "You go, Leopold Borisovich, and I'll take care of the electricity. I'll check the wire. Don't take off the sign saying we're doing an experiment, though!"

"Sure thing."

I went outside, slamming the door behind me and hurried to the armored car. All the running around today had left me fairly fatigued, but driving the police carriage up to the back door of the shop seemed an overly brave tack. In the inventor's place, I personally wouldn't have considered such a suggestion, and would have thrown whoever asked me out by the neck.

The trunk unlocked, I pulled out the already open box of hand-held mortar rounds, counted them and decided that twenty-two would be more than enough. I didn't need to start a war, after all.

The box wrapped in my canvas coat, I hurried back to the shop, muttering curses to myself the whole way back, damning the rain falling from the sky, the weight of the rounds and my poor mangled leg. But mainly, of course, the rain.

On the way back, I got soaked through; I even had to take off my jacket.

"Here Alexander, look," I said, setting the box of rounds on the workbench. "Just be careful, they're already armed, and the detonator is very sensitive."

"What is this for?" the shop owner asked in amazement.

I gave a condensed description of how the hand-held mortar worked; the inventor got one of the rounds, spun it in his hands and snorted in confusion.

"How interesting!" he muttered as he tightened it in the clamps. "This must be the propellant charge, and here's the main explosive, which gets primed by the launch. I can't imagine it will be a problem to replace the main combustibles with white phosphorus. Just remember: the rounds have to be stored at a temperature below thirty-five degrees. I cannot possibly guarantee the requisite level of hermetic seal otherwise."

"I'll figure something out," I decided and looked at my time-piece.

I still had two hours left before the meeting with my uncle, but I didn't plan on spending them in the shop. Alexander Dyak confidently dismantled the round. Next to it, there were another twenty of the explosive goodies, and I didn't even want to think about what would happen to us if the inventor made a mistake.

"I'll probably be going then," I muttered.

"Of course, of course," the inventor called back, deeply immersed in his work. "Close the door on your way out."

"Naturally," I promised and took the cane I'd left against the wall. But before I reached the hanger, the lights went out with a loud thud.

"Oh no!" Alexander Dyak gasped out with unhidden fear.

By then, he was already messing with the insides of the disassembled round. The hair on the back of my head started standing on end in horror. One false move and we'd be blown sky high!

"Hold up! Don't move!" I said in alarm and started looking for the kerosene lighter in one of my pockets. "I'll give you some light!"

"That's not the problem," the shop owner muttered. Even in the uneven flickering of the flame, it was becoming clear just how quickly his face was filing with lifeless pallor. "The generator..."

"What generator?" I asked and almost fell when the floor beneath my feet started shaking.

Lots of little knick-knacks fell off the shelves. Tools flew about the room, and another bump immediately followed. And another, and another! With every thud, the bashing became stronger, as if some force was in a hurry to burst out of the shop basement straight through the floorboards.

What the devil? An earthquake?!

"Get out of here!" Alexander Dyak ordered, turning on his electric torch. "Get out of here at once, if life is precious to you!"

Huge drops of sweat were rolling down his dead pale face, and it became clear to me that it was some new invention of his going haywire and threatening to destroy the whole building.

After putting out my lighter, I leaned on the wall and demanded an explanation:

"What is happening? What the hell is this? Tell me now!"

The inventor pointed his torch beam at the back-room door and exhaled:

"This is what I get for my pride."

"What's down there?" I grabbed him by the shoulder and turned him toward me. "The steam boiler? A generator of the most modern construction? A dynamo?"

"Get out of here! Get out of here while you still can!"

"What's down there?!"

"A poltergeist," replied Alexander Dyak,

blindsiding me with the unexpected answer. "It's trying to get free. When it's done, there won't be two stones left of this building to stack together."

"What the devil were you doing with an evil spirit?" I asked, cursing and waving my hand. "No, you don't have to answer. I already know. You were researching the effect of electric currents on otherworldly creatures and didn't want to take typical precautions. Drawing pentagrams in blood is outmoded and unscientific, after all! To hell with that obscurantism, right?"

"Leopold Borisovich!" the shop owner hurried me along. "Go on then, out!"

But I just moved him aside. Now, with the risk of the unrecognized genius's invention exploding suddenly past, I calmed down and demanded:

"Just give me some light!"

"What are you planning to do?" Alexander was taken aback.

"I've faced off against a poltergeist before," I said, remembering Inspector White's words of encouragement, he being a man with the custom of latching on to the most doubtful affairs. "Just give me light and stay out of the way."

"But, what are you pla...?"

I pushed the inventor aside and broke the cane he'd once made me in two. And though I no longer had the police electric baton, this shock device had made a very strong case for itself.

"How were you holding the spirit in place?" I asked, opening the door of the back room.

A hatch interred in the floor was bouncing up and down furiously, shaken by the terrible blows of the infernal creature trying to escape from below.

"I surrounded it with a chain of electric shock devices," Alexander Dyak told me. "You have to get it back and hold it there until I can get the generator started."

"Wonderful!" I snorted, not at all burning with the desire to go rooting around this basement with a spirit enraged by prolonged confinement.

Devil, I didn't like empty basements as it was, but this one had a poltergeist!

The next blow nearly blasted the hatch off. The latch was bending up in a sharper and sharper angle. The iron loops it was attached to were almost half way out of the concrete. One of them even totally broke out with a whole piece of crumbling flooring.

"Well, what are you waiting for?" the inventor asked in surprise when I took off my dark glasses and froze near the hatch with the cane held out in front of me.

"I want to let it blow off a little steam," I called back and then the hatch flew off and slammed full force into the wall.

After that, I got straight to work. I took a step forward and jabbed my cane into the black hole of the hatch. I was immediately pulled down as if some unseen creature had latched into the stick and was attempting to rip it away, but an electric shock sparked up between the steel needles, and the poltergeist was sent abruptly backward. Following it, I ran down the rickety wooden stairs into the basement and shouted to Alexander:

"Light!"

The evil spirit was hiding among the huge mechanisms. For normal people, it was practically invisible, but my colorless *illustrious* eyes could discern a lot that wasn't there to the vision of mere mortals. The electric light helped too. Probably more than anything else.

From up above, Alexander Dyak pointed the torch into the small room with beaten-up leaden sheets for walls, and the evil spirit's former prison immediately caught my eye. It took the form of a jutting stockade of electrodes arranged around a copper ball hanging down on a chain from the ceiling. There was a bundle of wires that led down from it to the generator. And the generator, for the record, was still puffing away, it's pistons in motion. The damaged component was the dynamo.

I only got distracted for a moment, but the poltergeist chose that very moment to dash for the exit. From behind the iron body of the incomprehensible device, a cloudy stripe dashed to the stairs, and I sharply waved the cane, blocking its path. A blinding shock flashed. The spirit dodged sharply to the side, and nearly managed to knock me down with a gear sent flying at my head. The improvised thrown weapon hit the wall and left a deep mark in the lead lining.

The spirit gave a malicious, reverberating howl. My teeth started aching, and the device screwed to the floor shook with the impotent rage of the ghostly being. The walls rocked, the generator started jumping around, and the store owner spoke up:

"Quick, before he turns the whole place upside-down."

The inventor ran off the stairs and started trying to find the gear the spirit had thrown on the floor. I, meanwhile, tried to chase the poltergeist into the corner. He easily dodged the sparking needles of the cane and went the other way.

"Faster!" Dyak cried again as he started messing with the generator, placing some element back in place.

The poltergeist flew at his back, but I was on guard and caught the ghost with a counterstrike. The cane nearly flew out of my hands, but the unquiet spirit was flung into the corner with its deactivated prison.

The ghostly shadow grew thicker and darker and, just then, the wheels of the dynamo started spinning, and the electrodes in the floor rained forth sparks. The spirit shot up to the ceiling, but unfortunately for it, the copper ball hanging from that chain was already enshrouded with a whole cloud of manmade lightning. Then, the poltergeist collapsed onto the floor and began to dart rapidly from one electrode of its prison to the next.

"I still think you should draw a pentagram in blood on the floor, just to be safe," I joked, wiping the sweat from my face. "Next time, I might not be available."

Alexander Dyak turned on the light on the ceiling and just shook his head:

"I do not understand how such a thing could have happened! The spirit couldn't have pulled the gear out! That's impossible!"

"Mechanisms do tend to work themselves free," I said with a shrug of my shoulders. Just then, a hand-rolled cigarette caught my eye, and I ground it into the floor with my boot. I chose not to share my guess on the true cause of this incident.

"A surprising coincidence!" the inventor gasped, sitting on a stool and pressing his hand to his heart. "The electricity was shut off because of the thunder, and the generator broke at the same time. Simply astonishing!"

I laid out the cane and asked:

"Where'd you get the poltergeist?"

"Leopold Borisovich!"

"Don't worry, I'm gonna run to the police."

Alexander Dyak sighed and answered unwillingly:

"Your friend Albert has introduced me to some reliable people. And no, I didn't bring them here. I'm not that naive. We met in the city."

I took a seat on a strange iron box and continued my interrogation:

"Why do you need it? And why are the walls covered in lead sheets? Why all the precautions?"

"Would you be opposed to us going back upstairs?" the inventor suggested.

I didn't object. When I returned to the workshop, Alexander immediately pulled a bottle of Russian vodka from a secret drawer and poured himself fifty grams.

"Not to get drunk, just to calm the nerves," he joked nervously, then gulped it down.

I threw a mint ice drop in my mouth and repeated my question again:

"Why do you need a poltergeist?"

The inventor sighed heavily, put the bottle back in the cabinet and warned me:

"It's a long story."

I looked at my timepiece and sat down on the chair.

"I've got time."

Alexander Dyak walked from corner to corner, then asked:

"Do you know how a telegraph works?"

"In essence – yes."

"Well, I'm working on a device that can send signals without wires."

"Is such a thing possible?" I asked, not impressed at the inventor's discovery.

"Is it ever!" he said, throwing up his hands. "I've even made a few prototypes. Just imagine the possibilities such an invention could reveal! We could communicate with dirigibles from land, or even ships! We simply wouldn't need wires any longer!"

I threw one leg over the other and wondered with unhidden skepticism:

"Why has no one heard of this miracle invention then? Why have you not shared it with society?"

"I have!" Alexander flared up. "Fifteen years ago, I published a work in Russia under the name 'Device for detecting and registering electronic disturbances!' And do you know what happened? Department Three issued a warrant for my arrest! I had to flee! I left my work and my house! Can you imagine it?"

It took a bit of effort to believe it.

"You are sure that your supposed arrest was connected with these findings precisely, and not a sympathy for socialists, for example?" I wondered.

"Leopold Borisovich!" the shop owner said with unhidden reproach. "They wrote whatever they wanted in the arrest warrant, but I know perfectly well what the true reason was!"

"Is that so? Another conspiracy theory, like with Mr. Diesel?"

"It all started with Hertz," Alexander Dyak sighed, ignoring the sarcasm coming through in my words. "He proved Maxwell's theory on a vortex magnetic field or, if you will, on electromagnetic waves. After that was Branly with the radio-conductor, Lodge, Rutherford and Marconi. Do these names mean anything to you?"

"Marconi?" I frowned. "I seem to remember a big trial fifteen years ago in Italy. One of the first accusations that someone was working as an Egyptian spy?"

"Complete nonsense!" the inventor snorted. "It's just that, after sixty-two, the topic was made top secret. Lots of the facts surrounding Hertz's death were suspicious, and then the accidents and arrests became business as usual. It was as if someone had opened Pandora's box. The only people untouched by the scandals were Tesla and Edison. By a strange series of coincidences, they managed to remain entirely distanced from the topic. Coincidence? Not likely."

I couldn't resist a vexed grimace and looked down at my timepiece.

His words did nothing to convince me. As I'd already managed to notice, Alexander had an unhealthy tendency to see the threads of conspiracy in everything. And also, imprisoning an evil spirit in the basement of your own home was an idea that would never occur to a normal person.

I was far from convinced that Dyak had lost his mind, but the boundary between eccentricity and madness, beyond all doubt, had been crossed. And I really didn't want to be near if tight-lipped Department Three officers came by or, even worse, if the store was launched sky-high.

Alexander noted my skepticism and was insulted to the depths of his soul.

"Let's go, Leopold Borisovich!" he said, dragging me after him into the back room. "Come with me, and you can see it for yourself!"

"No need," I tried to refuse, but the crusty old man dragged me after him with surprising strength, and I had to go back down into the basement.

And it was a good thing I did. It made little sense to start a fight with this man, who'd taken it on himself to prepare me two dozen incendiary rounds, after all.

"What's the lead for?" I asked when the inventor started messing with the casing of some apparatus.

"Extra protection," he answered simply.

"Extra?"

"Yes, there's also a grounded Faraday cage," Alexander Dyak explained. "My first device was called the 'lightning detector.' It registered disturbances in the electrical field. This time, I wanted to keep all the disturbances in, for understandable reasons."

"To keep the experiment pure?"

"That was one reason, yes," the inventor confirmed. "And also to make sure the radiation of my apparatus wouldn't hurt anyone else."

I just sighed.

At the same time, the shop owner hooked the apparatus up to the generator and asked:

"Leopold Borisovich, can you see the spirit? I need to use special lenses to see it but you, I suppose, have no need for them, is that right?"

"Yes, I see it perfectly as it is," I confirmed.

The immobile poltergeist was frozen in the middle of its prison at an equal distance from all of the spark-sprinkling electrodes. I had never before had the chance to see spirits in a calm state; normally these creatures were in constant motion, changing shape, throbbing and stretching from one position to the next.

"Is it static?" Dyak asked, turning on the device.

"Yes."

"Watch what happens next."

I heard a quiet humming, but the fleshless spirit didn't even budge.

"Is something the matter?" I smirked.

"Just wait!" The inventor demanded. "In the course of the experiments, I determined that the important factor was not the radiation in itself, but its frequency. And now, I'm starting to change it..."

"In what way?"

Dyak just laughed:

"I'm afraid that any explanation of how this device works would take the rest of the day, and you're already anxiously glancing at the time as it is."

"Yeah, I've got an important meeting scheduled at four."

"This won't take that long!" the inventor reassured me and started very slowly turning a knob. "Now, you can see it with your own eyes. Look!"

For some time, nothing happened, then the poltergeist started rippling. Alexander Dyak continued his manipulations and quietly muttered to himself:

"At these frequencies, it usually starts to take effect..."

"There's something happening..." I admitted.

The spirit faded out and was constantly twitching as if invisible gusts of wind were tearing it to pieces, thrashing it hither and thither. For a certain moment, it even seemed that it had disappeared from our world, pressed back into the underworld, but no – the power of the effect went on the decline, and soon the ghostly being had returned to its former state of immobility.

"Stunning!" I muttered, immeasurably surprised by the successful end to the experiment.

"As I said!" the inventor forwarded, melting into a happy smile, as he turned off the transmitter. "I propose a celebration!"

We went upstairs and, while I took the "experiment in progress" sign from the door, the store owner put on a fresh pot of tea. He placed the teapot directly on the counter and offered me some shortbread cookies.

"Are you convinced now, Leopold Borisovich?" asked the inventor, pouring the aromatic drink into teacups. "The electromagnetic field has an effect on otherworldly creatures! It is a scientific fact!"

"How has that just reached you now?" I replied, shaking my head and glancing at my watch. My window of time was growing razor thin.

Alexander Dyak didn't notice my glance and laughed softly:

"Leopold Borisovich, you still think me an addle-brained old man, but if I expound upon my theory, you'll certainly consider me a madman."

"After the demonstration of your device, I'm prepared to believe anything," I admitted and finished drinking my hot tea. "But I won't insist. Tell me when you think it necessary."

The inventor nodded, then walked around the shopping floor, looking over the shelves of goods and said distantly:

"I've always been interested in the topic of the insurrection. For what reason were *the fallen* deprived of their power? How did the conspirators manage to rise up everywhere around the world at the same time – in the Old and New World, Zuid-India and even the Celestial Kingdom? Especially in the Celestial Kingdom, where, according to the memoirs of one of Clement's supporters, they had no truly like-minded allies whatsoever?"

"Good organization?"

"Good organization could have helped them rise up simultaneously at an agreed-upon date," Dyak replied, "but then it would seem that Clement and his close companions knew in advance the precise date *the fallen* would lose a large portion of their powers." "Perhaps," I supposed, "they had a hand in it?"

I winced skeptically.

"Not convinced?" the inventor smiled understandingly. "And meanwhile, my data is in full agreement with that theory. The only thing I don't know is how such a strong signal was sent that it reached the whole planet."

"Did it really reach the whole planet, though?"

"You're right, Leopold Borisovich," the shop owner nodded, "we don't have any reliable evidence about what precisely happened in Alexandria and Tenochtitlan when *the fallen* were defeated."

"Then, the way I see it, there is one weak point in your judgments," I said, shaking my head. "Based on the results of the experiment, disturbances in the electromagnetic field are not fatal, even to ethereal spirits. What might that mean for *the fallen*? And by the way, though there were no conspirators among the Egyptians or the Aztecs, *the fallen* were also defeated there. And since that time, no one has seen them."

"The pyramids," Alexander Dyak said simply.

"What, excuse me?"

"Electromagnetic disturbances cannot penetrate deep into the earth," the inventor stated. "*The fallen* were able to take shelter in hidden chambers under the pyramids. And that is the complete explanation for the subsequent armed conflicts between our countries."

"I do not know, I do not know," I doubted. "*The fallen* were omnipotent, do you think some mere electromagnetic waves could deprive them of their powers?"

"We all have our weak points," the shop owner shrugged his shoulders. "They say every piece of glass has a small spot you can lightly tap to break the whole piece. My studies are not yet finished. I have to find the proper frequency."

I set the empty cup down and smiled:

"What if not only the frequency is important, but the contents of the signal? Perhaps, the problem is in the message."

"Are you suggesting curses, transmitted via electromagnetic disturbance?" the inventor frowned. "Leopold Borisovich, with all due respect, you should not mix science with magic. It's irrational."

"The very presence of *the fallen* in our world is irrational."

Alexander Dyak thought over my assertion, then waved his hand:

"In any case, my apparatus does not allow for the transmission of sound. This is no telephone."

"But what about a telegraph?" I reminded him. "Like those electric pulses and signals from Morse. Could that be done?"

"Yes," the shop owner agreed. "But, curses...? I'm a scientist! I don't know any curses. I don't believe in them and I am not prepared to use them! I believe in the primacy of knowledge and the power of science!"

"Let's not dig into the theological implications," I suggested. "Just send the message I write for you, okay? Think of it as just another experiment. Just a series of short and long pulses, that's all."

"If you insist, Leopold Borisovich..."

"I do!" I said, walking up to the counter. Then I demanded: "Paper and quill!"

After getting what I asked for, I started writing out the order of the signals:

"Dot-dash-dash-dot; dot-dash; dash; dot; dot-dash-dot; dash-dot; dash-dash-dash; dot-dot-dot; dash; dot; dot-dash-dot..."

Alexander Dyak accepted the paper from me, acquainted himself with its message and looked with unhidden skepticism.

"Are you sure, Leopold Borisovich?" he asked, stroking his gray beard in perplexity.

"Treat like with like, isn't that right?" I smiled carelessly in reply. "It's just an experiment."

"I never could wrap my mind around Morse code," the inventor sighed, "and now, at this age, my fingers are starting to lose their dexterity. I'm afraid I'd make a mistake and violate the purity of the experiment."

"Well, you could inscribe it into a mechanism, like the one in a music box."

"Now there's an idea!" Alexander Dyak lit up. "I'll try! Why not?"

"Please do," I nodded and headed to the exit but, already at the door, I was stopped by a cautious question from the shop owner.

"Leopold Borisovich! I can count on you not telling anyone about the experiments I'm carrying out on the poltergeist, right? At my age, stays in prison are hazardous for the health."

"Don't worry, I won't tell," I promised him. "But I need something from you in return."

"I'm listening."

"Nothing serious, I would just like to park a self-propelled carriage in your back yard. It'd only be for a day or two."

"Nothing could be easier," the shop owner caught his breath with relief. "You could even come now!"

"In that case, I'll make use of your kind offer in short order," I nodded and went out the door.

My head was spinning in the most natural fashion, but there was not enough time left to gather my thoughts and really think everything over. I had to hurry to the meeting with my uncle. And before that, I had to get ready for the meeting.

That was precisely why I took the armored carriage there. There was a distinct chance that the invitation was an ingenious trap, and I had no desire to leave this world with a knife driven under my shoulder blade.

Who could say what my uncle wanted from me?

3

THE RAIN started coming down all the harder. There were rivers of run-off gushing down the streets as the storm front gradually crept over the center of town. There weren't many people outside. The inhabitants were hidden in their homes. I only saw the odd courier or patrolman catching cold in a rubberized cloak.

That was precisely why it was no work at all to pick out the hired observers. One was a boy sitting bored in the doorway of the building opposite the lawyer's office. Another was taking shelter from the rain under an overhang not far from the back door. I noticed them as soon as I came around the corner to the awkward building that housed Maître LaSalle's rented office.

I didn't fall into a panic. The fact that my uncle had taken such precautions was no sure indication of bad intentions; also, it was possible that these observers had been hired to watch Maître LaSalle's office by the detectives investigating the bank robbery.

None of the observers could have seen me through my rain-covered windshield, so I drove calmly into the neighboring yard and parked the armored car under an archway. I locked it and went up the fire escape to the roof. The buildings in this neighborhood stood one against the next. The distance between their sloping roofs did not exceed half a meter, and getting from one to the next was no problem at all. The main danger was presented by the extreme slipperiness of the tiles underfoot and the sharp gusts of wind, constantly shifting direction.

Cursing the bad weather, I jumped over to the neighboring building, got over to the other side of the roof and jumped from it to the roof of the maître's office. To the sound of the next thunder blast, I jimmied open the attic door and went inside the dark dusty room. I took a listen – it was quiet. The only sound was the odd plunk of drops falling from the leaky ceiling.

Then, I pulled back the bolt of my Roth-Steyr and checked if I had a round in the chamber, took the Cerberus off safety and returned it to my left coat pocket; the incendiary grenade was in the right pocket. After that, trying not to stomp, I found a hatch to the floor below and easily jimmied it open. I simply stuck the split end of my short crowbar between the frame and the lid, carefully leaned on it, and the mortise lock gave with a quiet rasp. No one could have heard a thing.

I didn't have to jump: there was a little ladder in the wall leading to the hatch. I went down into a secluded nook on the upper floor and looked cautiously down the hall. The office door was clearly visible.

I looked at my timepiece. It was three fifty. I leaned on the wall and unholstered my Roth-Steyr just in case. I wasn't particularly hoping for the Count to be punctual so, when I saw him walking up the stairs five minutes before the scheduled time, he surprised me a good deal. Characteristically, he came alone. The observers stayed below to keep watch.

My uncle knocked on the office door. The lawyer let him inside with no delay and informed him laconically:

"He hasn't showed up yet."

I then jumped up from my cover and, before the door managed to slam shut behind them, dashed into the office with my pistol in hand.

"No stupid stuff!" I warned my uncle and commanded: "Go!"

Maître LaSalle puffed out his cheeks vehemently, but didn't raise a stink, instead walking into the office. Count Kósice, though, was not able to maintain his calm demeanor; he stared at me, flashed his eyes dully and demanded explanations:

"Just what do you think you're doing, young man?!"

"Go!" I repeated. "Or are you planning on conducting negotiations in the entryway?"

My uncle frowned, but didn't insist and followed after his lawyer. In the antique-furniture laden office of the maître, he immediately turned back and spat out the annoyance clearly filling him up:

"What is the meaning of these tricks?!"

I walked up in silence to the window and looked outside. The observer was still at the neighboring building and hadn't lowered his eye from the back door.

"You're the one playing tricks, not me," I snorted, pointing down.

The Count went red in indignation, but didn't lose his presence of mind, just shrugged his shoulders:

"A simple precautionary measure."

"And so you see I also took... a precautionary measure."

"What are you talking about, sir?" the lawyer shuddered.

My uncle looked in disappointment at him and asked:

"Maître, please leave us."

"But, Count..."

"This is a private conversation!"

The lawyer pursed his lips and reminded him:

"If you haven't forgotten, Count, I'm still in

the crosshairs!"

"Oh, no!" I smiled, putting my pistol back in the holster. "I beg your pardon, good sirs, if my actions made you afraid. You may be absolutely free in your actions."

"Maître!" Count Kósice repeated. "This is a one-on-one conversation."

"Tête–à–tête," I agreed, taking a seat on the wide windowsill.

My uncle gave a sniffle and lowered down in the maître 's seat.

"Well?" he hurried the lawyer along.

The maître shrugged his shoulders and went into the reception. The door closed tightly behind him.

"What was it you wanted to talk about?" I asked, not feeling like wasting time on long and cautious inquiries.

The Count unbuttoned a traveling bag he'd brought, pulled some rolled paper tubes out of it and threw them on the table.

"My decree transferring you your part of the family fund," he told me.

"Generous!" I said in immeasurable surprise. "What do you want in return?"

"First, call off your laughable injunctions," my uncle demanded.

"I'll call them off today," I said, agreeing to his condition. "But that's the least of your problems, right? The police are now after you, and they'd like to ask you all kinds of uncomfortable questions, isn't that so?"

"What on earth for?" asked my uncle, not

even raising an eyebrow.

"About the bank robbery," I hinted.

"Proving I wasn't involved in that sordid little affair is no effort."

"I believe they now have some tangible evidence. Clues, if you will."

"Clues?" the Count laughed back. "Come off it! The investigators have nothing to suggest it wasn't planted in my ruined mansion by the criminals!"

I nodded, beginning to understand what exact line of defense my prudent relative was taking.

"And if that's what they're talking about," my uncle smiled unpleasantly, "where were you on the night my manor was broken into?"

"Don't you worry about that, I have an iron-clad alibi," I answered calmly. "And don't pretend you're so innocent. Your participation in this affair has long been an open secret."

"Don't think me an idiot!" Count Kósice sniffed. "The fact that you have the check is more eloquent than any words."

"Exactly," I nodded. "So then, what is the second condition?"

"A mere trifle really."

"Just a trifle?" I asked, jumping down from the window sill and taking the documents from the table. I began to look through them, having begun to suspect a nasty trick, but no. All the signatures and stamps were in the right place. I also had no problem with the wording.

"And this trifle," I grumbled, putting the

papers back in my pocket, "means enough for you to sacrifice twenty thousand a year in income?"

"I warn you in advance," said Count Kósice, "if we do not come to an agreement, I'll declare this document signed under threat of violence, and the maître will corroborate."

"Get to the point! Just tell me about the box. The aluminum box with black runic lightning on top. What interests me most is what was inside it."

"Just to clear this all up," my uncle frowned, "the only one who can profit from the box is me and me alone. You'll have to be satisfied with twenty thousand in yearly income or rely on alms when I declare you a fraud and impostor."

Not so long ago, such a threat could have knocked me right off my feet, but now I just snorted contemptuously and repeated my question:

"What was in the box?"

The Count shot back a strange look in reply, then got out his wallet and placed an old yellowed photograph on the table, ripped unevenly from the bottom.

"Look for yourself," he allowed.

On the photograph was a fit lady in an old-fashioned dress holding a light-haired girl of nine or ten years old by the hand. I recognized the gaunt strong-willed face of the woman. It was the Countess Kósice, my grandmother. The pair looked like two peas in a pod.

Mom. That was my mom.

I looked at the back and spent a long time reading its dedication: "My child, Diana, remember: your future is in your hands."

At the bottom, there was a laconic signature: "Emile," and a series of incomprehensible numbers.

"Emile?!" the realization dawned on me suddenly.

It was *the* Emile Rie, Duke of Arabia, the brother of Emperor Clement?!

But then why the address: "My child?" And why would the eminent chancellor have had such a photograph?

I remembered the words of the head robber: "In respect to the memory of Emile Rie," and finally my head started spinning.

Count Kósice, who was watching me with a slight half-smirk, his look even having become a bit lazy, nodded:

"I admit with regret that my mother didn't always maintain her faithfulness to father. Diana was fathered by another man."

My uncle supposed it was someone I'd never heard of some mysterious 'other man' – I mean there were quite a few Emiles in the Empire! – and I didn't disabuse him of that notion. I just asked:

"How did you find out?"

"I overheard a random conversation. Not long before mother died, this man visited our manor," said the Count, a shadow running across his face. But he immediately got himself together and continued: "We were talking about Diana.

Some kind of risky arrangement was under way, but the need to provide for her future arose."

I even snorted in annoyance.

"Are you planning to give me my inheritance? That isn't just not fair, it's walking the line between good and evil!"

The Count just shrugged his shoulders:

"I'm not giving you anything. I'm making a deal with you. And note, I'm taking on all the risk. If my sister's father did not take the necessary measures, I'll come away empty handed. But you get twenty thousand a year in income no matter what!"

"That money is mine no matter what! This is a worse deal than selling one's birthright for a mess of pottage!"

"My father deserved the money!" my uncle objected, slamming his hand on the table. "Agree to that or get nothing!"

"I'll track down my own inheritance!"

"Complete nonsense!" Count Kósice laughed. "I tore off a part of the code! You'll never get to the second part of the photo."

My uncle's precaution made an unpleasant impression; I looked at the code and asked:

"What do you need from me?"

"A book from your library."

"Which one?" I asked and smiled with a snort: "I'm surprised you haven't tried to steal it yet."

My uncle's eyelid twitched and I guessed:

"Ah, that's right! You did try to steal it!"

"I sent three people," the Count

confirmed. "None of them returned."

Three people? I only had one burglar in my ice-house. What had happened to the others? The leprechaun hadn't really fed them to stray dogs, had he?

"Your lack of scruples makes an impression," I frowned.

"As if you're an example of moral virtue!"

"Alright. What book do you need?"

"I have no idea," my uncle suddenly declared. "Look at the picture. Your mother is holding it."

The girl in the photograph really was holding a book of some kind in her hands, but I couldn't make out the name or the illustration on the cover.

I walked over to the window, moved my glasses down to the tip of my nose and squinted. No, couldn't see it.

"How can I find a book if I don't know what it's called?" I objected.

"Are you mocking me?!"

The Count frowned in annoyance:

"I don't see how this could be so hard!" he announced. "Diana didn't throw out a single book her whole life, and when she moved, she brought her whole library with her. Finding the book by the ex-libris is a few hour's work. I'm sure very few books in your library would be appealing to a ten-year-old girl. At the end of the day, compare the covers. I wouldn't be surprised if you discovered a dedication in one of them from that Emile but, if not, the part of the code on the photograph I left will be the final test. When decoded, you should get words, not a random set of letters."

"What do these numbers mean?"

"Page number, line number, word number," my uncle explained. "You write the first letter, then move on. Is that clear?"

"You must have had extremely sharp hearing in your youth," I laughed, looking at the photograph.

The book's cover looked dimly familiar, but I couldn't place it exactly.

"It's not for you to judge me!" my uncle flew into a temper. "Either agree or go to hell for all I care! I won't get anything, but I'm well enough off as it is. You, though, will have to live on the streets. As your sister's only legal heir, I can order your manor demolished!"

"Easy now, uncle," I warned him. "Don't try to scare me."

"I'm not the one who started it!"

Just then, the door flew open and the lawyer stepped into the office with a revolver in hand.

"Pistol on the floor, Viscount!" he ordered.

Count Kósice jumped to his knees and objected:

"Maître, I asked you not to bother us!"

The lawyer didn't even look at him.

"Pistol!" he demanded.

With two fingers of my left hand, I pulled my Roth-Steyr from its holster and lowered it to the floor. My uncle came out from behind the table and walked over to his attorney.

"Maître, this is overstepping!" he shouted. "Why the devil did you interrupt us?"

The revolver barrel quickly swung toward the Count's chest.

"Please do be quiet, Count," the lawyer demanded and stepped aside, letting into the room an imposing looking gentleman of middling years, completely bald with thin eyebrows and lashes.

It felt like I was struck by lightning! Lazarus!

I didn't hesitate for even a second. With full force, I leaned into the window pane with my elbow and, when it shattered with a deafening crash, I stuck my hand with the photograph outside.

"One more step and I'll throw it!" I warned the vampire.

"Don't be stupid, Viscount," Lazarus winced. "The Count knows the code from beginning to end even without your photograph. In fact, just jump. You'd save me the trouble of ripping your head off."

"What is happening?" Count Kósice exclaimed nervously. "Who are you, devil take you?"

Lazarus turned, and the gaze of his impenetrably black eyes instantly sapped my uncle's will. The Count jumped back to the wall. The vampire moved up to him and demanded:

"The numbers! Tell me the numbers!"

"I don't remember!" my uncle babbled. "I just don't remember!"

"You do remember!" Lazarus assured

him. "People are not inclined to forget truly important things."

Now, with all the vampire's attention concentrated on my uncle, I stuck my hand into the pocket of my jacket, but the lawyer quickly ordered:

"Back!"

I had to hold my open hand in front of myself; I was still holding the photograph out the window.

"Lazarus, how did you come to know about this meeting?" I asked, wanting to buy us some time.

"The maître has been working for us for many years," the vampire said.

"So, that's who blabbed about the contents of the safe and the aluminum box!"

"I didn't blab, I reported!" the lawyer replied, offended.

"To the Convent?" I asked, throwing out a feeler.

"Enough chit-chat!" Lazarus barked, again demanding from the Count: "The numbers!"

"I don't remember!"

"What a pity," the vampire said quietly, suddenly grabbing the Count by the back of the head.

His clawed fingers pierced the skin with surprising ease. Blood started dripping out and my uncle froze. His face went slack, and his eyes went dead, becoming like a pair of transparent marbles with crimson blood-vessel cracks.

"Write!" Lazarus demanded, starting to move

his hand, still deeply embedded in the Count's yielding flesh.

The Count, moving like a marionette, grabbed the quill and started writing groups of numbers on the first piece of paper he came across.

Lazarus got distracted by me and smiled:

"See Viscount, you're just soaking that photograph for no good reason."

I heeded the vampire's words and stuck the picture into my inner pocket.

"Give it here!" the lawyer instantly demanded with a threatening shake of his revolver but, just then, Count Kósice threw his quill down on the table and slid the paper over to the vampire.

"How did you find out about the code?" Lazarus asked him, calling the maître to silence with a gesture.

"From a conversation I overheard between my mother and the Duke of Arabia," my uncle answered in a voice deprived of all intonation.

"What's written in this code?"

"The future," the Count exhaled. "He said it was their future."

Lazarus laughed wholeheartedly with a satisfied look and stashed the paper in his pocket.

"The photo, Viscount!" the lawyer again demanded, poking me with the revolver.

Then, two stocky brutes with pistols at the ready dashed into the entryway!

The maître turned sharply and pulled the trigger without warning. The first to step into the office was knocked off his feet, but before the lawyer had managed to plunk down the revolver's heavy trigger again, the still-living partner sunk two bullets right into him. After that, he quickly stepped over the threshold and aimed at the vampire.

"Don't move!" he commanded. "Get back! Now!"

Lazarus freed his hand from my uncle's head with a fastidious motion, and he flopped down under the table like a lifeless sack. The man stepped back toward the exit in horror, and the vampire went after him.

I, meanwhile, didn't want to stick around for the imminent conclusion. To the sounds of disordered shooting, I got up on the window sill and leapt over to the fire escape of a neighboring building. My chest slammed full force into the hand rail and I nearly lost my grip, but I managed to latch into the iron rod and crawled up onto the platform. There, with no delay, I grabbed the incendiary grenade from my pocket, ripped out the pin and threw the aluminum cylinder into the broken window of the office.

There was a boom. Tongues of colorless flame licked out onto the street, and a thick white smoke immediately followed. I got up from my knees just as a piece of plaster flew off the wall next to my head. I looked down with fear and saw a gunman in a raincoat and a wide-brimmed canvas hat on the street. He racked the slide and pointed his rifle up again.

A moment later, another shot blasted out.

But I jumped aside and rushed up the fire escape onto the roof of the building. I slipped on the wet tile, crawled away from the edge and froze, gathering my strength. At that very moment, though, shards of ceramic began flying up all around me; an invisible lash whipped the roof a few meters from my body and was heading in my direction. I got up and froze in horror: hovering over the buildings, there was a dirigible rocking in the wind, its name written across the whole side of the body, *Syracuse!*

Oh, devil!

The dual barrels of the machine gun in the cabin started sparking out again, but its turbulent flight made it hard to keep good aim and the bullets flew in a rather haphazard fashion. In the space of an instant, I jumped over the crest of the roof, lost my balance and fell downward. Thankfully, I landed on the roof slope though, sliding amid the flying rubble. The machine gunner was now obscured from view on the other side of the building.

After reaching the bottom on my back, I braced my boots on the eave, turned over onto my stomach and crawled to a nearby dormer window. But the gunner easily guessed my trick and didn't wait for the dirigible to come around the building. He shot out a long lash randomly around where he supposed I'd be moving.

Crushing tile, the bullets lapped against the sloped roof. I had to jump into nearby smoke for cover. A leaden lash whipped out behind me, and for a certain moment, the gunner got distracted. I then slammed into the dormer window with all my might, breaking it, and dashed into the attic.

I collapsed on the floor and turned my head, coming to. That second of delay nearly cost me my life. The machine-gunner drew two long diagonal lines across the roof, a crisscross. Dust and wooden splinters flew up. The attic was lit up with dim beams of light coming through the bullet holes.

I ran over to the stairs and a new path of bullet holes came to meet me. I only managed to jump aside at the very last moment. After flying into a pile of some kind of rubble, I fell to the floor and, on all fours, walked over to the floor hatch; I tried flinging it toward myself, but it was locked.

And then, the shots died down. Supposing that the machine-gunner was changing the belt, I kicked through a dormer window, got outside and threw myself to the fire-escape handles sticking out under the edge of the roof. As soon as I jumped onto the upper platform, tile shards rained down on my head; the wall protected me from the shooting. Not for long, but while the dirigible was flying to a new place, I had reliable cover.

So I went down the stairs. Once on the ground floor, I jumped across the sickly little lawn and dashed away. Hovering above the buildings, the belly of the dirigible shone like a beacon. Coils of rope flew down, unfurling, but it was still too high for the boarding team to reach the ground, so the machine gun thundered into action once again.

I darted around the corner of the building and almost ran into the gunman in the rain-coat. He started turning and then my Cerberus gave a grumble. The hired man fell face-down on the wet paving stone. The water around his shot-through head was instantly tinged a brownish red. I jumped over him and ran on.

Fortunately, I didn't come across anyone else on the way to the archway I'd parked the armored car under. Once there, I unlocked the door and got behind the wheel. I started up the motor and immediately slammed down on the acceleration pedal then, just as sharply, stomped on the brake when I saw a barrage of machine-gun fire dash against the paving stones before me.

The armor wouldn't be able to stand up to the dirigible's guns, and the Gatling in the trunk was mounted to fight against earthbound targets; its barrels wouldn't be able to aim high enough.

I cursed and jumped out of the car, intending to arm myself with the hand-held mortar in the trunk, but then I caught my gaze on the long wooden box containing the launch tube.

"Why not?" I asked myself, unpacking the box of strange elongated rounds with iron-blade stabilizers. The launch tube broke into two parts. The round fit easily inside. I snapped the locking mechanism, strapped a leather mask with glass eyepieces onto my face – what was this for, exactly? – and, bending under the weight of the weapon, left the carriage.

The launch tube secure on my shoulder, I took a decisive step out from under the arch into open sky. With a noticeable delay, the machine gun up above lit up with dual sparks. By that time, I already had the belly of the dirigible in the lattice sights. My fingers pulled the trigger and, with a roar and a cloud of fire from the launch tube, the missile shot out.

The eyepieces of the mask were instantly covered with sooty residue from the powder round, and the missile flew steadily upward, leaving a thick smoky trail behind it. When it reached its mark, an explosion thundered out!

My aim was true. The dirigible gondola simply broke in two; wreckage started flying all around and people were falling overboard. The body of the aircraft was punctured in several places; it began deflating and folding in on itself, but the inert helium gas didn't catch fire and the dirigible gradually fell faster and faster until it collapsed somewhere beyond the next building.

By that point, I was no longer moving slow. I threw the launch tube in the rear, raised the tailboard and ran into the front seat. The armored car's engine barked, and the vehicle flew out of the archway. Just then, from out of nowhere, the burnt figure of Lazarus appeared in my path. Before my eyes, his ghastly face flashed by, burnt up on one side. And then, the self-propelled carriage hit the vampire, flung him aside and kept on driving.

I DROVE full-speed until the police sirens quieted down. A few times, I nicked the sides of horse-drawn carriages. Once, I nearly drove into a steam tram that was blocking the road, but I managed to get control, only avoiding a serious accident by a miracle. My clarity of mind gradually returned, then I drove off the lively road and parked the armored vehicle in the first alley I came across. I wiped the sweat from my face, calmed my breathing and took my uncle's picture out of my pocket.

My grandmother, mom, the mysterious book, the note on the back.

"My child." "Emile."

Curses! It's not every day you find out you're a grandnephew of the Emperor! That meant I would have been third in line to the throne, not considering the minor fact that bastards have no rights to thrones at all.

And that meant this was not at all to do with courtly intrigues. But if the Duke decided to take care of my mother in his old age, what untold riches might he have left her for inheritance? After all, there were still people tearing each other's throats out for it sixteen years later!

"The future." What did he mean with that ambiguous statement? And why was this future of such vivacious interest to malefics and the mysterious gang of *illustrious*?

What was the code hiding?

"What is the code hiding?" I thought, clearly aware that I'd never find out. My uncle had torn off the lower part of the photograph as a precaution, so I wouldn't have the whole code.

I'd never get it. But, maybe I didn't have to.

Lazarus had the full code, and he definitely would be dropping by for a visit soon enough. He needed the book. The book and my hide.

Thinking about that put me beside myself, but I didn't start panicking prematurely and drove back to Alexander Dyak's shop. When the vampire came, I'd at least have something to greet him with. Based on his burned face, white phosphorus was not to Lazarus' taste.

But, no matter how badly I wanted to load the incendiary grenades into the car and hole up in my manor, that plan was destined not to come to fruition. It was a miracle the carriage reached the inventor's shop at all. Approximately half way there, a thick white steam started billowing out from under the hood of the self-propelled vehicle. I even had to stick my head out of the window under the pouring rain because the windshield was covered in condensation.

It was the radiator, broken in the fight with the vampire; when I'd parked the armored car in Alexander Dyak's back yard, he immediately pointed out the reason for the defect.

"It needs soldering."

"How much?" I asked, not knowing whether to worry about high cost or thank the heavens that I only had a leaky radiator.

"Come now, Leopold Borisovich!" the inventor said, insulted, hiding from the rain under an unfolded umbrella. "There can be no talk of money!"

"Alexander!" I responded, taking my turn to claim wounded honor. "I am no blackmailer and am not preparing to report you to the police regardless of what conditions our partnership continues under and whether it in fact continues or not."

The shop owner nodded, calculated something fast in his head and announced:

"Fifty franks."

"I've got it."

Through the back door, we walked into the shop. There, I got out my wallet and counted out five tenners.

"When can I come pick it up?" I asked, leaving my cane against the wall and pulling off my cold, wet jacket.

"Tomorrow lunchtime," the inventor decided.

"No way you could make it earlier?"

"Nope. Am I correct in understanding that you'd prefer to keep it out of official repair shops?"

"Yes."

"So, then. I will need to scare up some tools. The work itself will take up a pretty good chunk of time, too."

"Alright. I'll come by tomorrow," I sighed, looking through the window at the rain-covered street, gray and unpeopled.

"Tea?" Alexander asked.

"I wouldn't say no," I nodded and looked at my outstretched hand.

My fingers were barely shivering. And that was very bad. After all I'd gone through, I should have been a nervous wreck, shaking all over from head to toe. But I didn't feel anything in particular, as if I discovered I was a member of the royal family every day. Twice on the weekends, even: once before lunch and once after.

Shock. It should have been a shock.

Curses! I'm the grandnephew of Emperor Clement! And though I'd never manage to extract any preference from that, there was one factor that made that valuable.

Blood is thicker than water!

"Tea's ready!" the shop owner said, interrupting my contemplation.

I walked over to the counter and drank down the hot tannic beverage. I didn't add any sugar; I'm not sure why, but I didn't want anything sweet.

I wanted vodka. And that was on a purely genetic level – I had never drunk vodka in my life as, it should be said, I had never tried any other alcoholic beverages. My dad set me an example that inspired a healthy aversion to such excesses. Also, my *illustrious talent* necessitated that I maintain a certain degree of self-control. Even sober, it made leprechauns.

"Is something bothering you, Leopold Borisovich?" Alexander Dyak asked.

"My day's been going all wrong!" I laughed, hiding my nervousness with laughter.

"Would you like some mint in your tea?" the inventor suggested.

"No, thank you."

"Then feel free to take an oatmeal cookie."

I followed that advice and returned to the counter with a mug of tea. The rain wouldn't quiet down for anything. From time to time, lightning flashed and the windows shook from strong blasts of thunder.

"I guess I won't keep distracting you, then," I sighed. "Are the incendiary rounds ready yet?"

Alexander Dyak faltered self-consciously.

"You see, Leopold Borisovich," he said with downcast eyes, "your theory about transmitting signals got me so off track that I completely forgot about everything else, and focused my efforts entirely on that. But I do have five grenades ready right now."

"Reproaching you for that would be base ingratitude, Alexander!" I called back, realizing that without my armored car, getting the handheld mortar to my estate would be an affair that was not only burdensome, but also fraught with utterly unnecessary legal issues. "I've put too much on your shoulders as it is! You're already forgetting about the shop!"

"If I'm getting paid for interesting work, why not?" the inventor said with a philosophical shrug of his shoulders.

"I don't pay you that much."

"That's neither here nor there. In this weather, there won't be any customers anyway."

"That's true," I nodded, looking at the street and shivering from the cold.

What did I care about customers? Finding a cab now, that was my mission!

Alexander Dyak went into the back room and quickly returned with a small canvas bag.

"The grenades," he said, setting the bag on the table with a respectable metallic clang.

"Great!" I put on my coat, no less wet than before, hid the bag of incendiary rounds under it and asked: "Alexander, if your theory is correct and *the fallen* were destroyed by electromagnetic waves, then what secret would the people involved in that find most frightening?"

"The very fact that electromagnetic radiation has an effect on *the fallen*," the inventor answered simply. "And if you delve into the details, the wavelength optimal for affecting otherworldly creatures. Finding it experimentally would be very, very difficult."

"But possible?"

"Yes," the shop owner confirmed. "Do you think they consider the contents of the signal important? If I knew the right frequencies, with a bit of fine tuning, I could capture a signal and rebroadcast it."

"Perhaps, in their mind, the secret is the design of an oscillator of such great power," I guessed.

"It could be anything," said the inventor, throwing up his hands. "One can't very well climb into another person's head without knowing a damn thing about them."

I nodded. I couldn't climb into the Duke of Arabia's head.

Why had he entrusted such an important secret to his lover? I suspected that the Dowager

Empress didn't want to give up influence. Or maybe, he simply wanted to provide a decent existence to an out-of-wedlock child.

What moved him? I didn't know.

And I didn't guess. I squeezed Alexander's hand farewell and went out in the rain.

As I had supposed, catching a cab in the torrential downpour was impossible. There were steam trams, though, splashing up water from deep puddles as they rolled over wet rails.

I rode a steam tram up to Dürer-Platz and started walking up Calvary, leaning heavily on my cane. Dirty streams carried cloudy water down from the hill, but the ditches were still not overflowing, and the road was clear. However, the worst was yet to come.

Holding tight on the incendiary grenade bag under my coat, I stepped out to meet the sharp gusts of wind and cold, dreaming of taking a hot bath or, at the very least, crawling into a warm and dry bed. Conspiracies and riddles were now of little concern to me, I was worried only about crossing paths with Lazarus. That fear was making me nervously look around and fitfully grab at the incendiary device in my coat pocket.

I didn't have much hope for the grenade under the torrential rain, but when the dark figure of a sopping person stepped out of the bushes by the bridge, that was what I grabbed for. It was the wrong choice, though. The Cerberus would have been better...

"Drop it!" ordered a Chinese man, holding me in the sights of a sawed-off double-barreled twelve-gage hunting shotgun. Mr. Chan's henchman had wooden poles tied to his shot-through leg, and was leaning on a crutch.

I hesitated for a second, then threw the incendiary grenade down in the ditch and watched the aluminum cylinder quickly drown in viscous muck.

"Well then, white-eyes, are you happy?" the cutthroat faded into a malevolent smile.

"Easy with the trigger," I asked him. "The fund is mine, now I can pay my debts."

"I don't give a damn!" the cutthroat laughed. "Mr. Chan has already written off your debts, white-eyes. It will be a good lesson for the others!"

"You won't get away with murdering an *illustrious* gentleman!"

"The only ones here are you and me!"

"Yeah, but you won't be able to keep your mouth shut!"

The cutthroat didn't answer, just stuck the butt of his sawed-off into his shoulder in silence, but didn't have time to shoot. Through the sound of the wind and rain, there came the familiar crackling of a powder engine. Then, I saw the roof of an armored police carriage flicker by down below. The self-propelled carriage crawled slowly down the road, obscured by bushes, but soon came out in the open after rounding a bend.

"How are you gonna run from the cops with only one good leg?" I chuckled with untold relief.

"Get over here!" The Chinese man demanded. "Say one word and I shoot!"

But, before I had time to carry out the cutthroat's demand, the leprechaun pipsqueak, deftly and quickly spinning his arms and legs like a circus monkey, climbed up onto the Chinese man's back and plunged a kitchen knife into his neck with all his might.

The sawed-off boomed out twice. The shot blasted a clod of dirt from under my foot, and Mr. Chan's henchman fell lifeless into the ditch. The leprechaun jumped down from his back and calmly wiped the knife on the sleeve of his badly soiled frock coat.

"Cool, right?" he asked with a grin, vanishing into the shrubbery, disappearing from view instantly.

"Curses!" I cried.

There was a dead Chinese man with his throat slit, and a police armored carriage coming up the hill. To make matters worse, it was just me and no witnesses other than my imaginary friend.

Was he even a friend? More like pain in the ass!

After throwing the grenade bag on the side of the road, I hobbled over to the corpse and, in that there wasn't time to hide the body in the bushes, grabbed the dead body under the armpits and dragged it to the bridge.

The phrase "feed stray animals" flickered in my head, as I pushed the Chinese man over the edge and sent him tumbling into the water below.

There, I fed them! From down below, there came a plunk and a confused roar.

I didn't wait by the bridge, just went off in search of the incendiary grenade bag. Relief rolled over me with a pleasant relaxation and, when the police armored car started slowing down, I didn't assign that fact any meaning, just covered my eyes with my hand to block the bright headlights coming around the bend.

"Everything's fine!" I shouted to the constable on his way out of the passenger seat in a waterproof cloak. "I'm just heading home!"

The police man nodded and suddenly threw up a short crossbow. The string twanged and a wooden bar with iron pins and wires slammed painfully into my chest. A moment later, I was pierced through from head to toe by a powerful electric shock, like I had been struck by lightning!

Well, I wish it were lighting...

4

I WOKE UP in the back of the armored vehicle with a jolting pain in my numb muscles.

My head was splitting devilishly. My throat was very dried out. I couldn't move my arms or legs at all. Curses! Even my fingers wouldn't move. It felt like they had been tied down with ropes. My eyes were covered by a thick blindfold. There was a gag stuck in my mouth.

"Why such attention to detail?" I thought, trying to loosen the straps, but I soon suffered another blow to the temples from something substantial and fell unconscious yet again.

I was carried out of the vehicle on a stretcher. I could have gotten out myself, I just wasn't asked.

Where they brought me, I couldn't tell, but something told me that this was not just some mere kidnapping and that we were now arriving to the Newton-Markt. There was something particular in the air; familiar smells and sounds.

And I didn't even know whether to be glad about that or not. No matter how I spun it, I had committed lots of sins recently, enough for a hanging and a lifetime of work camp thrown in to boot. That dirigible explosion, how many people had died in that? I was defending myself, sure, but that would have to be proved.

In the cell, I was finally unlatched from the stretcher, moved to a table, had my arms and legs cuffed, and at chest level, had a thick belt tied around my back. I was immediately reminded of the electric chair, but in the end, managed to put on a calm demeanor, filled with chilly rage.

"Leave us!" demanded Inspector General von Nalz.

I heard the sound of footsteps. The door slammed shut. Then the blindfold was torn from my eyes and the gag was yanked from my mouth.

I moved my jaw, stretching the cramped muscles, looked at the Inspector General and joked gloomily:

"It seems this is becoming something of a

tradition..."

"Silence!" Friedrich von Nalz shouted out sharply, slamming his hand on the table. "Where is my daughter, you scoundrel?!"

"You couldn't think up a better pretext to bring me in?" I asked in a stupor.

"Silence!" the old man barked again, and the transparent flame filling him spilled over, lashing out at me with its impossible heat, bringing to mind Jimmy, baked from the inside.

Friedrich von Nalz was capable of frying a person without any curses or black magic, but what had scared me even a week earlier, had now lost all meaning.

"Where is my daughter?" the inspector general demanded an answer, and somehow instantly I was left without even the slightest doubt of his sincerity.

I just squeezed out:

"Has something happened to Elizabeth-Maria? Is she alright?!"

"You're asking me?!" the Inspector General balked in rage.

"Yes, I am!" I frowned, feeling annoyed, and in some measure, squeamish. "Please explain the reason for my arrest! My second arrest in a week, just imagine! And yet, not one person has apologized! I'm getting the impression this isn't a police department, but a coven of lunatics!"

The old man was fast. I didn't even manage to blink before he hit me with a forceful slap. I tasted blood.

"Blown off your steam?" I asked after

that. "Can we talk now?"

"No!" the Inspector General barked.

"You haven't blown off your steam, or we can't talk?"

Friedrich von Nalz took a heavy sigh, then turned away as if my damaged face was unpleasant to him, and suddenly rasped out:

"Is something the matter with you, Viscount?"

"So, it's Viscount now!" I snorted, at an impasse after the unexpected question. "I guess I graduated from scoundrel pretty quick..."

"There are plenty of scoundrel viscounts about," the inspector general cut me off, barely able to resist hitting me again. "What is this game you've conceived?"

"That I conceived?" My surprise had no end. "You stunned me with electricity and dragged me down here! I didn't ask for that!"

"Are you trying to say you've done nothing wrong?"

"I'm trying to say that it would be nice to hear some charges for starters!" I growled back.

Friedrich von Nalz waved his hand wearily:

"Drop the act, Viscount. You know perfectly well what this is about."

"As for now, I understand only that your daughter has disappeared. Where you got the suspicion of my guilt remains a mystery."

"Is that so?"

"Yes, indeed."

"You don't think we'll find any clues against you?"

"I would never do anything to harm Elizabeth-Maria," I answered with utter sincerity, even though my words now sounded slightly out of place.

"Youth is characterized by thoughtlessness. Young people often don't think about the consequences of their actions."

I closed my eyes, thought over what I'd heard, then asked:

"Are you accusing me of having ties with your daughter? Do you think she ran away with me, not wanting to marry a man she didn't love? Utter nonsense! If that were the case, we would be together, don't you think?"

"Perhaps you already got what you wanted from her."

"What do you think I could get from her?" I blurted out without thinking, and immediately caught another severe blow. "Curses! I could have gotten by without that quite well!"

"Enough of the comedy! Answer the questions!"

"Let's calm down," I suggested, gathering my thoughts. "You're supposing you can find out from me where Elizabeth-Maria is. Let's say I do have access to that information. Let's say that, before I make a deal, I want to figure out what proof you have of my guilt. Put my back up against the wall and I'll start working with the investigation right away but, first, I'd like you to explain what the devil is going on here!"

I shouted out the last words as loud as possible, and the face of the inspector general instantly filled with bad blood. He could barely hold back. It seemed he really had been counting on getting this information from me.

"In the end, it could save us a significant amount of time," I said, now totally calm.

Friedrich von Nalz crunched his bony fingers and warned me:

"You will not leave this cell alive," he said calmly, "if you do not tell me where my daughter is. I would be happy to sacrifice my career to get her back, if need be."

"What happened?" I asked.

"Enough!"

"Friedrich," I sighed, "you must understand that these accusations against me do not stand up to criticism. Otherwise, you wouldn't be here. These kinds of interrogations are normally done by detectives, after all. Remember what you said about Elizabeth-Maria's taste! Do you really think she'd suddenly think me a suitable partner? I cannot possibly compare with the minister of justice's nephew, right?"

The inspector general frowned, took a seat at the table and got out a cigarette case that contained pills instead of cigarettes.

"For my heart," he said, tossing one down his throat. "Everything's all mixed up, Viscount. The situation has flown directly into the depths of hell. But if you give me my daughter back, I'll try to forget about personal slights."

"Get to the point," I demanded. "What happened? Just the facts."

"Did you read about the robbery of the Dürer

factory a few weeks ago?"

"Yes, I read about it."

"In the interest of security, the patent documents containing the formula and production process for duralumin were transferred to the Baron's urban manor."

"And?"

"They were stolen."

"So, why am I here? I wasn't at Dürer's reception. I am understanding correctly that the theft occurred at yesterday's dinner party, right?"

"But Elizabeth-Maria was there!" the inspector general clenched his fists. "You told her to use her *talent* to convince the Baron to unlock the safe!"

"Complete nonsense!" I shot back, unable to restrain myself. "In that case, I'd have already left the country!"

"The storm upset all your plans, Viscount."

"And I was dumb enough to go back home?"

"You thought no one would connect you with the crime. Your second error."

"And my first?"

"My daughter isn't wretched enough to convince a person to kill himself. The Baron's attempt to take his own life was unsuccessful."

"Nonsense!" I muttered. "This is all just complete nonsense! And so, where is Elizabeth-Maria?"

"That's what I want you to tell me!"

"Alright, alright," I repeated a few times. "Elizabeth-Maria has the *talent* of convincing, but how could I convince her to commit such a dastardly crime? I don't have such a *talent*!"

"She thought you were fun. You made her head spin."

"Me?"

The inspector general looked at my rumpled countenance, overly angular and big-nosed, moved his gaze to my mud-caked clothing and sighed:

"I'd never have though so, but we have evidence to the contrary."

"Evidence!" I laughed with unhidden sarcasm. "Naturally, you must have some incontrovertible evidence! How could I forget!"

"That's exactly right," Friedrich von Nalz moved up to me and blew with a fierce fire. "You wouldn't have known, but Elizabeth-Maria kept a diary. She wrote all her doubts and hesitations in it. When searching her room, I found her notes and immediately put out a warrant for your arrest. Your third error, Viscount!"

"Nonsense," I sighed, the tips of my fingers going numb in terror.

I couldn't understand what was going on. I just did not understand.

Elizabeth-Maria, love, a diary, the patent theft...

None of it could be true! These were the stuff of my dreams!

I forced myself to calm down and asked:

"Is my name mentioned in the diary?"

"Unambiguously."

"And Elizabeth-Maria wrote that she loved

me?"

"Yes."

"Hard to believe," I snorted. The inspector general said nothing in reply, so I asked him: "You're sure it's her handwriting?"

"Beyond all doubt."

"May I have a look?"

"To what end?"

"I won't believe it until I've seen it with my own eyes."

"Do you think I'm bluffing?" Friedrich von Nalz smiled bitterly and took a swollen notebook from his pocket with a purple cover and a broken little silver lock. "Well, have a look!"

The inspector general held up his daughter's diary to my face and opened it to the right page.

The story started at the spring ball where I read Elizabeth-Maria a poem written by Albert Brandt. The romance developed quickly, we saw one another almost every day. After meeting at the hippodrome, we spent our first evening together. I told her my criminal intentions on our next encounter at the circus. Elizabeth-Maria agreed. We were then supposed to flee to Zuid-India.

The most sorrowful fact was that the handwriting in all the entries, whether made a year ago, or the day before yesterday, was exactly the same. Elizabeth-Maria had written it, but what the devil for? What ghoulish game was she playing? Who had told her to do this?

"None of this is true," I said directly.

"You didn't meet with my daughter?"

"I saw her in the city a couple of times," I admitted, "but we never spent much time together. We usually didn't even talk."

"This says otherwise."

Refuting a blatant lie is simplicity itself. Half-truths are much more insidious. Elizabeth-Maria and I did talk, and dozens of random witnesses could attest to that. So, how could I now prove that I hadn't incited her to crime? How could I prove it...?

"Stop!" I gasped, visited by an unexpected thought. "Go back a page!"

"Hippodrome," "walk around town," "all evening he didn't let go of my hand..."

"A-ha!" I sighed loudly. "I have an alibi!"

"Is that so?" Friedrich von Nalz started at me in disbelief, tucking the diary back in his pocket. "Regardless of what happened, I believe my daughter incomparably more than any of your witnesses!"

"Even if they are the head of the CID and senior inspector of Department Three? You yourself know they have no lost love for me!" I smirked. "And another investigator and five or so random constables? Which is to say nothing of the plainclothes officers working surveillance?"

"What are you talking about, Viscount?"

"The entry from the twelfth of April. I was at the hippodrome at the same time as your daughter, but I didn't talk with her. Right after the races, I went to the raising of the armored car from the Yarden, the one from the Witstein Banking House robbery. It was the twelfth! We started at four and were there until nearly five or six in the evening. Then, the surveillance officers saw me walking into Levinson's house. The exact time is written in the report. I'm no devil. I cannot be in two places at the same time! And the circus! After the circus, I had a talk with Senior Inspector Moran on the burglary of my uncle's estate! He'll tell you the same!"

The inspector general stared at me and percolated:

"If this is some kind of ploy..."

"Ask LeBrun, ask Moran. Bring out the report from my last arrest. There's no time to waste, I beg you!"

Friedrich von Nalz left the chamber in silence, and I was left alone with my unhappy thoughts. One thing, at least, made me glad, though. Lazarus would definitely not be catching up with me today.

TO THE INSPECTOR GENERAL'S credit, he did end up apologizing. His apology was dry and brief, but the fact remained. He didn't relegate the unpleasant business to a subordinate. And it would have all ended on a good note, but near the end, the ghastly old man came up right close to me and whispered:

"If you are involved in this, I'll burn you alive with no court or evidence," he warned, then afterward said out loud in an official tone: "Viscount, Senior Inspector Moran would like to see you."

That didn't make me any happier, but I

didn't show it. I just nodded and, rubbing my raw wrists demonstratively, headed for the exit.

A patrolman instantly blocked my path.

"What now?" I grew surprised.

"First, talk with Moran," the inspector general reminded me and left the room.

I shrugged my shoulders and grudgingly took a seat, secretly hoping that I wouldn't be in shackles by the end of my talk with the senior inspector.

Bastian Moran appeared five minutes later. He looked at me with a smirk, then asked the wardens to leave us alone and took out a pack of cigarettes.

"The inspector general warned me that you were an extremely elusive young man," he said, lighting a cigarette. "It's always nice to hear that a superior shares your point of view."

"Very funny!" I grimaced. "Two arrests for contrived reasons in one week is obvious overshot, don't you think?"

"For contrived reasons?" the senior inspector warped his peaked brow in astonishment. "You should not have said that!"

"Just don't tell me I'm going back through the wringer!" I threw up my hands. "It has been formally established that Levinson and his family were killed by Procrustes!"

Bastian Moran sat on the edge of the table and shook the narrow little tip of his lacquered ankle-boots in the air.

"I am not here to talk about Levinson," he suddenly announced. "We're talking about the theft of the duralumin patents."

"For goodness sake!" I groaned. "Did you not just confirm my alibi?"

"That is precisely what's got me worried," the inspector general admitted. "Quite the fortunate coincidence, isn't it? Elizabeth-Maria writes about clandestine meetings with you, but every time, the entries are easily refuted by undeniably reliable and neutral witnesses. A surprising coincidence."

"Not every time," I objected, "only on two occasions."

"And that is enough."

"You're accusing me of intentionally attracting suspicion? Why the devil would I want to do that?"

"You're vain," Bastian Moran reminded. "You thirst for societal attention. Having the whole metropolitan police wrapped around your finger and gaining notoriety – would that not be reason enough to bear certain inconveniences?"

I rubbed my bruised chest.

"Have you ever been electrocuted, senior inspector? If you had, I strongly doubt you'd be calling it a mere inconvenience! What's more, if I had stolen the secret patents on the aluminum alloy, I'd have been on my way to the continent long ago!"

"The storm. It's impossible to predict bad weather."

"Oh, come off it!"

"Alright, we'll drop the topic," Bastian Moran agreed, tapping his ash onto the floor. "By the way, speaking of flying. Today, your uncle's dirigible, *Syracuse*, met with an accident. On the site of the crash, we discovered the personal effects and documents of the Count Kósice."

"What are you trying to say?" I asked, shaking my head. "You'd do well to consider your earlier statement: one cannot predict bad weather!"

"There's a lot of strange circumstances surrounding the accident, Viscount," the senior inspector said, looking me penetratingly in the eyes. "Could you tell me where you were at four o'clock this afternoon?"

I turned away, pitying the fact my glasses had been confiscated, then laughed quietly:

"If you're hinting at my involvement in that unfortunate event, I'm afraid I have to disappoint you. My uncle and I resolved our conflict."

"Yes, I saw the documents we confiscated on your arrest," Bastian Moran nodded. "When did you receive them?"

"Between three and four this afternoon, in the office of the Count's attorney. I didn't see my uncle there."

"And you're not worried for his fate?"

"I am indifferent to it. Though we smoothed over our conflict, our personal feelings remain complicated. I tend to hold grudges, you know."

"Is there anyone who could back up your story?"

"Only my uncle's attorney, Maître LaSalle. His secretary wasn't working today."

"The maître gave him the day off," the senior

inspector confirmed.

"If you've already spoken with the maître, what the devil are these interrogations for?" I objected with righteous indignation. "I'm getting the feeling that you're just running up the clock!"

"Nothing of the sort," Bastian Moran shook his head and threw out the cigarette butt in the far corner of the room. "At around four this afternoon, there was a fire in the office of Maître Lasalle. Four people died."

"That's horrible!" I said, hunching up my shoulders with no acting. It really did make me feel out of sorts.

"The bodies were very badly burnt. It's made identifying them complicated, but it is thought that one of the dead is your uncle, the Count Kósice, and a second is the maître himself."

"A grizzly death."

"Oh no, Viscount," Bastian Moran shook his head. "The maître and one of the unidentified corpses had been shot. The coroner's assistant found signs of trauma on the back of the Count's head. It was split. The last dead man had been strangled. There is evidence of shooting everywhere."

"I don't understand this at all!"

"And that was approximately the same time the dirigible had an accident."

"Are you suggesting this was no mere coincidence?"

The senior inspector didn't answer, just stared at me stubbornly and continued:

"And also, on the neighboring street, we

discovered the body of a man by the name of Samuel Borto, a bounty hunter. He had been shot in the back. A ten-caliber bullet was removed from his corpse."

"Where are you going with this?" I asked, getting on edge.

"When you were detained, a Cerberus was confiscated from you with one chamber empty, Viscount. I see a definite connection between these two facts."

"That connection seems pretty thin to me."

"And the holster?"

"What about the holster?"

"The holster on your belt was empty when you were arrested. Meanwhile, a Roth-Steyr pistol was discovered in the burnt office."

"It's all quite simple," I smiled, at ease. "I wanted to buy a new pistol, but couldn't find anything at a reasonable price. I turned in my service Roth-Steyr, don't you remember?"

"Then for what reason were you carrying a full clip of eight-millimeter rounds?"

"As I said, I was looking to buy a new eight-millimeter pistol! What kind of spendthrift do you take me for?"

"It's all very suspicious, that's all."

"Am I being charged with anything?"

"Not yet," the senior inspector smiled calmly. "But I don't think this will be the end. I'm firmly convinced you were there. Only a person as elusive, yet short-sighted as you could have jumped from roof to roof, running from a dirigible-mounted machine gun."

"What are you saying?" I asked, gaping in false surprise. "What machine gun?"

"Where were you at four o'clock this afternoon, Viscount?"

"Walking home!" I flared up. "Have you ever tried catching a cab in this weather? I have! It's a deadly endeavor!"

I wasn't at all afraid to be caught in my lies. If I'd gone straight from maître's, I'd still have gotten to Calvary at about the same time, if not later.

But my words did nothing to convince Bastian Moran. The senior inspector was looking at me like he saw through all my tricks, and walked back to the door.

"One last question, Viscount," he said as he turned. "Do you know why your uncle would have wanted to hire twenty mercenaries?"

"Senior inspector, you have the habit of asking me questions I don't have the answer to."

"Is that so?"

I got up from the chair and confirmed:

"That's right. But you're asking the right questions. My uncle can't seriously have been so afraid of me that he felt it necessary to bear such expenses. Good mercenaries usually cost a lot. Either he was working on an illegal scheme, or had a reason to expect an attack."

Bastian Moran nodded.

"You're free to go, Viscount," he said, and walked out the door.

I immediately ran after him.

"Senior inspector!" I shouted, jumping out

into the hallway. "What about my things?"

One of the patrolmen answered instead of Moran.

"Let's go," he said, calling me after him. "You'll get everything back."

I was awaited in the CID evidence room by a familiar detective sergeant with a red mustache and yellow eyes. He took the ledger from a folder, asked me to familiarize myself with it, then started setting one piece after the other on the counter. My knife, lighter, wallet, bank notes and coins, sugar drop tin, dark glasses, inheritance documents, Cerberus with an extra cartridge containing two rounds, an untouched cartridge with silver bullets, an empty holster, a Roth-Steyr clip, my cane and a photograph with the elegant signature, "Emile..."

I stuck the photograph nervously into the inner pocket of my jacket. The detective sergeant didn't pay that any mind and demanded:

"If this is all correct, write that you have no grievances and sign."

So I did. Then, I quickly redistributed my effects in my pockets and shot out of the Newton-Markt like a bat out of hell. I practically leapt into the courtyard, divided from the street by its colonnaded portico, and stuck my face out into the water coming down from above.

It had eased up, but not by much.

The unexpected discovery that I was related to the Imperial family, the attack of Lazarus and the disappearance of Elizabeth-Maria without a trace had torn my tormented soul to bits, and my head was just spinning.

What is happening? And why am I precisely at the center of all this devilry?

And most importantly: why had Elizabeth-Maria slandered me? Stoking my own ego, I could call her journal entries the inoffensive fantasies of a girl vexed by an unwanted marriage, but the fact of her participation in the secret patent theft did not fit into this scheme at all.

She can't seriously have been deflecting suspicion from someone else, right?

Who would that even be?

And just then, I felt as if struck by lightning.

Albert Brandt! The *talented* and charming Don Juan, who was with me at all the alleged unexpected meetings with Elizabeth-Maria. Beyond that, he wrote her a poem. When I considered how easily he tended to get carried away, and his bitter split with Kira, I realized he easily could have transferred his feelings onto a new object.

The mystery girl! So, he was talking about the daughter of Friedrich von Nalz all along, just trying not to upset my relationship with him?

My pace started quickening, and I even would have started running if my thoughts hadn't returned to the strange robbery of Baron Dürer. Why the devil would the poet want the duralumin patent? He had never been caught up in illegal stuff before!

Money? Did Albert really need money that badly? Or was he simply intending to run away with my lady love?

My lady love?!

A sharp pain pierced my heart. I took a step back and even leaned on a marble column of the portico. My eyes grew dark. The world grew gray. The sound of rain was replaced by an eerie ringing. Shame and resentment swept through my head. I wanted to kill someone.

Someone? Oh no! I wanted to kill Albert!

I held his friendship dear, but I could never forgive such treachery. I couldn't kill him, either though. My arm simply wouldn't raise to harm him. And how could I ever live with such a heavy weight on my soul after that? Only a bullet in the forehead...

But I didn't want to die at all. I wanted to live. I wanted it more than ever.

I exchanged the spent round in the Cerberus magazine with a silver bullet, and headed to the Greek Quarter. The chance of catching Albert in the *Charming Bacchante* wasn't great, but storms really could upset any plan. I had to look him in the eyes and decide how to act from then on.

I just had to, and that was that.

5

THE *CHARMING BACCHANTE* was packed to the rafters. There wasn't a single open table. All around, the audience members were hunkering down, taking shelter from the storm. I ordered a cup of coffee, gulped it down, threw a few coins on the bar and walked up to the second story.

His apartment door was not locked. Albert was standing before a mirror getting dressed and preparing to make an appearance.

"Greetings!" I squeezed from myself against my own will. "Are you alone?"

"Oh, Leo!" The poet grew joyful. "You've come at the perfect time! Let's go to the thermae!"

His warm reception threw me off. I hesitated and couldn't make up my mind to say the words still burning me from the inside.

In the end, I might have been wrong. It might have just been a coincidence. Such things were known to happen, after all.

Perhaps, but I didn't believe in them.

I felt quite sure, yet I didn't want make a scene. Was my sheepishness leading me astray, or had good sense awoken? I do not even know...

"To the thermae?" I asked, just expressing my surprise at the poet's unexpected suggestion and throwing my derby hat over the billiard ball lying on the shelf. "But why?"

"Oh, it's a fantastic story." Albert laughed. "Do you know where I spent last night and most of the day? You'll never guess! Behind bars! Can you imagine?"

"What did you do this time?"

"That's the thing, I didn't do anything! During yesterday's reception at Baron Dürer's, someone opened the safe and all the guests were searched like hardened criminals. Inconceivable! And then we were... what did they call it? *Isolated* while they conducted preliminary interrogations!"

I forced a smile.

"But there's also a good thing there, no? Your mystery girl was forced to give up the incognito."

The poet tied on his neckerchief and turned away from the mirror.

"Fortunately, she left the reception before the police arrived," he said. "But if only you could have seen what a furor my veiled lady made among the guests."

I pressed my hand to my unbearably aching heart, and Albert wondered compassionately:

"Leo, is everything in order with you?"

"It's nothing. Just the end of a stressful day."

"So, shall we go to the thermae?"

"Let's go," I nodded. "Just take a cloak. It's dog's weather out there."

"Well, naturally!"

Albert took his long cloak from the hanger; we walked into the hallway and went to down to the first floor.

"Curses!" I swore out. "My derby hat! I forgot it at your place!"

The poet handed me his keys thoughtlessly.

"Run!" he allowed. "I'll send someone out after a cab while you go."

I ran back up to the second floor in an instant, unlocked the apartment and lit the candles on the desk. Albert had the custom of keeping his work drafts in the top drawer of his desk, so I broke it open first of all.

On top, there was an unfinished draft of

Inhabitant of the Night. It was of no interest to me, but after that, I discovered sheets of writing paper covered with sketches of a fine female figure. A narrow waist, a high chest, and curvy thighs. Her alluring body was sprawled out in luxury. Sprawled out on this very couch!

I started shaking, but just after I turned over the sheet, my eyes went totally cloudy. A woman's face was looking up at me from the page. It wasn't as expertly done as Charles's drawings, but still easily recognizable.

The face staring back of me was that of Elizabeth-Maria.

My Elizabeth-Maria! The succubus, and not the daughter of the inspector general!

There couldn't be the slightest doubt.

My legs gave out. I fell back in the chair, reached out for a decanter and poured myself a glass of water with my hands shaking. I drained the glass greedily and tried to gather my thoughts.

Albert wasn't playing any games, that was obvious now. The overly impressionable poet had simply succumbed to the unnatural charm of the succubus. He was not involved in the theft of the patent, or the mysterious disappearance of the inspector general's daughter. He hadn't attempted to send the police down a false trail, or done anything wrong at all, with the exception of falling in love with the wrong woman.

But then me... I had believed in his guilt all too easily, and that burned fiercer than red-hot iron.

I threw the papers on the table, broke open one drawer, another, and a third. I rifled through their contents, then took a bottle of rum from the cupboard, threw open the window and broke it with the bottle so the glass would fall inside. I tossed the bottle outside and quickly left the apartment, not forgetting to grab the derby hat I'd thrown on the floor.

Someone just broke in, that was all.

But in my soul I felt uncommonly vile. Getting involved with a succubus had yet to lead anyone to anything good; I'd have to save the poet.

When I was back down on the first floor, Albert was drinking wine at the bar and admiring the half-naked beauties prancing about on stage. The poet didn't pay the slightest attention to my delay; he'd always been inspired by the sight of fine female legs regardless of whether he was in love with someone or not.

And even with my delay, we still had to wait at least another quarter hour for the cab.

"The most prudent are waiting in the neighboring taverns for the end of the show and are about to take the audience for triple normal prices," Albert told me with a smirk after we'd gotten into a covered carriage and were rolling down the rain-slicked alleys of the Greek Quarter.

The cabby, who smelled robustly of wine, was pretending not to have heard the acrid remark, and didn't intervene on behalf of his colleagues' honor. But perhaps, he really just didn't hear. He was pecking with his nose here and there, giving a shake and wiping the rain off his face, only to repeat the procedure all over again.

For some reason, that observation put the poet into a state of indescribable elation. He was overjoyed and started stacking one tall tale on top of the other. He couldn't even stop joking around in the thermae, where he, thankfully, was a familiar face. For that reason, we were let inside without having to wait in the huge line that started all the way back on the veranda of the huge public bath building built in Ancient Greek style. The idea of warming our bones in such bad weather hadn't been quite as unique as we'd supposed.

In the spacious vestibule, it was so crowded you couldn't move. There was a nimble little boy ducking around there with a stack of papers, shaking an evening edition of the *Capital Times*.

"Mysterious happenings!" he shouted over the din. "Bodies disappearing from the city morgue! Police stumped! Storm coming over the city! Port closed!"

Albert bought a paper, but didn't read it. He turned it over and stuck it in his cloak pocket. After choking by the crowded concession area, we headed directly to the changing room. We left our clothes in a locker there, wrapped ourselves in togas and walked into the steamy room. The hot air enshrouded me from all sides. A moist heat came down, chasing away the dank cold outside. I was forced to calm down and forget all my problems and cares.

But I didn't manage to cast the weighty thoughts from my mind. One thing was certain: I didn't know how to tell my friend that his beloved was a succubus.

We set up on some hot stones near the entrance, where the air was comparatively mild in temperature; I was drinking lemonade, and Albert was nipping at a goblet of wine. The wisps of steam enshrouded us, hid the other visitors, and muddied the speech, turning all the conversations around us into one uninterrupted din. I normally felt out of my element in the thermae and was careful to have my robe covering all my tattoos, but today, that worry took the back seat. I had to tell my friend everything, but couldn't find the right words.

"You know what, Leo?!" the poet suddenly asked. "I decided to shake off the dust and head off on a trip. Spring in Paris, summer in London, fall in Persia or the New World, and return to New Babylon in the winter. It would be a truly marvelous voyage!"

I nodded and inquired carefully:

"And how does the lady of your heart feel about that?"

Albert laughed carelessly:

"She supported me whole-heartedly! She'll be free in the next few days and we'll fly out of this smoky cesspool like birds from a cage – to freedom. Just her and me. Don't you get upset though. I'll send you postcards."

"How very sweet of you," I smiled sourly.

The succubus was intending to be free in the next few days? Considering that only death could separate us, that was a bit disheartening.

"The chestnuts in bloom on Montmartre!" said Albert, staring dreamily at the ceiling, his hands behind his head. "The foggy London nights! I know such places there, you'd be surprised! We'll be happy and carefree."

And my tongue just couldn't turn to dash these dreams. I got cold feet. I was afraid of hurting my friend. I decided to wait for the situation to resolve itself.

It was surprising, but no matter how well I knew others' fears, it was beyond me to overcome my own. Cowardice is like an invisible brand one can never be rid of.

But I could no longer bear looking at the poet's serene face, so I decided to bring him to his senses at least a bit.

"Albert, old friend," I said, unable to hold back an acrid snicker, "are you sure you'll be allowed to travel to the continent? Didn't you just spend the night in the police station?"

The poet just waved it off:

"Do you think I was the only one thrown into a cell?" He sat on the stones, leaning his back on the warm wall. "Everyone was checked. Distinguished guests were released earlier. Staff and invited artists only after lunch. I actually got off easy, Leo! I'm considered trustworthy!"

"Well, well," I smiled with half of my mouth. "Did the investigators not have any questions for the lady of your heart?"

"I'm telling you: she left me long before the theft."

"And you yourself didn't notice anything suspicious at the reception?"

Albert tilted his head to the side:

"Why are you asking, Leo?"

"Discounting my normal worldly curiosity?" I shrugged my shoulders, "I'm feeling moved by professional instinct. Don't forget that, for a private investigator, to solve such a prominent case is the same as drawing a winning lottery ticket."

"Procrustes wasn't enough for you?"

"I already spent the reward from that to the last franc. By the way, you might congratulate me. Certain things have happened with my inheritance. I'll soon be living high on the horse."

"On twenty thousand francs a year?" Albert asked incredulously, his mood now lighter. "Some socialites have been known to drop that much on cards in one night!"

"Money begets money," I smiled, again filling my glass with lemonade. "If I make a bundle, I'll buy you a couple of first class steamer tickets to Lisbon."

"Dirigible tickets," the poet corrected me. "We'll be traveling in style!"

"As you say. So then, was there nothing suspicious?"

Albert finished his wine, fell deep into thought, but soon waved a hand:

"What the devil, Leo? Do I look like a detective to you? I didn't see anything suspicious.

At the beginning, I was concentrated on wooing my lady, and after that, I was slaking the bitterness of parting with wine. Nearer the end, I went on stage and stunned all the buffoons who performed before me with my *talent*. Sorry, Leo, I wasn't really paying attention."

I had no doubt in the poet's sincerity, so I just sighed. Somehow unnoticed, the conversation shifted to the arrival of Tesla and Edison, then we discussed the bad weather. When we drifted into politics, though, Albert finished his wine and stood decisively to his feet.

"I think it's time to go home," he told me. "I have an important meeting tomorrow morning."

"Is that so?"

"Yes, I'm going to buy a traveling outfit for my little bunny."

I turned away, covering up a morbid grimace and adjusting my toga.

"What are you talking about?" Albert got on guard, having noticed a dissatisfied air pass over my face. "Is something the matter?"

"The life of a private investigator is not sweet," I frowned. "Have you ever been electrocuted?"

"You know, somehow I've managed to avoid it."

"It's extremely unpleasant. That much I can tell you, old friend."

"I'll take your word," the poet laughed. He then asked: "But, is everything alright?"

"Yes! Of course! It's just that one of my former colleagues has expressed a bit too much zeal."

We headed to the changing room, and Albert whistled when he saw the huge bruise on my chest; the electrode-laden bolt shot out by the crossbow had kicked my ribcage almost as hard as a rogue stallion kicking a ranger.

"You've come into quite a noble inheritance, my friend!" the poet shook his head.

"You're telling me," I sighed, getting dressed. "Shall we take a cab?"

"Were you planning on walking in this weather?"

I shrugged my shoulders and felt for my wallet, but Albert stopped me.

"Let me tell you a secret, Leo," he said, cocking his eye. "Today, on my way out of the Newton-Markt, I went to a publisher and collected my fee for the publishing rights to the poem about you-know-who."

"Congrats," I snorted. "Surprising, even."

"What exactly do you find surprising?"

"That such naive publishers could possibly exist. Paying such a fee as an advance is basically the same as chaining a poet to a barrel of wine! Throwing money to the wind! And I'm not even talking now about their unassuming taste."

Albert trained his pointer finger at me and declared:

"That is all envy talking, old buddy."

"Truth hurts, doesn't it?"

"Look who's talking!"

Trading insults, we left the thermae and sent a boy, who'd been dawdling around nearby, after a free cab. The cab drivers here fancied a certain tavern on the opposite side of the square and were drinking grog, warm and dry, having abandoned their carriages under the pouring rain.

"Just make sure to get a covered one!" Albert shouted after the boy. He then turned to me and asked: "What are your plans for tonight?"

"Weren't you about to go to sleep?" I asked in surprise.

"Sleep isn't such a fundamental concern."

I shook my head:

"If I go with you, it will be. So, I'm going home."

"As you say."

A carriage drove up to us with its top raised. We loaded ourselves into it and rolled away from the thermae. On Dürer-Platz, I left the poet and started up Calvary, nervously glancing from side to side. My hand was clenched around the handle of the Cerberus in my pocket, but time and time again, when I saw an impenetrable darkness in the rain, or a lightning strike blasted the tower on top of the hill, my heart started racing and my soul wanted to jump out of my skin.

I was afraid. Very afraid. There was Lazarus and the Convent with him, Mr. Chan and his helpers and the *illustrious* gentlemen with their police infiltrator. They were all trying to murder me. There was no negotiating, either. It was either them or me.

That was precisely why I spent a good ten minutes looking in the dark wet grass along the roadside for the bag of incendiary grenades I'd left there. In the end, I did scare up the canvas sack, but the fifth grenade, which I'd thrown in the ditch, was nowhere to be found.

Alas.

So then, the bag strap over my shoulder, I hurried home. I undid the latch and walked through the dead garden, all black and wet, up to the manor, which greeted me with a warm light from all the first-story windows.

Bewildered at the waste of electricity – what had Elizabeth-Maria managed to think up now? – I got up on the veranda, walked into the entryway and locked the door. I set my bag on the floor, then sat down on an ottoman and held my face in my hands, not knowing how I could frame the upcoming conversation with the succubus. I wanted to go on a rampage, but the bonds that held us placed certain restrictions.

I couldn't kill the girl, no matter how much I wanted to.

With a fated sigh, I pulled off my wet jacket, put it on the hanger and headed off in search of the succubus. But as soon as I entered the hallway, I immediately ran into my butler.

And Theodor was just lying there, looking lifelessly at the ceiling with glassy eyes. He was dead.

I immediately pulled my Cerberus from my pocket and froze, tensely listening to the silence of my empty manor. My first urge was to jump for the bag of incendiary grenades, but I overcame it and stayed still.

There were no wounds on the butler's body, no bullet holes, no crimson drops of blood, so it seemed a most doubtful proposition that my servant had been done in by Lazarus. But at that, I was reminded of Albert's assertion that his flame intended to obtain her long-awaited freedom in the very nearest future, going with him to the continent.

Was this just Elizabeth-Maria playing some new game? What if she was looking for a way to get out of the oath that bound us?

That thought forced me to shiver uncomfortably, and I first slipped into the guest room. But no, my grandfather's saber was still hanging over the fireplace, right where it should have been.

Squeezing the Cerberus to my chest in order not to have it torn from my hands, I popped into the dining room. There was no one there either. In the silence of the empty house, I heard rolls of thunder blasting out. Every time, the window panes started shaking, and I got the sense that there was raging battle underway not particularly far away. That didn't help my already fraying nerves.

Finally confounded, I headed into the kitchen and froze in the doorway like I was interred. Elizabeth-Maria was lying on the floor, her face pale as chalk and her lips turned blue. The girl's arms and legs were convulsing. Her eyes were rolled back so far that her pupils were nowhere to be seen.

The hair on the back of my head stood on

end in horror. Whoever had been fighting with my servant and houseguest, they were such an expert at their craft that he had managed to kill a living corpse and overpower a succubus, and now they were waiting for me...

Run!

I took a step back, jumped into the hallway and tore into the entryway. With the corner of my eye, I caught a blurry motion in the doors of the library. I spun in place, throwing up my pistol and suddenly, not really comprehending how, found myself on the floor.

My head was spinning. Everything before my eyes was swimming, and the Cerberus lying not far from my outstretched hand looked like nothing more than a blurry dot. Not able to feel my own body, I tried to reach for it, but couldn't. Just then, a pair of lacquered ankle-boots came into my field of view, covered in blotches of dried mud.

The uninvited guest slid my pistol away with a careless movement of his foot and said calmly:

"You're now experiencing a weak semblance of a stroke, Viscount. Nothing to worry about. Yet."

I tried to get up, but the pain shooting from the left side of my chest was so forceful that all I could do was collapse back onto the floor and limply press my cheek to the cold parquet.

"And that heart," the voice repeated, still cracking like an old man's. "The heart is a surprising muscle, I can tell you that! It pumps blood for days on end with no break, day in, day out, month after month. A lifetime. It gets tired, of course. And some have natural defects. Incurable even, like her highness's."

"Go to hell!" I exhaled, trying to get up on all fours, but my left arm just gave out, and I was turned over onto my back with a careless poke of his shoe.

"The heart grows tired, Viscount," the old man towering over me repeated, gray-haired and wrinkled. "Do you not think yours might have already run its course?"

I looked at the *illustrious* gentleman's colorless eyes and shook my head.

"That's right!" he laughed. "That's just my tricks, my *talent*. Viscount, one small clot is enough to paralyze you until the end of the day, so I beg of you – don't do anything stupid."

The pain started to gradually recede. My heart stopped skipping beats. My ability to move my arms and legs came back.

I crawled away from the *illustrious* gentleman, leaning my back against the wall and asking, not especially careful in my expressions:

"What the devil do you want? The box? Well, I don't have it!"

"Viscount, don't play games with me. It's rather a bad idea," the old man demanded. I recognized him as one of the men who had tied me up to the electric chair. "And don't hope for the manor's curse to protect you. The Diabolic Plague can't hurt me."

"What do you want?" I repeated.

"The book!"

"What book are you talking about?"

I felt like my heart was in a steel vice. The pain left me dumbfounded and, for a moment, I simply lost control over my own body. That gave the *illustrious* man enough time to bow down over me, rifle through my pockets and take the torn photograph.

"I need the book this girl is holding," the old man announced.

"That is my mother," I sighed hoarsely.

"All the worse for you, Viscount," the old man frowned. "Otherwise, I wouldn't have come here."

"What do you need the book for?"

"You're in no position to be asking questions."

"But, all the same?"

The old man removed his jacket and hung it on the door handle; pulled massive golden cuff links from his expensive dress shirt and started unhurriedly rolling back the sleeves.

"Give me the book," he suggested, "and I'll spare your girlfriend's life."

"Not mine?"

"Oh no! The only way for your life to be saved, is if you act stubborn. Unfortunately for you, though, a blood vessel will burst in your head, and you will be left paralyzed to spend the rest of your days in a beggar's hospital. I'll even come by once or twice a week to ask you if you want to end your suffering. In exchange for the book, naturally. So, why complicate things?"

"A curious perspective," I muttered. "Am I to

assume you've already searched the library?"

"I didn't find anything that looked right," the *illustrious* man admitted. "Where is it?"

I grabbed the doorjamb, and exerted a good bit of effort getting to my feet before I peeked into the library. There was not a single book on the shelves. They were all lying on the floor, arranged into uneven stacks.

"You checked them all?" I asked, guessing how exactly the *illustrious* gentleman had gone about the search knowing nothing at all about the book he intended to find.

"Yes," confirmed the old man.

"Then, let's go!" I called to him, stepping away from the wall. The old man took a deft step back.

"Drop the knife!" he demanded.

I cursed out silently, took out my titanium blade and threw it on the floor.

"After you!" the *illustrious* man ordered, removing his jacket from the door handle. "And no stupid stuff!"

We got over to the stairs, went up to the third floor, and I suffered another heart attack in the hallway. While I endured the convulsions, the old man went first into the bedroom, looked around and went back.

"It isn't here!" he said, accusing me of lying with unhidden rage. "There aren't any books in this room at all!"

"Well, of course there aren't!" I rasped out, getting up from my knees. "This is where I keep my magnifying glass, idiot!"

"And what of it?"

"For want of money," I winced, massaging my chest with my hand, "I had to sell off parts of my library to booksellers. Who got which book is something only I remember. So, be a bit more careful with your *talent*. And, if you think it will be enough to simply find out the name, let me tell you something – different editions of the same book may not be the exact same. And the pagination is certain to be different!"

The old man's transparent, light eyes started glowing with a fell fire, but he held back from another burst of torture and just pointed at the door:

"Please go!"

I went into the bedroom, sat at the desk and tried to open its top drawer, but my arm suddenly went slack like a limp lash. The old man himself opened it, took out the magnifying glass and set about taking a closer look at the photo.

"I can't make out a thing!" he announced.

"Old age is no blessing," I snorted back.

"Not everyone lives to see it," the *illustrious* man parried.

The allusion was as transparent as they come. I demanded:

"Give it to me."

I took the photo and magnifier, looked close and suddenly, by some inspiration, guessed what book my mom had been holding in her hands.

I didn't hesitate, even for a moment. I quickly stuck the yellowed photo in my mouth and started chewing, trying to tear up the thick paper with my teeth, or better yet swallow it, leaving the *illustrious* man playing the fool.

But I couldn't. My eyes clouded over, I slid off the chair and thudded onto the floor. The old man took a seat next to me and, without particular ceremony, pried open my jaw with the blade of a pen knife. After removing the bespittled wad from my mouth, he smoothed it out and threw it with annoyance into the far corner.

"Why did you do that, Viscount?" the *illustrious* man asked, vexed and pacing the room nervously.

My stun slightly retreated, and I rasped out:

"You'll never figure it out without me..."

"Oh, come off it!" he replied dismissively. "You didn't even have the whole number!" And he added with unhidden superiority: "But I do!"

I tore my head from the floor, looked closely and discovered with unhidden surprise that the *illustrious* gentleman had somehow acquired a copy not only of my photo, but also of the piece my uncle had torn off.

"You don't have the book!" I then squeezed out, trying to get up from the floor.

"Is that so?" the old man snorted, picking up the copy of *Alice's Adventures in Wonderland* the leprechaun had left on the chair. "It seems to me I have everything I need."

The old man took a seat in the armchair, laid both photographs on the wide armrest and started leafing through my mother's favorite book, writing down something in his notebook as he did.

"You are a very self-assured young man, Viscount," he muttered to himself in passing, "you clearly took after your grandfather. Emile was known for his flighty nature. His head was always in the clouds, always scheming. He made a good foil to his brother, but was worth nothing on his own. He was an unremarkable personage inclined toward poorly-thought-out adventurism."

I carefully filled my lungs with air and allowed myself an uncomfortable question:

"Then why are you all so concerned with the secrets of this supposed non-entity?"

"Non-entity? Nothing of the sort," the old man objected. "He was a decent person in his own way. The life of the party, and a favorite with the ladies. He wasn't talentless. He was just short-sighted. He was a masterful card player, but he never knew how to think out his play too far in advance. And that was his ruin."

"He did a great job hiding his secret, then."

"This isn't his secret!" the *illustrious* man suddenly barked back. "This is our secret. Our shared secret! Emile blackmailed us, pulled us into his worthless intrigues, and put us in the line of fire! We have lived all the last years with an ax hanging over our necks, but now is when it all ends! Now is when it all ends!"

It all ends? I was afraid that might have been true.

What a shame. Not even one drop of me wanted to die.

"He must have had you by the nuts," I laughed, wanting to at least somewhat distract the *illustrious* man and draw out my time, but he suddenly shot up from the chair and stared at the writing in his notebook in confusion.

"This cannot be!" he whispered, now white as chalk. "This simply cannot be! Unfathomable!"

The old man walked over to the table, poured himself some water from the decanter, drank it and paced the room, rubbing his sweaty face with a kerchief.

"This cannot be!" the *illustrious* man insisted stubbornly, visibly aging before my very eyes. "Damned half-wit!" he cursed out, rifling through the pockets of the jacket left on the bed. He got a box of matches from it and started the photo on fire. "Burn in hell, Emile! Burn in hell!"

The gaze of the *illustrious* man's colorless eyes fixated on me and, not wanting to go out on my knees, I got up from the floor and leaned heavily on the back of the chair, not strong enough to take a single step. The old man held his empty hand out with an unpleasant smile and balled it up into a fist. I shuddered, expecting trenchant pain, but no – this time, it came on slowly, letting me feel every little prick, every spark.

"Emile orchestrated all this for nothing," the *illustrious* man exhaled. He now looked just a little better than me.

And I looked obviously unwell. My eyes grew dark. My legs started giving out, and I had to grab onto the back of the chair in order not to fall back down onto all fours. The figure of the leprechaun appeared in the doorway. He looked at me with incomprehension, made a "screw loose" gesture and hid from view.

"The heart," stated the old man. "Your heart is no longer beating, Viscount."

And silence came over the room. All sounds died out. The patter of rain on the roof, the rolling thunder, the rustling of branches on the blinds and the shuddering of the window panes.

The sounds died out but, looking at the *illustrious* man's uncomprehending face, I suddenly realized that the strange flood of silence had also caught him.

"Isn't *your* heart wearing out, too?" I whispered out and in one, perhaps my last, breath said: "Just look at yourself – pale, sweaty, panting, elevated heart rate. Are you afraid of dying from a heart attack? Dying before you get what you're after?"

The old man was afraid. I didn't even have to kindle his fear with my *talent* in earnest. Just his very deep disappointment was enough. The *illustrious* man fell to his knees, then slowly moved forward and collapsed face-first on the floor.

A new convulsion shook through me. My chest was pierced with pain. Unlike the earlier attacks, I got the sensation that my heart was being turned inside out and, all the same, after an unthinkably long pause, it started beating again, sending blood coursing through my veins.

But the sounds of the surrounding world

still hadn't returned. I could only make out muffled strikes from outside and a strange crackling.

I looked out the window and immediately decided I was going insane. There were black shadows climbing over the fence one after the other.

I saw a silent flash of lightning, breaking up the darkness of the night and, only then was I able to make out the intruders. From head to toe, their unnaturally gaunt bodies were wrapped tightly in blackened bandages.

Mummies, seriously?!

I couldn't be sure, but I had a pretty good idea why these ghastly restless souls had appeared at my estate.

Curses! Lazarus had come for my soul!

A banging on the front door forced me to cast off my consternation. By that time, the mummies running from the fence had already bounded through the dead garden and were beginning to climb up the walls, but the windows of the first floor were affixed with iron grates, and the second floor had been empty for many years, the windows shuttered behind sturdy blinds.

Not losing time, I slammed the blinds shut and started running toward the front door. I ran up to the stairs and almost fell down them after running into the leprechaun as he dragged a weighty box of some kind up to the attic. I jumped past, then realized that the pipsqueak had been hauling the hand-grenade box from the carriage-house. But I didn't go after him, just ran down to the first floor.

Strange as it may seem, Theodor had already come back around and was wiping off his dusty frock with incomprehension.

"Viscount?" he stuttered at my appearance.

"Get your gun!" I snapped. "We're under attack!"

I then jumped into the entryway, braced a cupboard against the door, grabbed a canvas bag of incendiary grenades and ran into the kitchen. Elizabeth-Maria was convulsing on the floor as before; I bent down next to her and tried to find some hidden fear to stoke in the girl's mind. I knew she had a fear of helplessness and being completely dependent on another's will, for example.

Then, I simply laid into her with a slap to the cheek straight from the shoulder.

"Hey, wake up! Wake up!"

Elizabeth-Maria winced several times, and her transparent watery eyes lit up with a dim glow.

I commanded:

"Follow me!" And ran into the carriage-house through the door from inside the house.

"What is happening?" the girl shouted, having chased me into the hallway. "What games are you playing?!"

"There's been an attack!" I replied, throwing open the box containing the hand-held Madsen machine-gun, then loading the weighty, cumbersome object on my shoulder. "Don't forget rounds! And pistols!"

"Why the devil do we need all that?" Elizabeth-Maria snarled.

"Faster!"

Elizabeth-Maria's eyes flickered in rage, but she didn't smart off. She stuck both of the pre-loaded Mausers into the ammo-bag next to the machine-gun magazines, and grabbed the semi-automatic carbine with fixed magazine.

"Are you satisfied?"

"Run!"

We went back in the house and, just then, somewhere up above, heard the sound of glass breaking and a muted crashing.

"The blinds!" I gasped, having just realized that my bedroom wasn't the only occupied area on the third floor – Elizabeth-Maria slept there as well. "Did you close your blinds?"

"Why on earth would I have done that?" the girl asked in surprise.

"Devilry!" The mummies were in the house. My whole defense plan was scuttled on the rocks!

The pounding at the front door was growing sharper and clearer, but now, there was a threat coming at us from the upper floors as well.

"To the guest room!" I decided and ran down the hallway, hunching under the weight of the hand-held machine gun.

As I ran, I simply didn't notice a black figure. It appeared from out of nowhere, wrapped in dark bandages and holding its unnaturally gaunt arms in front of itself. But before it got to me, it was sent flying backward with its head blown off. Elizabeth-Maria had hit it with the semi-automatic carbine with such force that the stock broke to pieces. Ruddy blood spattered on the walls, and the hallway filled with the smell of rotten meat.

A second mummy jumped past its defeated comrade and ran at the girl, who'd lost her balance after the powerful bash. But the succubus managed to stay standing and slammed the barrel of the rifle into the puffy eye of the undead creature with a blistering lunge. And when the restless soul grabbed the foregrip with both hands, it didn't move the weapon away, it instead just pulled the trigger.

A muffled shot rang out, and the back of the mummy's head flew off.

"Faster!" I hurried the girl on, jumping over the corpse with a busted head and hurrying into the guest room. Elizabeth-Maria threw away the ruined carbine and ran after me.

A third mummy charged at us from the stairs just as a deafening shot blasted out from the side hallway. The buckshot knocked the horrifying creature off its feet; it was still down on all fours when Theodor came right up close, aimed the double-barreled hunting shotgun at its bandaged face and pulled the trigger. The undead man's head was torn to pieces. Meanwhile, my butler cracked the hunting shotgun in two and took a pair of new shells from his frock pocket, as if he were just hunting woodcocks.

"Theodor!" I snapped. "Follow me!"

I jumped into the guest room, laid out the tripod and set the machine gun near the door.

From there, I had a line of fire on the whole entryway and hallway leading into it. I took the ammo bag from Elizabeth-Maria and popped a mag into the gun with trembling hands.

"Hold the second door!" I ordered my companions.

The girl quickly took the saber down from the wall, unfazed as if she were death itself. My butler was standing opposite the passage with his gun in his hands. I heard quick footsteps. Theodor braced the stock of his double-barrel on his shoulder and shot once, twice, then quickly stepped aside for the succubus.

The mummy that ran in impaled itself on the saber, losing all its speed at once. Another strike, this time relaxed and from the side, easily split its head wide open.

Soon after, our head start lost all significance; the front door flew off its hinges, and an avalanche of black figures flooded into the room. By then, an extra magazine already loaded, I was sitting spread-eagled behind the machine gun. I immediately opened fire in distinct, two-to-three-bullet bursts.

The gun shook. The stock was kicking me painfully in the shoulder. Casings were flying around the floor as I confidently shot down the undead pouring in from outside. The bullets mangled the bodies. Their watery blood splattered everywhere. Chunks of rotting flesh flew, and yet the mummies just kept coming.

After again changing out the mag, I followed my butler's example and started aiming for their heads. The barrel was recoiling, causing the bullets to go higher and higher, but when I hit my target, the bullet easily went through several bodies. The corridor became a meat grinder; the attack of the living dead had suffered a setback.

I risked pulling away from the machine gun, and saw with relief that Theodor and Elizabeth-Maria had driven back the attack; the girl was wiping the saber on the arm-chair cover. My butler placed his remaining four shells on the fireplace shelf and reloaded his double-barrel. The room was full of wisps of gun smoke. There were blood spatters coloring everything a ruddy shade and lopped-off appendages lying about. In the doorway, there were quite a few mutilated mummies just piled up.

"It's never a bore with you, Leo!" Elizabeth-Maria laughed. "You have a surprising talent for making new friends!"

I couldn't find a good answer, but then an explosion rang out from outside and I no longer cared for mental exercises.

I jumped over to the window and was blown away: while the mummies had our attention, a whole horde of undead wrapped in non-matching rags had come into the yard through the open gates. These restless souls weren't as fast or deft, but their eyes were glowing with a transparent fire all the same. And there were many of them. Too many.

A whole army was walking through the garden. At least fifty.

Before my eyes, a grenade fell into the

crowd, thrown from up above. I heard an explosion. Five mummies were thrown back in a wave. The others were struck with fragments. But it wasn't enough to stop Lazarus' horde of filth.

"Hold the doors!" I cried to my companions. I jumped over to the machine gun and gasped after grabbing it by the barrel. With a curse, my arm shot back from the red-hot steel. I took it by the grip and pulled the gun over to the window, set out the tripod and opened fire on the dead walking through my garden.

My bursts mowed down the restless souls. One after the other, another three grenades plopped down. When the mummies started getting up close to the house, I stuck a hand out the grate with an incendiary grenade of my own. I wound up and threw the aluminum cylinder far from my manor.

A white flame gushed forth. Dozens of the undead caught fire, and immediately picked up their pace, now moving too quickly and sharply to be normal dead. I cast a second incendiary grenade in their direction and got on the machine gun.

The leprechaun was supporting me from the roof. Theodor walked back from the door to the window, unloading the double-barrel in a business-like fashion on the mummies, who were now up on the veranda. The buckshot knocked them off their feet, but before the butler reloaded, a few of the restless souls managed to come inside.

I cursed out to myself and threw a third

incendiary white-phosphorus grenade outside. The spark of white flame dispersed the corpses hobbling toward the front door, and Elizabeth-Maria noted calmly:

"That's the last of them."

Then, I armed myself with the Mausers, one pistol in each hand and commanded:

"Follow me!" and went out into the hallway.

The four ambling mummies who'd made it in started off in my direction, but I didn't even slow my pace, just threw up my pistols and opened fire with both hands, aiming at their heads. The clumsy corpses were great targets at short distance even for a relatively unrefined shot such as myself, so clearing out the corridor was a matter of just a few moments. Then, we jumped outside.

I went first with a Mauser and incendiary grenade, then Theodor armed with the double-barrel and finally Elizabeth-Maria, covered head to toe in blood.

It was quite the ugly spectacle. There were motionless bodies lying all around the yard. It smelled unbearably of burnt flesh. Many of the once restless dead were badly burned by the incendiary grenades and cut to pieces. I felt sick.

"Looks like somebody raided the morgue!" Elizabeth-Maria decided, looking all around. "And this was all for our sake? Quite flattering, really!"

"Not so much for our sake as mine," I corrected the succubus. And I wasn't bragging, just stating the facts. Lazarus wanted me and no one else.

"We need to check everything here," Theodor said wearily. "Some might still be alive."

"Not very likely," I said with a shake of my head. I put the last incendiary grenade into the ammo bag hanging around my neck. Lazarus had fled. He'd fled and wouldn't hesitate to repeat his attempt. That scared me.

But suddenly, I heard a raspy voice from the roof:

"Uh... hey!"

I threw up my head, looking at the leprechaun, and a moment later, Lazarus jumped out of the darkness. He simply wove himself out of the shadows of the rainy evening and would have surely been breaking my neck if Elizabeth-Maria weren't in his way. With a skillful twist of the saber, she met the vampire with a powerful side strike and, an instant later, flew away, knocked off her feet by a no-less-forceful jab.

Throwing up my Mauser, I started turning toward the vampire. But before I managed to shoot, the pistol was ripped from my hands. Lazarus missed me, and Theodor shot twice, blasting the vampire a few steps backward.

After grabbing an incendiary grenade out of the ammo bag, I lobbed it at the blood sucker and tried to lay into him with my *illustrious talent*, but Lazarus didn't even notice my attempts to control his mind. With a sharp, calculating kick, he knocked the aluminum cylinder away; the incendiary bomb somersaulted in the air, fell into the dead black bushes and spilled out a blinding white phosphorus explosion.

My last incendiary grenade burnt up for nothing!

The horribly burned countenance of the vampire twisted into a self-satisfied smile. Frightening stigmata on his cheek were bursting and streaming with ichor.

"Payback time!" Lazarus creaked out as he walked forward, knocking Elizabeth-Maria from her feet with a careless motion before she could stand up. "We have the whole night ahead of us, *illustrious* one!"

I took a step back in fear, and Theodor, opposite me, took a step forward and even managed to swing the unloaded double-barrel before the vampire hit him with a powerful blow, fracturing his chest with his bare hand and pulling out his heart to the crack of his ribs.

"Oh, how I adore this!" he snarled out, clenching his fist. Next, he bit into the heart with his teeth and pulled a fair chunk out of it. "You, though, won't get away so easily!"

On Lazarus' disfigured face, there was a mixture of his own blood mixed with Theodor's. It was hardly even a face anymore, having now transformed into a demonic mask. His nails had grown sharper, and a great many razor-sharp needle fangs were poking out from under his lips, disfigured by the fire.

I took a step back, feverishly searching my consciousness for a fear appropriate to the situation. And although my *illustrious talent* was capable of turning the long-rotted heart of the living dead into a piece of fresh meat dripping with blood, no man can truly scare that which is pining away impatiently to disembowel him and strangle him with his own intestines.

And that is precisely what Lazarus wanted to do to me. After flinging Theodor's heart aside, he stepped toward me and, blinded by hate, didn't notice the white-haired pipsqueak appear behind him. In the space of an instant, the leprechaun hopped over to Lazarus, tucked a mud-caked aluminum cylinder under his belt and swiftly ran away to a safe distance.

Lazarus shot up like he'd been stung by a bee and stuck his hand in in his pants, but before he managed to pull the incendiary grenade out, the detonator activated and the white phosphorus blew violently. The powerful blast tore the vampire in two. The searing flame enveloped him head to toe, burning through his skin, muscles and flesh to the very bone. There was almost nothing left of him.

And suddenly, the blanket of silence enveloping my manor and dividing it from the rest of the world started thinning. Thunder rolled over again and the wind started whistling.

"Bugger, it's windy!" the leprechaun gave an admiring whistle, watching the dying bloodsucker convulse. "Went up like a firework, that one!"

I caught my breath with untold relief and asked:

"Did you pull that out of the ditch?"

"I wasn't gonna let it go to waste,

bugger!" the pipsqueak declared proudly and hid inside.

I was left alone in the yard. First of all, I picked up the pistol that had been ripped out of my hands and walked over to the garden filled with piles of corpses. The garden was black and wet. It had bald patches where bushes had burned and wood chips from broken trees, but signs of life – or afterlife? – were nowhere to be found.

All the corpses, carelessly wrapped in dirty rags in the manner of Egyptian mummies were spread-eagled on the earth motionless. In places, I saw livor mortis spots peeking out from under their bands; apparently, Lazarus hadn't been too discerning when selecting his army of the dead.

I walked through the garden to the wide-open gates, closed them and returned to the manor, not knowing what to do first: check the house or help my maimed companions. And was it really worth helping Elizabeth-Maria?

She was still alive; Lazarus' masterful attack had damaged her trachea and spine, but the succubus could still follow me with her gaze.

"It's for the best," I decided, but then Elizabeth-Maria got up on an elbow, wheezed and grabbed me by the arm.

"What the devil was that?!" she gasped out hoarsely.

"A vampire," I answered with some disappointment.

"Unbelievable!" Elizabeth-Maria croaked, letting me go and lying down on her back. The girl's chest was heaving rapidly, as if she couldn't catch her breath.

I left her, stuck my Mauser into the empty sack, found Theodor's heart with clear marks from Lazarus' teeth, and stuck it back in his torn-up chest. There wasn't any real necessity, but it seemed the right thing to do.

I closed my eyes and restored the living image of my servant in my memory. I didn't manage to even get near his fears before Theodor's chest gave a shudder under my hand and my fingers picked up a feverish heartbeat. My butler returned to life. He wasn't resurrected, he just stopped being finally and irrevocably dead.

"Thank you, Viscount," he whispered.

I opened my eyes and saw with surprise that there was a gray patch in Theodor's thick hair, and his face had grown noticeably older and sickly, as if two deaths in one day had robbed him of a good portion of his life force.

"Leo!" Elizabeth-Maria shouted back to me, unraveling the bandages from the nearest corpse's head. She was looking with fastidious curiosity at a symbol carved in the middle of its forehead.

I came up close, took a look and immediately felt nauseous.

"Black magic?" I supposed, turning away.

"Black as it comes," the girl confirmed. "Though, that's actually fortunate."

"How so?" I asked in surprise.

"Leo!" Elizabeth-Maria looked over her

shoulder. "Tell me, where were you preparing to store fifty rotting corpses? We'd simply never fit that many into the icehouse!"

"We'll have to take them out of town."

"No, we won't," the girl said, shaking her head. "These charms squeezed the dead dry. In the sun, they'll just smolder to ash."

"In the sun?" I laughed, wiping my face, smearing the dirt and drops of rain around it. "There's a storm brewing!"

"Doesn't matter," Elizabeth-Maria waved it off. "After a few days under open skies, all that will be left of them is bones."

I nodded, taking it into account.

"I'm more worried about the vampire," I said after that. "Do you think he'll come back to life?"

"I've never come up against anyone from that brotherhood before," the girl answered, walking over to the burnt remains of Lazarus and asking: "How'd you get him to burn?"

"I have my ways," I winced. "So, should we worry about him or not?"

The girl looked at the corpse and shook her head:

"It seems to me you did him in."

"Great!" I grew joyful and shouted to my butler: "Theodor! Drag the corpses outside, would you!" After that I called Elizabeth-Maria: "Let's go inside."

"Aren't you going to help Theodor with the bodies?" the succubus asked, confused, as we got to the stairs and started up to the third floor.

"There's another body up here I have to drag

down to the icehouse," I said and led the girl to the bedroom where the dead *illustrious* gentleman was lying. The old man was frozen in an unnatural pose. His feverishly clenched fingers were squeezing the edges of the rug.

"I remember him!" Elizabeth-Maria jumped up. "This is the old guy, who showed up before I started feeling bad!"

"That was his *talent*," I explained, and fell into the armchair without any strength left. I felt something under me and pulled the *illustrious* man's notebook out. In mute silence, I then stared at the uneven letters, reading their unbelievable words:

"Loy and Coe, Zurich. Ten million francs in bearer deposits. To be claimed by..."

PART THREE
DEMON

High-Voltage Shocks and Morse Code

1

G REED IS BAD. The sin of money-making is unbefitting of a noble person. There's no happiness in money, at the end of the day.

I knew that. I knew it, but I couldn't tear my gaze from the three scant lines.

"Loy and Coe, Zurich. Ten million francs in bearer deposits. To be claimed by..."

And what was there to be claimed? What did I have to send to the bank to get this pile of money? Also, considering the years of interest, how much might it have been now? Curses! Not even all African colonies can boast of such a yearly income!

This was riches! True riches, and they belonged to me by birthright!

But the old man didn't write anything further. He got up to where the picture was ripped, then lit and burned the copy of the encoded message.

And that caused me unbearable spiritual torment.

The *illustrious* gentleman was counting on finding traces of the materials the Duke of Arabia had once used to blackmail them, but instead of that, he found a rainy-day nest egg. The old man's money was of no interest to him, but it had clearly driven my uncle to utter madness.

The Count Kósice had bet on that card and lost. I wouldn't like to meet the same fate as him, but I couldn't forget about the ten million francs either. It was just eating me up inside.

Ten million! Ten million, devil take me!

I stood from the armchair, stuck the notebook in the back pocket of my pants and walked up to the desk where the pieces of burnt photo were lying. It hadn't burned all the way but, no matter how closely I stared, I couldn't make out a single digit.

"Leo!" Elizabeth-Maria shouted in surprise. "Are you going to help with the body?"

"One second," I called back, smoothing out the remnants of the photos.

It suddenly occurred to me that these copies were still slightly damp, as if they had been printed just a few hours earlier.

As if? Not at all, that was it!

And that could have only one explanation: the piece of the photograph my uncle had kept was found on the site of the dirigible crash. And beyond that – the robbers' accomplice from the Newton-Markt not only had access to the ponderous evidence, he had also been able to copy the photographs confiscated from me on my arrest.

"Leo!" Elizabeth-Maria frowned. "I'm getting the impression you're not being totally honest with me, dear."

Anger rolled over me in a prickly wave. I turned to the girl, and she immediately took a step back from the ill reflection of my eyes.

"What about you?" I asked in reply.

"We all have our secrets, beloved," the succubus smiled carelessly, masking a feeling of confusion, or perhaps also fear.

"Albert Brandt!" I suddenly declared in reply

to her chest-thumping.

Elizabeth-Maria pretended she was thinking.

"The poet?" she contorted a brow after a short pause.

"You've been meeting with him!" I exclaimed. "Behind my back!"

"Did he tell you that?"

"Don't try to fool me! I worked it all out on my own!"

The girl twirled a lock of her red hair around a finger, then laughed carelessly.

"And what of it?" she asked.

"We had an agreement!"

"Leo, my sweet!" Elizabeth-Maria took a step toward me and led her mud and blood caked fingers over my cheek. "Our agreement is extremely simple. I don't hunt for people, that is my end of the bargain."

"So, leave Albert alone!"

"We have a relationship," the girl answered calmly. "What does that matter to you?"

"Don't try to play word games with me!"

"I wasn't using my... special powers," Elizabeth-Maria announced, "and I didn't break our agreement. Albert and I like spending time together, what's the harm in that?"

"Nonsense!"

"So, you're getting jealous, Leo!" the succubus laughed uncontrollably. "I just can't figure out who exactly you're jealous of, him or me?"

"I don't want you to drag his soul to hell!"

"Our relationship has nothing to do with

you!" the girl cut me off. "You upset all my attempts to make an agreement, and I am not preparing to stay in this house just to play the unwanted servant girl."

"Find someone else!"

"I don't want anyone else. Want me to leave Albert alone? Then you'll have to work to defeat me. If you can do it, I'll forget all other men then and there."

Such unabashed blackmail enraged me. I took a step toward the girl, intending to grab her by the neck and squeeze, but instead, I fell to my knees with the fierce pain that suddenly struck inside my head.

"Leo, my Leo!" Elizabeth-Maria shook her head. "We cannot harm one another. Such is our agreement. And don't be afraid, I won't do wrong by your poet. We really do just have fun together. He's fun."

I buried my forehead in the floor, clenched my teeth, and waited for the pain to subside. Then I demanded:

"Leave him alone."

"I'd never dream of it."

"Leave him!"

The girl came up closer, grabbed me by the chin and raised my head.

"You can only ask. Do you want to beat me on Albert's terms? Let's see how good you are in bed."

I threw back my hand, understanding perfectly that it was just a scheme to make me and the poet fight.

"No?" Elizabeth-Maria laughed hoarsely as she walked away from me. She then squeezed out contemptuously: "Weakling!"

Letting the insult go unnoticed, I got up from the floor and flopped into bed in exhaustion. And when the succubus went for the exit, I asked:

"So, you say you weren't using charms?"

"That's right," the girl answered, throwing open the door and only then catching the hidden meaning in my words. "Do you mean to tell Albert about my true nature?" she asked, now facing me again.

"You're missing one fairly important thing."

"And what might that be?"

I tapped my finger on my temple.

"Elizabeth-Maria is entirely in my head. Entirely! To the last hair!"

The girl stared at me gloomily, then shook her head and announced:

"You are not capable of changing my appearance! That is not one of your powers!"

"That's right," I confirmed, falling onto my back. "Your image is too bright. Sometimes, I even think you and I have known each other for many years. In fact, it's as if I've known you my whole life."

"Where are you going with this, Leo?" Elizabeth-Maria got on guard.

"People do tend to change with time though," I answered, closing my eyes. "Your body is mortal. What will it look like in two decades?"

"No!"

I got up and looked at the girl.

"I've known you for many years. Many long years..."

"No!" Elizabeth-Maria exclaimed as she ran toward me, but then she was struck with an attack of fierce pain. Now, her muscles were tied in a knot, and her body was shaking in an unbearable fit.

I waited for her to come back to her senses, then smiled ruthlessly:

"If memory serves, Albert never did like ladies past a certain age."

"No!" the girl exhaled again, rubbing out her cheek with her fingers to find it had now lost its formerly taught surface. Her skin, now covered in a web of the finest wrinkles, dried up once and for all. "No!" Elizabeth-Maria shouted out and ran away. A moment later, thunder rang out, the door to her bedroom slamming shut.

I just shrugged my shoulders. My imagination had treated Elizabeth-Maria fairly mercifully. Now, she looked like a ripe lady, just over forty years of age. But for the girl, it was a crushing blow.

And what a shock this would be to Albert!

For a moment, I even felt slightly bad for my unlucky friend. But he'd survive another breakup, even if it would be hard on him. The poet never did get used to splitting with girlfriends.

With a fateful sigh, I grabbed the old man by the legs and dragged him out of the room. On the stairs, the back of his head slapped against every step with an unpleasant thud, but it no longer mattered to me; I was too tired. After leaving the corpse by the hatch to the basement, I found Theodor and ordered him to bring it down to the icehouse.

The manor was gradually becoming a burial ground.

I didn't have dinner. The slaughter had completely destroyed my appetite, and the strong smell of corpses caused profound nausea.

Fortunately, on the third floor, the smell of dead flesh wasn't quite so strong; I locked the bedroom door, set my knife and pistols on the bedside table, then checked the blinds and fell powerless onto the bed. I recovered my breath and picked up the old man's jacket which had been lying there all that time. Beyond unremarkable baubles, in one of his pockets I discovered a wallet. And in the wallet, there were business cards. His business cards.

The *illustrious* man was named William Mathew. The name was unfamiliar to me, but the phrase "judge emeritus" was a clear indication that this was an important person, and his disappearance would surely be noticed. There would be people looking for him; not only his *illustrious* co-conspirators, but also his relatives.

"We need to get rid of the bodies!" I decided, stashing the dead man's money in my wallet. I put back a photograph of two twins, a boy and a girl in modern clothing, then wiped off my fingerprints and threw the wallet on top of his jacket on the floor.

No part of this caused me any real emotions

whatsoever. It wasn't me that killed the old man; his past did him in. He lived many years in fear of being uncovered, but would have died his own death surrounded by relatives and friends, if he had not decided to try and trick fate.

The *illustrious* man's fortune was of little concern to me; the ten million francs in the Swiss deposit box was all I could think about. It was burning my soul. Possessing such a grandiose fortune without being able to use it – is that not the greatest torture you could imagine for an honest person?

I cursed aloud, put out the gas lamps and went to sleep with a feeling of extreme pessimism.

MY MOOD was no better in the morning, either. I laid in bed for a long time, listening to the rustling in the empty manor, then reached for the bedside table and looked at my timepiece.

It was nine forty-five.

I should have been up long ago, but when I remembered yesterday's events, I suddenly wanted to wrap up under the comforter and hunker down in the hope that the hardships would just pass me by.

Baloney! I shouldn't be acting like a caricatural ostrich with my head stuck in the sand. If I didn't get myself together and deal with these troubles right away, an avalanche of problems would entomb me in and pull me down so low I'd reach the very bottom. Straight to the underworld.

And first thing I had to do was get rid of the *illustrious* man's body. The disappearance of a retired judge was not the kind of event that went unnoticed. The police might even come to my quarantined estate if they thought I had him. All it would take is one anonymous tip. And I should not be doubting that it would soon follow: the old man's co-conspirators certainly knew where he was headed before he disappeared.

But if the body turned up in some canal without signs of a violent death, there wouldn't be much of an investigation. Bad weather, an elderly man, a heart attack. Such things were known to happen. But that meant I had to go get the armored car I'd left at Dyak's right away and take the dead man into town.

After that, I'd deal with the money. No, not the money I'd pulled out of the old man's wallet and part of which I put back with some measure of pity, but the deposit for ten million francs that promised me a new life, free from want.

Staying in New Babylon was now extremely dangerous, but if I got control over the funds in Zurich, I'd be able to get at least to the New World, or the continent. I'd even have enough to make it to Zuid-India. The problem was that getting it required the second part of the number. The fragment with it was apparently among the personal effects of Count Kósice found on the dirigible crash site. But it didn't seem possible for me to get to it. After the recent events, I wasn't particularly popular in the Newton-Markt.

I remembered Elizabeth-Maria von Nalz and

my heart was overcome with a fatal sorrow. Why had she written about me in her diary? Did she want to harm me, or had she been forced? Maybe it was a cry for help? Oh, if only I knew where to find the girl...

Empty dreams! Without hesitation, I threw out the imagined tale of me rescuing my beloved from captivity and confessing my love to her. I got out of bed and walked over to the window. The blinds opened with a creak, but not all the way, as if someone had tried to break them yesterday and nearly found success in that endeavor. Outside, it was damp and gloomy; there was no rain, but the sky was stretched over with thunder clouds. There was a drizzle hanging in the air. A piercing wind blew. The bad weather had just given the city a small breather, no more. By the evening, or maybe even earlier, there would be a storm.

I quickly shaved and brushed my teeth, got dressed then put my Cerberus and knife in my pockets and started considering what to do with the Mauser. I didn't want to leave home with just the three-round snub-nose. I had to find my traveling bag and put the pistol in it.

After that, I went down to the first floor, and there, my somber butler was washing the kitchen floor.

"Your little hellspawn made this puddle right in the middle of the room!" he declared with distaste, clearly referring to the leprechaun.

"Well, Theodor! That is the least of our problems!" I said, trying to cheer up my abnormally nervous servant and throwing the *illustrious* man's jacket over a chair. "Put this down with the body in the icehouse."

"Yes sir, Viscount," he nodded, gone gray after all he'd been through.

Despite the open windows, there was still a strong corpse stench, but it was no longer quite as pungent as last night. Theodor had dragged all the rag-wrapped corpses out to the yard last night, and he even managed, with what strength he had left, to mop the floor and clean the walls.

The butler himself wasn't looking too good: he was somehow peaked, gloomy and strangely angry.

"We need to find the leprechaun's treasure!" Theodor declared, wiping his hands off with a rag. "This cannot go on!"

Elizabeth-Maria came noiselessly down the stairs like a ghost, looked at us and encouraged the servant:

"Theodor, I'll help you look for it."

Abnormally, the girl was wearing a floor-length black dress, gloves and a hat with a thick veil. I couldn't see her face, but her faint voice let me know that yesterday's metamorphosis had been irreversible.

I poured myself some water from the teapot and smiled:

"Best of luck in your search."

I didn't try to talk them out of it. I also was curious to see what would be found in the troublesome pipsqueak's treasure. But when I started for the exit, Elizabeth-Maria suddenly added significantly:

"There's nothing you want to say to me, Leo?"

"No," I answered shortly.

"You have no heart!"

And on that note, our conversation ended.

I wasn't experiencing even the slightest pangs of conscience over how I had treated the succubus; beyond that – I was preparing to rid myself of her once and for all. That creature was seriously intending to drag my soul down to hell and I could not count on any other outcome. Her look of insulted innocence was all the work of the Deceiver...

After ducking into the guest room for the hand-held machine gun, I carried it into the carriage-house. On my way, I picked up the rifle whose butt-stock had broken over the head of the first mummy. I added a couple of Mauser clips to my traveling bag and went outside.

The garden was a pitiful and unsavory spectacle. Among the black trees, cut down by bullets and shrapnel, there were dead bodies lying everywhere, their appendages strewn about haphazardly. There were dark bald patches in the lawn covered with fresh ash from the burnt phosphorus. In the yard, there was a towering pile of corpses. They were gradually degrading; their rotting flesh was soaking through the rags and forming foul-smelling puddles on the ground.

All that remained was to hope that, when the sun came out, this mess would rot away and dry up as Elizabeth-Maria claimed.

I went back home, cleaned my boots, grabbed my canvas jacket and cane and headed to Leonardo-da-Vinci-Platz. I had to get rid of the *illustrious* man's body post haste. And it wouldn't have been an issue, but Alexander Dyak hadn't yet started on the repair work.

"A thousand pardons, Leopold Borisovich," he muttered, wiping his puffy face with his hands, "there just wasn't time. First, I was dealing with the incendiary mortar rounds. Then, I just couldn't wait and started work on the electromagnetic wave transmitter. And, would you believe it? It's completely finished!"

"That's great," I sighed, "but I need the armored car now."

"Soldering the radiator is no problem. I just need the right tool. I promise it will be ready by lunch time!" The inventor came out from behind the counter and locked the door behind him. "Leopold Borisovich, there's something you have to see!"

"What exactly?"

"I attached a cylinder to the transmitter like that of a music box, the pins arranged in the order you suggested. I'm positively burning with desire to test it out!"

"I'm afraid I don't have any time now..." I said, trying to refuse, but the shop owner was implacable.

"You have to see this!" he repeated, trotting out a trusty argument: "Leopold Borisovich, are you personally not intrigued?"

Curses! I was intrigued, and how!

I looked at my timepiece and asked:

"But will the armored car be ready by lunchtime?"

"You have my word!" the inventor promised.

"Alright, I'm with you!"

We went down into the basement. In the far corner, between the spark-showering electrodes, I saw the shadow of the frozen poltergeist. Alexander Dyak demonstrated his apparatus with pride.

"Here, look, Leopold Borisovich!" he said, pointing at the cylinder with two kinds of pins, some thin and some thicker. "The electric wire turns the axle at a constant speed. The pins lift the metal strip and complete the circuit, thus broadcasting either a dot or a dash."

"Have you tested it yet?"

"I have, but without power to the transmitter." The inventor looked at me and, as if apologizing, said: "I don't even know what I'm more afraid of: success or failure. I actually only called you so I could be sure my observations were objective. It's all so near anti-scientific mysticism..."

"Treat it like a code," I advised him.

"That is an utterly unscientific approach, Leopold Borisovich!" Alexander Dyak grew gloomy, falling into a bad state of mind. "And I'm a bit embarrassed to be grasping at it like straws. I'm hoping for a miracle, but I should be relying on my mental prowess!"

"Your mental prowess and sublime electricity," I nodded. "Maybe we should start?"

"I'm afraid," the shop owner admitted, but immediately got himself together and switched on the power.

The apparatus hummed to life, then the inventor sent a few short signals as a test. Effected by the electromagnetic-field disturbances, the transparent shadow of the poltergeist broke into layers and started to vibrate. Then slowly, it came into balance, frozen in its former immobility.

"Alright, let's go!" Alexander Dyak exhaled, putting the axle into motion.

The pins started lifting the metal strip one after the other, completing the transmitter's circuit, and the poltergeist started sparking like a heat lamp after turning the power on and off repeatedly.

Short-long-long-short...

The electromagnetic disturbances shook the shadow, digging into it with pellets of light. In time with the flickering, something started quietly ticking in my head, but the evil spirit was doing incomparably worse. His transparent mirage separated into layers and poured over, flaring up like the northern lights, before it gradually burnt up in a strange fluorescence. Soon, the measured rhythm of the flashes started growing slower, and the bursts of light began penetrating the poltergeist with ever greater frequency. The ghost suddenly fell out of our world, then appeared again. But, after that, it started to shine with a blinding light that cut painfully into my eyes, even through my darkened lenses.

Alexander Dyak buried his face in his hands and stretched out to the off switch, and the evil spirit exploded, blasting the metal needles surrounding it around the whole basement.

One second it was there, and the next it was gone, no longer in this world. And its power gushed out in all directions, bending and breaking everything in a small radius. The huge body of the dynamo gave a shudder, having taken the brunt of the pressure wave. It was even moved from place and slowly dragged over the concrete-covered floor. The iron top flew off and cut into the wall, then slammed onto the floor with a deafening clang.

Alexander and I were not hit.

We spent some time sitting in complete silence, then Dyak turned to me with a chalk-pale face and exhaled:

"*Otche Nash*! It worked! Did you see, Leopold? It worked!"

I nodded in silence. The steel needle of one of the electrodes was sticking out of the lead wall lining a few hands away from my head; if it had gone just a bit more to the left, two lost souls would have just been sent to hell: that of the poltergeist and my own.

"It worked!" the inventor exclaimed. "It worked, do you hear me?!"

"I do," I answered, wiping my sweaty face with a kerchief.

I didn't have much hope for the *Pater Noster* translated into Morse code, but the poltergeist was dispelled even before Dyak's apparatus had finished the prayer left to us by the Savior.

"Stunning!" the shop owner said, continuing to delight in the result of the experiment. "I don't know how, and I don't know why, but it worked! Electromagnetic-field disturbances with that same wavelength were not able to drive out the poltergeist on their own, but that combination of short and long signals led to the complete destruction of the object under study! How can you explain that?"

"Without falling back on theology?" I smiled. "I'm afraid you cannot. But inventing a scientific basis for a discovery once made is easier than making the breakthrough itself."

"You're completely right, Leopold Borisovich! Completely right!" the inventor agreed. "But there's more work to be done here!"

We went up from the basement into Alexander Dyak's workshop. Once there Dyak, overjoyed, opened a bottle of Shustov brandy.

"Have a drink?" he offered me.

"I'll refrain," I shook my head. "I hope our agreement on the armored car remains in force?"

The inventor was obviously impatient to put his thoughts and theories to paper, but he exerted some effort over himself and confirmed:

"Yeah, come by at two."

"Thank you."

"Don't thank me yet!" Alexander Dyak laughed, pouring himself another glass of brandy.

I bid him farewell, went outside and started thinking about what to do with my free time. There was no use in going back home; in the end,

I decided to drop by Albert Brandt's and prepare him for parting with yet another lady of his heart.

There was a slight drizzle, but it wasn't very strong, so I went to the poet's on foot. In comparison with yesterday, there were many more people out; there were patrolmen hanging around on every corner, students rushing to class, and hawkers and street sellers taking advantage of the moment of calm.

"Horrible catastrophe! Dirigible crash! Aircraft explodes!" one of the paperboys called out. "Buy an *Atlantic Telegraph*!"

"Brazen robbery of Baron Dürer! Theft during dinner party! Inspector general's daughter disappears mysteriously!" his competitor echoed. "Only in the *Capital Times*!"

No longer able to resist, I bought a fresh edition of the *Capital Times* and went into the *Helen of Troy* coffee shop to have breakfast and acquaint myself with the news. Tea was not served there, only coffee, but my heart was already pounding and my temples aching; I didn't order a coffee. Instead, I requested a bag of frosted profiteroles be brought out. And while they prepared my order, I quickly leafed through the paper.

As it turned out, no one was connecting Elizabeth-Maria von Nalz with the theft. The only content in any of the articles about her disappearance was the fact that she could not be found, and no one knew where to look for her. The inspector general had used all his influence to make sure the truth wouldn't leak out, and now, every low-level constable in town, when looking at beautiful girls, was holding the portrait of the missing lady in mind. If she was still in the city, she would be found.

The word "if" caused a sharp pain in my heart, and I forced myself to cast the thoughts about Elizabeth-Maria from my head.

"Everything in its time. First, I should settle urgent matters, and what to do after that will become clear," I muttered, trying to convince myself as I walked over the drizzly streets.

Anyway, I wasn't the only one in a horrible mood: Albert Brandt was cursing like a boot-maker, arguing with the owner of the cabaret over who should pay to fix the broken window and dry the rain-soaked furniture after his apartment was robbed.

It even made me a bit ashamed.

"Madame!" Albert said in his low voice, his patience gone. His eyes started lighting up in the semi-dark of the room like two transparent flames.

But the voluptuous lady knew the poet better than that; she immediately came up to him, poked at his high chest and covered his mouth with her hand.

"Albert!" the landlady purred. "Another word in that tone and I'll have to knee you between the legs. You'll go straight to falsetto!"

The poet threw back his hand, but stopped using his *illustrious talent*.

"Split the costs, then?" he suggested.

"You're such a sweetheart, Albert!" the lady

smiled, then went off to give orders.

My friend, extremely vexed at the unexpected expense, threw up his hands and turned to me.

"Where is this world headed, Leo, tell me. Trying to rob a poet, just think! Inconceivable."

I nodded after the landlady and asked:

"Did you and her ever get together?"

The poet just laughed:

"Leo, men and women cannot live together under one roof even one day without a certain kind of relationship taking shape, and I've been renting this apartment for three years running! Of course her and I have been together!"

"Philanderer."

"I'm a one-woman man!" Albert Brandt declared with honor. "At any given moment, I love only one woman. To be honest, I once lost my head over a pair of twins, but that's a different story. The thing is, Leo, my current beloved is supposed to be dropping by at any moment, but everything up in my apartment is topsy-turvy. There's just no time."

"Did you not sleep here?" I smirked.

"I'll sleep when I'm dead," the poet joked. "You're not offended?"

"No problem," I replied, slapping him across the shoulder. "I was just walking by and wanted to find out how you were doing."

"I'm doing great, Leo! Everything is good! Try to come by some other time!" Albert shouted and ran upstairs.

I didn't stop him. I didn't tell him a thing. I

just shook my head and went out the door. And there, my eyes met with a female figure in a black cloak and hat with thick veil. Elizabeth-Maria looked like she was headed to a funeral.

Shivering either from foreboding, or the chilly breeze, I walked over to the succubus and asked in a rude tone:

"What the devil do you want here?"

"That's not for you to know," the girl called back just as ungraciously.

"You're taking the risk of showing yourself to him like this?"

Elizabeth-Maria just snorted.

"Leo, I have an offer for you," she announced. "It benefits the both of us."

"Hard to believe," I retorted, turning around and walking down the street.

"The daughter of the inspector general has disappeared," she called out suddenly from behind me. "Don't you want to find her?"

I felt as if struck by an epileptic seizure. I slowly turned and said ponderously:

"You know nothing about that."

"Leo, my sweet Leo!" Elizabeth-Maria laughed sonorously, just as before. "That *illustrious* string bean has disappeared, and the only question is how badly you want to find her."

"You read about that in the newspaper!"

"I did," the girl confirmed. "You did say I should try reading the papers, after all. They don't have such things in hell, remember, Leo? Those were your words."

"Come off it!"

Elizabeth-Maria walked up to me and whispered quietly:

"I saw someone at the reception. I'm sure it could help you find your dummy."

"What do you want in return?" ripped out of me against my own will.

"I want my youth back!" the succubus demanded, as I expected. "Return my youth and give me your word that you'll never take it again!"

I shook my head.

"Not gonna happen."

"May I ask why?"

"You've got this all worked out. Do you think you can wrap me around your finger? It won't work."

"I give you my word," Elizabeth-Maria said very seriously. "I give you my word, and you give me yours. If my information doesn't lead you to the girl within forty-eight hours, you can do as you please."

"Forty-eight hours?"

"Yes."

"Curious..."

I wanted to believe. Oh, how I wanted to believe the succubus' words, but I just couldn't trust her. That said, what did I stand to lose? If this was a deception, everything would be back to normal in two days. But, if Elizabeth-Maria really had seen something important, I might find the daughter of the inspector general. I do not know if I could earn Elizabeth-Maria von Nalz's favor in this case, but I could absolutely count on the thankfulness of her father. And that was what decided it.

The succubus noticed my eyes starting to glow and licked her lips.

"Well, Leo? Do you agree?"

"You leave Albert," I said, adding a condition. "And it isn't up for discussion."

"As you say, dear," Elizabeth-Maria agreed appeasingly, pining with impatience to return to her former girlish looks, and threw back the veil.

We exchanged oaths, and before I even managed to do anything, the wrinkle-covered skin of the girl started smoothing out, regaining its freshness and spring before my very eyes.

"Tell me!" I demanded, feeling like a right idiot. "Or our deal is finished!"

Elizabeth-Maria sighed a few times with a full chest, then laughed again, but immediately faltered, having caught my gaze full of fierce rage.

"Leo, calm down!" she asked. "I always keep my word!"

"Tell me!"

"At the reception, the inspector general's daughter didn't seem quite right to me," Elizabeth-Maria said, giving a broad statement. "When I saw her at the police ball, her gaze was completely different. At the Baron's, she seemed like she'd drunk laudanum."

"Enough!"

"It's not my fault if your delicate psyche is traumatized by these details! Even ladies of the highest nobility are sometimes known to be drug addicts!"

"Get to the point!"

"Knowing your attachment to this girl, I tried not to let her out of sight," the girl continued. "The only person she was talking to at the reception other than her fiancé was Maestro Marlini, the magician."

"The hypnotist."

"The charlatan."

"Where did you see them?"

"I went into the ladies' room to powder my nose and I ran into them in the hallway."

"That doesn't mean anything yet."

"My instincts say otherwise," Elizabeth-Maria objected. "And now, leave me. I need to go break up with the poet."

"Go easy on him!"

"Forty-eight hours!" the succubus reminded me as she walked toward the cabaret.

I cursed out loud. I first started following after her, then dismissed the idea and headed off to find a cab.

Moon Circus was supposed to have left the city right after their final performance, but the bad weather had stopped them from starting off on their slow path to the continent. And that meant I had no time to lose. Every minute was valuable.

I caught myself on that thought and shook my head. Elizabeth-Maria had manipulated me, and that was fraught with serious problems. What if she wanted revenge one day? Or just lied, trying to make time?

Naturally, I could have asked Ramon for help, but decided not to. In this situation, I had to be sure to stay strictly within the bounds of the law; new problems were the last thing I needed.

In the end, I caught a cab and told the driver to make for Newtonstraat. But I wasn't going to the metropolitan police headquarters, not at all. I was interested in *The Blue Ostrich* restaurant.

I gave a careless nod to the doorman, walked into the establishment, not at all embarrassed at my inappropriate appearance, and asked the maître 'd:

"Has Senior Inspector Moran shown up yet?"

"Yes, come in."

Bastian Moran nearly choked when he saw me. He'd just started eating, savoring the subtle flavor of truffles in wine sauce, but he immediately set his knife and fork aside, wiped his lips with a napkin and announced:

"Viscount, you're the last person I was expecting to see here." After a brief pause, he added: "And you're the also the last, no – the second to last person I'd like to see here."

"Believe me, senior inspector," I smiled back, "seeing your face brings me no joy, either."

"Then, to what do I owe the pleasure?"

I took a seat opposite him and asked:

"How is the search going for the robbers' mole in the Newton-Markt?"

Bastian Moran glanced coldly at me, raised a high brow and retorted snappishly:

"I am not prepared to speak on that topic now."

"That means you've gotten nowhere."

"Is that all you wanted to see me for?"

"To be honest," I sighed, "I didn't want to see you at all, I just didn't have anyone else to take this to."

"Is that so?" snorted the senior inspector.

"I have a mutually beneficial proposition. I give you a clue that allows you to significantly shrink the circle of suspects, and you help me with a certain affair."

Bastian Moran shook his head:

"You know, Viscount, you are not only vain, but also excessively self-assured."

"I repeat: my proposal will benefit the both of us."

"Forgive me if I doubt your words."

I sighed hopelessly and risked showing my cards:

"It has to do with the daughter of the inspector general. Perhaps, I have a clue. Perhaps, I know where she is now."

"I'm not sure I want to be the one to arrest the daughter of the inspector general," Bastian Moran shook his head. "You're a frightening man, Viscount! You want me to help you get rid of a person, who threatens your interests. And in a show of gratitude, you want to drag me into another problem that will destroy my career once and for all! You call that mutually beneficial?"

"Yes, listen!" I said, raising my voice. I immediately caught myself though, then said, now calm: "Elizabeth-Maria is not guilty. She was not aware of her actions. She was just used."

"If that line of defense makes it to court, the

scandal will be enormous. I do not want anything to do with this. And also, you're gonna need a scapegoat to pin all her sins on. It's a dirty game you're playing, Viscount."

"I'm not planning on falsely accusing anyone. I'm sure of what I said!"

"Just yesterday, you claimed to know nothing about that unfortunate incident!"

"That was yesterday! I haven't just spent all day wearing out my trouser seat in an office, you know. I was out, talking with people, and I uncovered some information."

A flash of interest flickered by in the senior inspector's eyes.

"Alright, tell me."

"First, give me your word that you will tell the inspector general about my involvement. Unofficially, naturally. You can have the laurels."

"You want to come back to work?" Bastian Moran squinted. "That's a new one!"

"And what do you care?" I frowned.

"Not one bit," the inventor shrugged his shoulders and promised: "If this endeavor is successful, I'll provide you an audience with the inspector general. Satisfied? And now, stop wasting my time or get out of here and go straight to hell!"

I didn't go anywhere, though. I reclined in my chair and said:

"The robbers' informant had access to the effects confiscated on my last arrest, and also to Count Kósice's documents found on the site of the dirigible crash. He definitely wasn't at the crash site, and didn't personally dig through my pockets, otherwise he'd just have confiscated the piece of paper, not made a photo-copy."

"Photo-copies were made?" Bastian Moran perked up his ears. "Are you certain?"

"I am."

"And how did you become aware of that?"

"A certain elderly gentleman shoved them in my face."

"And you didn't apprehend him?"

"He was so insistent that I lost consciousness."

The senior inspector turned up a high brow:

"And you weren't hurt? Why?"

"They were talking about some papers that had once belonged to my grandmother," I lied slightly. "Perhaps the robbers think they'll still turn up somewhere and I'll get access to them."

"What papers precisely?"

"That is of no importance."

"I could now arrest you for withholding evidence, Viscount. Your uncle has been killed, and the Banking House – demolished. To my eye, there's already been more than enough casualties."

"It's a family matter that I still have yet to figure out all the way," I stated matter-of-factly. "I suggest we move on to rescuing the daughter of the inspector general."

"One more question, Viscount," Bastian Moran snubbed, getting out a notepad and pencil. "What did the elderly man look like?"

"He was *illustrious*. Very old. Well dressed.

Seemed to be an important personage. That was all I could make out. It was dark." I was purposely trying not to describe the appearance of the old man who'd died from a heart attack. Then I asked: "Have I satisfied your curiosity, senior inspector?"

"Partially," he snorted, taking a few gulps of Pino noir and waving a hand without particular interest. "Recount what you have there!"

Such treatment frankly grated on me, but I didn't say anything, just told him about Elizabeth-Maria's conversation with Maestro Marlini at Baron Dürer's reception.

"And that's all?" Bastian Moran winced after hearing me out. "Viscount, you're surprising me! The suspect was speaking with a famous person, who gets approached for autographs on the order of ten times each day, and on that basis, you've made these far-reaching conclusions? Utter nonsense!"

I was not going to give in so easily, though, and I reminded him:

"That conversation fits perfectly into the overall scheme! The hypnotist forced her to commit the crime!"

"He forced her to use her own *talent*?"

"And why not?"

"It's a stretch."

"Senior inspector," I frowned, "I'm getting the impression that you aren't interested in solving this robbery! Shall I tell as much to the inspector general?"

"Viscount!" Bastian Moran smiled calmly in

reply. "I'm not taking part in the investigation. And the identity of the suspect could not be of less importance to me. Above all else, I value rule of law. I repeat: your conclusions don't seem convincing to me."

"You aren't even trying to figure it all out?"

"You've got the wrong number. Department Three isn't taking part in this investigation, and I'm trying to stay as far away from it as possible. So, you go and tell the inspector general."

"Are you sure he won't fall out of his chair?"

"That is of no importance. Rule of law is above all else," Bastian Moran shrugged his shoulders and asked: "And now, if you'd be so kind, please leave me to my meal."

I stayed sitting and said thoughtfully:

"Duralumin is the latest word in dirigible manufacturing, isn't that so? What if the manufacturing documentation ended up sold to the Egyptians or Persians? Isn't it obvious that they precisely must be behind this crime?"

I remembered something the senior inspector had once said about the fervent activity of foreign spy agencies, so I was sure I'd hit my mark. And hit it I did. His eyelid started twitching blatantly.

"That is an argument," he sighed, thoughtfully smoothing out his napkin, "but Maestro Marlini has many influential admirers. Accusing such a person without sufficient basis is fraught with serious problems. And what makes things worse is that it would be a public scandal. That is the exact thing the inspector general is trying so hard to avoid! I'm afraid, Viscount, that you are doing him a disservice."

"What's the difference? Isn't rule of law of utmost importance to you?"

"There's no evidence. No basis for a search. Nothing at all to go on."

"So, that means you shouldn't do anything?"

"It seems to me that you have a personal stake in this matter," Bastian Moran sighed. "Here's what I have to say to you: any citizen in possession of information on a crime is legally obliged to take measures to apprehend the criminals. You don't need me at all. You're perfectly free to ask any old patrolman for help. And I encourage you in that endeavor! Find clues, and I'll happily help you direct the investigation where it needs to go. Is that good enough for you?"

"No!" I shouted, shooting up too sharply from my seat and spilling the senior inspector's wine on his jacket.

"Curses!" he swore, blotting the expensive fabric with a napkin; a waiter appeared next to him almost immediately.

"Allow me," he asked, helping his valued guest with the wine-stained clothing.

When the waiter had gone, Bastian Moran stared gloomily at me and whispered out:

"You're unbearable, Viscount! Get out of here or I can no longer be held accountable for my actions!"

"We'll see each other again," I called back, stepping into the restaurant foyer. Then, my dark glasses perched on my nose, I stood in front of a panoramic window.

The rain outside was pouring. I was feeling no less nasty inside. My evidence wasn't solid enough to attract the help of any patrolmen for the arrest. Such officers were not inclined to listen to private detectives, especially when talking about such a famous and popular personage.

At that moment, a waiter emerged from the men's room with the senior inspector's jacket. I crossed his path and outstretched a hand.

"Please, allow me to beg my forgiveness."

For a certain moment, he hesitated, then handed it to me. I nodded and headed into the room, but almost immediately turned back and shook my head:

"I'm afraid that would only make matters worse. My apologies."

"Nothing to worry about," the waiter answered with absolutely serene calm, accepting the jacket from me and bringing it over to Bastian Moran.

I then calmly went out under the awning, opened the wallet I'd borrowed from the senior inspector and called the doorman.

"My good man!" I said, handing him the wallet, but keeping the badge. "Someone must have dropped this. Ask your patrons on their way out the door."

"Without fail," he promised, not suspecting any tom-foolery in my innocent request.

I nodded and hurried of in search of a cab. I

had just a sliver of time.

2

A NIGHTMARE for any policeman, even an inveterate careerist, is to attract the attention of the top brass just as your shift is coming to an end. Especially if it's dog's weather, rain and wind, and you've already sat down in a cozy tavern with a mug of beer or a glass of warm grog. And I knew that first-hand. I'd once walked a beat in a pair of uniform boots myself.

That was precisely why, after coming up to the area of the old circus, I headed directly to the nearest establishment that served liquor. I had no need whatsoever for vigilant wardens who'd start doubting and asking uncomfortable questions. No, I was intending to play it safe.

Entering *King of Clowns*, a pretentiously named establishment of middling shabbiness, I found five Newton-Markt employees drinking wine together. I coughed and showed off the stolen badge.

"Department Three, Senior Inspector Moran," I said significantly. "Gentlemen, to the exit."

And they all obeyed. None of them were surprised at the senior inspector's young age or his visit to such a low-rent establishment. They didn't seem to think about why such an important figure was not accompanied by a horde of underlings, or why he didn't ask a single question, either.

"Insolence gives you half the world," as my grandfather loved to repeat; and beyond insolence, I also had an *illustrious talent*. Fear of upsetting the upper leadership constricted the constables, forcing them to carry out the impostor's orders unquestioningly.

Outside, I arranged the patrolmen in a row and pointed at the circus dome.

"We're conducting a search. For the inspector generals' daughter."

"But, how can that be...?" one of the constables babbled out.

"Do you not read the papers?" I asked coldly, and the light-haired bull instantly checked himself. "Move out!"

And my little division started rushing across the square.

With a perfect understanding that I couldn't keep the wool over their eyes for long, I hurried to split them up and get to business. The light-haired constable headed to the back door, his friend stayed in the foyer, and the others I led backstage.

"You can't go back there!" cried an alarmed doorman as he ran after us.

"Police!" I threw out as I walked. I then barked just like my former boss, who'd taught me to play nice with commoners: "Out of the way, you feckless ingrate!"

The doorman instantly stepped back. The sentries looked with envious respect. Such treatment of a circus person was to their liking. Circus people and police had a long tradition of mutual acrimony.

At the approach to the backstage, we were caught by the theater manager. But I'd encountered pompous individuals like him plenty of times in my childhood. And I saw through them. I could guess all their fears perfectly.

"My good man!" I said, pulling the fop over by a gilded frock button. "One of your people did something they really shouldn't have. If you get in the way, you'll make yourself an accomplice. Get the message?"

And again, I hit the mark. In any circus, in any troupe, even the most respectable, you can always find a black sheep. If not among the circus folk themselves, then among the ancillary staff. The leadership, naturally, would find out about the dark dealings, but where else could they find someone willing to work for such a comical salary? Also, this was a mere trifle...

But such trifles only seem small until the police get involved.

"What do you think you're doing?" the theater manager objected, having gone very pale. "I know many important people! I will be complaining!"

"Do you have a telephone?" I asked, throwing him off with the unexpected question.

"Yes, and what of it?"

"Start calling around to your friends, while they still remember you."

"This is ridiculous!" the fop exclaimed with a

step back. "I'm calling a lawyer!"

"Such is your right!" I smiled and called a constable after me: "Let's go! Come on! Faster!"

Even my *talent* couldn't hold the theater manager for long; the contentiousness of such individuals surpassed all rational bounds. Soon, he'd come to his senses and kick up such a scandal that the very demons in hell would get nauseous.

A little boy came backstage to meet us, probably an assistant of one of the artistes; I quickly stopped him and bid him take us to Maestro Marlini. The carny hesitated, then I clamped down his shoulder and reminded him:

"You're about to start a big tour, right? It would be a shame to end up in the slammer and miss out on all the fun."

The boy shuddered in horror, and quickly took us through the confusing passages of the circus. And that was just wonderful. The police gradually stepped back from their initial shock and looked at me with unhidden incomprehension.

Well, move it!

MAESTRO MARLINI was expecting us.

We dashed into the spacious room to find it filled with boxes of stage props packed for the voyage. He was just smiling an unconcerned smile:

"Ah, the valorous guardians of public order! To what do I owe your visit?"

"Search the place top to bottom!" I ordered

the patrolmen. "Look for the girl and Baron Dürer's documents."

The police exchanged confused glances and went in different directions.

"Stop!" the hypnotist said simply, and my underlings stopped in place.

"Are you intending to impede the execution of justice?" I snorted. "That is fraught with serious consequences, maestro."

"First, introduce yourself!" the magician demanded.

I waved my badge before his face and announced:

"Senior Inspector Moran, Department Three!"

My assertion didn't have even the slightest effect on the hypnotist. His face didn't even change. Moreover, though we'd never been introduced, I started to get the impression that the magician knew for certain who I really was.

"So then, I'm sure you have a warrant for this search, Senior Inspector Moran." the magician intuited, curious, unfurling the last of my doubts about whether he was guilty or not.

He was mocking me! Simply mocking me!

But I didn't express any annoyance and, in response to the jeering in his question, calmly declared, no longer for the carny, but for the patrolmen:

"A warrant is not necessary in suspected cases of unlawful detention."

"Are you accusing me of kidnapping?" the maestro smiled softly.

He didn't say anything in particular, or move his arm. He didn't even move from place, but the police took an involuntary step back toward the exit. If my *talent* weren't still holding them, they'd surely have been running away as fast as possible.

"Who said this was about you?" I asked in surprise. "Are you the only one with access back here?"

"Naturally, I am not!" the hypnotist announced, clapping his hands. Three young men came out of the neighboring room. "These are my assistants, Mickey, Don and Leon," said the maestro, introducing them.

"Then you have nothing to worry about. No one is accusing you of anything," I shrugged and ordered the constables: "Commence the search!"

"Stop! One minute!" the magician demanded. "My assistants will show you around." He assigned one assistant per police man and, when they'd begun searching the building, he turned back to me: "May I be so curious as to inquire who you mean to find here?"

I looked carefully at him and said pointedly:

"Elizabeth-Maria von Nalz."

"Oh, I read about her disappearance!" the hypnotist called back just then. "What a tragedy!"

"We'll find her."

"But why here exactly?"

"Investigatory privilege."

"Don't think I'm doubting your competency, inspector general..."

"Senior inspector."

Maestro Marlini smiled:

"As someone who's led a strictly civilian life, I think it a forgivable error, senior inspector. You've just been hoodwinked." He walked over to a table with a partially drunk bottle of wine and a bowl of fruit. He filled a glass and suggested: "Have a drink?"

"I'm working."

"Admirable restraint! It can't have been easy to work your way up to senior inspector at such a young age, can it?"

"Appearances can be deceiving, maestro, you of all people should know that," I parried without hesitation, carefully observing the patrolmen's actions. They were checking all the boxes a person could fit into, and yet something in their movements around the room was making me restless.

"And your glasses?" the hypnotist distracted me again. "I've never seen such a thing before. Mind if I take a look?"

My arm started moving toward the glasses loop against my will, but I stopped it in time and rubbed my cheek.

Maestro Marlini laughed:

"I'll have to order a pair for myself."

"They'll hardly be of any use to you at the labor camp," I said, shaking my head.

"And what of the presumption of innocence?"

"The daughter of the inspector general of the metropolitan police is not the kind of person you can kidnap, then expect leniency."

"I don't understand this escalation," the magician huffed. "Do you have a personal stake in this matter... Senior Inspector Moran?"

"Oh, yes!" I smiled, having suddenly realized what exactly was causing the feeling that something wasn't right here. The center of the room was free of boxes, but both the constables and the maestro's assistants were only walking along the walls.

"Personal interest can spoil a case," the hypnotist noted perceptively, clearly surreptitiously making fun of the doltish blockhead he took me for.

I didn't answer, just waved a hand, calling for the police man looking over the stack of boxes in the far corner.

"Constable! Come over here!"

The sentry shuddered and hurried to carry out my order. But he didn't come straight over, he went along the wall again, as if the middle of the room was being blocked by some kind of obstacle he was going around without realizing it.

"Yes, senior inspector?" the police man rapped off, now near me.

"Find anything?"

"Nothing."

"Keep it up!" I let him go and returned to the maestro, who had been watching our conversation with unhidden curiosity.

"You won't find anything," the magician assured me. "And you really don't have any right to search me. I'm sure our stage manager has already called a lawyer. I advise you to leave the circus before he arrives."

"You're giving me advice?" I laughed quietly and picked three small oranges from the fruit bowl. "You know something? I used to live with a circus. My father represented the interests of their field manager. Naturally, our troupe was no match for your circus but, regardless, my father's least favorite part of that job was intervening in conflicts the circus folk had with the police."

"That does not characterize your father in the best light!" the maestro threw out sharply.

"I'm afraid such is the character of all attorneys. They prefer to wait for a situation to resolve itself. You lot hit the road, and they stay here to live."

"Is that a threat?"

"Nothing of the sort. Do you know what else I learned in the circus?"

The hypnotist shrugged.

"The constables have finished their search," he announced. "You'd better leave."

I pretended not to hear the reply, threw one orange into the air first, then another, and another, beginning to juggle them in my left hand.

"My right hand was in a cast back then," I told him. "I still haven't learned to juggle with it."

"I do not understand what this has to do with your accusations!"

"Nothing," I answered; all my attention now fixed on the oranges flying up into the air and falling again into my hand.

One-two-three,   one-two-three,   one-two-three. This primitive rhythm completely occupied my conscious and put me in a trance. My mind was clear. The only thing that remained in the whole world were the orange balls with cold, slightly rough peels. They flew up and fell, then flew up and fell again.

"Cut the buffoonery!" the maestro finally lost control, and I threw an orange at him and turned sharply, taking in the whole room with my gaze.

Maestro Marlini was good and even, I'm not afraid to say it, a genius. Without any preparation, and with just a few meaningless phrases and banal gestures, he had managed to get into the minds of a group of people he didn't know, and force them to ignore a cabinet towering in the very middle of the room on a spinning foundation. We saw it well enough to walk around it, but didn't pay it any mind. Only the idiotic orange game had allowed me to slip out from under the web of his skilled hypnosis.

"What is that?" I inquired loudly, thus immediately attracting the baffled gazes of the constables.

"What are you talking about?!" the magician asked in surprise, now much less careless and blasé than before.

"Have you searched that cabinet?" I asked, pointing to the middle of the room. Only then did the police notice the great big box that had been sitting in plain sight the whole time.

"We missed it, senior inspector," one of the constables admitted. "I do not understand how such a thing could have happened..."

"He's not the senior inspector!" Maestro Marlini suddenly spit out. "I remember this guy. He was fired from the police!"

But it was too late. One moment later, I was next to the cabinet throwing open its doors.

Empty! Inside, it was empty! Worse than that, the cry of the hypnotist had finally put an end to my power over the constables. Realizing I was an impostor, the policemen stared at me with muted amazement and would have certainly thrown themselves at me to punch, but I had a fair understanding of the stage props used by magicians and easily found and broke out the partition that divided the cabinet in two.

And just then, who should tumble out but Elizabeth-Maria!

I gasped in surprise, grabbed the girl and carefully set her down in an armchair. Then, I pressed my hand to her neck in alarm and exhaled loudly when I started feeling a weak pulse.

After that, I gave a shudder and turned my head from side to side, but the maestro's trail had already gone cold.

"Where is he?" I snapped. "Where did the hypnotist get off to?!"

The constables just threw up their hands. The magician's assistants, meanwhile, fell into a complete stupor.

"You!" I poked my finger into one of the policemen. "Get a doctor, fast! The rest of you, don't let her out of your sight!"

I then jumped out into the hallway and

immediately ran into Bastian Moran.

"Not now!" I waved him off, running past, but the senior inspector grabbed me by the shoulder and turned me around. There, two sturdy constables were leading Maestro Marlini to us down the hallway with his hands bound behind his back; there was a hefty bruise swelling up under the magician's eye.

"As a matter of fact," Bastian Moran snorted, "I came here to arrest you, but the maestro was trying to leave the circus in such a hurry that it seemed a good idea to detain him as well. I hope I won't live to regret that."

"Look for yourself!" I pointed to the thrown-open door.

The senior inspector stepped over the threshold and whistled in surprise upon seeing Elizabeth-Maria von Nalz, still unconscious.

"You know? I'd never have thought it but, sometimes, you know what you're talking about, Viscount!" He shook his head.

"Is our agreement still in force, then?" I asked, returning the borrowed badge.

"I'll think about it," said Bastian Moran, cooling my ardor. Then, he shouted to the constables: "Out of the way! Give her more air!"

"Make way! Let me through!" the circus doctor said, pushing his way through the police crowding up the hallway. He knelt down near the girl and got out the smelling salts. "She'll be just fine!" he reassured us. "She's simply fainted!"

Elizabeth-Maria's eyelashes started batting, and my heart fluttered, surprised to see her orange-flecked gray eyes.

"Viscount!" Bastian Moran elbowed me in the side. "Take the lady to the carriage. She must be brought to a hospital at once!"

"I'm completely fine!" the girl tried to object, barely able to stay on her feet.

I offered her my hand and led her outside. Two Department Three officers came after us; Bastian Moran obviously still didn't trust me.

"What is happening, Viscount?" Elizabeth-Maria babbled out. "I was at the reception, and now I'm waking up here. Where are we? What is happening?"

"That's all behind you," I assured her. "Someone poisoned your drink. They were trying to kidnap you for ransom, but we arrested the scoundrel."

"But who? Who was it?!"

"Your father can tell you that," I replied, not wanting to upset her delicate sensibilities with excessive detail.

We went outside. A fresh wind had blown in, and rain was lashing. Elizabeth-Maria's gaze grew clear, she looked around and gasped:

"We were in the circus?"

I led her to the police carriage, helped her get inside and sat down next to her.

"Viscount!" one of the officers called out to me. "You have to go back inside!"

"Just a second!" I called back in annoyance and closed the door. "Elizabeth-Maria, I have something to admit to you..."

"What happened?" the inspector general's

daughter gasped, starting to worry.

"Do you remember that newspaper blurb about Albert Brandt writing a poem dedicated to you? I asked him to write it. I... I love you, Elizabeth-Maria! I've loved you for a long time!"

I don't know what I was expecting. I just had to say my peace. The languor of love was burning me from the inside and I could no longer bear to keep it all a secret. And that was all despite my fear of being refused.

I confessed.

Elizabeth-Maria drew back from me. Her gaze was now cold and distant.

"Viscount," she said, the usual warmth no longer present in her voice, "I am very grateful to you for rescuing me, but I have to say that I do not feel the same about you." Then she went silent, not even mentioning her fiancé.

It was a heavy blow, but I set myself up for it, so I overpowered my feelings, stretched my lips out into a careless smile, and said in parting:

"Forgive my lack of restraint. You can always count on me," and got out of the carriage, closing the door and commanding the driver: "To the hospital!"

The carriage rolled off, and together with it went the Department Three officers, bouncing up and down on the running-boards. And also with them went my heart, ripped to shreds.

There was nothing more holding me here but, unlike flighty creative types, people of noble origin tend to be characterized a healthy pragmatism. So, I didn't throw myself off the embankment into the river like I wanted, and just went back into the circus.

Maestro Marlini was brought out to meet me; his hands were cuffed, and the lower half of his face had a half-mask gag over it.

Bastian Moran looked with a smirk at my droopy countenance and wondered:

"Are you still interested in an audience with the inspector general, Viscount?"

"More than ever," I answered calmly and pointed at the maestro. "Did he confess?"

"No, but there's no need. He was keeping the stolen documents on his person."

"What surprising arrogance."

"Such things are known to happen with people who think themselves of superior intelligence," the senior inspector threw out pointedly in reply. He then added quietly, just for me: "It'd be better if you'd just shot him when he tried to run, Viscount. There's no way for this not to gain wide publicity now. After a trial, no one's good name will remain intact, believe you me."

"Give me five minutes," I asked.

Bastian Moran shook his head:

"You missed the chance."

"I'm not planning to kill him!" I whispered. "I'm just gonna drive home the possible consequences."

"Aren't you afraid he'll hypnotize you?"

"I'm afraid of too many things to give any importance to my fears."

"He's all yours until we get to the Newton-Markt," the senior inspector decided. "Make good use of the time."

I got into the police carriage after the hypnotist, and the locks immediately clicked from outside. Maestro Marlini looked at me sidelong and turned away.

I didn't pull the gag out of his mouth. I just leaned back in the uncomfortable seat and said:

"Claiming innocence will not bring you significant advantage."

The magician stayed silent.

"I mean," I continued, "you could claim the daughter of the inspector general is guilty of anything, but who would believe that such a young creature with such a flawless reputation could ever do such a thing? Are you going to try and use mind control on the jury? Come off it! Everyone knows you have a *talent* for hypnotism. You won't even be allowed to speak. You'll just sit out the whole trial in a jail cell, your hands and feet in cuffs."

The maestro started gurgling expressively, so I pulled out the gag.

"Love of art can make one bear such things!" the magician declared.

"Love of art?" I asked in surprise.

"I've just staged quite the production! Two people, secretly in love, confess their inner feelings to one another. He – a poor private detective, and she – already promised to another. So, they decide to flee and start planning a robbery. He's caught, and she confesses it all in court but, not able to bear being apart from her beloved, she stabs herself. Now that is art!

Shakespeare has nothing on me!"

His words grated on me, but I just shook my head:

"If you pretend to be mad, they'll lock you in the insane asylum until the end of your days. I advise you to opt for hard labor."

"You don't understand a thing of the great power of art! Not a thing! You're mediocre, Viscount, just like everyone else! You carry on a friendship with a famous poet. You must appreciate the grandiosity of my intention. My story would make you immortal!"

"Drop the act!" I demanded. "We don't have much time left."

"Do you mean to offer me a deal?" the maestro inquired, his interest piqued. "You know, there are all kinds of things in the mind of your beloved. Would you like me to make her fall in love with you? I could do that."

"If you bring that up again, I'll hit you," I warned him. "I need you to confess your guilt, and that is all."

"Not gonna happen! I won't sign anything, even under threat of death."

"Why would I want to kill you? Death by hanging is quite a lot more torturous and humiliating."

"Balderdash!"

But I'd already found the hypnotist's weak spot, so I laid into it with all the power of my *talent*, repeatedly widening the breach in his desolate defenses.

"The theft is a relatively minor charge. A

charming thief can always plead his case before an unassuming public, pretending to be a gentleman-robber of some kind, a modern-day Robin Hood or Arsène Lupin. And the attempt to convince Baron Dürer to commit suicide isn't so frightening either. At the end of the day, it's quite hard to prove your criminal intent in that. And really, who cares what happens to fat-cats like him? No one. But the accusation that you were colluding with Egyptian spies gives you no chance for acquittal. That is high treason. There won't be any pliant jurors, crowds of supporters or letters from influential admirers. It will be a closed trial, then the noose. Everyone will forget about you. Everyone. Forever."

"Nonsense!" Maestro Marlini shouted out. "I am not in contact with foreign spies in any fashion!"

"But who else would have wanted the duralumin patent?" I noted reasonably. "It's a top-secret document, didn't you know that? It was found in your things when they searched you. It will be very, very hard for you to twist your way out of the hangman's noose this time. Even if you accused an innocent girl of every deadly sin in the book, the fact would remain – the documents were found on your person."

The hypnotist closed his eyes and started thinking.

"But what if I picked the papers up by mistake? They might have just been sitting under my bills of exchange or obligations. I was keeping them on my person because I was intending to return them to the Baron."

I melted into a smile and chummily poked the magician in the shoulder:

"So! I knew you and I would find a common tongue! Of course, you picked up the patent on accident!" And then, now totally serious, I added: "*You* took it, not Elizabeth-Maria."

The maestro winced in pain.

"What could I get for that?"

"Five years' hard labor," I supposed. "Because you weren't in cahoots with anyone, were you? Elizabeth-Maria merely saw you leaving the Baron's office. And you weren't planning to kidnap her, she just got so worried she fainted. You had to give her first aid. There was no agreement, nor kidnapping. You took the patent by mistake, so there wasn't any high treason either. And Baron Dürer tried to slit his own wrist only because of his personal tribulations. There remains the theft, but everything stolen was returned in full measure. You'd be out in three to five."

"That's quite a long time."

"It's better than certain hanging and biased interrogations."

"Will Baron Dürer agree not to puff up a scandal?"

"After the patent is returned? He'll be in seventh heaven!"

"You're speaking so confidently, my friend..."

When he called me that, I nearly squirmed, but I held myself together.

"What are you shrinking back for?" I asked,

moving toward the magician. "The most important thing for you is to save your life. A person with your talents can't be held in a work camp for long. Escaping such a place would be a mere trifle in comparison with your other tricks."

"I'll make the confession," the maestro then decided, clearly fearing that he could be called right into a judge's chambers.

"Write it down!" I demanded and handed the hypnotist a pad and pencil.

He thought it over briefly, then started writing out his nervous confession on his knees with his hands still shackled, claiming his deepest repentance for what he'd done.

"Perhaps, someone from Department Three will express the desire to speak with you," I said, taking the notepad. "Unofficially, naturally. I insist that you inform them with no reservations who theoretically could've been interested in the patent. After all, you were holding onto the document only to make sure it wouldn't fall into the wrong hands, weren't you?"

The maestro promised:

"I'll think it over."

"Negotiate," I advised him and, having heard the sound of the locks opening. I opened the door, and saw that the carriage had arrived to the back of the Newton-Markt.

Bastian Moran came up, carefully looked at me and asked:

"Well?"

"I don't have anything for you, senior inspector." I shook my head.

"It was stupid to think otherwise," Moran sighed. "I'll fill out the arrest papers, and you go up to the inspector general's reception. Don't doubt that I'll keep my word."

3

BASTIAN MORAN came by only one hour later. I had already thoroughly lost hope of seeing the inspector general, and the looks his bewildered secretary was shooting me had become inappropriately curious. The senior inspector immediately ducked into his office, left a short while later and announced:

"You're expected, Viscount!"

He didn't go in after me.

I walked in the door with my legs feeling like wet cotton. I had no idea how Friedrich von Nalz would react to my appearance, but it all turned out easier than I was expecting. The sickly old man didn't even raise an eye. He was sifting through papers and barking orders into a telephone at the same time.

"Senior Inspector Moran told me about your involvement in this case, Viscount," said the inspector general, having left the phone on the hook. "And I am immeasurably grateful to you for the help in rescuing my daughter, but if you came to ask to be rehired, I'm afraid now is not the best time. Next week, we'll convene the ethics committee and we can discuss the issue there."

"No need," I replied, shaking my head. "I don't think I'm experiencing the desire to return to work."

"Is that so?" The old man asked in surprise. "So then, what was it you wanted?"

I set the maestro's confession on the inspector general's desk.

Friedrich von Nalz skimmed it over and stared at me with unhidden astonishment:

"Am I to understand, then, that your involvement in this affair was somewhat more substantial than Moran reported?"

"Forget about it," I waved it off.

"But the thing you're offering..." the old man frowned. "A confession to the theft alone? It isn't enough to break this scoundrel on the wheel!"

"I wholeheartedly share your righteous indignation," I sighed, "especially considering the role he assigned me, but accepting this admission point blank is your only chance to avoid a big scandal. If your own career doesn't worry you, think about your daughter. Think about what she'll have to go through."

Friedrich von Nalz smoothed out the sheet and muttered:

"She's but a chance witness to the crime, not involved in anything reprehensible. I'll have to discuss this with Baron Dürer."

"Discuss it," I nodded, and advised: "But if you decide to contest the confession, my advice to you is: don't set up a kangaroo court, just strangle the bastard in his cell quietly and announce that he committed suicide. You already have his confession."

"How cynical the youth of today are," the old man sighed, then threw himself back into his chair and asked: "So what did you want from me, Viscount?"

"I've got a request, a mere trifle really..."

On hearing these words, the inspector general put up his guard, but still nodded:

"I'm listening."

The old man had seriously deteriorated in the last few days; he no longer called up images of a big, strong tangle of pine roots, and had turned into a shadow of his former self. But, still, his *talent* had no less luster than before. Playing a game of doublespeak with him wasn't worth doing, so I didn't.

"My uncle, the Count Kósice... I'm sure you've heard about the unfortunate events that have befallen him recently, inspector general."

"I have," the *illustrious* man confirmed.

"So then, my uncle had a piece of a photograph that belongs to me. It was discovered by the police among the Count's possessions on the dirigible crash site. I'd like to have it back."

Friedrich von Nalz looked at me with doubt, clearly deciding whether to throw me right out the door or find out the details first; his professional curiosity got the better of him.

"What is depicted in the photo, Viscount?" asked the inspector general.

"My grandmother and mother," I answered with the pure truth. "It's an old picture from forty years ago. It was the only picture I had left of my mom before she got married. Her family was against the marriage. All the pictures after she moved stayed with the Count and Countess. Of course, it's hard to even call it a picture. The piece in evidence only shows their legs. I have most of the photo, and I'd like to put it back together."

The old man relented.

"How did such a thing happen?" he answered, no longer so harsh.

"The Count and I had a little scuffle at our last encounter," I shrugged. "But if you doubt my words, ask someone to check the ledger from my last arrest. I had the whole picture then."

"I see no reason to doubt your words, Viscount," Friedrich von Nalz announced. "But you'd better tell me one thing: does the picture have any value at all to the direct heirs of the Count?"

I threw up my hands.

"What value could a fragment of a photograph of their grandmother's and aunt's legs have? In any case, the Count's whole office was full of such photos. But it's of value to me as a memory."

The inspector general hesitated, but not for long. In the end, the old man decided to settle accounts, having considered the old photograph fragment a fully acceptable price.

He raised the phone, told them to get him Maurice LeBrun and ordered my request fulfilled.

"Go to the evidence lock-up, Viscount," the inspector general told me after hearing the head of the CID's answer. "And I thank you again for the help in rescuing Elizabeth-Maria."

"It was my duty," I smiled, though a pang shot through my heart when I heard the name of the inspector general's daughter.

I took a bow and left the office, then hurried to evidence before the old man changed his mind or one of his subordinates suspected something. Being slow with such things could only make it worse.

And I was fast enough. Immeasurably surprised at the order, the red-mustached detective sergeant passed me the photo fragment under signature and tried to accost me with questions; I didn't play along, though. I signed the ledger and hurried to the exit.

While I was walking to the guard post, I memorized the number combinations written in even columns, then stashed the valuable photo fragment in my wallet, caught a free cab and told him to take me to the Greek Quarter.

Yes! I was overflowing with emotions. I wanted to spit them out, share my experiences with someone at least, and who better than Albert? Though I couldn't tell him the whole truth, I had to share my joy with someone! My joy and... my sorrow.

I remembered Elizabeth-Maria von Nalz's parting words and grew gloomy.

I could see lightning once again on the outskirts. The rain was getting stronger, and the streets were gradually darkening. The only sounds were the clanking of the steam tram's steel wheels on the rail joints and the clopping of horse hooves on the wet causeway. There were almost no pedestrians to be found. And that was no wonder. There was another storm brewing over the city. The wind was whistling between the buildings and wailing down the chimneys. Everyone who could was waiting out the bad weather at home. But I was so strongly opposed to returning to my dead-flesh reeking manor that my teeth were grinding.

And why did I have to? There was nothing more holding me there. Nothing other than the old edition of *Alice's Adventures in Wonderland*.

After letting the cab go, I walked into the cabaret, shaking the water off my hat in a habitual motion and carelessly nodding to the barkeep.

"Is he home?" I asked, pointing at the ceiling.

"He's in a very bad mood," she replied.

I just laughed. I went up to the second floor, threw open the door and announced from the threshold:

"Albert! I have wonderful news: I've come into my inheritance!"

The poet didn't react to that in any way. He just kept standing by the window and looking out of it.

"Has something happened?" I then wondered.

"Yes," Brandt nodded. He turned around and his glowing eyes pierced through the gloom of the room like two colorless flames. "You lied to me,

Leo! I thought you were my friend, and you lied to me!"

"About what?" I clarified.

"Please don't play games, now least of all!" snapped the poet. "I know everything!"

"Well shit," I thought to myself, wanting to curse out loud when I realized what precisely could have caused this attack of rage, but it all turned out much worse.

"She said we cannot be together! She said she gave you her word and that she was your property until the end of days! That's dishonorable, Leo!"

"Wait!" I tried to cut into the poet's monologue. "You've got it all wrong!"

But Albert wasn't listening to me.

"You took advantage of my lack of experience and trampled over the girl's innocence, destroying her dreams! She was counting on my help, but you won't let her have it!"

"What is this nonsense?!" I shouted out and suddenly realized it really was just that – nonsense.

The poet was out of his mind.

"There's only one way for us to settle this issue now," Albert Brandt continued in the meantime. He picked his dueling sabers up from the table, set one on the floor and sent the other to me with a sharp kick. "En garde!"

"Stop!" I screamed. "Albert, stop! It's me! How many years have we known one another? Just hear me out for a start!"

The poet shook his head and suddenly said

with a strong tone, straight from the chest:

"Take the saber and fight me, devil take you!"

His *talent* overwhelmed me, and tried control my actions, forcing me to take a step forward and drop my cane. But I didn't bend down for the weapon.

"No!"

"Take it!" Albert demanded again, raising his blade to the very ceiling. "Now!"

He was definitely out of his mind. I, meanwhile, couldn't shoot him, nor run and leave him in such a state. I could only raise the saber and defend, but I didn't, despite all his *talented* admonishments.

"You're under a spell, Albert!" I shouted to the poet. "Wake up!"

"I'm under a spell?" he laughed. "I met the love of my whole entire life, and you stole her from me! But we will be together no matter what!"

Albert Brandt had always had the tendency for recklessness, and had fallen in love to the point of memory loss many times before; the succubus easily played on his feelings. The poet was burning with desire to cut his opponent to bits and was planning to do just that.

Either he would kill me and find favor with the hangman, or I would shoot him and lose my only friend forever. Elizabeth-Maria had set the ideal trap.

"En garde!" the poet again ordered, and the force of his *talent* made me reach for the weapon. But an empty bottle rolled out from under the couch at that very moment; it rolled into Albert's boot and forced him to lower his *illustrious* eyes to floor for just a moment.

I didn't hesitate; I grabbed the billiard ball I'd forgotten there long ago and threw it at the poet with my left hand with all my might. It hit him right in the forehead; Albert's head took the blow; his legs gave out and he collapsed to the floor.

Nothing to worry about! The nimbler the mind, the stronger the skull, as they say. And in that regard, poets were probably more a confirmation of the rule than an exception to it.

And it was proven right – I managed to feel a pulse on Albert's neck without particular effort.

He was alive.

At that moment, the leprechaun came out from under the sofa. He shook the dust from his rumpled accordion top-hat and snorted:

"Bugger, he's a right messy chap!"

"What are you doing here? Did you leave something?" I asked, but immediately waved my hand. "Doesn't matter. I'd actually rather you didn't answer."

And the leprechaun didn't answer; instead, he started rummaging in the liquor cabinet for a bottle of rum.

I, meanwhile, picked up my cane, ran down to the first floor and, with a careless salute farewell to the barkeep, went outside. But I didn't head home. I went to bring Alexander Dyak up to speed. I suddenly had an urgent job for him.

WHEN I CAME into the back yard of *Mechanisms and Rarities*, the inventor was already finishing the solder on the radiator and showed me his handiwork with well-earned pride.

"Tell me what you think, Leopold Borisovich!" he said, but I just threw up my hands.

"I don't really understand engines," I admitted with a clean conscious.

Dyak put the steel hood back in place, slapped it with his hand and smiled:

"And you don't have to. I guarantee that it's fixed."

After a successful completion to his experiment, the inventor found himself in an elevated state of spirit and reeked thickly with the noble aroma of brandy. But he had approached the radiator repair job with all due seriousness and, beyond the blowtorch, had dug out a bunch of other tools. I didn't doubt his words.

"Would you come in for a glass of tea, Leopold Borisovich?" Alexander offered, wiping his mechanical-grease-covered hands with a piece of rag.

"If it's only tea," I agreed, not knowing the best way to approach the store owner with my request.

We hid in his workshop from the rain; Alexander left me alone briefly, then came back with a tea pot, tea cups and a plate of short-bread cookies. He was still drinking brandy.

"For medical purposes," he winked at

me. "Helps reduce stress!"

I was planning to reduce my stress with a much more radical method, by parting once and for all with its main cause but, before I managed to start my request, the inventor coughed, stroked his gray beard and said carefully:

"Leopold Borisovich, I actually have one request of you..."

"I'm listening, Alexander."

After a moment of hesitation, he laid out bluntly:

"One successful experiment isn't really proof of anything. The scientific method demands that a series of experiments be performed and their results compared, but I simply have no one to perform them on. Do you think maybe you could help me with that?"

I stared at him in confusion.

"What, excuse me?"

"I understand how barbaric it sounds," the inventor sighed, "but it is extremely important for me to get access to several infernal creatures and subject them to the effects of regulated electromagnetic disturbances."

"The idea is not without merit," I admitted after brief consideration of the extremely unusual proposal. "But actually doing that would have certain complications."

"I understand!" Alexander Dyak admitted. "I understand! But judge for yourself what kind of perspectives this reveals!"

"This reveals the perspective of us being eaten alive or being thrown in a work camp, depending on our luck," I retorted with a shake of my head. "Bringing an infernal creature to your shop would not only be extremely difficult to accomplish, but also just plain dangerous."

"Well, what else can I do?" the inventor said, at a loss.

I shrugged my shoulders.

"I don't know." So, I asked: "Just how cumbersome is your device? Would it fit in the back of the armored car?"

"Are you suggesting we conduct field experiments?" the shop owner gasped. "That could be one way around this but, if the broadcasts we make are detected, they'll try to track us down."

"Hold up!" I cut the inventor off, not wanting to brush this idea aside out of hand. "You said the first device was called a lightning detector, right? It could detect electric discharges in the atmosphere, right? Doesn't that mean there should be an extremely high amount of interference in weather like this?"

Alexander Dyak shot up from his chair and started pacing from corner to corner.

"You're right, I didn't consider that!" he decided a bit later. "But the storm won't last long. Do you think we can do a second experiment with the transmitter before the end of the day?"

I nodded.

"Most assuredly."

"Great!" the shop owner replied joyfully. "Absolutely marvelous!"

"So, will the device fit in the back of the

armored vehicle?"

"Without a doubt," Dyak confirmed. "If I replace the dynamo with a powerful electric battery, we could even conceal it in a traveling suitcase." the inventor said with a shudder. "Leopold Borisovich, do you have time for this right now?"

"How much time will it take?"

"A quarter hour at most!"

"Alright," I decided. "Get to work."

The inventor took the little box of tools and called me after him:

"I'm gonna need your help!"

I set the traveling bag on the workbench and followed the shop owner into the basement. Alexander Dyak deftly detached the dynamo wire from the transmitter. The device wasn't so big on its own, but lifting it was quite a serious task. In order to protect the fragile equipment from breaking, we first had to place the transmitter into a traveling suitcase to drag it up the stairs.

But we managed. And when the inventor was done screwing in the massive electric battery, I loaded the apparatus into the back of the truck myself.

"Where are we going?" Alexander Dyak asked, running out after me under the pouring rain and pulling on his raincoat.

"We're not going anywhere. You're staying here"

"Please, Leopold Borisovich!" the inventor objected. "How do you mean?"

"I assure you, I'll tell you everything," I

promised. "But it would be too dangerous for you to come with me."

"You're hiding something from me!"

I sighed fatefully.

"Has Albert ever told you about my home?" I asked, already knowing the answer.

"He said something about a curse, but that's unscientific..."

"And yet, nevertheless, something is contaminating the manor and the property attached to it. It cannot harm me, but you must never go there. I'll start up the transmitter in my own yard, and tell you about what happens."

"Ah, so that's it!" the inventor said, drawing out his words. "I see, I see! Well, I won't try to talk you out of it. It will serve as a good initial test of how well the apparatus works. But I beg you not to draw it out: I need a test of the effect of electromagnetic disturbances directly on infernal creatures."

I clapped him on the shoulder and warned:

"Don't you worry, Alexander. This won't leave you wanting."

"You oblige me greatly, Leopold Borisovich."

The shop owner went to open the gates; I sat at the wheel, threw my traveling bag on the passenger seat and started up the powder engine. In idle, the engine worked like a Swiss timepiece; neither the visit to the vampire, nor the subsequent repair had done any permanent damage. I waved goodbye to Alexander and started off on my way.

The rain was coming down as if being

poured from a barrel. Behind the sheet of water falling from the sky, I occasionally saw branching lightning strikes flicker by. But there were certain advantages in the bad weather – there were no passenger carriages or carts on the streets, so driving to Calvary took a quarter hour at most. It only took a bit more time than getting up the hill, though, as it had been quite washed out over the last few days. The wheels were skidding in the mud. The massive armored vehicle was snarling angrily, and just barely crawling forward.

But I made it.

I left the self-propelled carriage on the little platform before the gates, threw open the latch, walked past the fence and opened the rusty, creaking gate for the car. I parked it on my property and ran to close the gates before some random passerby glanced into the disfigured garden and saw all the corpses, which I still had yet to get rid of.

The armored car stopped at the porch and I dragged the hefty suitcase into the house. I unlatched it right in the entryway and gave some power to both it and the code cylinder, but I didn't broadcast the Morse code prayer just yet. All I did was shout out:

"I'm back!"

In reply – silence.

Reminded of recent events, I immediately pulled the Cerberus from my pocket, switched the safety off and listened. Nothing, just the sound of rain outside.

What the hell had happened now?

I stepped back to the entrance and looked into the yard. There were huge raindrops smacking the lawn and dead flower beds, and streams gushing from the gutters, soaking the neatly stacked mummies. Quiet and calm. However, there had been nothing outside to warn me of yesterday's events, either...

I decided to take precautions, ran up to the armored car, threw open the doors from the passenger side and nearly cursed in surprise when I found the leprechaun. The pipsqueak, his top-hat sitting rakishly back on his head, was distractedly turning the wheel and snorting recklessly, imitating the crackling of a working engine. He didn't even look at me.

And I didn't touch him. I just pulled my Mauser from the traveling bag, chambered a round and went back inside with my weapon at the ready. I was starting to like this less and less. But when I noticed the icehouse hatch thrown back, it felt like my legs were suddenly glued to the floor. I got the urge to go back for grenades.

But instead, as if under a spell, I slowly and carefully walked up to the black maw of the basement, got down on my knees and glanced into the ominous darkness...

But actually – it was quite bright down there. The light of two kerosene lamps was quivering in the ice chunks stuck to the walls and floor and, in the uneven glow, I immediately saw two figures rummaging about in the far corner. Based on the holes dug all around the floor, they'd already checked all the other parts.

I was so surprised that I even forgot my age-old fear of basements for a moment.

"What are you doing?" I shouted, running down the stairs. "Theodor!"

My butler turned and answered with dignity:

"We're trying to find the leprechaun's treasure, Viscount."

"Oh yeah?" I asked, taken aback, but immediately waved my hand. "Excellent, carry on. But then you, Elizabeth-Maria, we need to have a serious conversation. Let's go!"

The succubus, beyond all doubt, had noticed the hints of rage peeking through in my voice. Also, I'd never called her by name before, but she didn't even raise an eyebrow.

"I'm helping Theodor, if you didn't notice, Leo!" she announced.

"Up, now!" I snapped, no longer pretending that everything was alright.

"Is something the matter, dear?" the girl smiled charmingly. "Did you not find the inspector general's daughter?"

"I did."

"So, you see! And that is only thanks to my help! Why are you so upset? Did you not have the brass to confess your true feelings, or did she reject you?"

"Listen!"

"Oh, how sad!" Elizabeth-Maria broke me off, placing a hand to my mouth. "Unrequited love just breaks my heart!"

I wasn't preparing to have an argument in the basement, but before I even knew it, I was standing right in front of the girl.

"Listen, you!" I yelled in her face. "You thought you could poison my relationship with Albert? Well, no such luck! We didn't duel!"

Elizabeth-Maria's nose shot up.

"Really? It's a shame to hear that," she said, extremely ambiguously, "but I didn't do anything blameworthy. I just parted ways with Albert and explained why we cannot be together."

"He misunderstood the whole situation!"

"People tend to do that," the succubus burned me. "You, I hope, managed to dispel his error?"

The girl's poison-dripping voice made me want to stand up and start the transmitter right then, but I wasn't sure the electromagnetic waves would fully penetrate the basement, and I had to get myself together.

"You should not have done that!"

Elizabeth-Maria folded her hands demonstratively and turned away from me to my butler as he dug in the ice chunks.

"I didn't break any of your rules or our agreements, my sweet Leo," she told me. "If your friend is too amorous or hot-tempered, that's not my fault. You pick your own friends. I suggest you be a bit more prudent in the future."

I didn't give in to the provocation, or jump into a fight. But before I managed to find a dignified response, the girl suddenly said to my butler:

"Hey! There it is!"

"Where?" Theodor shuddered, turning his

head in confusion from side to side.

"There, it's sticking out!" Elizabeth-Maria pointed at a silver fork handle protruding from the ice.

Having instantly forgotten about me, they started raking away the ice and had soon dug up the tip of a man's shoe.

"Original choice for a hoard," the girl snorted and made a totally natural squeal.

The shoe was on a foot; the fork was pinning a frozen pant leg to the ankle and stuck into the icy flesh all the way to the end of the tines.

My vision grew hazy. I suddenly felt the cold in full measure. The lamp flames became dull and diffuse, and the light spot of the hatch was covered by someone's shadow.

"Bugger!" I heard distinctly from the other side.

"The pipsqueak himself even dropped by!" Elizabeth-Maria said, lighting up in joy.

The leprechaun cursed out dirtily and hid from view. The girl laughed sonorously. Theodor continued disinterring the corpse. And meanwhile, a ghastly sensation rolled over me of inevitable misfortune.

Shaking from nervous chill, I walked up to the butler, intending to order him to leave the basement, but my tongue felt stuck pointing up.

To Elizabeth-Maria, this was all child's play.

"You weren't the first one to think of storing corpses here!" she laughed uncontrollably.

It should be said that even the succubus was affected when my butler had dug up the torso. The stomach of the unknown man was torn open and had silverware sticking out of it in an orderless fashion: forks, spoons, and knives – all silver.

"Unbelievable," she shivered.

Theodor, meanwhile, didn't stop; he dug out the left hand, its wrist pierced through with a silver fork, started throwing the ice chunks away, and soon revealed another ghastly wound – the neck of the unfortunate man had been sliced open from ear to ear in a steady, deep cut that reached all the way to the white bones of the spinal column.

"Leo, how am I to understand this?" Elizabeth-Maria cried out in alarm, but I didn't stir, intently observing as the corpse's white face emerged from the ice.

"I know this man," I whispered when a half-forgotten memory dislodged itself from the depths of my conscious. "He was our chef!"

"Devil!" the girl cursed. "This all smells disgusting, even by underworld standards!"

"Not funny," I finally pressed out of my numb lips.

I was enshrouded in an unbearable cold. It froze me to my bones, rolling over me with an incomprehensible consternation. The rustling of the ice chunks was abrasive to my stripped-bare nerves. The shadows scared me half to death and awoke long-forgotten memories. It suddenly seemed this had all happened to me before. As if I had already stood over a lifeless body just like this one, but not in this life, in another that I had forgotten so painstakingly that it had ceased to exist.

"This is no place for me," I suddenly thought, but I carried on standing and watching Theodor gather the silver, not disgusted at tucking his hands into the chest cavity of the dead man, split from the center of his rib cage to the groin.

All of our attention was fixed on the ghastly spectacle, so when we heard a sonorous metallic clank on the stairs, it came as a complete surprise.

"Bugger!" the leprechaun cursed with a grenade in his hand. "Get the hell out of there!"

"And what if I don't?" Elizabeth-Maria bared her teeth.

Instead of answering, the pipsqueak pulled the pin and started counting down:

"Three!"

My consternation cast aside, I pushed the girl to the exit and rushed for Theodor's hand.

"Let's get out of here!"

I did not doubt the leprechaun's threat. He was going to do this regardless of the consequences.

"Two!" sounded out from the stairs.

"One last piece of silver!" Theodor groaned out, tearing a fork from the corpse's right arm as I dragged him to the exit.

We were still on the stairs when the albino exhaled:

"Bugger!" and tossed the grenade at the corpse.

I pushed my butler up and jumped out after him, slamming the hatch. Just then, an explosion blasted out, but the sound was unexpectedly muffled. The floor underfoot just gave a slight shudder and some dust came down from the ceiling.

"Where is that bastard?" Elizabeth-Maria bared her teeth, but the leprechaun's trail had already gone cold. "Leo, what does all this mean?" the girl suddenly harangued me. "How'd the chef end up in the basement with his belly and throat cut open and full of silverware?"

"How should I know anything about that? I was only five!" I objected and called out to my butler, who was sorting the silverware: "Theodor, what do you say?"

"I haven't the slightest idea," my servant answered, not raising an eye.

"What a family!" the girl snorted. "Dignified people tend to have skeletons in the closet, sure, but you keep corpses in the icehouse!"

"Why the devil'd you even start rooting around down there?" I demanded an answer.

"Theodor called me to search for the leprechaun's treasure."

I was suddenly overcome by a wave of disgust, and I wanted unbearably to change the topic.

"Alright, to hell with the corpse, then! You put a spell on Albert!"

The girl laughed in my face.

"Nothing of the sort!" she replied. "I wouldn't have had to! He's got quite a compulsive personality. I was just blown away! I really did like spending time with him. You don't even know."

"I don't believe you!"

"My sweet Leo, trust is a decidedly intimate matter," Elizabeth-Maria noted caustically and turned to the butler standing behind her. "Has something happened, Theodor?"

"No," he answered calmly. But when the girl turned back to me, he suddenly grabbed her by the head and snapped her neck in one sharp motion. Her spine cracked with a sickening snap, and her body fell lifeless to the floor.

In a panic, I stepped back and grabbed the Mauser on my belt, but immediately regained my composure.

"What are you doing?" I exclaimed, not understanding what was going on.

Theodor shrugged his shoulders and calmly stepped over the girl's body.

"Otherwise, it never would have ended," he said in a voice not his own.

"You're not Theodor!"

"Clever boy," smiled the thing from the *other* side, and my servant's eyes lit up with a dark flame of an unpleasant shade.

I didn't shoot, just concentrated, trying to imagine Theodor dead once and for all, but found no success.

"You can't really have believed that pedant was staying in this world just because of a sense of duty, right?" the unquiet spirit asked in surprise. "Nope! It was all his twin brother. I connected their souls with an invisible thread, created a loophole out of hell and spent all these years clutching onto it, my soul squirming in unbearable torment, and my body wallowing in the icehouse, stuffed with silver. I couldn't move an inch, or force this dummy to search for me. I couldn't even see myself until your girlfriend noticed the fork! But I knew I'd get free sooner or later!"

"Who are you?" I asked and immediately guessed: "The chef!"

"To you, I was just the chef," the underworld native confirmed and took another step forward.

I took a nimble step back and quickly drew my pistol.

"The death of his brother was quite lamentable," the chef continued, "but fortune smiled on me. Now, I am free and I will have what's mine!"

"What are you talking about?"

"The secret of your grandfather, Emile Rie," said the unquiet spirit, stretching out the butler's lips into an avaricious smile. "Why else would I get a job in this house? I knew the answer to the riddle was somewhere nearby. I was looking for it, but I made a little mistake..." he trailed off, his eyes burning with a fell light. His piercing gaze went all the way in to my liver. "Eating your pitiful little heart was a bad idea. I should have just ripped your head clean off!"

The creature controlling my butler made a jump, intending to surprise me, but I was holding "Theodor" in my sights the whole time and opened fire as soon as he stepped forward.

Shots thundered out, and though the bullets didn't do any harm to the unquiet spirit, just made pointless holes in his frock and vest, he was knocked back. Without letting him push me into a corner, I jumped aside, grabbed a silver fork from the floor and pulled my Cerberus from my pocket with my other hand.

"You're playing with me again!" Theodor laughed in the strange voice. "Do you need to be reminded how this all ended last time?"

"Probably in your death," I answered, taking a step toward the window.

The creature was afraid of silver, but my *talent* would never have managed to grab this spark and light a flame of boundless horror with it. I simply didn't have time.

"Yes, I did die," the unquiet spirit admitted, "but I took all the inhabitants of this house with me except for two degenerates – you and your father! I sapped the life force of everyone nearby! And I have continued to do so for many long years. The only one not to feel it was your girlfriend. What's wrong with her, boy? Will you tell me, before you die?"

Of course, there really was something wrong with Elizabeth-Maria. The girl was holding her head in both hands, and setting it back in place with a quiet snap, as if fixing a mannequin damaged by vandals.

The chef, fortunately, didn't notice a thing, so I hurried to distract him with a question, playing on his desire to say his fill after the long years of imprisonment in the icy underworld.

"I'd rather you tell me why it was necessary."

"You're asking me why I wanted the secret of the weapon that did in *the fallen*?" The unquiet spirit asked in surprise. "I intend to destroy it, you silly person, and thus clear the way for the true sovereigns of this world!"

"The ancient gods?"

"The great ones have many names," the chef smiled. And just then, Elizabeth-Maria flew at him from behind.

She threw a noose around the unquiet spirit's neck made of the braided strips of enchanted Moor skin, pulled on it, and dug her knee into his lower back, not letting him turn around.

The butler's face instantly went a violet-black shade; he stepped back and pushed the girl against the wall. She didn't even wince.

"The saber!" she shouted to me.

I dashed into the guest room, yanked my grandfather's saber down from the wall and ran back. I struck him from my running start, putting all of my momentum into the slash, but the chef managed to throw up an arm, stopping the blade at the cost of a sliced muscle and radius.

A strong slap to the face knocked me off my feet; I was spread-eagled on the floor, and when the unquiet spirit managed to throw the succubus off his back, I unloaded my Cerberus in him. The first two shots did nothing, but the third bullet was silver, and the servant's body went numb for a moment. And that was because the silver bullet managed to spark a fear in him, set alight by my *talent*. He had a fear of the noble metal.

The seizure lasted just an instant, but that short moment was enough for Elizabeth-Maria to grab the saber, and swing it with an inhuman might, utterly destroying Theodor's head. It went straight through from top to bottom.

The well-sharpened blade had entirely split his skull and was now embedded half way down the chest. Then, the girl pulled it out in one strenuous motion and struck him again, this time horizontally, taking the head off the shoulders.

The decapitated body, whose horrible wounds didn't give forth even a drop of blood, froze in place for a second, then collapsed on the floor with a thud. And I immediately stopped sensing the presence of the underworld native.

"Leo, it's extremely humiliating to hear from a stranger that you aren't a fellow's first," Elizabeth-Maria said viscously. "How could we have any secrets?"

Before I managed to answer, the house shook. Clocks and pictures flew onto the floor. A cupboard fell down, nearly crushing me. The chandeliers shook, and a wide crack ran down the wall of the guest room. Then another, stronger impact broke through the floor, turning it into a stockade of broken boards.

Elizabeth-Maria jumped nimbly back from the dangerous place and grabbed the mantel, but a slimy tentacle suddenly shot up out of the hole. It wrapped around the girl, bashed her head on a cabinet, stunning her, and tossed her outside through a gap in the collapsed wall.

I darted into the hallway; the detestable appendage of the demonic creature cut into the walls, dashing through them with such ease, it seemed they were made of construction paper. One of the chunks of wall hit me and knocked me off my feet.

The tentacle shot upward and fell down, trying to flatten me out on the parquet. It missed by just a few hand-lengths and hit the silver lying on the floor. It shot right back up, but now there was an acrid smoke in the room. An instant later, its smooth violet-black skin had dozens of pus-swollen burns on it.

The manor shook from yet another blow. The floor in the guest room shuddered and curved in. The demonic guise of the dead chef crawled through the hole, hauling its disgusting shapeless carcass out. A second tentacle appeared. Then I saw a stinking mouth hole.

But I didn't step back. I knew this creature's weakness and was planning to give combat.

Silver! I picked up a silver fork from the floor. It was massive, carved and of ancient providence. I clenched it in my hand so hard it hurt. The demon had a fear of silver, and I always got along well with fear.

At that moment, the leprechaun popped out of the entryway. His tongue was lolling out as he dragged the suitcase containing Alexander Dyak's transmitter into the room, unlatched the belts and snapped his fingers, intending to start the thing up.

"Don't you dare!" I barked, not knowing how far the electromagnetic waves would reach. I was still nursing the hope that I could kill two birds with one stone.

I was only distracted for a moment, but I immediately paid for my gaffe. One of the tentacles slid into the hallway, wrapped around my ankle and dragged me into the guest room, right into the demon's embrace. The sharp jerk didn't leave me any chance to stay on my feet. I collapsed backward, but immediately turned onto my stomach and latched my free hand into the doorframe.

But it was of little use! The grasp of the otherworldly being was too strong.

My fingers started slipping. Then I bent low, contorting my body, and full-force jabbed the fork into the tentacle grabbing my leg. The silver tines went deep into the slimy flesh. It jerked back, nearly pulling off my boots, but the pain forced the demon to yank the appendage back and start smacking it at random against the walls in an attempt to free itself of the hateful metal.

Taking advantage of the opportunity, I got off my knees and filled my whole consciousness with thoughts of molten silver being poured into the basement, cleansing it. Like a sharp spear, my *talent* embedded the image in the demonic consciousness, and the undead chef froze for a few seconds, shocked at the horrifying image.

His puzzlement didn't last long, though. The bloated carcass soon burst from the basement with such force that the whole house shook, but by that time, Elizabeth-Maria was back from outside to help me. Her red curls disheveled, she walked over the rubble, saber in hand. She looked surprisingly like one of the legendary northern Valkyries, and I gave a signal to the leprechaun with a certain degree of irrational pity:

"Fire it up!"

The girl cut off the outgrowth that shot at her; the pipsqueak flipped the breaker and I darted away, hurrying to take shelter in the corridor. The demonic incarnation of the chef pulsed with a transparent flame in time with the Morse-code signals being broadcast. And these signals were repeated in my head:

Short-long-long-short...

The electromagnetic pulses tore through the bloated body of the underworld native, washed it away, and deprived it of reality. It shook harder and harder, first becoming semi-transparent, then suddenly disappearing in a blinding flash of light. Ghostly voices yelped in my head like a horrifying choir. For a moment, I was blinded by the constant flickering and, when I regained my vision, I found myself kneeling in the guest-room doorframe for some reason.

Threaten to kill me, I still wouldn't remember how it happened.

The smell of burnt wire coating and strong tobacco filled the house. I tried to look around, but my neck was asleep as if I'd spent several hours in this uncomfortable position. Standing proved difficult.

I walked cautiously over to the hole in the floor, looked into the basement and caught my breath with relief when the only thing I saw down there was ice. The demon had disappeared without a trace. Not even the slime from its tentacles was left. And what was more important – I no longer felt the presence of the curse filling the house. Not in the slightest.

"Bugger, your hurdy-gurdy's toast!" the leprechaun announced, sitting on the suitcase as he threw a hand-rolled cigarette on the floor. "Now we're in a bad way..."

I nodded and suddenly froze, having noticed Elizabeth-Maria. Contrary to my hopes, the electromagnetic disturbances had not sent the succubus to hell.

Curses!

But then, Elizabeth-Maria took her blood-soaked hand from her face and stared at me with the whites of two blind eyes. The girl had ceased to be *illustrious*. The otherworldly essence had left her, and that scared me half to death.

I had created her as an image in my head, but the strength of the succubus had helped it be embodied in reality. Now, the infernal creature had been driven out, but Elizabeth-Maria hadn't disappeared, she'd become a normal girl! Demonic charm no longer surrounded her with its seductive veil. The once fatal beauty had been replaced by a sweet, cute young woman. Sweet, cute and blind.

"What is happening?" Elizabeth-Maria asked, undercutting my theory that she'd totally lost her senses. "What is happening?"

The girl's voice sounded unusually vulnerable, as if it was someone else entirely. When I tried to take Elizabeth-Maria by the hand, she quickly wriggled free and cried out:

"Don't touch me!"

"Calm yourself!" I demanded, but the girl took a step back. Then, she just ran down the hallway, blindly running into furniture.

I didn't follow after her. I simply didn't know how to behave now. Though I'd gotten what I wanted, for some reason, my conscience made me feel uncomfortable.

The leprechaun was also feeling out of sorts; he lit a new rollie and said, drawing out his words in perplexity:

"Bugger, what a situation!"

I kicked the pipsqueak away in silence and bent down over the apparatus, which reeked unbearably of burnt electrical wire. The leprechaun frowned aggrievedly and went to walk around the manor. I, meanwhile, had to pull the melted electric battery from the suitcase; the transmitter itself, to my untold relief, looked undamaged.

I got the desire to simply take it and rip out the wires, but instead, I unfolded my knife and carefully cut through them. It took some time, but the transmitter now looked somewhat more presentable than before. I had no desire to upset

Alexander Dyak too badly.

I latched up the suitcase, dragged it back to the trunk of the armored vehicle and went up into the bedroom for *Alice's Adventures in Wonderland*. I didn't try to unscramble the code, just stuck the book in my bag and stared at the pencil portrait of Elizabeth-Maria von Nalz in contemplation.

" I do not feel the same about you, Viscount," her voice called out in my head painfully. In a rage, I rumpled up the sheet of paper and threw it into the trash bin. I quickly got it back out and smoothed it over as much as I could, then put it in my bag.

After that, I started gathering my things.

I did not plan to return to this house again. It made my skin crawl.

I didn't remember.

I didn't remember what happened in that basement sixteen years ago. But along with that, I was sure that I had seen a throat cut open in such away before. It was the same way the leprechaun had cut the Chinese enforcer's throat. And that fact scared me all the more.

I didn't remember, and didn't want to remember.

I wanted to leave here as fast as possible, but first, I had to get rid of some evidence. The curse was no longer protecting the manor, and anyone could come inside now to look for weapons and dead bodies. The last thing I wanted was to have to spend the rest of my life fleeing from investigators. To hell with the mummies, though. What I really needed to get out of here was the human corpses and weapons.

At first, I parked the armored car in the carriage-house and loaded all the boxes into it. Then, I searched for the hand-held machine gun and warped rifle, threw them into the trunk and went inside the house.

There was rain sprinkling in through a hole in the guest-room wall. Water was flowing through the broken floor into the basement and gradually covering the chunks of ice. I threw back the reinforced hatch, went down and gave an involuntary shudder. And though there was daylight driving back the darkness of the icehouse, I still didn't want to go down there. My fear of basements was right where it had always been.

I overpowered it, ran down the hoar-frosted stairs and dragged the corpses outside, first the retired judge, then the robber the leprechaun had cut up and, finally, I returned for the Moor. There wasn't even a wisp remaining of the chef.

After loading the dead bodies into the back of the car, I went into the house and, there, I was shouted out to by the leprechaun.

"Boy, are you sure you didn't forget anything?" pointing to the frosted-line jar containing the *fallen one*'s heart.

"Leave it," I said with a wave of my hand.

The pipsqueak shrugged his shoulders and threw the jar over his back. I winced, expecting to hear the sound of breaking glass, but the vessel landed with a quiet thud, sunk down into the ice chunks, and went out of view.

And to hell with that heart, even if it had broken to pieces.

I couldn't have cared less.

I ran through the whole house, but didn't find a single trace of Elizabeth-Maria; it was as if the girl had sunk down into the earth. I checked the garden – she definitely wasn't there. Then, I stood over the graves of my mother and father for a short time, promising that I would one day return and got into the armored car.

It was time to get out of here.

4

THE STORM rolled over the city. Every minute, there was a new lightning strike on the iron tower at the top of Calvary; the bright flashes blinded the eye. The thunder caused the windows of the self-propelled carriage to shudder, and the gusts of wind nearly blew us off the road.

I didn't look back even one time. I just drove down from the hill and maneuvered the vehicle down the wet and homely streets to Leonardo-da-Vinci-Platz. That said, calling what I did "maneuvering" was rather overstating it. The rain was pouring over the windshield and, even with the armor plate thrown back, I had to stick my head out the window just to get the slightest notion of the road ahead.

On the way, I stopped at the embankment of

one of the canals that led to the Yarden and threw the thoroughly frozen bodies in. This way, there wouldn't be any uncomfortable questions at Alexander Dyak's when he helped me unload the suitcase with the transmitter. When I arrived to the inventor's, he just shook his head at the many boxes filled with weaponry.

"I hope, Leopold Borisovich," he asked when we had gone inside, "that you do not have any ties with the anarchists." And immediately, he waved his hand. "I beg of you, pay no mind to my old-man's humor! You, rightly, need to put yourself in order. You don't look yourself!"

I decisively set a glass of brandy he stuck in my hand on the workbench and looked in the mirror. On my pale face, you could see a swollen nose, and my shirt collar was spattered with dried blood.

When did this happen to me?

After washing up, I asked the inventor for a towel, wiped the water off my face and took a seat at his desk with the photograph fragment and the worn edition of *Alice's Adventures in Wonderland*. I started decrypting the instructions for claiming the deposit, taking sips of hot, strong tea as I did, chasing it by nipping at a spoon of sugar in the Russian fashion. Alexander Dyak, meanwhile, took a look into the suitcase. After seeing the transmitter, he asked with voracious interest:

"Did it work?!"

"In full measure," I affirmed.

"And how was it?"

I shrugged my shoulders:

"Just like with the poltergeist. You're a genius, Alexander."

"You're flattering me, Leopold Borisovich."

"A genius!" I repeated. "But what exactly became of the electric battery, I cannot say precisely. It burned out."

"I'll figure it out," the inventor reassured me.

At the same time, I was nearing the end of the code. I read the text a few times, trying my very hardest to memorize the fairly basic instructions, flicked my lighter and burned the paper and photo up. I didn't want to take any unnecessary risks.

"What are your plans for the next few days, Leopold Borisovich?" Dyak asked, checking the components of his device. "I'd like to carry on our work together, but I need to order a few parts. The battery wasn't the only thing that burned out."

"Our work is sure to carry on," I promised, "but first, I need to take a trip to Zurich. Would you object to me leaving the car in your back yard?"

"For a long time?"

"If need be," I shrugged, not knowing whether it was worth coming back at all.

Alexander Dyak nodded, wiped his face with the rag and took a seat at his desk.

"Then allow me to quiz you a bit more, Leopold Borisovich," he smiled, opening a spreadsheet. "Every detail is important to science!"

I spent around a quarter hour describing the

details to the inventor, then pulled out the white-phosphorus hand-held mortar rounds from the back of the armored vehicle, – what need did I have for them now? – bid the old man farewell and went outside.

The wind immediately bared down on me, the cold rain whipping and crawling under my shirt collar. The wind was trying to pull off my hat. I slouched and, leaning on the cane, hurried to the nearest steam-tram line. Beyond the storm, which had caused all travel to the continent to be suspended, my hasty departure to Switzerland was also impeded by a simple lack of money.

I had plenty of cash for a steam-ship ticket, but I didn't want to beg for alms the whole way to Zurich. And my attorney could help with that.

To my good fortune, the trams hadn't stopped running in the rain, and most of the trip was spent warm and dry. And that was simply wonderful: the rain outside was clearly stronger. The storm-drain system could no longer manage it. There were ruddy streams gushing down the street, and lightning flashing and booming with all the fury of an artillery cannonade.

The wind rushed between the high buildings with an unbelievable force, nearly knocking me off my feet and forcing me to duck down. When I got into my attorney's little office, the water was streaming off me like a brook.

"Viscount?" the lawyer was taken aback by my appearance. "Has something happened?"

"Horrible weather," I muttered, getting the

late Count's agreement to me coming into my inheritance from my traveling bag. "Here, take all necessary measures."

My attorney quickly looked at the papers and raised his surprised, round eyes to me:

"Viscount, how did you do this?"

"The injunctions helped," I smiled simply.

"I'll take care of this, Viscount," the lawyer promised and faltered, "but does it have to be today? I'm only still in the office because I'm afraid I won't make it home! I'll never catch the right people at work now!"

"Alright," I nodded. "See you tomorrow, then. I'll be in touch. Most likely, I'll send a telegram saying where to send the first allotment."

"Yes sir, Viscount!" my attorney repeated.

I bid him farewell and went out into the hallway, intending to wait out the bad weather at Central Station and go from there to port as soon as the weather improved. I no longer had to worry about money. The allowances from the family fund would be quite enough for the upcoming trip to Zurich. And there, everything would work itself out.

It would work itself out!

My head was full of such big ideas that I only paid any mind to the man walking up to meet me in the vestibule when he said:

"Viscount Cruce! I've been looking for you everywhere!"

Awoken in an instant, I stuck my hand in my pocket and stared cautiously at the familiar detective sergeant with red mustache and yellow eyes.

"To what end?" I asked him.

"The inspector general would like to see you," the police man answered, shaking the raindrops off his cap. "I wasn't told the reason."

"Wasn't he planning to go home?"

"As a matter of fact, he's asking for you to be brought to his home," the detective sergeant confirmed. "Perhaps this is somehow connected with his daughter. I do not know."

Upon hearing mention of Elizabeth-Maria, my heart gave a moan, but I didn't show it. I got my tin of sugar drops from my pocket and tossed one unhurriedly into my mouth, only saying after that:

"Great! Let's not leave the inspector general waiting, then."

And so, went outside, ran over to a carriage parked right on the porch and hurried to take shelter in it from the rain.

"Some weather, eh!" the detective sergeant shook his head, rubbing his mustache.

I just nodded, not really trying to keep up the conversation. My thoughts were occupied with something else entirely. I mean, I couldn't really hope for anything. Elizabeth-Maria had said her fill in this regard clearly and unambiguously. Yet the whole way there, I was anticipating seeing her again, regardless. Stupid! Devilishly stupid! But, it is a well-known fact that hope is the last thing to die.

I was hoping for a miracle. I was hoping while we rolled over wet causeways. Hoping as we looped around the confusing little streets of the Old Town. Hoping as I looked out the rain-slicked window at the inspector general's manor. And, walking through the yard, I continued to console myself with illusions, as if I'd just caught luck by the tail. An overly developed imagination in such circumstances brought nothing but problems.

A cold shower washed over me in the fabric-draped hallway, though, when I heard the cracking sound of a gun being cocked behind me. A second later, the detective sergeant demanded:

"Don't move, Viscount!" I felt the steel of the gun poke into my waist and another command sounded out: "Hands up!"

I obeyed and tried to get an explanation, but the investigator didn't explain anything, just ordered:

"Silence!"

He pulled the traveling bag from my hands and threw it on the floor, then patted down my pockets and took the Cerberus. He found my knife, as well. The detective sergeant must have known perfectly what was in each of my pockets.

"Walk and don't turn around!" he ordered, taking a step back. "Forward!"

And I started down the hallway again. But now, I was not nursing any illusions about my near future. There were unanswerable questions tearing through my head – what the devil was going on?! – my legs gave out; my heart was almost jumping out of my chest.

What had the inspector general thought up now? What had Elizabeth-Maria told him about me? And if it wasn't her, then who? When we parted, the inspector general and I had been getting along famously. What had gotten into him?!

It all turned out much simpler than I ever could have imagined.

When I got to the spacious reception hall, the man I met, was not Friedrich von Nalz at all, but an old *illustrious* gentleman I didn't recognize. To be more accurate, I only didn't recognize the narrow noble face of the withered old aristocrat; the colorless-glowing eyes I recognized on first glance. It was the boss of the bank-robber gang.

But I didn't show that I knew that, just asked:

"So, am I to understand that this is not the inspector general's home?"

"Indeed, Viscount," the *illustrious* man answered and pointed me to a chair opposite his. "Take a seat."

I obeyed, then the man turned to the detective sergeant who'd delivered me:

"How'd it all go?"

"The target left home in the armored car you were already aware of and parked it in back of the shop *Mechanisms and Rarities*, which is off Leonardo-da-Vinci-Platz. On his way, he threw three bodies into a canal." The investigator sighed and said pointedly: "One of them was Mathew's."

"Oh, Viscount," the *illustrious* man muttered and turned back to the rain-slicked window. "That is so unfortunate..."

I looked at the huge chandelier with electric candles under the ceiling and snorted:

"In my defense, I can say that your Mathew died from a heart attack."

"Is that so?" the manor owner asked, seemingly without particular interest.

"He couldn't bear the disappointment. Such things happen when you're starting from bad assumptions."

The *illustrious* man shook his head.

"What irony!" he laughed quietly. "A heart attack was the ruin of a man who caused dozens of them!"

"Your radiance," said the detective sergeant, drawing attention to himself. "What are your orders?"

"Viscount," the manor owner stared at me stubbornly, and his eyes lit up to full transparency, "for what reason did you park the armored vehicle in the back yard of that shop?"

"The radiator was leaking," I answered the nearly pure truth. "The owner said he could help fix it."

"You really trust him that much?"

"He's not a talkative man."

"How are we to get our property back, then?"

I considered for a moment whether I would manage to send an encoded message to Dyak, then threw the idea aside and advised:

"Just tell him I sent you for it. It won't be an issue."

"Is that so?"

"I guarantee it."

"Deal with that," the *illustrious* man ordered the detective as he pulled a cigar case out of the interior pocket of his smoking jacket. He opened it, took out an elongated electric bulb and clenched his fingers on the metal base. "But before we're left alone, Viscount," he said, "I'd like to demonstrate a small trick."

The bulb suddenly flickered on and, at the same time, the colorless eyes of the manor's owner lit up nearly as brightly.

"Once upon a time, this primitive gimmick provided me the affection of ladies in salons," the *illustrious* man chuckled quietly, "but believe me, my *talent* can do more than that. You definitely won't like to feel its effects. I'm told they're rather... unpleasant."

The old man shifted his gaze to a floor lamp near the window. The bulb under red fabric first lit up with a blinding glow, then burnt out with a loud clap.

"I hope you can manage to avoid doing anything foolish, Viscount?"

I evaluated the distance between us and nodded:

"I can."

The *illustrious* man's *talent* made an impression on me. After all, the extreme pain that can be caused by electric shock was still fresh in my memory.

A living generator, holy crap!

"Go fetch the armored vehicle," the manor owner ordered the detective sergeant, who was still here.

"Are you sure, your radiance?" the red-mustached investigator doubted, not wanting to leave his master alone with me.

"Go!"

The detective sergeant stuck his police-issue revolver in its holster and went outside. The quiet patter of his steps soon grew quiet, then the *illustrious* man got out of his chair and walked over to the window, beyond which there where bright lightning bursts flashing out from time to time.

"Would you like something to drink?" he asked, talking over the howling of the wind, and his voice resonated in the spacious room.

"No thank you," I refused, guessing why I had been brought here.

They could have just killed me on the way; popping a few bullets into me and dropping my body in the river was about the easiest thing one could imagine. Did that mean this was all about that ill-fated box?

"You look just like him," the aristocrat suddenly said.

"Excuse me?" I asked, not knowing what he was driving at.

"Your grandfather. You look just like him," the old man repeated.

"Did you know him?"

"Did I know Emile?" the *illustrious* man laughed. "We were friends! He always beat me at cards, the old rogue."

I gave a nervous shiver and corrected him:

"Neither of my grandfathers were named

Emile."

"Drop the act, Viscount," the manor owner waved a hand, returned to his chair and leaned on its high back. "Anyhow, it seems we got off on the wrong foot. Allow me to introduce myself: Duke Talm. You can call me Duncan."

"How pleasant to make your acquaintance, your radiance," I said, evaluating my chance of getting out of this fix alive. To be straight – it was quite small.

"Leave the formalities for official receptions," the Duke winced. "And stop looking at me like a sheep looks at a wolf. I'm not planning to kill you!"

I shrugged my shoulders.

"After everything that's happened, I find that rather hard to believe."

"That was nothing more than expediency!" the manor owner declared. "Nothing personal, Viscount. It's just how the stars aligned. If it's of any consolation, I was opposed to such aggressive tactics, but the situation started spinning out of control almost instantly."

"And what changed now?"

"Nothing. Actually, I'm currently saving your life, Viscount. A document of the utmost importance has fallen into your hands. There are very many who would stop at nothing to have it. Soon, they will make their play, and the safest thing for you is to remain in this very place, in my company."

"Remember what I said about bad assumptions?" I sighed. "Well, it was really all one big misunderstanding, your radiance."

Duke Talm stared stubbornly at me and demanded:

"Explain yourself!"

I got the dead *illustrious* man's notebook from my pocket, opened it to the right page and got up from the chair.

"May I?" I asked. After getting permission, I walked up to the buffet table, set the notepad on it and returned to my place. "I suppose this handwriting is familiar to you."

The manor owner familiarized himself with the decrypted message, ripped out the page, crumpled it up and threw it ferociously on the floor. The old man's face acquired an incomprehensible expression, as if disappointment and relief were battling inside him.

"Viscount, do you know what exactly we were hoping to find?" He asked.

"I have no idea," I answered with a slight lie.

"Mathew didn't tell you?"

"No."

"Well then," the Duke said, drawing out his words, "our conversation will be a bit longer than I supposed."

"I don't want to hear your secrets!" I hurried to assure the man, but he didn't even listen.

"Take a seat, Viscount!" he demanded, lowering down in his armchair. "You can't escape fate! No one can, Viscount, not you, and not me."

"Your words do not inspire confidence in the future."

The *illustrious* man laughed:

"Viscount, nothing bad will happen to you. I promise. I just wanna have a chat."

"What for? What if I don't want to know anything?"

"Do you really want to spend the rest of your life on the run? Are you counting on making it to Zurich? An empty hope! You'll be caught and disemboweled. These people are accustomed to getting what's theirs."

"These people?" I snorted. "Are you talking about yourself?"

"No, the Convent," the old man said weightily. "They think you have all the information they need. I have no idea how you'd ever be able to convince them otherwise." The Duke arrived at a bad mental state and pointed to the door. "Leave, you no longer interest me! Leave, but know this – you won't live to see sunup!"

I didn't move an inch.

Duke Talm made several loud sighs, then placed a hand behind his back and started pacing the room.

"I ordered you brought here, thinking that you were in possession of our secret. But Emile was bluffing! Curses! No one knew how to bluff like him! He bamboozled us all! We were hunting for nothing, just a gift he gave his illegitimate daughter! You may go, Viscount. I was doing this out of respect for the memory of your grandfather, but if you don't want my help – leave right now!"

I shook my head.

"It's raining out, and I don't have an umbrella."

"Would you like one? I've got plenty."

"I'd rather wait it out," I answered, suspecting that any attempt on my part to leave this room would lead to nothing but more trouble.

"Wise decision," the old man said with a strange look on his face. "But swear to keep our conversation secret."

"You just take me at my word?"

"Why not?" the manor owner shrugged. "After all, revealing it will bring you no good, just more trouble."

"Good," I promised. "I'll hold my tongue."

"I'm counting on your good sense, Viscount," Duke Talm sighed, lowering down into the armchair. He then suddenly asked: "What do you know about *the fallen*?"

"Strange question," I snorted. "The same things as everyone, I suppose."

"Considering your father's views, I strongly doubt that," the *illustrious* man said with a shake of his head. "You'd be surprised, Viscount, how paltry the average person's knowledge of the history of our world can be. Even the educated public often cannot boast of particular erudition when it comes to the events of our recent past. The reductionists are more concerned with the future. They do not understand that the future doesn't exist yet, that it is completely dependent not only on the present, but also on by-gone times. To be more accurate, on how our society thinks of those times!"

I looked at the window with sorrow. The rain there was pouring down. Lightning was flashing, and the trees in the garden were bending under the gusts of wind.

"So then, what do you know about *the fallen*?" Duke Talm repeated his question.

"Which of the generally accepted points of view would you like me to parrot off?" I shrugged. "The Christians say *the fallen* were divine punishment, sent down to us for killing the Savior. Everyone else thinks that, after the resurrection of the Savior from the cross, the Creator ceased caring for this world, and *the fallen* simply descended to earth in order to set up shop and rule."

The *illustrious* man nodded, leaned back in his chair and smiled.

"The history of our world, Viscount, was written in the epoch of the Renaissance and consists of omissions, confusions and obvious lies. 'Pious lies,' or so thought the first reductionists. At that time, they were already anticipating the upcoming changes and were preparing the ground for them."

"I have a hard time believing in a conspiracy of that magnitude."

"There was no conspiracy, it's just that a few like-minded individuals, the brightest minds of their times, were laying the foundations for a grandiose falsification. As I've already said, the average person doesn't know much history. It's always been like that. But *the fallen... The fallen* burnt cities, turned humans into pillars of salt, and caused rivers and seas to evaporate. They frightened us. And no one understood the motivation for their actions."

"Humanity's punishment for its sins?"

"But what about forgiveness?" the old man parried. "And if it is a punishment, where's the divine hand of the Great Flood? All scholars speak of the oppressions suffered under *the fallen*, yet none of the authors is capable of explaining just how humanity developed and grew over the course of its history. Perhaps *the fallen* weren't such bad shepherds for our lost herd after all."

"Or maybe they simply couldn't bear the temptation and yearned for power?"

Duke Talm melted into a satisfied smile.

"That's right!" he confirmed. "The path of the Most High is unknowable. After the crucifixion of his son, his mercy left this world. And only his heavenly host remained to hold back the underworld. They came down to earth, created Atlantis, their indestructible bulwark, and started the struggle against the forces of evil! They destroyed the darkness everywhere they could reach it, but the people simply couldn't understand why these heavenly emissaries were burning their cities. They did not realize that darkness reigned there, that devils and witches had enslaved the minds of men and were preparing to spread their influence like gangrene throughout a body. There's only one treatment for such an ailment – cauterization by red-hot iron! But *the fallen* didn't explain anything to anyone. For long centuries, they did nothing to intervene in daily life, just protected humanity from infernal creatures. The Christians weren't always persecuted by them. But everything changes. And one day, *the fallen* also changed. Their essence became corrupted. The angels of the Lord, protectors of humanity, considered themselves the powerful leaders of this world. No one can say the exact date when their fall to sin was completed, but the fact remains – they became *the fallen*."

"Quite a bold point of view," I noted neutrally, thinking over what I'd heard in agitation.

"Everything started to change at the beginning of this millennium. The more profoundly *the fallen* were overcome by their thirst for power, the less attention they paid to the fight against the natives of the underworld. As contemporary written sources bear out, people simply found it impossible to live with all the witches, werebeasts, vampires and malefics about, so the church tried to remedy the situation. An inquisition was launched."

I smiled involuntarily.

"Yes, yes!" the *illustrious* man nodded. "An inquisition. The bogeyman of our current enlightened society. Though it was over the top, they started cleansing the cities and villages of evil-doers and their allies. *The fallen* thought it an encroachment on their power. Religion was then forbidden. The Christians bore persecutions even harsher than those at the very dawn of the church. *The fallen* became like we remember them. They finally were no better than the underworld natives and did not scorn making deals with them. They sold human beings like cattle."

"I do not understand the need for this excursion through history," I admitted.

Duke Talm smiled:

"*The fallen* became evil, yet the only thing keeping hell itself from invading our world was their power. They hindered humanity, disfigured it but, at the same time, protected it from an incomparably greater evil: death itself."

I had an idea of where the conversation would go from there, but still I sat stone-faced, not showing any emotion.

The *illustrious* man picked up the light bulb from the armrest. It was still lit. He shifted his gaze to the chandelier under the ceiling and sighed.

"At that time, it seemed unacceptable to us," he sighed a little while later. "We were young and thirsted for freedom. And we got it. Yes we did..."

"Are you talking about the uprising?" I asked directly.

"The uprising was just the tip of the iceberg," Duke Talm said with an unhappy smile. "I am not authorized to tell you everything, but we received a weapon against *the fallen*. The power of science and sublime electricity helped us cast off their loathsome yoke, and ever since then, we've kept our secret. Would you like to know why?"

"Power," I supposed. "Otherwise, it would be impossible to get the provinces to submit."

"Oh, yes!" the *illustrious* man smiled. "We taught the little local power brokers a lesson, depriving them of their protection against the underworld! And not even a month later, they were crawling to us on their hands and knees, recognizing Clement as Emperor."

I crossed my arms on my chest and asked:

"What does this story have to do with our situation? And who is this 'we' you keep mentioning?"

"Everything in due time," the Duke assured me. "Everything was wonderful while Clement was in good health. Nature had awarded him a resilient constitution, but his only daughter died in childbirth. And her only daughter, the Emperor's granddaughter, was discovered to have a heart defect while she was still a baby. That laid him low. He burnt up in bitterness in a matter of days. And then Emile expressed the desire to occupy the throne. 'Brother succeeds brother, what's so strange about that?' he asked us."

"Am I to understand that the widowed Empress was against it?"

"Not only her," said the Duke, growing gloomy. "A rift grew in the old guard. Some of us supposed we should just let it run its course, others demanded we support Emile. He was one of us, and the Empress was not. But there was no unity. We did not have time to come to a decision."

"Then grandfather pulled the trump card from his sleeve..."

"Emile went all in. He promised to publicize our secret if we didn't support his claim to the throne. He threatened to destroy everything we achieved!"

"And so you did away with him?" I guessed. "There was no African flu?"

"Not at all!" the *illustrious* man objected. "We obeyed him, because he knew all our deepest fears."

"Then what went wrong?"

"Someone must have talked," the manor owner shrugged. "The flu was raging that year. Sudden deaths didn't surprise anyone. Former advisers of Clement had their whole families die. There was nothing we could do to change it."

"Why were you not arrested?"

"Well, we weren't just some mere aristocratic club!" the Duke laughed. "When we first started, just one bad word about the authorities could lead to disemboweling and quartering, then resurrection just to be disemboweled again and burned alive. We always took certain precautionary measures. Only the most prudent survived. Those who never relaxed for many years of calm life."

"Paranoiacs," I said, knowing fully well what kind of people I was dealing with. They'd been following me, the illegitimate grandson of a former associate ever since he'd died fifteen years ago, after all!

"We knew that Emile hid the documents in a safe place. We could not allow them to fall into the wrong hands. And it wasn't even a matter of power. The very survival of the human race is at stake. We are the only force stopping all hell from breaking loose. Us alone. And we aren't getting any younger. What's more, the Empress must know something about us from her dead husband. She is still searching for the traces of our society. We could not risk accepting new members. We got old."

"But what did Emile Rie know about you?" I asked directly.

"We defeated *the fallen* with the help of science, but that which one genius invents, sooner or later, will be invented by another," the Duke said, slowly and full of sorrow, looking out the window. "I am not strong in technical details. All these electromagnetic waves and frequencies are just a dark forest to me. We still have reliable people in the Sublime Electricity movement. We provide them with money, they repair the equipment. Emile knew everything. People, how it worked, the frequency, the code, the locations of the transmitters. If that information were to get out, destroying the network would be no trouble at all."

"And what about asking the Empress for protection?"

"None of us have gotten better with time," Duke Talm smiled sadly. "Victoria thinks us her enemies. She'd sooner destroy everything than trust the purity of our intentions."

"But why?" I asked. "Why did you tell me this? I knew nothing about your affairs, so what the devil?"

"I think you have the right to know why this is all happening."

"What are you talking about?"

Duke Talm turned away to the window, then sighed:

"Emile was my friend, Viscount. I should have talked him out of that adventure, I should have done everything in my power, but I didn't even try. I wanted to see him on the throne, old fool! And in the end, it all flew straight to hell. We carry on living through our descendants, Viscount. You are Emile's only living descendant, so in some measure you are all that remains of him."

I caught a quick glance from the man toward the window and gave an unwilling shudder.

"Allow me to express doubt in the sincerity of your words, Duncan."

"Dear Leopold, the very fact that you are still alive is better confirmation of my sincerity than any assurance I could give you."

But I didn't believe it. I felt the echoes of distant fears, and I didn't like that one bit. The old man was afraid of something. He was expecting something, and it definitely was not the return of the detective sergeant he'd sent out for the armored vehicle. Also, it was hard to square what he was now saying with the electric chair I'd once had the distinct pleasure of being strapped into.

I looked at the window, and cast my gaze into the spacious hall. The rich decoration aroused envious respect. The composed mahogany parquet was shining with a fresh coat of wax, and a certain desolation could be sensed in with that. No balls had been held here for a very, very long time.

Duke Talm sensed the doubts plaguing my mind and suggested:

"Wine?"

"No, thank you," I refused, tossing a mint sugar drop into my mouth. I didn't say anything more.

"Alright!" said the manor owner with a hand wave. "I admit, I wasn't being totally honest with you. But do you understand what kind of responsibility I have on my shoulders? For the last half century, the only thing keeping infernal creatures from humanity was our society! The engineers of the Sublime Electricity were just servicing the equipment, changing the worn-out parts, and providing power. They do not know what it is all doing, and so it must remain. The only thing keeping us from being revealed is the fact that none of our enemies knows what exactly to look for. Vampires now cower in the very farthest corners of the Empire. Witches have degenerated into illiterate herbalists, malefics suffer from migraines and can only cast the most primitive of spells! Werebeasts are confined to life in the provincial backwoods, and all other underworld filth doesn't even have a modicum of the powers they once did! And how were we rewarded for that? We were driven into hiding, not only from the Convent's bloodhounds, but also from the police and Imperial Guard secret service. We were not ready for the present crisis. It caught us completely by surprise! So, Leopold, I beg you – please be understanding of our old-timer follies!"

I just shook my head:

"In your words, I see only contradiction. The Empire is great – I will not dispute that, but what about the rest of the world? Who is protecting them from the forces of the underworld? The Aztecs, Egypt, the Celestial Kingdom, Persia – how are we to deal with them?"

"Our equipment covers the entire globe," the manor owner answered calmly. "Inside the Empire, it is stronger. Its effect grows weaker the farther you get from our borders, but the fact remains – we are protecting humanity. In its entirety."

"How noble!"

"Nobility has nothing to do with it," the *illustrious* man shook his head. "That is more of a side effect. Otherwise, the Emperor of the Celestial Kingdom would have long ago sworn his allegiance to us as a vassal."

"And the others?"

"Viscount, you see to the root of the problem, as always!" the old man smiled bitterly. "A very significant number of *the fallen* survived the Night of the Titanium Blades. And though they were deprived of their powers, they maintained their former influence over the rulers of the Egyptians and Aztecs. Many thirst for the return of the old order, Viscount. Very many."

"The Convent?"

"The Convent is not homogeneous in its aims. They're just a group of the Empire's most notorious sons of bitches, joined together for survival. But, as soon as they achieve success, they'll start tearing each other to pieces. If we back down, rivers of blood will flow. That cannot be allowed! Under no circumstances!"

"Why am I here, Duncan?" I asked again, though I was afraid to hear the honest answer.

Duke Talm got out of his chair and walked to the window. There was a raging storm outside. Rain covered the window. Lightning flashed.

"Simple coincidence and nothing more," he finally said. "We're all playthings in the hands of fate."

"Sounds ominous."

"And it is," the manor owner confirmed. "You wouldn't have survived the night, Viscount. Despite all your success, it was not fated."

"What are you talking about?"

"Protection from the forces of evil built on electromagnetic radiation," the Duke said, "but sometimes, it doesn't work very well. Look out the window, Viscount! Lightning! Lightning strikes create disturbances. The equipment turns off due to surges, wires break, electricity goes out. In such weather, malefics are not limited in their abilities. It would be no work for them to send hellhounds or a Wild Hunt out after their intended victim. You have nowhere to hide from these diabolic beasts."

"And you brought me to your home..."

"Actually, this is the home of one of my deceased friends," Duke Talm smiled. "There's nothing to tie it to my name."

"That hardly clears anything up."

"A demon is being sent for you, and I can stop it. Fate itself brought us together."

The Duke's voice sounded so solemn in the empty room, I felt ants crawling up my spine.

"And if you cannot manage?" I asked.

"Then this will all end here and now," Duncan answered with an unconcerned tone.

"You thought I had Emile's papers. Now, you know that isn't the case. Why take the risk?"

"This isn't only about you, Viscount. The Convent needs to be taught a lesson. I need to tear the poisonous fangs from these scoundrels while I still can. Today, they aren't expecting a trap. They're sure of their success. This will make their defeat all the more bitter. We'll get a breather and we can take advantage of that."

"You're that sure of your own powers?"

"This isn't my first time. And also, better to die in a skirmish than to live out a century watching everything fall to pieces. Today, we can still fix something. Tomorrow, that will not be possible."

I nodded in silence, having begun to expect that this could all be explained by the Duke's desire to die in battle. The old man didn't look capable of standing up to a demon.

The *illustrious* gentleman sensed my doubts,

turned away from the window and declared with an unconcerned smile:

"Chin up, Viscount! An old gambler like me always has an ace up his sleeve. I'll be ready when the underworld fiend appears."

"Are you able to sense the demon's approach?"

"It's easier than you think," Duke Talm replied, waving carelessly as he pointed at the chandelier filling the whole room with bright light. "See?"

The light of the electric candles had already been uneven and flickering for some time.

"Power fluctuations," I supposed.

"Demons and electricity don't pair well together," the old man laughed. "Wherever you find one, there's no room for the other."

"I'm not convinced."

"Well, then trust my experience."

At that moment, the doors behind me opened loudly, and I nearly jumped in the seat from surprise.

"Calm yourself, Viscount!" the *illustrious* man said. He then asked the detective sergeant who'd just entered: "What of the armored carriage?"

"I got it, your radiance," the investigator said. There was a whole puddle of water pouring down off his rain-slicker onto the parquet floor.

I looked around and inquired:

"What about the shop owner?"

The detective sergeant looked at the Duke and, only after a positive nod from his boss, he answered:

"No one opened the door. I had to break in."

"No one noticed?"

"In this weather?" the detective laughed, wiping his red mustache and looking at the chandelier. "Has it begun?"

"It will soon," the Duke confirmed.

"Isn't it time for you to get ready?"

"I'm about to get started."

The electric candles in the chandelier started flickering more and more. Their light became dim and sparse. The shadows in the corners grew thicker. I got uncomfortable. I now wanted to get out of here fast. The last thing I wanted was to play the live bait for a demon.

Just then, some of the bulbs went out. The others started glowing many times stronger, filling with an unbearable light and starting to burst with a quiet tinkling sound, one after the next. A few seconds, and the room was immersed in darkness. Just one bulb was still on: the one on the buffet table; the *illustrious* man's *talent* did not depend on electrical fluctuations whatsoever.

I stood up from the chair, deciding whether or not to high-tail it out under cover of darkness, but then I saw the flicker of a gun's steel in the gloom.

"Back in your seat!" the detective sergeant demanded, aiming his issued revolver at me.

"Calm yourself, Viscount!" Duke Talm laughed quietly, and immediately the electric candles in the chandelier filled with an unnatural white light; those which hadn't burned out, that is.

I gave an unwilling gasp and covered my eyes with my hand.

"Now, I have to leave you, Viscount. Business, you see. It was nice knowing you," said Duke Talm with a rigid bow before he left the room. "Forgive me!"

5

THE DUKE was now gone, but his last word was still hanging in the air, and it was not at all to my liking. But what could I do? Nothing. Just sit and wait to see how this crazy story would end.

The detective sergeant unbuttoned his rain-slicker, sat down in the armchair and set his revolver arm on the broad armrest, aiming the barrel at my chest.

"Is this all really necessary?" I grimaced. "We're kind of in the same boat now, right? We're in this together!"

"Silence!" the detective demanded; his yellow eyes looking unusually wicked.

"Are you nervous?"

"He'll manage."

"And if he doesn't?"

"We'll die."

"Such an outcome does not suit me."

A contemptuous grimace crawled over his face.

"Nothing will change for you in any case,"

the detective sergeant said. "The Duke is sentimental, but he's not senile. You are a threat. Threats are to be eliminated."

"The Duke ordered you to shoot me?"

The detective went silent, but the revolver barrel spoke more eloquently than any words.

I leaned back in my chair and went silent. We were sitting and looking at one another like two card players trying to figure out who was bluffing, and who really had the upper hand.

Had the red-mustached man really been ordered to shoot me, or was he trying to provoke me to reckless action? And if he really did consider me a threat, wouldn't he shoot me no matter what?

The situation scared me with its uncertainty, but I didn't fall into hysterics. I calmly tossed one leg over the other and asked:

"Has Senior Inspector Moran been showing heightened interest in you recently?"

For a moment, the inspector's tough exterior started to crack. But before I managed to grab onto his sudden fear and set it alight with my *illustrious talent*, the detective sergeant had already gotten himself together.

He was smiling carelessly and shaking his head.

"No," he answered. But then, he couldn't help asking: "What did you hear?"

"You should know better than me," I replied with a shrug of my shoulders. "When you copied those documents, you were aware how many other people had access to them."

The investigator laughed:

"Good try, but I know about your *talent*. You won't be frightening me."

Before dying from a heart attack, William Mathew thought the exact same thing, but I didn't bring that up, just started enumerating in a monotone voice:

"The copy of the expert report on the contents of the Countess's safe deposit box; I found it on the old man in the warehouse. The photocopy of the picture confiscated from me, the photocopy of the picture from my uncle's effects; I found those on your Mathew. One to one odds, detective sergeant. One to one odds!"

"Do you mean to say that you told Moran about those things?"

"As soon as I could."

The investigator jumped to his feet and exclaimed in rage:

"You're lying!"

"Why would I do that?" I smiled calmly. "I just suggest you think about the consequences and not do anything reckless. We can still end this all on good terms."

"And why shouldn't I just shoot you right now?!" the detective sergeant cried out, starting to get worried. He pointed his issued revolver back at me.

"What would that change? Nothing. But I, on the other hand, might lie to the senior inspector that I made it all up to defame you. He doesn't have the highest opinion of me. He'd believe it."

"Hell no!" the investigator growled, and then

the door behind him flew open. The detective sergeant turned around and jerked his revolver into position. Just then, I heard a quiet popping snap, and blood spilled onto my face.

The detective, his head shot through, fell dead to the floor. I raised my arms in silence, not wanting to share his fate.

"It's comforting to hear that you do not suffer any delusions in regards to my opinion of you," said Bastian Moran, continuing to hold me in the sights of his double-barrel gun, which had a bulbous barrel receiver and a little handle hanging down, making it look like a medieval crossbow with a crank. For the record, when it shot, it was totally silent.

The senior inspector stepped aside, and heavily armed policemen started running into the room in steel helmets and cuirasses. They quickly fanned out, then Bastian Moran approached me and asked:

"Where are the others?"

"And just who..." I prattled out, immeasurably taken aback by the unexpected turn of events. "Just who did you expect to find here, senior inspector?"

Bastian Moran's eyebrow snapped up high in surprise and he said significantly:

"We came to arrest the gang responsible for the robbery of the Witstein Banking House. But if you were not kidnapped and are here of your own free will..."

"I was kidnapped, I was kidnapped!" I immediately assured him. "I am here against my will. The detective sergeant told me the inspector general wanted to see me here."

"And nothing made you think twice?"

"I was too blown away by the honor of being invited to the inspector general's home!" I chuckled and ran my hand over my face; my fingers were caked in blood. "Also, it'd be nice if you stopped poking me with that thing, whatever it is."

Bastian Moran extended a handkerchief and said:

"It's an air gun. Indispensable for jobs that require silence."

I cleaned off my face and returned the kerchief, but the senior inspector just winced fastidiously.

"Throw it away!" he ordered.

"It looks expensive..."

"Viscount!" he snapped, having lost his patience. "Answer me at once. Where are the others!"

"I have no idea," I confessed. "There was an elderly *illustrious* man here. He introduced himself as Duke Talm. There was also a coachman, but I didn't see him come inside."

The senior inspector looked over the policemen, who'd taken position at the doors and windows. Moran pumped the lever of the air rifle a few times with strain, then pulled back the bolt and placed an elongated revolver bullet into the barrel.

"I was hoping you'd have some more useful information," he grumbled. But as soon as I reached for the weapon of the late detective, he ordered: "Hands off!"

"But why?"

"Don't touch it, or I'll order you cuffed!"

"If you say so," I said, stepping back from the detective sergeant's body. "Did you come in through the main entrance?"

"Yes."

"I was taken in through the back door. Last time I saw the Duke, he was heading that way."

"Stay on me!" Bastian Moran ordered, and pointed the police to the second exit. "No noise!" he reminded the soldiers running past.

To the clop of their heavy boots, the constables, armed with air guns and semi-automatic-carbines, lined up along the walls in anticipation of an order to go deeper into the manor. One of the sturdy fellows even had a hand-held Madsen machine gun over his shoulder; all of them, without exception, had a grenade pouch. The senior inspector had taken past errors into account and was not preparing to allow the robbers to outgun his division this time.

I looked at the detective sergeant's body and couldn't resist an entirely irrelevant question:

"Where'd you learn to shoot like that?"

"In the army," Bastian Moran answered, fairly perplexed by the question.

His sophisticated appearance seemed to utterly preclude severe army bunks.

The senior inspector stopped being distracted by me, and issued an order:

"Move out!"

The police ran out into the hallway and once again quickly fanned out along the wall to keep themselves out of their comrades' lines of fire. But, as it turned out, there was no one to shoot at, and the division slowly moved onward. The lights in the manor all flickered off, and our path was now lit only by the beams of portable torches.

"You outmaneuvered me with the hypnotist," Bastian Moran suddenly recalled. "I arrested him, but it was you that brought the inspector general his confession."

"What would it have cost you to head to the circus with me?"

"I'll be invoicing you for the suit."

"If you say so."

At the intersection of two hallways, the police stopped and I pointed out:

"The door into the back yard is up ahead."

A mustached sergeant shone his light on the stairs and asked:

"What's up there?"

"I have no idea," I answered at half voice, not wanting to make a sound.

My heart was sinking. I couldn't get the Duke's words out of my head about how an actual demon would soon be coming to lay claim to my soul. And I didn't have the miraculous electromagnetic-disturbance transmitter, or weapons, or anything.

"What shall we do, senior inspector?" the sergeant clarified.

"We're going into the back yard," Bastian

decided.

The police hurried down the hallway. I, meanwhile, caught up with the senior inspector and quietly whispered out:

"The Duke believed a demon might be turning up here. I suggest you call for reinforcements."

"Old wives' tales," the Department Three man said with a hand wave, not really listening.

I suddenly heard a muted knock, a couple muffled blows, and a couple of constables dragged over a middle-aged man with his hands cuffed behind his back and a gag in his mouth.

"This man was sitting in the footman's room," the sergeant said, jerking the man's head up by his long hair to reveal the face of his captive.

Lit by the bright light of the electric torch, I saw a familiar face.

"The coachman," I said.

"Great!" Bastian Moran rejoiced. "Let's keep going through the first floor toward the back yard! Don't go outside!"

Checking every room we came across along the way, we walked down the hall. And soon, a gallery led us into an abandoned botanical garden with dried out plants, but fully intact glass. It stuck out into an inner courtyard, surrounded by the gloomy walls of the manor; there was also a vehicle entrance through a gated archway.

In the far corner of the yard, under the overhang, there were glowing electric bulbs.

Through the glass wall, we could clearly make out the figures of a group of people getting up to something. So, the senior inspector immediately ordered:

"Torches off!"

But it was too late – one of them had noticed the suspicious glint on the glass of the orangery and pointed in our direction.

"Don't shoot!" Moran whispered out, enraged by the blunder. "Take positions and await further orders!"

The policemen quickly dispersed throughout the botanical garden and knelt behind barrels of dried out plants, but our patience was not rewarded. The vigilant sentry ran through the yard with his rifle held horizontally. The others started picking up their weapons. Meanwhile, I took note of a metal statue they were all crowded up around. I couldn't get a clear look, but something in it seemed strangely familiar...

And then, the lookout froze stone-stiff and threw up his rifle. He aimed directly at me, and by some kind of inspiration, it occurred to me that, for some unfathomable reason, I must have been the only one he could see.

Unfathomable? Dolt! Think about it! He could see my glowing eyes!

I quickly slunk behind a tub of soil. A moment later, a shot clapped out. Shards of glass showered down. The barrel that took the brunt of it shuddered.

A half a dozen officers fired a volley of bullets, knocking the lookout off his feet. And before his bullet-honeycombed body managed to collapse onto the rain-soaked ground, the criminals had fanned out throughout the yard, and were opening fire in return. Broken glass cascaded down into the greenhouse. Stray bullets whistled overhead, cutting down dried-out saplings and biting into the stone wall behind my back.

The police surpassed the bandits not only in number, but also in training. They'd brought plenty of rounds, and the stone flowerbeds and tubs of soil provided incomparably better cover than the frames of half-destroyed carriages. Those two factors reduced the amount of return fire significantly before the firefight really managed to even get off the ground. Three of our opponents were shot in the first minute, while the others pinned themselves down to the earth and didn't dare peek out from behind their unsound shelter. Only one of the bandits managed to run into the house, and he was now pestering us with shots from a first story window.

One of the constables hurriedly stuck a grenade onto the end of his carbine, loaded a blank and, with a sure shot, sent the explosive sailing across the whole yard. A blast rang out. The firing went quiet.

"Now they won't get away!" said Bastian Moran, melting into a satisfied smile and shouting out: "The manor is surrounded! Surrender! Drop your weapons and come out with your hands up!"

But then the metal statue under the awning

started moving.

It was huge, no smaller than three meters high. The human-like figure straightened up with a loud clank, and a pair of spotlights on its shoulders switched on.

"What devilry is that?" one of the constables exhaled, and I agreed with him fully.

It really was just that – devilry. The statue resembled an enlarged suit of medieval armor, but there was no man alive that could move while wearing such a heap of metal. Steel sheets covered the figure from all sides. There were black slits in the round helmet for eyes, and the arms ended in stumps. There were two electrodes protruding from one, and a hulking device made of crisscrossed copper wires attached to the other. Based on the ponderous barrel and long belt trailing from the back end, it was a machine-gun.

The armored figure moved slightly, and I heard the crackling buzzing of an electric motor. But – curses! – there was no generator on earth that could fit inside that suit of armor and produce the requisite amount of energy!

And then it occurred to me! Duke Talm was inside the armor suit.

The spotlight beams on the figure's shoulders crawled over the ruined botanical garden, and the policemen's nerves gave out. Shots started clapping, bullets ricocheted off the steel sheet covering Talm's chest, giving forth a hail of sparks, then the figure seemed to wake up. It raised the machine gun mounted on its arm, and a long burst of bullets came racing toward us, but the gun itself wasn't making any noise.

The heavy bullets went right through the decorative flower beds, pots and tubs. Shards of ceramic flew in all directions, and my face was covered with a fine soil. Someone shouted out in pain. I heard a noise come off the wall behind us that sounded like someone was scraping it with a fine-toothed metal comb.

Chhhhhhh!

One of the constables jumped out of his cover and tossed a hand grenade into the yard, immediately caught two or three bullets in his chest and collapsed backward. Meanwhile, the steel monster didn't even sway, though the explosion was right under his feet. Beyond that, thin orange threads of electricity started meandering between the electrodes on his left hand.

"Retreat into the house!" Bastian Moran shouted. "Cover me!"

The constables remained in formation and released a hail of bullets. The iron figure kept snapping out short distinct bursts of fire, and the first policeman to dash for the doors was nearly cut in two by one of them.

"Torches!" the senior inspector ordered, crawling to the exit behind the cover of a long flowerbed. I crawled after him.

The spotlights were blinding, so the constables were now aiming at them. Almost immediately, one shattered, followed quickly by the second – darkness reigned in the yard once again. The steel monster continued shooting the botanical garden, but now, he was just shooting at random, responding to the odd shot of the soldiers covering our retreat.

"Run for it!" Bastian Moran shouted.

I dallied for just a moment to get the truncheon and grenade bag off the dead constable, and jumped into the house. The police fanned out along the windows and started shooting the iron blockhead with a renewed force. Now, covered by thick stone walls, their peace of mind had returned.

"Don't lean out!" the senior inspector ordered and glanced at the phosphorus-illuminated hands of his pocket watch. "We need to hold out for a few more minutes!"

I came over to him and showed him a bullet I'd picked up from the floor. It was half a centimeter in diameter, and no less than four centimeters long. Based on its appearance, it was titanium-jacketed with an iron core.

"A Gauss cannon," Bastian Moran told me. "His electric jar will run out of power any second now, then we'll be able take him with our bare hands!"

I tried to take exception – but, just then, the gates flew off their hinges with a savage gnashing sound, and a police armored vehicle of a design I didn't recognize crash-dived into the yard. It had three axles, and treads stretched over the back pair of wheels with an awkward tower on top. However, the cannon barrel jutting out inspired respect with its caliber alone.

The cannon started turning toward Duke Talm in his steel armor suit but, suddenly, all the torches went out at once. The heavens split and a clod of darkness fell onto the armored vehicle. The huge winged demon flattened the self-propelled carriage, pushed it into the earth, tore out the tower with a careless swing of its huge paws, and threw it at the Duke.

It seemed as if his actions were doubled by space itself. Darkness descended like a ghostly cloak, and my heart almost stopped in fear. But the *illustrious* man made no blunders; he easily dodged and opened fire in return from his Gauss cannons. The titanium-coated rounds lashed his opponent like a deadly whip. Clumps of black feathers from the demon's wings started flying all around along with splatters of its no-less-black blood.

The infernal creature threw itself on the attack, and then the steel blockhead's free hand flickered with electric charge. A blinding arc hit the demon and threw it aside.

"Devilry..." one of the policemen croaked out.

The Duke was hurrying to finish off his wounded opponent, but the demon easily jumped up from the ground onto the house wall. The building shook from a powerful blow. A column collapsed from a flap of its wing, then the demon threw a marble statue of Atlas at the steel-suited man, jumping after it and dealing a crushing blow with its interlinked hands.

Atlas crashed into the dirt and flew to

pieces, the Duke blocked the blow with his free hand, stuck the barrel in the chest of the demon and blasted a burst of a couple dozen bullets right through it.

The pair started grappling, and a nightmarish beast suddenly jumped through the broken window of the gallery and instantly bit half the face off a gaping constable. I jerked up my weapon and blasted the hellhound back outside, but that turned out to have been only the first in a horde of hellspawn.

"Retreat!" Bastian Moran commanded, having unloaded his air rifle into one of the creatures. He then took out a strange looking pistol, its grip attached to a cylindrical receiver at a sharp angle.

Everyone ran into the corridor and I, much to my surprise, found myself taking up the rear. Without hesitation, I grabbed a hand grenade from the ammo bag and, after tearing out the pin, threw it on the floor, then dashed off after my comrades.

There was a bang, then a wail and the door flew off its hinges, but I had already jumped out. From the side passage, another hellhound dashed in front of us. I shot as I ran, aiming for the crimson glow of its eyes. The buckshot knocked the infernal creature from its feet. I managed to jump past and charge off after the police.

Another grenade rolled down the floor. I curled up behind a corner and almost ran right into a free-for-all skirmish. The hellspawn had intercepted our division, and they were now fighting it out ferociously. Shots thundered, the constables were shooting from all barrels and dashing for the exit, but the infernal creatures were too many, and the normal rounds couldn't hold them for long or, for that matter, kill them.

I jumped up to Bastian Moran and pulled him back.

"After me!"

The hellhounds slashed up by the grenade blast were still no threat, but new monsters were already giving soul-chilling howls from the gallery, and we were running as fast as we could down a side corridor.

"To the back yard!" I shouted, only managing to find my place in the impenetrable darkness of the empty house by a miracle.

The senior inspector overtook me. I also picked up the pace, and even managed to load another twelve-caliber round into the Winchester's tube magazine before the door flew open with a rumble and a beast only distantly reminiscent of a dog ran at us, charging with its disproportionately huge, bulbous head first.

I shot right into its gaping maw, tripped over a carcass underfoot and rolled on the floor. I immediately turned over onto my back and managed to throw my hands up, the Winchester clutched by the barrel and buttstock, just a moment before a set of terrifying fangs as long as a pinky finger managed to close around my throat.

The teeth of the hellhound easily rumpled

the steel of the gun, but couldn't get through the frame. Then, Bastian Moran returned. He placed the barrel of his pistol to the head of the infernal creature and blasted out its brains.

"Hurry up!" shouted the senior inspector, yanking me to my feet as we jumped outside.

To the ghastly wail and rumble of the subsiding firefight, we tore through the back yard over to my former armored car, which had been parked there by the detective sergeant. One of the hellbeasts was trying to catch us out in the open, but the senior inspector really was an excellent shot: running, in pitch black and under pouring rain, he put a bullet right between its crimson-flame eyes.

It seemed that the master of the hellish pack was now expending all its energy on the confrontation with the Duke, because the diabolical mutts it was holding in the physical realm with its powers started to grow weaker. Reality assigned them nothing more than the boundless rage of dead souls. Even normal bullets now took them out of commission for a significant time.

"Get behind the wheel!" I shouted, catching up with Bastian Moran.

He threw open the door and got in the driver's seat. I, meanwhile, threw open the back door, crawled into the trunk and collapsed, sapped of strength, among the many boxes; my lungs felt on fire, and my arms and legs refused to obey.

The powder engine crackled to life. The self-propelled carriage started trembling in time with it and turned around toward the gates. But it was too late. Glass exploded out of the manor window, and the ghostly pack shot out after us, hot on the trail.

I got up from the boxes. The armored car was picking up speed unexpectedly quickly, and a strong bump threw me onto my back. The wheels popped over the knocked-down gates. I almost fell again, got behind the Gatling gun, switched on the barrel assembly drive and – what a miracle! – the electric jar wasn't fully discharged; the rotor hummed into action, gradually picking up speed.

The hellhounds had already made it through the yard, but I was in no hurry to open fire. Despite the constant bouncing, I was obstinately holding the cross hairs over the gate. Only when the infernal creatures gushed out to the street did I push down on the trigger. The Gatling gun shuddered, vomiting out a hail of lead that sliced through the pack like a scythe. All that remained now was to take aim and shoot down the most persistent, saving as many bullets as possible, as they were almost gone.

And so we tore down the deserted road, gradually distancing ourselves from the hounds and, from time to time, snarling forth fire. We drove like that for a short while, then were overtaken by a deafening rumble.

It overtook us, and rushed past at a blistering pace before quickly returning in an echo from the houses. Over the manor, there arose an elevated fiery mushroom, but we didn't have to wonder who had emerged victorious from the fight for long: a moment later, on the dark backdrop of the cloud-covered sky, there appeared an incomparably darker spot. The demon threw open its black wings and lunged off in pursuit.

In horror, I got out from behind the machine gun, crawled over to the grated window between the rear and cabin and shouted:

"The demon! It's flying after us! Drive!"

Bastian Moran cursed out and stepped on the pedal, clutching at the handle. I stuck my head out, but the cursed abomination had already hidden among the low clouds.

"Bastian! Where are we going?"

"To the Sublime Electricity lyceum!" the senior inspector called back, turning the wheel in agitation. On the rain-slicked causeways, the armored car skidded from time to time, but Moran managed to keep it on the roadway by some kind of miracle, and just kept driving, never reducing speed. Must have been evidence of his army experience.

The whole city was immersed in darkness; both the gas jets and electric bulbs were all off. The only thing breaking up the dark of the night was the frequent bolts of lightning but, after we dashed past the Imperial Theater, we started to see a white luster before us through the sheet of rain.

The Sublime Electricity lyceum towered in the center of its square like an ancient citadel. Its windows shone forth with a bright light, and the copper balls on the poles that wreathed the giant Nicola Tesla coil were occasionally enshrouded in translucent flashes of electricity.

There, salvation awaited. But the armored car was still driving up to the square when a black shadow nosedived from the heavens. Paving stones from the causeway flew in all directions from the terrifying blow. The neighboring homes shuddered. The lyceum, meanwhile, caved in. It looked as if the shaking caused by the demon had caused its expansive basements to collapse. The light in the high windows flickered and went out.

"Devil!" Bastian Moran cried, sharply turning the wheel.

In the headlights, the body of the demonic being flickered by, clearly ravaged by the battle with its steel opponent. I then flew onto the floor. The powder engine revved, and the we dashed clear.

The demon gathered his strength, threw open his wings and took off into the air, but its flying was now somehow faltering and labored. I was puzzled over whether it had missed us intentionally or not but, the second time, it was clearly intending to take a less risky approach – it didn't go up too high, just gliding over the roofs of nearby buildings, gaining speed.

"Drive!" I shouted to the senior inspector, taking a seat behind the Gatling gun and shooting the rest of the machine-gun belt at our pursuer, but without any success.

Curses! Why hadn't the Duke's titanium bullets stopped him?!

That question didn't occupy me for long, though. I threw open the box with the launch tube. It had already gotten me out of one jam, so why not? After I got the launcher out, I started hammering on the partition between the rear and cabin of the car.

"Moran!" I barked over the rumbling of the engine. "Drive up Calvary!"

"We won't find shelter in your manor!"

"Drive!" I insisted. "It's our only chance!"

After taking a missile from the box, I crammed it into the tube, snapped it shut and locked it. Then, I clipped the mask on my face and went over to the open back. The demon was tailing our armored car down the little winding narrow streets of the Old City, waiting for the right moment to make a blistering dive.

I set the launch tube on my shoulder and, when the self-propelled carriage was flying full steam onto Dürer-Platz, I caught the infernal creature in the thrown-back crosshairs. At that very moment, it folded its wings and plunged downward like a stone; I also took immediate action. The spark of the electric igniter flickered up. The tube gave a kick and the trunk of the vehicle filled with a cloud of acrid gas.

Leaving a trail of smoke behind it, the missile tore upward, caught the infernal creature coming down to meet us, and exploded with a grumble. A blinding flash blazed forth. The demon was sent flying away. It crashed to the earth and inertia rolled it another good twenty meters, crushing its wings, making it shed black feathers, and causing blood to gush out, glowing with a transparent flame.

If it had been a mortal being, the flesh would have been scraped back to the bone, and the bones themselves would have been milled to dust. But instead, the paving stones cracked and crumbled into shards. The terrifying blow to the fountain, meanwhile, completely shattered its marble basin.

Before the armored car flew off the square, I managed to see the demon getting up from the paving stones and trying to take off into the sky. Fortunately, one of its wings was seriously damaged and now, the infernal creature was forced to come after us in bounding leaps, each of which required significant forethought. We then managed to catch a tailwind.

But we also had problems of our own: the engine wasn't able to manage the weight, and the armored self-propelled carriage struggled up the hill against the stream of water coming down it. Our pursuer was gradually closing in on us.

"Faster!" I shouted as I threw the semi-automatic-rifle box from the back. They wouldn't be able to help us in the present situation anyway, and only added unnecessary weight to the vehicle. After it, the box of cartridges went overboard. Then, the Madsen machine-gun met the same fate and, soon, the only thing left in our arsenal was the hand-held mortar and its white-phosphorus rounds.

Cranking the drum, I loaded the incendiary rounds one after the other and aimed, but the demon was too far away; hitting it from this distance didn't seem possible.

"Where to now?" the senior inspector cried out to me as the armored car rolled over the bridge up to the fence of my estate.

"Keep going up!" I called back. "To the very top!"

Around a turn, another bend, and the engine revved. The shaking reached its absolute limit. The path to the top was horribly broken, but thanks to the exotic-seeking tourists, extravagant newly-weds and occasional visits of an inspector to the rusty tower, it hadn't grown over once and for all and the self-propelled carriage was able to pass at a speed only slightly lower than our hell-bent race through the city.

Behind us, over the manors nearest the summit, the black wings of the demon flickered past. I pressed myself to the grated window and shouted over the sound of the engine and the thunder blasts:

"Pull over quick in front of the tower and drive around it!"

Bastian Moran nodded, and a little while later reduced his speed, giving me the chance to jump out. Then, he steered the armored vehicle onto the path around it, which was broken up and uncared for.

The tower was depressing. Its tons of rusty iron stretched up for more than two hundred meters, and now, with lightning bolts striking its top from the thunderous sky almost constantly, it was even slightly illuminated in the darkness by the red-hot metal. There was steam coming off in every direction.

I gathered my strength and rushed forward.

It smelled strongly of ozone. The raging wind nearly knocked me off my feet. My ears were ringing from the thunder. I couldn't even raise my eyes due to the blinding flashes of lightning. The air was humming from the atmospheric electricity all around. Suddenly, my hair stood on end.

But I stopped and turned around only when I sensed the approach of evil with my back. The world instantly turned gray. The sounds died down. Lightning was striking the tower very high up.

I turned and shivered involuntarily – the demon was climbing to the top.

There was no way to play on his fears or buy my way out of this one, the infernal creature wanted only one thing – to take me and drag me down with it to the very farthest depths of hell. I didn't have a single chance to stand up to it in battle, but I wasn't preparing to give up, either.

I had a plan.

The demon stood up to its full height, threw open its shredded wings and stretched out a clawed paw. Its eyes were burning with a crimson flame. Its gaping maw was filled with darkness. And it even became darkness itself, by some absurd misunderstanding having been incarnated in our world.

I was mindlessly afraid of it. I was afraid of it, and intended to destroy it.

The infernal creature was approaching slowly and falteringly. On its smooth hide, overflowing with all shades of darkness, I could make out the wounds left by titanium bullets. Its chest was adorned with deep burns from the electric shocks. Its muzzle, which elicited horror by its appearance alone, grimaced with every lightning strike to the tower behind me. But the creature wasn't planning to give up. As if against its own will, it started getting closer and, with its presence alone, warped the laws of the universe.

I started shooting when the distance between us was only one hundred steps.

With a dull clap, one of the incendiary rounds blasted off toward the demon, then a second, third and, just then, the hellspawn tore from place and threw itself on the attack with a movement imperceptible to the human eye.

I miscalculated. I thought I had enough time to flee, but I had underestimated the crafty beast. The demonic creature seemed to flow from one point in space to the next. If no mortar rounds hit it now, it would tear me to shreds.

But then, an explosion lit up bright. The burning flame spilled out around its powerful torso and lit its snout on fire, then another two incendiary charges went off. Smoke plumed down, white and stinking. The demon, devoured by the fire, gave a piercing howl. But I didn't stay to watch its convulsions and ran off at full speed.

It was a good thing I did, too. A moment

later, the partially blinded creature darted off after me, despite the flames still enshrouding it.

I was racing without turning my head, trying to make it to the foundation of the open-work tower, directly under the lightning and praying as I ran, more sincerely than I'd every prayed before. No, I didn't ask the Most High to rid me of the demon, nor appeal for holy power, nor did I even think about begging to be brought to a different part of the planet by supernatural means.

No! I prayed for just one thing – to run under the tower and not end up fried by a lightning bolt. Just to get to the opposite side unharmed. Nothing more...

The iron foundation of the colossal construction started smoking overhead. The air was humming with electricity. The atmospheric charge enshrouded me from all sides as the reinforced iron beams shuddered from the electricity flowing down them.

One spark flew up, then another. Then, small nips of electricity started burning through my whole body like fire, but I didn't stop for even one moment. The lightning flashed right overhead. There was a terrifying boom and groan, and a hateful shriek rang out from behind me accompanied by the crackling of electrical shocks.

I jumped under the beams of the first platform. The huge demon clutched onto them and gave a sudden shudder. Electric arcs flared up, and a thick smoke emanated from the demon's hide. The infernal beast was trying to get out of the insidious trap, but couldn't.

Without hesitation, I started running faster than ever. I jumped out from under the tower onto the road and nearly ended up under the wheels of the self-propelled carriage. The brakes squealed as the armored car deftly skidded off the perimeter path. It soon straightened out, and stopped right next to me. I flung open the door, tossed the hand-held mortar into the cabin, jumped in after it myself and shouted:

"Drive!"

I didn't have to ask Moran twice. He slammed down on the pedal and the self-propelled carriage started flying down the hill somewhat quicker than it had gone up.

"What happened?" the senior inspector demanded an answer.

"The demon is in a trap, but for some reason, it didn't die!" I answered. "It should have just been blown to smithereens but, look, it's escaping!"

"The titanium bullets didn't affect it either," Bastian Moran reminded me, turning the wheel in agitation. "It appears it was summoned to this world, and the summoners are holding it in this world."

"So, this is malefics performing a ritual?"

"Yes!"

"The demon will destroy half the city before we find them," I said, my mood soured.

The senior inspector tore his right hand from the wheel and stuck a pack of Egyptian guineas under my nose.

"What is this?" He asked.

"A trophy," I shrugged my shoulders.

"Is it somehow connected with the malefics?"

"I got it off a vampire. I recently toasted him along with some Moorish underlings," I admitted, caution thrown to the wind.

"What is this all for, Viscount?" Bastian Moran continued the interrogation. Without waiting for an answer, he flew into a rage: "Just tell me what was in that aluminum box! No more bullshit about family secrets or, I swear, I'll throw you right onto the road!"

I looked doubtfully at the man, then said:

"Someone supposed that was where the secret of the vulnerability of *the fallen* was kept."

The senior inspector looked with surprise at me and asked suddenly:

"And the Egyptians might be interested in this secret?"

"And how!" I admitted, remembering Duke Talm's revelation on the true powerbrokers in Alexandria.

"Curses!" the senior inspector swore, making a sharp turn onto Dürer-Platz.

I nearly flew out of the chair and shouted:

"What the hell? What do you think you're doing?"

"We confiscated a packet of freshly minted guineas with similar numeration when arresting Maestro Marlini!" Bastian Moran declared, pushing the vehicle to its limit. "The magician confessed, off the record, but he confessed that it was an advance for stealing the patent. And he got the money from the second secretary of the Egyptian embassy!"

"Oh no!" I moaned out. "Are you suggesting we assault the embassy? That would lead to war!"

"There's no avoiding war now, and the victors are free from judgment!" the senior inspector snapped back and pursed his lips obstinately. He was not planning to retreat.

And I had no other choice either; I recognized that with perfect clarity.

"Before we're in front of the embassy, I'll have to crawl back into the trunk," I warned him, "to the Gatling gun."

"Alright," Moran nodded, gloomy and detached.

We raced through the empty city, throwing up high splashes of water. The armored car's hood was giving off more and more white steam. The soldered radiator couldn't bear the extreme workload, and we risked being left without a mode of transportation at any moment.

"The guardhouse is right past the gates," the senior inspector warned me on the street neighboring the embassy. "There are no less than ten Mauritanian guards on duty there. If you cannot immediately suppress them with fire – we're done for."

"I'll try," I promised.

The upcoming attack on the embassy of our southern neighbor scared me so much my knees were shivering, but I was much more afraid of the thought that the demon was already out of the trap and racing off after us. I had no doubt whatsoever of his abilities to find his victim, even on the other side of the world.

In the trunk, I loaded another belt into the Gatling gun, took a seat behind it and clutched tightly onto the bench. Even still, hitting the embassy gates nearly smeared me against the partition with the cabin. The radiator burst in the blow, and steam shot out, ensconcing us in a white cloud. But Bastian Moran managed to complete the maneuver and turn the armored car's back end toward the ivy-covered barracks. That left the sentries in the entrance watchtower for him. I, meanwhile, pressed down on the trigger and traced an "X" on the wall of the wooden barracks from corner to corner; splinters sprayed in all directions and the windows shattered. Occasional shots popped out from the gates. Our steel armor sheet took the brunt, sounding out with a clinking sound, and the senior inspector immediately opened return fire through the viewing slit.

I didn't get distracted, either.

The door flew open, and the second the black-skinned guard had his weapon pointed at me, he immediately fell to the earth, honeycombed with high-caliber bullets. A figure flew out of the bushes. I quickly released a long burst in that direction, then covered Moran as he jumped out of the cabin, bearing down on the Moor. The senior inspector, ducking down, ran up to the barracks, which had been shot full of holes, and threw a few grenades in.

Muted explosions blasted out. The firing

finally died down.

Then, I loosed the rest of the belt into the embassy building, grabbed the hand-held mortar, ammo bag and grenades, and joined Bastian Moran.

He then helped himself to a short-bayoneted Enfield rifle off a dead guard, and called me after him:

"Run for it!"

Some of the embassy workers jumped out onto the mansion's veranda. A revolver clapped out, but the senior inspector, only slowing his run for a moment, took the Egyptian down with one accurate shot and hurried on, pulling back and releasing the bolt as he went.

We had already run up to the blood-soaked veranda when the sphinxes on the roof of the building suddenly came to life, a transparent light shining forth from their eyes. I jerked the mortar in their direction and shot an incendiary round. It blasted out with unexpected ferocity. One of the stone beasts was torn to shreds, and burning white phosphorus was cast in all directions. But the rain stopped it from spreading to the building.

The second sphinx tore out a part of the stone gutter with its powerful paw and lobbed it at us, then nosedived down in our direction. The heavy landing shattered the marble steps of the veranda. A flap of its ponderous wings nearly lopped off Moran's head; he only managed to duck at the very last moment, then somersaulted aside. I ran in the opposite direction, pulling the handle as I ran, cranking the massive drum.

The sphinx hesitated for a moment, then went after the senior inspector, but I had already run away to a safe distance and shot the beast in the back. The explosion blew the hulking creature to pieces; we went around the phosphorus burning on the earth and ran into the manor.

"Where to now?" I asked, catching my expended breath.

"Malefics love basements," Bastian Moran decided. "We need to find a way down!"

Now, we were left with no doubt that we were on the right track; stone statues don't typically come to life all on their own, after all. Damn that Egyptian magic!

But we just had to go a bit down the hallway before shots started ringing out in front of us, and we were forced to take shelter in the niches for ceramic vases. One of the embassy guards had blocked the passage with an overturned desk and was shooting recklessly from behind his improvised barricade.

I tried to lean behind it with the mortar, but Bastian Moran stopped me.

"You trying to get us burned?" he shouted, boiling over as he took yet another grenade from his ammo bag.

With a sharp toss, the senior inspector sent it past the overturned desk, waited for the explosion and ran on the attack. While I was jumping over the shrapnel-riddled desk, Bastian reached the blood-soaked guard and stabbed him with his bayonet, clearly trying to save bullets.

"Faster!" Moran shouted, running onward.

In the next room, we discovered a stairway to the basement but, almost immediately, a few shots came up at us from down below. Then, when we tried to run down it, they opened fire with a hail of bullets, ricocheting off the marble panels and whistling past.

"Let's clear the first stairway, then we can go on," Bastian Moran announced calmly. From his demeanor, one might think Moran had spent his whole life storming well-armed embassies.

That said, what did we have to worry about now?

He and I had already earned the death penalty regardless of the outcome...

I chucked a hand grenade down. It jumped back from the wall and bounced around the corner. Moran sent another grenade after it. The two explosions amplified one another; we ran down without delay, and the senior inspector, already accustomed to the bayonet, plunged it into the contused gunner.

The other guards managed to escape to the stairwell below. Another few grenades were sent after them, but when we were down the stairs, we ran into a heavy armored door; locked, naturally.

"Shit!" Bastian Moran exclaimed, unable to bite back the curse. He then started digging through his grenade bag, saying, "Get out all your explosives, now!"

Not wanting to nit-pick, I added my whole ammo bag to it, grenades and incendiary rounds alike; the door looked sturdy.

"Let's get out of here!" the senior inspector hurried me along.

We went up to the overturned desk. There, Bastian Moran pulled the pin and tossed a grenade down. A few seconds later, the building walls were shaking from the strong explosion. Acrid smoke billowed up to us.

"Careful!" I warned the senior inspector. "The smoke is toxic!"

"Curses!" Bastian Moran swore out again and extended me a couple revolvers he'd taken off the dead guards. "Take these!"

I threw the hand-held mortar onto my back, loosened the belt cutting into my shoulder and armed myself with the five-shot Colts.

The roar of the flames gradually died down and the smoke started coming out the broken windows onto the street. But before going down, we wrapped kerchiefs around our faces.

"Will this help?" the senior inspector asked.

"I have no idea," I confessed honestly.

"We can't wait any longer!" Bastian Moran announced, and here the manor gave another shudder, as if its facade had just been struck by a steam-tram going full speed off the rails.

The demon had caught up to us, so we had no time to delay. We ran down the stairs, jumped over the door, which had been twisted and melted in the explosion, and made a blistering dash through the smoky corridor.

A guardsman emerged from the dust lingering in the air; I shot him in the head, ran into a small recess for cover and opened fire, now with both hands. Bastian Moran supported me a moment later; the contused guards were not able to offer any kind of resistance.

One of the Moors jumped into the far door. The senior inspector caught up to him, poked him in the back with the rifle bayonet and threw him over the iron barricade of the upper level of the vault. After tossing the unloaded the revolvers, I pulled the hand-held mortar off my back and poked my head into the spacious room with my weapon at the ready. The room, immersed in semi-dark, impressed with its dimensions. But my attention was immediately drawn by a hulking construction in the very middle of it. It was a frame, welded of metal bars, covered with a fine copper mesh that led into wire bundles snaking into holes in the floor.

A Faraday cage! A chamber, completely protected from external electromagnetic disturbances! The malefics inside wouldn't have to worry about signals transmitted through the air, storm or no.

Inside that cage, standing on the corners of a huge five-pointed star, there were five dark figures frozen in a trance. In its very center, there was a sparkling ball of immaterial fire.

Another jolt shook the manor from basement to attic; the demon was still after us, tearing down walls and plowing through the narrow doorframes in rage. I was sent reeling, and would have surely flown down after the unfortunate Moor, but I grabbed onto a hand-hold just in the nick of time.

Bastian Moran was also affected. He could barely stay on his feet. His pistol flew from his hands and bounced away to the wall.

"Devil!" the senior inspector cursed out, trying to find his dropped weapon in the pitch dark.

The din grew. The clawed paw of the demon suddenly stuck through the door, latched into the barricade and tore a good-sized chunk from it, easily breaking the iron frame. I threw up the hand-held mortar and shot. My first round landed on the copper mesh. It exploded there and sent burning phosphorus flying in all directions. The glowing ball in the center of the pentagram went out for a moment, but the malefics were still immersed in a trance didn't seem to notice the rain of fire coming down on them; they stayed in their places like monuments embraced in flame.

I turned the drum and shot a second time. The explosion sent the conjurers flying, and a heart-rending wail rolled through the room. The demon was being dragged forcefully back down to the underworld. The malefics' conjuration spell was no longer holding it in our world. It reeled in a circle, then desiccated instantly. With a shudder, it turned to ash and instantly scattered.

"Let's get out of here!" Bastian Moran commanded, picking up his fallen pistol. "You can say that again!"

So, we rushed to the exit. The demon evaporated. The embassy guards had all been taken out in the assault, and no one was left to stop us from coming up to ground level and jumping outside.

The armored car's rumpled hood was grinning out at us. There was no hope we'd get it to run again, so I ran out beyond the gates, turned around and sent my last incendiary mortar round into it. A flame sparked up in the back and Gatling gun rounds started shooting off at random. I then, with a calm mind, raced after Moran as he beat a hasty retreat. As I ran, I threw the mortar away into a gutter. Just after I jumped to the corner of the building opposite, I heard a deafening roar from behind me. The armored car exploded and sent twisted metal flying around the whole embassy grounds.

My lungs were on fire. My legs refused to bend but, all the same, I pushed myself harder and caught up with the senior inspector. We ran into some kind of gateway and started greedily gulping down fresh air with our mouths wide open.

"Some night, eh!" I rasped, looking out at the street.

And just then, a pistol barrel poked into my back.

"Hands!" Bastian Moran demanded, shackling my wrists in steel cuffs with a quiet chuckle: "How long I've awaited this moment, Viscount! You're under arrest!"

PART FOUR

HEART

Surgical Scalpel and Kitchen Knife

1

GETTING STABBED in the back is always an unpleasant and devilishly painful experience. You trusted this person, and they betrayed you, betrayed your trust, and trampled on your friendship. Such things always leave indelible scars on the soul.

But that's if you trusted the person in the first place, and weren't expecting any tricks. Otherwise, all you can do is throw up your hands and admit that you've been outplayed.

I never harbored any illusions in relation to Bastian Moran, so, locked in a lonely cell, I didn't indulge in self-flagellation.

Nothing of the sort! The last days had brought so many unpleasant surprises that, in comparison, being arrested didn't actually seem such a crushing blow. As soon as the iron door slammed behind me, I laid down on the uncomfortable bench, closed my eyes and immediately fell asleep.

It was a dreamless sleep but, when I opened my eyes, my first thought was that I must have gone mad, or was in a waking dream.

In the middle of the cell, sitting on a folding chair, was Friedrich von Nalz in the flesh. He was smiling sheepishly and immediately apologized to me:

"Forgive me, Viscount. I didn't mean to wake you."

"That's new," I muttered out, having ascribed the inspector general's presence to a trick of my *talent*. There was no other way to explain it.

The bare stone walls didn't have a single window, and the lamp grate was all rusted. The door before me looked sturdy, and the bench I was lying on – dingy... On the backdrop of all this mess, the ceremonial uniform of the head of the metropolitan police, shining back at me with all manner of medals, looked quite out of place.

Was this a delusion? Clearly.

"So, I take it you weren't expecting my visit," Friedrich von Nalz smiled.

I'd have been less surprised to wake up in front of a firing squad, but I didn't say that out loud, just admitted shortly:

"I was not."

"Well, why not?" the ghastly old man asked in surprise. In his colorless eyes, I could see the far-off glow of his burning *talent*. "Senior Inspector Moran only had the highest praise for about you."

Considering that it had been the senior inspector precisely that put me behind bars, hearing that was, at the very least, strange.

"And where is the senior inspector?" I asked, trying to at least somewhat come to grips with my reality.

"In the hospital," Friedrich von Nalz said. "The doctors suspect he was poisoned by the combustion products of white phosphorus, but he'll recover."

"Is that right?" I asked in confusion, practically falling off the bench as I listened to my own sensations. There was nothing worrying me.

"The senior inspector gave a full account of your actions," the old man said significantly.

"That's what I was afraid of."

The inspector general laughed.

"There's nothing to fear, Viscount!" he announced. "You won't be charged with anything for the attack on the embassy of Great Egypt."

"Just don't tell me you were able to play this all off," I replied, blown away at the unexpected statement.

"The newspapers are calling the whole episode a random demon attack. It moved through the city like a hurricane and attacked the Egyptian embassy. There's no reason to be worried, Viscount. The papers never lie."

"And the Egyptians are swallowing that?"

"Considering certain factors you're already aware of, they're avoiding adversarial maneuvers."

I tilted my head to the side and asked:

"Then, why am I still here?"

"Senior Inspector Moran thought it necessary to isolate you from society to protect you from reckless actions. In his opinion, you are marked by excessive vanity, and overly frank discussions with the press are not what we want in this situation."

The allusion was clear as day, and I nodded hurriedly:

"I'll keep clammed up."

"It's in your best interest, Viscount."

"I have no doubt."

The inspector general got to his feet and

suddenly asked:

"Why didn't you tell me, Viscount?"

A cold sweat came over me and I babbled out:

"Why didn't I tell you about what?"

"About your kinship with Emile Rie. I actually knew him back before he became chancellor. And I even managed to talk with him afterward. He was a surprising man."

"Where did you get that idea?" I asked, taken aback. Then I guessed: "The photograph!"

"Your request caught my interest, Viscount," Friedrich von Nalz confirmed. "I looked at the copies of materials and recognized the signature on the back at first glance." He chuckled. "I've got the exact same signature on my promotion papers."

"To be honest, inspector general, I only found out I was related to the preeminent man a few days ago, and wasn't planning to spread that information around. It doesn't seem like a good idea."

"What are you on about, Viscount?!" the old man slapped me on the shoulder. "I took it upon myself to inform her Imperial Majesty's chancellery. The message caught their attention greatly."

"You didn't have to..."

"Balderdash!" said the inspector general, waving it off and walking over to the door. "You'll be asked a few questions now, then you can go. No charges, no grievances. Best of luck, Viscount."

The *illustrious* man walked out the door. He was immediately replaced by a horde of clerks. They took out the folding chair and placed a folding table and three stools in the middle of the room, after which they left the cell without saying a word.

A few minutes later, the door flew open again, and in came three young men in frock coats of an austere cut and identical ties. I sensed a certain military bearing in them, either from their carefully maintained cropped hair, or their direct manner.

One of them set out writing implements on the table and sat on the stool; his colleagues exchanged sour looks without sitting. Being in my company made them obviously uncomfortable. Or was it just their first time in a one-man cell?

Finally, a light-haired gentleman of twenty-five cast off his consternation and extended a hand:

"Allow me to introduce myself, lieutenant of the Imperial guard for her Imperial Majesty, William Grace."

I got up from the bench and shook his hand.

"Nice to meet you."

The lieutenant nodded, smiled politely and warned:

"Viscount, this is in no way an interrogation, but I urge you to answer the questions with all due seriousness."

"I'm as serious as they come," I snorted.

Then, the second gentleman to come into the

cell spoke. He was swarthy, with a pock-marked face. He caught the sarcasm in my voice and did not fail to express his disapproval:

"Viscount, we are aware of your supposed close kinship with the Imperial family, so I am obliged to remind you that illegitimate branches are not accorded any special status."

The grumbler, though, did not take the pains to introduce himself.

"Well then, sirs, what are you doing here?" I inquired, feeling the tension in the cell growing thicker.

"Her Imperial Majesty, the Princess Anna would like to meet you," the pockmarked one said with unhidden disapproval. "In connection with that, you'll have to undergo the requisite security screening."

"What for?" I asked, startled. "Why does her Imperial Majesty want to see me?"

William Grace sighed:

"Her Imperial Highness was very interested to hear about you."

"We had to obey," the pock-marked one added.

"Alright," I sighed, not seeing any chance to refuse the honor without being arrested for disrespecting my crown-bearing relative. "So, let's begin!"

Lieutenant Grace threw open the cell door and invited someone inside:

"Enter."

A tall, thin doctor walked in wearing a white robe with a bulbous leather traveling bag.

"Clothes off above the belt," he said, getting out a listening tube.

"What's all this for, then?" I frowned.

The Imperial guard lieutenant gave a soft smile and explained:

"The health of her Highness leaves something to be desired. Talking with a sick person, even if they just have the common cold, is categorically contraindicated."

"I've never been sick with anything," I grumbled, but the doctor just waited and I had to throw my jacket on the bench. I pulled my shirt off over my head and noticed without particular surprise the eyes of those present growing wide in amazement. They had never before seen such a fresco on a man's body.

"I say!" the pock-marked one exclaimed, drawing out his words, but immediately checked himself after catching the lieutenant's gaze.

The doctor calmly placed the wide end of the tube to the star on my chest, evaluating my heart beat, then listened to my lungs and asked me to turn around. Hearing no rasping, he looked into my mouth and announced:

"No pathologies detected."

"Continue," the lieutenant allowed.

He got a scalpel from his traveling bag along with a tourniquet and an empty syringe.

"Excuse me?" I asked, confused, taking a step back.

"The pathogens of many dangerous diseases can be detected by blood analysis," the doctor explained. "We'll have to take blood from a vein.

Don't be afraid. It won't hurt."

I allowed them to tie the tourniquet around my left bicep and clenched and unclenched my fist several times. The doctor disinfected a patch of skin with alcohol, then jabbed the needle in. It was utterly painless. A moment later, the syringe was full.

"Press down!" the doctor said, handing me a cotton ball and warning: "Hold it for five minutes."

Then, he gathered his tools and left the room. I, meanwhile, was left standing in the middle of the room with an arm bent at the elbow and naked to the waist.

I didn't like that one bit, but my interviewers looked quite pleased. They started piling questions on me at a galloping pace. Frequently, they repeated them with minor changes in the wording. The stenographer was ferociously scraping a quill on the paper, hardly managing to keep the record.

At first, their inquiries dealt with common matters, leaving me at peace with their methodology. But, when the conversation turned to the contents of the aluminum box and my conversation with Duke Talm, my patience ran out.

"One minute, sirs," I said, taking a pause to pull my shirt over my head. As I got dressed, I slightly gathered my thoughts and decided not to hide anything from them, so I wouldn't later end up with my foot in my mouth. "Continue!"

It should be said that I didn't end up telling

them anything seditious, having managed to smooth over a few tense moments and keeping some others concealed.

Lieutenant Grace was pacing the cell with his hands folded behind his back and asked me:

"And what is your opinion on the feasibility of electromagnetic radiation having an effect on otherworldly creatures?"

I was not in any mood to give my opinion on anything. Beyond that – I had no desire to meet with the heir to throne; I just wanted to get out of New Babylon as fast as possible and head to Zurich for the ten million francs that awaited me there.

Maybe, I should just be upfront and tell them that?

I sighed and shook my head.

"The problem isn't that the Most High has turned away from us and stopped caring for us. And it isn't even that we lost our faith in him. The reason for all the problems is that we're afraid to believe. And we're even more afraid that one day, *he* will come to believe in us anew. We consider sublime electricity a panacea against all our hardships, but if hell suddenly broke loose, all our weapons, all our inventions wouldn't be able to help. Only faith can save us. Faith, and faith alone."

A freethinker self-indulgent enough to make such a statement should not have even been allowed within cannon-range of the heiress to the throne, but the guards just exchanged sour glances and kept silent. They had no more questions for me.

The doctor returned soon, but didn't come into the cell, just glanced into the open door and said:

"It's a match."

"What's a match?" I grew surprised.

"That just means your bloodwork was all fine," explained Lieutenant Grace. "Gather your things, Viscount."

All I could do was sigh.

2

AT THE EXIT from the jail area, I was given back my confiscated property; I put the items back in my pockets as I walked, then we left the Newton-Markt, climbed into a four-horse carriage and rolled out to meet her Imperial Highness the Princess Anna. I was feeling devilishly beside myself.

In an effort to distract myself, I looked out the window from time to time. And though the storm had finished this morning, broken trees caught the eye everywhere, along with mud and cloudy pools on the sidewalks and streets. The city didn't look at all washed up by the bad weather, more the opposite.

At any rate, I was looking out the window occasionally, which gave me pause, making me suspect something was amiss.

"My good sirs!" I then addressed the

guards. "I may be mistaken, but I believe the Imperial Palace is the other way!"

"Do you not read the papers?" asked a pock-marked guard, staring at me with an expression of sincere incomprehension. "Her highness has spent the last week in the Central Hospital for screening."

"So, she's still in the hospital!" I thought to myself, cringing internally. But I didn't express my unhappiness in any way. I was still nursing the hope that the attendant doctors wouldn't allow our meeting to go on too long.

I mean, what did I even have to talk about with the heiress to the throne, a woman who'd spent her whole life surrounded by nothing but courtiers, tutors and doctors? Who was I to her? Certainly not a relative. An entertaining oddity, nothing more.

THE WHOLE AREA around the Central Hospital was surrounded by a high fence, but the boom barrier was sticking straight up, and the carriage passed unimpeded through the wide-open gates. No one was thinking of stopping us or even asking the purpose of our visit.

That said, the far building set aside for the needs of the Imperial court was being guarded somewhat more seriously. Sentries were standing guard there, and although they recognized my companions' faces beyond all doubt, they still asked them to get out of the carriage and studied their travel log and pass meticulously.

In the hospital vestibule, we were expected

by a whole delegation: doctors, assistants, and some inconspicuous individuals in white robes with the tenacious gazes of experienced investigators.

An important gentleman, mustached and pot-bellied, led me into one of the rooms on the first floor, surprised at the unremarkable decor, and pointed to an empty box.

"Get undressed and put your things in there," he demanded.

I turned to the guards:

"What the devil?!"

"Final check," Lieutenant Grace declared.

"Is this really necessary?"

The lieutenant shook his head.

"This is truly beyond the pale!" I grumbled.

"Your security clearance is still very much in question, Viscount," the pockmarked guard reminded me. "But her highness was unambiguous in expressing an interest in meeting with you. Don't make more problems for us, I beg you."

I didn't curse or call down thunder and lightning on the guards' heads. I just got undressed and accepted a hospital gown and slippers from a mustached gentleman.

"Come in, Viscount," said the doctor, pointing at the next door over.

A large part of that room was occupied by a huge apparatus with a thrown-back hood in the middle, which revealed an opening large enough for a person.

"Please!" said the fat doctor, pointing. "I

strongly encourage you not to fidget or move. The procedure won't take long."

"Procedure?" I groaned.

"We're going to send x-rays through your internals," the important gentleman explained calmly. "If there are any foreign objects inside you, we'll detect them. It's a radiography machine, ever heard of it?"

I had, in fact, read something about the latest word in diagnostic medicine a few years earlier, but asked about something else:

"Foreign objects – what do you mean by that?"

"Bombs, Viscount," the pock-marked guardsman answered calmly.

"And just how do you suppose that such a bomb could be detonated?"

"Using a timed mechanism, naturally," the lieutenant answered, utterly serious, and hurried me along: "Viscount, don't waste our time."

I got into the apparatus and the lid, internally lined with lead foil, immediately slammed down. The mustached gentleman advised me:

"There are handles, grab onto them. And I beg you: do not move!"

And so I did. Then, a low hum started sounding out. The fat man stood, watching me intensely for the duration of the procedure. I managed to curse both the heiress Princess and her guards at the same time with my last words, but also didn't forget von Nalz who'd drawn me into this whole episode.

When the humming faded away, I got out of the apparatus, and the assistant immediately crawled off to pull out the photo sheet. Meanwhile, the mustached gentleman asked:

"Would you please kindly wait in the reception?"

So, accompanied by the guards, I returned to the neighboring room and gave a cold shiver due to the chilly breeze that snuck in under my hospital gown but, when I went to get dressed, I was stopped.

"Do you intend to go to a meeting with her Highness in those rags?" the pock-marked guardsman laughed. "Viscount, you're quite the character!"

"These rags, as you so kindly put it, are my clothing."

"No worries," Lieutenant Grace smiled and rubbed his dandified mustache, "we'll provide you with new clothing. You'll be able to pick your clothes up again on your way out, if you so desire."

"Have you got my measurements?"

"Naturally!"

At that moment, the door of the apparatus flew open, and a mustached gentleman joined us with the photo plate.

"The heart is free of pathologies!" he declared. Then, he asked: "You're sure you didn't mess anything up with the blood type? It is of critical importance!"

"No, doctor, a perfect match," Lieutenant Grace called back.

I turned to him in surprise, intending to demand an explanation, but the pock-marked guardsman instantly put me in a headlock and pressed a damp cloth to my face. A sweetish ethereal smell struck me in the nose. My head started spinning and my consciousness was carried away to the unfathomable beyond, a place without troubles or worries, where the imagination easily stands in for the laws of physics, and words have different flavors and colors.

In other words, he knocked me out with chloroform.

FIRST THERE was nothing, then the darkness was cut through by a luster coming down from an unfathomable height. And so it continued for an indefinite length of time. Then, some intuition told me I was lying with my eyes wide open gazing at a glowing lamp hanging off the ceiling.

The light started causing a terrible splitting pain in my temples. I tried to squint, but couldn't. I tried to cover my face with my hand. My arm though, stretched out flaccid alongside my body, just slumped down. My numb fingers hit upon a strange vessel, causing a rattling steel sound.

And just then, a face hovered over me in a gauze face-mask.

There was fear spilling out of the stranger's eyes. He was trying to recoil, but didn't manage. My fingers touched a piece of iron and, in a blistering movement, stabbed it into the medic's neck.

Blood gushed out. His throat began to wheeze. He squeezed the wound with both hands and ran away from me. I followed him and stuck him in the back, facing the closed door. I pinned him down, struck him with the scalpel in the loins, between the ribs, and under the left shoulder.

I hit confidently. I hit to kill.

And that realization sobered me up instantly, forcing me to take a step back and throw the bloodied blade away.

I mean, I'd killed before, but not with my bare hands. Feeling how easily the blade entered the supple flesh, how it scraped on the ribs and how the handle shuddered in my clenched fist. And the death throes, pressing the body to the floor, was something I'd also never seen before. So then, why the devil did it feel so surprisingly familiar?!

I sighed loudly as I woke up yet again. The anesthesia was still stupefying my mind. The chloroform was leaving my body at a torturously slow pace, from time to time immersing me in the soft embrace of oblivion.

Now, my mind was getting clearer, and I nearly managed to suppress a scream that tore itself from me.

Completely nude, I was standing over the medic's bloody body. I was also covered in blood from head to toe.

What kind of devilry was afoot here?!

I turned my victim onto his back, but the

doctor was already beyond help. I then stood up straight and cast my gaze over the room I found myself in.

"Operation room," came some vaguely familiar words emerging from my memory.

The huge bulb under the ceiling filled the room with a blinding luster. In the middle, there was a table, covered with a sheet besmirched with crimson spots. A stand with a tray was pushed over on top of it. There were scalpels, surgical scissors, clamps and used napkins.

Having noticed a wash basin in the corner of the room with a mirror, I approached it, intending to wash up, but I froze in place on seeing my reflection.

It wasn't my pale corpse-like skin that scared me. What drove me to terror was the slash across my ribcage. There were ribs jutting out, hacked up and moved aside by the confident hand of an experienced surgeon. And, over my heart, there was a vast cavity.

Over? Nope – instead of!

I had no heart! My heart had been cut out!

I just gasped. No. No, no, no.

This simply could not be! It must have all been from the chloroform. This was just a crazy vision, created by the power of my imagination. Just a subconscious fear of death brought to life by my *illustrious talent.*

I turned on the water, washed up and quietly laughed at my absurd fit of anxiety.

My heart had been cut out? What complete nonsense!

I mean seriously, who would want my heart? Other than me, of course.

But then I quickly remembered the strange events of the past day, the medic's interrogation, the innuendo, and the blood sent out for analysis.

Well, what if they decided to transplant my heart into the heiress to the throne?

Wild horror shook me from head to toe. I clenched my fingers around my wrist, trying to detect a pulse, but didn't manage.

Curses! With a single jerk, I pulled the sink off the wall and threw it to the other end of the operation room.

I am not dead! I am moving, thinking and feeling.

I think, therefore I am!

But what to do about the heart? Where was my heart? Where had it been brought?!

And why wasn't I dead yet?

I felt an unbearable urge to run off in search of the scoundrels who'd disemboweled me, but a glimmer of good sense stopped me from committing this act of highest-order recklessness.

These people knew what they'd done. Seeing their organ donor back from the dead would hardly bring them any joy. They wouldn't put the heart back, or sew up the wound. They'd kill me. And this time, it would be for good.

Run! I needed to run out of here immediately!

And then it dawned on me. The heart of the *fallen one*!

That hellish thing was still beating, even after I'd ripped it from the chest of the infernal creature. Its strength was such that it didn't need surgeons, needles or stitches. I could just pop it in my chest and become alive again.

I could do that!

And it wasn't just that I could, that was exactly what I intended to do. I'd have plenty of time to think about revenge later.

I was overcome by hatred – my heart! They'd cut out my heart! But the ghastly desire to tear out someone else's throat with my bear hands, fortunately, soon subsided, and I knelt down in exhaustion next to the medic. His blood-soaked clothing was only fit to be thrown out now.

I cracked the door carefully, looked at the cabinet-jammed room, quietly slunk into it and picked out an outfit that more or less corresponded to my size. I got dressed, put on some shoes and, after loading the corpse onto a gurney, covered it with a sheet.

I threw a white robe on over my jacket and pants, covered my face with a gauze mask, snapped a white skull-cap onto my head and rolled the gurney down the corridor, not at all afraid to be discovered by staff.

And so it went – no one even looked at me.

I abandoned the corpse and gurney in a hidden nook, pulled the mask down onto my neck and stuck a cigarette into my mouth that I found in the pocket of the borrowed jacket. I clapped over my pockets in a businesslike manner, passed the post and hurried to get lost among the many buildings of the military hospital. The men in charge of the guard booth didn't even consider checking the documents of the medic leaving their zone of responsibility.

Getting past the gates outside was no work at all. The robe, mask and skull-cap had already long been sent into the first trash can I came across. I calmly walked around the boom barrier and walked off down the sidewalk.

There I was, a dead man rushing home. This dead man wanted a new heart.

Bugger!

3

THE ESTATE greeted me with a mess of trees that fell down in the storm, decayed mummy bodies and pieces of broken wall. The spectacle was even more unsightly than usual. Meanwhile, by some unknown force, the manor had grown older and more dilapidated. The whitewash was cracking and peeling, and the roof had grown dark with areas missing tile. Everything was covered in mud. The flower beds were washed out, the black dead flowers forming a partially rotten canopy.

The curse had retreated, and time had taken its due. Time always takes its due.

But that didn't matter. I was not planning to live here. All I needed now was the heart of the *fallen one.*

My heart.

Not wanting to deal with the front door, I came in through a hole in the wall, grabbed my grandfather's saber and, for some reason, returned it to its place over the mantle. I didn't get distracted by anything else, just went straight down to the basement.

There was enough light coming through the hole in the floor to see, but I still had to walk in knee-high water for some time before I found the glass jar with the heart. After finding it in the very darkest corner, I ran up the stairs and laughed nervously, squeezing the internally frosted vessel to my chest.

There it was! I found it!

But when I got the tight cap off, the *fallen one*'s heart was not in the jar. There were just some scraps glowing with an internal shimmer; scraps and that was it.

The moist glass slipped from my suddenly numb fingers, fell underfoot, and shattered.

I, meanwhile, froze, not feeling up to checking it with my own eyes.

Where was it? Where had it gone?

"Bugger, what a mess!" the leprechaun grumbled, having come out of nowhere. He lifted one of the pieces of glass, sniffed and stated authoritatively: "Rat poison!"

I stared at the pipsqueak in incomprehension, then grabbed the intact bottom, sniffed the scraps covering the glass and also caught a familiar scent. The succubus had generously seasoned her food with exotic spices, but I recognized this aroma immediately.

And then it dawned on me.

She had fed me the heart of *the fallen one*! Day after day, she had been cooking it, and I had been happily chowing down on the flesh of a supernatural creature, none the wiser! So, that was why I'd had such a persistent bout of the Diabolic Plague! That was the true reason I was sick, not just the blood I got on my arms!

A fit of maniacal laughter came over me. I laughed, and couldn't stop. I laughed, laughed and laughed like a madman.

And a madman was just what I'd become.

The succubus had been intending to damage my soul but, instead, she reinforced my *illustrious talent* to such a degree, that it had overcome death itself! The power of my thoughts alone turned out to be enough to support life in my body, even with no heart.

I think, therefore I am? Indeed!

But what now? Sew up the hole in my chest and remain among the living dead?

Did I want such a fate for myself?

In exhaustion, I sat down on a chair. But just then, with an unexpectedly biting slap, my hysteria was cut short.

"Don't you remember?" he asked. "Bugger! You really don't remember anything, do you?"

"Do I not remember what?" I asked, looking him from top to bottom. I then touched my split lip, but no blood came out. I mean, how could a dead man have blood?

"Everything!" the white-haired pipsqueak exclaimed angrily. "You don't remember, do you?"

"I don't remember!"

"Bugger!" cursed the leprechaun. "Bugger! Bugger! Bugger!"

He suddenly jerked the ratty green camisole off him, keeping his pants and pinafore on; his sinewy body was covered with tattoos just like mine, but mirrored and branded into him with red-hot iron.

It surprised and scared me, but I was somewhat more scared by the kitchen knife the pipsqueak pulled from his belt.

"Do you want to remember?" the leprechaun asked, drawing the blade in a sharp motion across the palm of his clenched fist. Crimson blood shot out and the albino extended the knife to me. "Give me your left hand!" He demanded. "Only the left!"

The left? The arm that hadn't received a single tattoo?

I didn't hesitate for even a second, took the knife and split my chalk-white skin with its sharp edge. I was expecting a bloodless cut, but my hand instantly gushed with black fluid. And from my wrist to my elbow and higher, right to the place where my heart should have been, a torturous pain shot out.

From there, the leprechaun did everything. He clenched my hand in his, like in a barbaric blood-brotherhood ritual, and rasped out:

"Well, do you remember now, dimwit?"

The markings on his skin suddenly filled with luster. A moment later, that fire transferred to me, but before my consciousness was devoured by the pitiless flame, I managed to answer:

"I do remember now!"

And I really did. Old memories, buried in the depths of my psyche, returned. And together with them, something more returned, a certain part of me...

A PIERCING COLD, dull reflections of a kerosene lamp on ice chunks; the frost covered door of the cellar slammed shut. No matter how I knocked or screamed – I'd never call for help through its thick barrier.

But I did scream, I know that for sure.

The chef with a ghastly kitchen knife, the cold steel in my chest, the frightening smile on the hellspawn in my house, my heart in his hand...

But I saw all this from another perspective, all from the eyes of my imaginary friend. And suddenly – a miniature hand on the handle of a knife stuck into the ice chunks, a blistering burst, blood spatters, creaks from a split throat. And – blank. After that, there was a gaping hole in my memory.

The leprechaun did everything after that on his own.

The memories flickered before my inner gaze in a flash; I tore off the appropriated shirt and, in muted amazement, stared at two terrifying gashes, splitting the eight-pointed star tattooed on my chest; the new one had traces of fresh blood, and the old was dark-blue, white and scarred.

Curse me!

The fear of the little boy was so strong that my *illustrious talent* had created him a new heart! A new, imaginary heart!

And I would have laughed if it wasn't so painful. The tattoos glowed and burned with a ferocious fire. I was shaken by convulsions. My ribs cracked, moving back into place, growing and stretching over with flesh. The wounds – both old and recent – covered over. Now, not even scars remained. But the metamorphosis didn't end there. The changes flowed over my body from the cut on the left hand as if mercury had been injected into my veins. Muscle fibers wrapped the bones, crawled under the skin and widened my shoulders, reshaping me, turning me into someone else.

Into the person I was meant to grow up into, if it hadn't been for that ill-fated evening in the basement of my father's manor...

When the tattoos stopped glowing and went gray, and the fit ended, I spread-eagled out in complete exhaustion on the cold floor. The clothing from the hospital was split at the seams and hanging off me in tatters; I was no longer a lean string-bean. I now looked like a complete copy of my father.

Tall, broad-shouldered, and strong.

And I became exactly like my father. Inside me, there now also lived a beast.

With the help of the tattoos, my father had managed to lock the hereditary condition inside me, depriving it of power, protecting his son from transforming into a blood-thirsty monster. The irony of fate is that my dark alter ego was already external, even then. My *illustrious talent* had placed it into an imaginary friend, and only now had everything come full circle.

I had become a werebeast. I was now a werebeast, and a heart was beating in my chest once more!

The hereditary disorder! That was exactly what had protected the dead chef from the curse. That was the exact reason he had called my father and I degenerates.

Sensing my weakness retreating gradually, I got up from the floor, reeled and nearly fell, but managed to lean my back against the wall. I glanced at the white mark of the residual scar, which stretched across my left hand, then ripped off the remainder of the other person's clothing and, stumbling, went up to the third floor.

In all the years I'd lived in this manor, I'd never entered my father's room. Everything there was just like the last day of his life in this house. Books, personal items, clothing...

And now, I was going for the clothing. Though it was damp and clumped, smelled of must and had long gone out of style, it fit my new body-size perfectly. I selected some underwear, trousers, a vest and a frock coat, then donned a pair of good-quality, slightly worn boots and returned to the first floor.

My new body moved with a grace beyond all understanding. It seemed someone was controlling it for me, and initially, that even scared me. The light got brighter, smells grew stronger, and I could now sense even the smallest nuances in aroma.

Not that I wanted to. It smelled of death in the house.

It smelled of death in the house, and I wasn't planning on sticking around. Not for one hour, or even one minute. Not at all.

In the wallet taken from the hospital, I discovered two ten-franc bank-notes and seven francs in change; I moved the money into the pocket of my old-fashioned frock coat. The wallet I threw on the floor, then went outside.

The sky was growing lighter. The sun was shining through the foggy smoke and I felt the habitual desire to set my dark glasses on my nose, but they were still in the hospital.

In the hospital, along with my cut-out heart. I wonder if the heiress to the throne would start having imaginary delusions? I mean, why not? It had served me in truth and faith for many long years.

I laughed and went out the gate. I glanced at the tower atop the hill gratefully. It was rusty, iron, homely and hadn't suffered one bit in yesterday's showdown. I turned around and started down the hill to the city, once again covered with a gray cloud of smog.

On Dürer-Platz, I kept my distance from the broken fountain basin with gawkers crowding around, and headed off to walk through the city, not especially wanting to go anywhere, just getting used to the unfamiliar sensations and enjoying my new life.

My legs took me on their own to the Greek Quarter, I stood on the embankment of the unnamed canal, looked from a distance at the *Charming Bacchante* cabaret and suddenly realized I simply could not just walk past.

Albert Brandt was my only friend. He understood me like no one else, and it would be wrong to allow our friendship to end because of the succubus's scheming.

She had us both wrapped around her finger, and we'd both messed things up! The poet had insisted on a duel, and I'd knocked him out by throwing the billiard ball. But I still could go and fix it! I could still find the right words. I could and I should!

I was certain of that, and yet still shivered uncomfortably while walking inside.

"Is Albert home?" I asked the owner's nephew, who was wiping down the bar.

If he noticed the changes in my appearance, he didn't show it.

"The poet?" he asked, wiping out a beer glass and shaking his head: "The poet moved out. This morning."

"What do you mean he moved out?" I froze. The left side of my chest shot through with pain.

"He moved out for good," the young man answered calmly. "He was warbling like a nightingale about some blind girl, Paris in spring and London at night. I heard him ask a cabby to bring him to the port."

I took a deep sigh, forcing myself to calm down and dug through my pockets for change.

"Pour me a..."

"Lemonade?" the owner's nephew suggested customarily.

"No," I cut him off sharply, setting a five-franc coin on the bar. "Pour me a vodka. Russian."

Immeasurably surprised at my choice, the boy didn't accost me with an interrogation. He obediently filled the crystal decanter and placed the shot glass next to it. I went outside, stood at a table under the awning, poured myself some vodka and froze for a short time with the glass just under my mouth.

I finally took a slight sip, winced from the detestable flavor of strong alcohol and clanged the shot glass down on the table. I stood for a bit, dumped it out in a sharp jerk and started decisively off down the street.

My new life had the familiar taste of disappointment, but I wasn't going to waste it on empty regrets. I would go on to do great deeds; great deeds, and no one could tell me otherwise.

End of Book Two

Want to be the first to know about our latest LitRPG, sci fi and fantasy titles from your favorite authors?

Subscribe to our **NEW RELEASES** newsletter:
http://eepurl.com/b7niIL

Thank you for reading *The Heartless!*
If you like what you've read, check out other
LitRPG novels published by Magic Dome Books.

Dark Paladin **LitRPG series by Vasily Mahanenko:**
The Beginning
The Quest

The Dark Herbalist **LitRPG series**
by Michael Atamanov:
Video Game Plotline Tester
Stay on the Wing

The Neuro **LitRPG series by Andrei Livadny:**
The Crystal Sphere
The Curse of Rion Castle

The Way of the Shaman **LitRPG series**
by Vasily Mahanenko:
Survival Quest
The Kartoss Gambit
The Secret of the Dark Forest
The Phantom Castle
The Karmadont Chess Set
The Hour of Pain (a bonus short story)

Galactogon **LitRPG series by Vasily Mahanenko:**
Start the Game!

Phantom Server **LitRPG series by Andrei Livadny:**
Edge of Reality
The Outlaw
Black Sun

Perimeter Defense **LitRPG series by Michael**
Atamanov:
Sector Eight
Beyond Death
New Contract

In order to have new books of the series translated faster, we need your help and support! Please consider leaving a review or spread the word by recommending *The Heartless* to your friends and posting the link on social media. The more people buy the book, the sooner we'll be able to make new translations available.

Thank you!

Till next time!